john
brosnan

MOTHERSHIP

Copyright © John Brosnan 2004

All rights reserved

The right of John Brosnan to be identified as the
author of this work has been asserted by him in accordance
with the Copyright, Designs and Patents Act 1988.

First published in Great Britain in 2004 by
Gollancz
An imprint of the Orion Publishing Group
Orion House, 5 Upper St Martin's Lane, London WC2H 9EA

This mass-market paperback edition
first published in 2005

A CIP catalogue record for this book is
available from the British Library

ISBN 0 575 07627 5

Typeset at Deltatype Ltd,
Birkenhead, Merseyside

Printed in Great Britain by
Clays Ltd, St Ives plc

www.orionbooks.co.uk

*To Ma and Pa Kettle and
the two little Toasters*

CHAPTER ONE

'Jad, you're an idiot,' Lord Krader told me.

'Thank you, sire. You know how much I always appreciate your invaluable criticism—'

'Shut up, you fawning cretin, and let me finish. You're an idiot, yes, but my son is an even bigger idiot. You, however, are also shrewd, devious, cunning and a born liar. You're a natural survivor. Hopefully, you'll keep my son alive while saving your own skin. That's why you're going with him on his hair-brained expedition.'

This was not good news. On the contrary, it was extremely bad news.

'I am? But Lord Krader, surely you jest!' I said, profoundly alarmed.

'I never jest,' he growled. 'Rumour has it that *you're* the court jester around here.' As usual, he wielded his heavy sarcasm as if it were a battle-axe.

But I persevered. 'I can't go, sire. I'm needed here. Who would keep your court entertained in my absence?'

'You know as well as I do that you're a lousy jester, Jad. We can all do without your bad jokes, abysmal juggling and clumsy pratfalls for a few months. In fact, it would be a distinct relief.'

That hurt. It might have been true, but that didn't mean I liked hearing it in such blunt terms. But then, Lord Krader had never particularly cared for me, even before I became his jester. For a warlord he was unusually fair-minded: a decent type of tyrant as tyrants go, I had to admit. I had many reasons to be grateful to him, but even as a child I'd inevitably managed to rub him up the wrong way. And I'd always found him an intimidating figure, both emotionally and physically. He was a barrel-chested man with massive arms; his imposing head was made larger by his thick grey hair and luxuriant beard. When he grinned, he seemed to have more teeth than any normal person. No one liked it when he grinned, particularly me.

'But my Lord, I wouldn't be of any use as an escort to the Prince,' I tried again. 'He needs the protection of an expert soldier. Captain Vilkter, for example. He'd be ideal!'

'Captain Vilkter is a good soldier, I agree. One of my best men. But he's also a bloodthirsty maniac. He'd be picking fights the whole time. He'd get himself killed, and my son along with him. No, you're the best choice for this assignment. You're an out and out coward.'

This catalogue of my character faults was being issued in Lord Krader's grisly trophy room, the walls of which were studded with the glassy-eyed heads of his hunting victims: bears, deer and various other unfortunate beasts. As far as Lord Krader was concerned, my faults were numerous, and so far he was only skimming the surface. I tried another approach. 'Sire, you know I'm a terrible rider. Horses and I just don't get along. To be honest, horses hate me.'

Lord Krader was seated in a high-backed, throne-like chair. I was seated on a small stool so that he could look down on me. He leaned forward, gave me a malicious smile and said, 'They've probably seen your act.'

I forced a laugh. 'Very good, sire. I must remember that one. But seriously, if I ride for any length of time I get nauseous.'

'The practice will do you good. By the time you return you'll be an expert horseman.'

He had said the key word: 'return'. There was no guarantee that we *would* return, of course, but I decided not to voice that grim possibility. After all, Prince Kender was his only son. I tried to think of yet another objection, but while I was doing so my gaze fell on the head of a ferocious-looking griffin mounted on the wall. It seemed to be looking directly at me, its silent message being: 'If this happened to *me* it sure as hell can happen to you too.'

Lord Krader said, 'My mind is made up. No more arguing. Now go and select a suitable horse. Preferably one that doesn't bite you on first sight.'

'Yes, my Lord,' I said miserably. I stood up and turned to go.

'Oh, and Jad—'

I stopped and turned to face him again. 'Yes, my Lord?'

'Don't come back alone.' And he grinned.

I got the message. He wasn't talking about the horse.

I left the trophy room in a mood that was equal parts pique and gloom. I was piqued partly because of what Lord Krader had said about my jestering abilities – but in fairness, I had to admit I was probably the worst court jester in all of Urba. My every appearance at Lord Krader's court induced groans and a number of shouted obscenities, most of them coming from Lord Krader himself. The fact that I hadn't even wanted to be his bloody jester didn't make me feel any better. But I'd much prefer continuing to try and make a fool of myself at court than to go off with Ken on a suicide mission.

I blamed the Day of Wonder. Nothing had been the same since the Day. Not that we in Capelia knew on the actual Day that the Day of Wonder was even taking place. The only out-of-the-ordinary thing that happened to us on the Day was that the magic light globes – a rare gift from the Elite – suddenly stopped working, plunging the entire castle into darkness. As a result, the town's candle and torch makers were doing great business, but the castle remained dim and gloomy no matter how many candles and torches were installed. It was some five weeks before news reached us of the wondrous and world-shattering events that had taken place on the Day, and the days that followed.

And now, thanks to the Day of Wonder, Ken had gone stark, raving mad.

As I wandered disconsolately through the now very badly lit castle, it struck me how quickly one's life can turn to shit. I'd woken up this morning, as usual, next to Tiri, one of the kitchen maids, without a care in the world. Well, with hardly a care in the world.

And now suddenly I was doomed. I began to feel angry. I decided to go in search of Ken rather than go and audition horses, as Lord Krader had ordered. Perhaps I could talk Ken out of his mad enterprise, I thought, though it was a somewhat futile hope. I was horribly afraid that Lord Krader was being overly optimistic in his belief that I would somehow keep his son alive. It was only a matter of luck that Ken hadn't managed to get us both killed by now – he was forever coming up with reckless schemes, even when we were children. There was the time when we were both twelve and he decided to launch a two-man raid on Vurgun, our biggest neighbour and traditional enemy – the raiding party consisted of himself and me. Of course we were quickly captured and Lord Krader had to pay Lord Vorgal, Vurgun's warlord, a hefty ransom for the return of his only son. It was touch and go whether I would be included in the package; fortunately I was, as a kind of afterthought. Then Ken had decided we should see how far we could up climb up the Wall. I was lucky to suffer only a broken leg that time – not by attempting to climb the Wall myself, but by breaking Ken's fall when he landed on top of me. Ken survived unscathed . . .

I checked my watch by the light of a flickering torch. It was close to eleven p.m. and I knew where he was likely to be. The archery range was currently the Prince's favourite haunt. He'd developed a new type of crossbow, capable of firing three bolts in rapid succession, and he delighted in testing his invention at every opportunity. While I had discovered a talent for conjuring in my late teenage years, Ken found he had a natural flair for engineering, though he applied this ability almost exclusively to weaponry. He'd come up with the idea for the three-in-one crossbow some time ago, but it was only since the demise of the Elite that he'd been able to build a working model. The Elite had had strict rules about how far we low-lifers were allowed to develop anything, and these rules were ruthlessly implemented. I shuddered as I recalled the fate of one of Lord Krader's wise men, a member of his council of advisors, a few years ago. He'd prised from a ceiling one of the magic light globes, and the metal box it was attached to; he'd intended to take it apart to try and discover how it worked. His attempts to open the box all failed, but even so a group of Elite turned up at the castle the following day, arrested him and took him away. He never returned.

Before I went in search of Ken, I made a swift detour downstairs to the kitchen. As usual it was stifling hot in there. I found Tiri plucking a large goose. Tiri was a fair-headed, well-upholstered girl who verged on being pretty.

'Tiri, I've got something important to tell you—' I began, and then I paused. The goose was twitching. 'Tiri, that bird's still *alive*.'

'No it's not,' she said as she continued her energetic plucking. Her face and bare, muscular arms were covered in sweat.

'But it's still moving!'

'I've only just wrung its neck. It's just nerves.'

'Nerves? No wonder it's feeling nervous. It's not dead and you're plucking it!'

'It's dead.'

'If you insist,' I said, feeling squeamish. 'Anyway, listen, I've got something important to tell you.'

'Jad, can't you see I'm busy?' she said irritably. 'Tell me later.'

'But it really is important!'

'I'm sure it is. You've finally learnt to juggle more than two balls at once?'

Stung, I said sulkily, 'It's even far more important than that.'

'Whatever it is, tell me tonight. Now go away, Jad, do. You're distracting me.'

Deeply offended, I searched for a sarcastic retort, then, failing to find a suitable response I turned and flounced haughtily out of the kitchen. As I left, it occurred to me that I had a lot in common with that hapless bird: my goose was going to be well and truly cooked too unless I could talk some sense into Prince Ken.

As expected, I found him on the archery range in the grounds at the rear of the castle. Also as expected, he was playing with his new toy. As I arrived he fired off three rounds, then shouted for the distant manservant to move the target even further away. He beamed at me as he cranked the crossbow back to full tautness.

'Look, Jad, look how quickly one can reset this beauty! The winding action on the windlass is so smooth a girl could do it!'

We are both twenty-three years old, but apart from being the same height, there all resemblances between us end. Ken is an exceedingly handsome young man, with a fine physique and a mane of thick black hair. He exudes vitality and good health and is so charismatic it's downright sickening. Not surprisingly, women can't resist him. I won't say I don't resent and envy him, because I do. I, on the other hand, may be just as tall, but I'm a thin, gangling figure with a long face and a ridiculous mop of red hair. It's an ironic joke on the part of the gods that I certainly *look* like a court jester . . .

'Ken, we have to talk,' I told him seriously.

He frowned. 'So talk away.'

'Your father has insisted that I go with you on your spying expedition.'

'Marvellous!' Ken grinned at me. 'I hoped he would. I had a word in his ear. We're going to have a fine old time, Jad.' He took aim and fired another three bolts, barely giving the servant time to clear the target area. 'Damn. They fell short!' he cried in disgust. 'Still, a range of over a hundred yards is pretty impressive, wouldn't you say?'

'Indeed it is. I'm truly thrilled for you. Look, Ken, won't you reconsider this entire plan of yours? It's too bloody dangerous. You could get killed. More importantly, you could get *me* killed. Leave it to the professionals.'

He gave me one of his newly minted aristocratic looks. He'd clearly been practising in the mirror. 'I *am* a professional, Jad.'

'You know what I mean. Your father has sent out his spies

already. There's no need for you to risk your life as well. To risk *our* lives.'

'I'm going to try and increase the tension,' he said, ignoring my last plea. He rewound the crossbow, took three more bolts from his ammunition belt and reloaded.

'Well, you've already increased *my* tension,' I told him, crossly.

He ignored my comment and said, 'My father's spies are all men of little imagination. I, on the other hand, will be able to establish the big picture. This isn't some minor skirmish between a few domains – the entire world is being affected by what has happened to the Elite. It's vital my father receives reliable information about any potential dangers that might arise.'

I had to admit this was true, though I was surprised to hear Ken put it so well. I assumed, rather unkindly, that he must have been present at a recent meeting between his father and his council of advisors.

'For example,' he continued, 'those timber merchants from Lexos who arrived last week said the warlord Camarra is busy launching a major campaign of conquest. He's moving his forces towards the Citadel; apparently he plans to eventually conquer all of Urba. We need to know if there's any truth in these rumours. And there are accounts of massed dragon attacks on domains at the other end of the world—' He fired the crossbow again. The servant threw himself on the ground, but again the bolts fell just short of the target. 'Damn,' Ken muttered.

'There hasn't been enough time since the Day of Wonder for any real information from the other end of the world to reach us,' I pointed out.

'I know, I know,' he said, irritably. 'The dragon story was probably just that – a story – but that doesn't mean we shouldn't try and learn as much as possible about what's going on.'

I tried a different approach, adopting a serious tone. 'Look, Ken—'

He held up a warning hand. 'You know I don't want you to call me that any longer. Especially when we're not alone.'

I looked around. 'But we *are* alone.'

He pointed at the distant manservant hovering by the target, no doubt dreading another fusillade. 'What about him?'

I sighed. 'Yes, your highness. Forgive me, sire.'

He laughed and clapped me on the back. 'Swallow your misgivings about our journey. We're going to have a grand adventure, I promise you!'

'I don't *want* a grand adventure,' I protested, 'I want to continue with my boring life right here.'

'Oh Jad, surely you'd like a break from people constantly sneering at your attempts to be a court jester? It has to be very depressing for you.'

'It's a challenge,' I said with a sniff. 'One of these days I'll make someone laugh. Apart from your mother.'

'People never stop laughing at you.'

'You know what I mean. I want the right *kind* of laughter.'

'When we return from our mission you'll get respect, not laughter.'

'I don't need any respect, your most royal of highnesses. And besides, you persist in this optimistic belief that we're going to return from this exercise; it's utter folly. It's dangerous out there – far more dangerous than it used to be. I've heard the rumours too: there have been rebellions in several domains. Your royal credentials may offer you – us – no protection at all if the normal diplomatic customs have broken down along with law and order.'

'Aha!' he said, triumphantly. 'You wrongly assume that I will be travelling as Prince Kender!'

'You'll be travelling as *Princess* Kender?'

He gave me a contemptuous glare. 'I'm going to disguise myself as a commoner. You are now looking at Gideron Blaze, mercenary soldier. A cynical, hard-bitten, freelance swordsman. No scruples, and capable of doing anything if the price is right.'

I stared at him. I wondered what illustrated adventure story he'd taken this character from. I'd long given up reading such juvenile fictions, but Ken still devoured them avidly.

'Yes, I see the likeness. Good choice of character. But who will I be? Black Basil, the notorious pirate?'

'Of course not. You don't need a disguise – you're already a commoner. You can be yourself.'

'Oh, thank you, your highness. So I'm a wandering jester, am I? A kind of freelance jokester?'

He thought it over. 'I don't see why not. You'll be like a wandering minstrel, except you tell jokes round the campfire for money rather than play an instrument. Except—' He broke off and gave me an apologetic look. 'Perhaps you shouldn't actually try to *tell* any jokes. Otherwise you'll destroy your credibility.'

I bristled at his slur. 'You want me to be a wandering jester who doesn't tell jokes? That doesn't seem very credible.'

'Jad, you're *not* credible as a court jester. You'll be staying in character.'

I kept sulkily silent.

'Just stick to doing magic tricks,' he continued, 'you're good at them.'

'You're too kind. So please tell me why a hard-bitten mercenary is travelling in the company of a non-joke-telling jester, such as myself, who can perform magic tricks? What do I do – distract your opponents with my famous disappearing egg routine before you hack them to pieces?'

The Prince waved a hand dismissively. 'We'll think of something.'

'Glad to hear it. When do you plan to begin this momentous expedition?'

'Tomorrow. First thing in the morning.'

'That soon?'

'Is that a problem?'

'I suppose not,' I admitted. 'It's not as if I have a lot of affairs to settle before we leave.' Actually, Tiri was the only thing I had to settle before I left. No doubt when I finally got to break the news of my departure and imminent death to her there would be tears aplenty; I intended spending the night consoling her. Actually, I thought I'd prefer it if she spent the night consoling *me*.

'Don't pack much,' Ken told me, 'we'll be travelling light. And we can pick up supplies and anything else we need from the garrison at the Vurgun border.'

'Fine. I'll probably just bring a pen, ink and some paper. Just in case I have to write my will in a hurry.'

Ken gave me another hearty clap on the back. He does that a lot. It's bloody annoying. 'Cheer up, Jad, one day you'll thank me for giving you this marvellous opportunity.'

'When that day arrives I don't know which one of us will be the more surprised,' I muttered, cursing him under my breath. Don't get me wrong: I love Ken like a brother. That's not surprising as we were raised together more or less as brothers. I was only two years old when my parents were killed by a band of Vurgun raiders; after that Lord Krader more or less adopted me. Well, it was really the idea of his kindly wife, Lady Kalina. But, like most people, she did have an ulterior motive: she wasn't able to have any more children after Ken, and she thought I would make a substitute brother and playmate: Ken was also two at the time I was orphaned. So I grew up in the castle with Ken, believing myself to be part of the royal family for several years, until the day I was taken aside by Lord Krader and told, in his customary blunt way, the reality of my situation. I was nine at the time. From then on I slept in the stables with the stable boys – and the bloody horses – though during the day I continued to be Ken's companion, with my usual free access to all the royal parts of the castle. I suppose it was a strange childhood, but it could have been a lot worse. However, when I reached the age of eighteen, Lord Krader decreed that it was time I took up a trade. My choices were limited: I could join the army or become a lumberjack.

Trees. Capelia has a lot of trees. This is due to its location: it lies next to one of the two great Walls of the Gods that bookend Urba like, well . . . bookends. The giant red jewels that lie at the centre of each vast, blue Wall are the sources of the sun that, during the day, stretches the entire length of the world, all eight thousand miles of it. As children, we learned that the gods had created the Walls at the same time that they'd created Urba, out of the solid rock that constitutes much of the entire Universe. Capelia's close proximity to the Wall was the reason it was cold the whole year round. Apart from the great jewel of the sun, the Wall had a circular series of huge holes, each several miles in diameter. From these holes torrents of cold air would periodically issue forth, and as a result of this cold climate, so the theory went, Capelia, like many areas that border the Wall, was thickly covered with trees. We have trees coming out of our arses. Stand anywhere in the domain and all you can see is what appears to be an endless forest curving upwards on either side of you. Capelia's unique type of high-quality timber is the domain's national asset, and its chief source of revenue. Well, its *only* source of revenue, really, so the profession of lumberjack is a pretty common one.

However, being a lumberjack involves a lot of scrambling up trees to lop off branches, and I have no head for heights. I also have no liking for falling long distances to the ground, which lumberjacks tend to do a lot. As for joining the army – again, I lack the necessary qualifications: namely, the complete lack of any ability when it comes to using any type of weapon. I am unable to engage anyone in a fencing match without closing my eyes, a distinct disadvantage. And the one time I tried to use a crossbow, Lord Krader almost declared a state of national emergency.

Again it was Lady Kalina, my substitute mother in a distant sort of way, who came up with a solution to the problem: she suggested I should be apprenticed to the court jester, who went under the stage name of Harius the Hilarious. Lord Krader, after a lot of pressure, I'm sure, from his wife, grudgingly agreed and so suddenly I had a new profession. I wasn't exactly thrilled by the idea, but it beat the hell out of falling from the top of a tree, or getting skewered by a sword or crossbow quarrel. And it also meant I got to move out of the stables and into one of Harius's small rooms at the top of the crumbling Green Tower. Harius had been the jester for years; Lord Krader had actually inherited him from his own father. He was a skilled performer in many ways: an expert juggler, he had an impressive range of conjuring tricks, did great impressions (his Lord Krader was a killer) and he could tumble in the most spectacular fashion. But not only was he getting very old, he also had a drinking problem. A very serious drinking problem.

I soon realised this once I became his apprentice. In theory, he was supposed to be passing on his skills to me, but this usually consisted of him handing me, say, a book called *Juggling Made Easy* before he headed off in the direction of the wine cellars. As a result, my skills as a jester didn't perceptibly improve during the whole year I was Harius's apprentice. As a juggler, I hadn't even advanced beyond being able to handle one ball or club at a time. And when Harius told me, as he frequently did, that I was coming along 'brilliantly', I took his compliments with a pinch of salt: it was pretty obvious his critical assessment was more than slightly coloured by his wine consumption.

Despite the all-round lack of tutoring, I did manage to become an accomplished conjurer: I had discovered my natural aptitude for sleight-of-hand. But this and a talent for picking locks that I used in my much-underrated escapology routine did not leave me massively overqualified as an all-round jester.

This wouldn't have mattered if Harius had managed to continue as the court jester, but, sadly for me, that wasn't the case: the inevitable happened one night, during a banquet being held in honour of some visiting – and very important – timber merchants. Harius had that day imbibed a particularly large proportion of the contents of one of the wine cellars; that night, when he made his usual entrance at the top of the main staircase, he did a spectacular tumble down the stairs. On this occasion, his tumble was *very* spectacular, a tumble of breathtaking dimensions. He ended up in a heap in front of Lord Krader's table, raised his head to issue a triumphant 'Ta-

dahhh!' and promptly died – though no one realised this until the applause had finished, when Harius didn't leap up to take his usual bow.

At least Harius went out on a high note; it also meant I abruptly inherited his mantle as court jester, a position for which I was far from ready. I've successfully blanked out all memory of my debut performance, though I'm certain it didn't involve any tumbles down the main staircase. I do remember that at the end of my act Lady Kalina clapped enthusiastically. She was quite alone in this.

I sighed, and turned my attention from our childhood back to the matter at hand. Ken was signalling to the manservant to collect the bolts he'd fired; the man's relief was obvious even from this distance.

'Finished with your practice?'

'For now,' Ken replied. 'I'm going to the Compound.'

'Again? You must know every inch of that place by now.'

'Well, I find it fascinating. Don't you?'

'It gives me the creeps. When I'm in there, I keep expecting the Elite to return at any moment.'

'No chance of that. Anyway, come with me.'

'Do I have to?'

'Yes. There's more I want to discuss with you about our journey.'

'Oh, good,' I muttered as the servant, panting alarmingly, finally reached us. Ken gave him the crossbow and told him to return it to his workshop, adding a warning that the man's life depended on the weapon reaching the armoury workshop undamaged.

Then we set off for the Compound together.

CHAPTER TWO

A s we strolled unescorted through the town of Carvel, Capelia's capital, people greeted Ken cheerily, the men bowing and the women curtseying as the Prince passed by. Children waved at him with no trace of fear or awe. Capelia, I've been told, is unusual among the domains in that the members of its ruling family are actually quite popular. True, Lord Krader has the odd bad egg lobbed at him, but that's the extent of any form of blatant insurrection.

On the way, we made a brief stop at the temple to pay our respects to the gods. Ken placed a gold coin in the bowl in front of his favourite, Maurice, the God of War, while I dropped a bronze coin in the bowl of Agnes, Goddess of Good Sex. The statue of Agnes had breasts the like of which I'd never encountered in real life . . . and probably never would.

The Elite Compound is located in the centre of a cleared area beyond the outskirts of the town. Every time I see it, I experience a trickle of unease running up my spine. Like the castle, it dominates its surroundings, but in an entirely different way. The castle, with its towers and high battlements, looms over the town, while the Compound is a low-lying structure that exerts its influence by its sheer unnatural appearance. With its inwardly sloping walls, made of a substance resembling black glass – but it isn't – the Compound is compelling because of the way it's in complete contrast with its bucolic environment. It simply doesn't *belong*. I'd grown up seeing the Compound quite frequently, but it still possesses an alien quality for me. I'd never got accustomed to it. And even though it was now empty and lifeless, its powers gone like the Elite themselves, it still exudes a sinister aura.

The Prince came to a stop when we were still some distance away and stood there staring at it. I don't think he found it sinister; I think he has always admired the place. But I could never forget the terrible incident that happened here when we were both about eight years old. We, along with most of Carvel's population, were forced to witness an act of Elite retribution. Lord Krader and Lady Kalina, being the ruling family, were obliged to take pride of place amongst the unwilling spectators; being a token member of the family at that time, I too was in a position to see everything exceptionally clearly. Twenty townsmen, chosen at random, had been lined up in front of the wall of the Compound. Exactly what transgression was being punished I can't remember, but then, the Elite were notoriously arbitrary in all their actions, which was one of the things that made them so frightening. When the men had been positioned, ten Elite, clad in their traditional black and scarlet uniforms, stood in front of them. Above the grim scene hovered a number of black air-cars. I may have been only eight, but I was well aware of how deadly these vehicles could be . . .

After a long, cruelly drawn out wait the word was finally given. The Elite opened fire with their hand weapons. The townsmen burst into flames and died screaming. Then all was quiet, apart from the sound of crackling from the smouldering corpses. The smell of burned flesh stayed with me for ages; I had nightmares about the atrocity for weeks afterward.

Ken broke into my reverie. 'I still can't get used to the idea,' he said, shaking his head. 'The Compound is *ours*. Never in my wildest dreams did I ever imagine the day would come when I could enter the Elite Compound at will. Don't you feel the same way, Jad?'

'The Elite never figured in any of my wildest dreams, only my nightmares,' I told him truthfully.

There was a large wooden ladder resting against one of the sloping walls of the Compound. It's the only way inside – the Elite never put gates in their walls. There were two soldiers at the foot of the ladder. They'd been sitting until they spotted the Prince; now they were standing at attention as we approached them.

'Anything to report?' Ken asked them.

'No. All quiet, sire,' replied one of the soldiers. There had been some trouble with would-be treasure hunters – not that there was much left in the Compound to remove. Lord Krader had had the place stripped of valuables as soon he'd learned of the Day of Wonder.

One of the drawbacks of living at the end of the world is that you're last to hear important news. Well, any news at all, actually. There were no Elite in Capelia on the Day of Wonder and so there was nothing to indicate to us the disaster that was befalling them throughout the rest of the world. Finally, weeks later, a group of traders arrived in a state of high excitement and I was amongst those who crowded into Lord Krader's court as the traders told him and his council of wise men what had happened to the Elite.

For as long as records have existed, the Elite had ruled Urba. According to legend, they were invaders from another world who had used their magical powers to tunnel from their own world to Urba – which they then proceeded to conquer. The Elite, on the other hand, insisted they had brought us civilisation, whilst eradicating most of the deadly diseases that had plagued us. And they claimed they'd also established Order, preventing us Urbans from slaughtering each other in a worldwide war that was threatening to obliterate mankind from the face of Urba. The Elite arrived in the nick of time. They were our saviours. They said.

I don't know how much of the old Elite legends I still believe in. I'm no longer as superstitious as I was when I was younger – I shed more superstitions with every passing year. These days I even have doubts about the existence of the gods.

Ken started up the ladder. I followed him. The Compound wall sloped at forty-five degrees, so it was a fairly easy climb. It was about fifteen yards high; I was relieved to get off the top of the ladder and onto the protected walkway that extended along the entire lengths of all four walls of the Compound. I couldn't help glancing at the nearest array of devices that sat on one of the several masts that protruded high above the wall. When Ken and I were boys, we used to enjoy watching the devices move to follow us as we ran around the base of the walls. We'd been warned they were weapons, but as we'd never seen them in action we were, as small boys tend to be, fearless.

Today, as I stood on the parapet with Ken and gazed across the Compound, we still didn't know whether they really were weapons – whatever their function had been, they were now completely inert, like all Elite devices had been since the Day of Wonder. The magic roof screens had also stopped working that Day. Before that, whenever someone tried to see into the Compound from some high vantage point, such as from the top of the castle's highest tower, they were stopped by a kind of canopy that looked like a muted rainbow of shimmering patterns of light: rather pretty, but if you stared at it for too long it gave you a headache. Typical of the Elite . . .

I'd been in the Compound on three previous occasions, but it never lost the capacity to both surprise and unnerve me. The outside's a fortress, but I wasn't expecting what I saw when I first climbed the outer wall. I don't know *what* I'd actually expected to see, but it certainly wasn't a garden of extraordinary beauty: trees and wild flowers, lawns and ponds, the latter complete with fountains, all laid out to create an atmosphere of serene peace.

At the centre of the gardens was a flat-roofed, one-storey building; with its columns and marbled patios, it was also a thing of beauty. But closer inspection had revealed that charm was deceptive; it was designed to function as part of the fortress complex. We'd worked out that a system of metal shutters could be instantly deployed, to render the building impregnable; the flat roof clearly served as a landing area for the Elite air-cars. Also on the roof were arrays of more of the mysterious devices, including tall masts and dish-like objects. Lord Krader's advisors had yet to determine what their function had been.

Ken and I descended a set of steps that led down from the parapet and began walking through the garden towards the building at the centre of the Compound. It might have been a beautiful setting but I still found it eerie, despite the familiar and reassuring sounds of birds in the trees. Apart from the birds, though, the Compound was devoid of life: no small animals of any kind, not even rats and mice, had yet been found.

And then the bird song suddenly ceased. A shadow passed over the ground ahead of us and for one terrible moment I thought it was an Elite air-car. We both drew in relieved breaths when we realised the shadow was caused by a young dragon flying over the Compound.

'Damn,' said Ken as he drew his sword, 'I should have brought the crossbow.'

'Yes, that's exactly what we need to round off a perfect day – one pissed-off dragon.'

We waited nervously, but the dragon flew on, paying us no attention at all; as it disappeared from sight, Ken slipped his sword back into its scabbard and the birds resumed their singing.

'It's as if the dragons know instinctively that the Elite are no more,' I said, still anxiously scanning the sky. 'They're becoming bolder by the day.'

'So what do you really think happened?' Prince Ken asked me.

It didn't take a genius to know that he was referring to the Day of Wonder; that was pretty much all anybody talked about these days.

'I haven't had a revelation since the last time you asked me that question,' I replied.

'Oh, come on, Jad. I know you. You must have some ideas by now. I'm sure you've had your nose in any number of Harius's books looking for a clue.'

As well as his living quarters, I'd also inherited the late Harius's extensive collection of books. When he'd first introduced me to his library, I'd been surprised at the wide variety of subjects it covered – apart from the piles of books dealing with the noble art of jestering, of course – but later in my apprenticeship I discovered a little of Harius's hidden past; it explained a lot about him, including the drinking. One of the advantages of growing up with Ken in the castle was that I picked up something of an education – a crude one, true, but it had included learning to read. And both my reading and my education improved during my exploration of Harius's library ... but none of his books could have helped explain what happened to the Elite.

'I really have no new ideas about the Day of Wonder, Ken.'

'Please don't call me that any more. Even when we're alone.'

'But I can't help it. I've always called you Ken ... Ken.'

'I know, but it's a childhood name. It's no longer ... *suitable*. So please stop. Call me Gideron from now on. It would be good for you to get into the habit before we leave.'

'Gideron,' I said slowly. I still thought it was an extremely silly name. 'So that's "Giddy" for short—'

'No! Definitely *not* "Giddy" for short,' he said firmly, '*Gideron*. Now tell me what you think about the Day of Wonder.'

I shrugged. 'Haven't a bloody clue, to be honest.'

We'd reached the building. Again we stared at the rectangular pond, very different from all the other ponds in the grounds, and wondered what it was for. A wide, columned verandah extended along three sides of the building. Originally there had been chairs and tables on the verandah but these were now all in the castle.

'You still don't have a special theory of your own?' Ken persisted as we entered the building through a wide doorway. I couldn't help shivering. It wasn't just because of the strange architecture – which looked like it belonged to a different world – it was also due to the lingering presence of the Elite. We walked into a small hall that ended in another doorway; mounted above it was the Elite's emblem: a black and silver dragon with its wings spread and its mouth open in a snarl.

'I suppose I accept the general theory,' I said, 'that somehow the Elite fell foul of the gods, who punished them by taking away all their magical powers in a single day.' We were now in a large room that, like the rest of the building, contained lavish furnishings and more mysterious Elite devices, this time large thin plates of a glass-like substance, mounted on adjustable pedestals. I guessed, like everyone else who'd explored the Compound, that it was some kind of communal leisure room, though what manner of leisure activities the Elite had pursued within it I couldn't even begin to imagine.

Ken said, 'You've told me many times that you aren't sure that the gods exist.'

'Well, maybe I've changed my mind in the light of the Day of Wonder. After centuries of ruling Urba, the Elite mysteriously losing all their powers simultaneously suggests a supernatural force at work. If not the gods, then who else could perform such a miracle?'

'If it was the gods, then it took them a bloody long time to answer our prayers. People have been begging them for centuries to deliver us from the Elite.'

'True,' I agreed, 'and so why did they finally act now, after letting us suffer under the Elite for such a long time? Like I said, the Elite must have done something really out of the ordinary to offend the gods, but I can't imagine what. Either that or there's an entirely different explanation.'

'Such as?' asked Ken as he wandered out of the room. I followed him into a corridor.

'I don't know. Some kind of natural catastrophe perhaps. If their powers weren't magical, but derived from another source, like some people think, then something drastic must have happened to affect that source—'

An overall picture of the Day's events had been painstakingly pieced together by Lord Krader's council of advisors, from all the traders, travellers and spies who had visited Capelia over the ensuing weeks. The one thing that was certain was that on the Day of Wonder, all the armoured air-cars of the Elite suddenly fell from the skies. The vehicles never went higher than three hundred feet, and often flew at lower altitudes, so many of the Elite travelling in the air-cars survived the fall, though most were apparently injured. Some were immediately attacked by low-lifers who couldn't resist the gods-given opportunity, no matter what the future consequences. In each case, the attackers thought they were involved in an isolated, one-off incident – a lucky accident – and had no idea their experience was being repeated right across the world. At least, the wise men presume this was the case, and so far they've had no evidence to the contrary. It seems safe to assume that the events of the Day of which we had subsequently received first-hand eyewitness accounts occurred simultaneously throughout Urba.

It wasn't just the air-cars that were hit: before long, the news that the Elite weapons – including those on the vehicles, their hand-weapons and those in the Compounds – were ceasing to function spread like a forest fire . . . and the slaughter began.

After all the Elite who'd been caught out in the open had been either killed or captured, attention then focused on the Compounds themselves; soon every Compound in every domain was under siege – and in every case, the siege was over very quickly. The only exception to this was the Citadel, the Elite stronghold. No one knew how many Elite were still living in the Citadel, but in theory, they too were helpless . . . or rather, everybody hoped they were. And there was the unpleasant possibility that there were surviving Elite in other unknown enclaves.

But as there were no Elite in Capelia at the time, no massacres occurred in our domain. When news of the Day of Wonder finally arrived, Lord Krader ordered an armed party into the Compound. Naturally, Ken volunteered to lead the party; I think he was more than a little disappointed to find that, as had been expected, the Compound was deserted.

In recent years the Elite had appeared – thankfully – to lose interest in Capelia; perhaps they found the place as boring as we did. It wasn't unusual for the domain to be an Elite-free zone for long periods at a time. It had been nearly a decade since they'd forced Lord Krader to launch a major military campaign against one of his neighbours, and even longer since there'd been any 'disappearances' – periodically, in every domain, young girls would mysteriously vanish, never to be seen again. As any mysterious event in Urba had to be the work of the Elite, everyone knew the Elite were responsible for these 'disappearances', despite their official denials.

There were plenty of ideas and rumours – none of them pleasant – about the reasons behind the ritual kidnapping of young low-lifer women, but no one could ever find out for sure what happened to them because none of the women ever returned.

The Elite had always encouraged – no, *insisted* on – wars between the domains. At any one time, there would be dozens of battles happening across the world, each one with its appreciative audience of Elite watching the carnage from the safety of their hovering air-cars. These campaigns were never allowed to get out of control, though: if a warlord became too successful and showed signs of succumbing to ambition – maybe indulging a desire to spread his area of conquest – the Elite would stop him and his army with ruthless efficiency.

Nobody in Capelia complained at the Elite's increasing lack of attention in our affairs.

'If it was some kind of mechanical malfunction and not an action of the gods,' I continued, 'I don't understand why the Elite didn't put it right – carried out emergency repairs or whatever. It just doesn't make sense.' They'd never let anything stop them before, let's face it.

'They obviously didn't have the time,' said Ken. He'd picked up a large candle, lit it and began heading down the stairs towards the part of the building that lay deep underground. I dutifully followed him.

'You're forgetting about the Citadel,' I said. 'The Elite in their stronghold might be putting matters right, from their point of view, even as we speak.'

'I haven't forgotten about the Citadel,' he said smugly. 'That's why our mission is so important.'

I stared at him in horror. 'You're going to the Citadel?' I exclaimed.

'We're going to have a damned good try.'

'We are? Oh joy.'

At the bottom of the stairs we entered another large, mysterious room. The feeble light our flickering candle cast couldn't dispel the menace I felt lurking in the surrounding shadows. This room was also filled with the unfathomable devices of the Elite, but this was clearly no place for recreation. The chairs that faced the two rows of mysterious equipment were strictly functional. The equipment might have been vitally important; now it was all completely dead and useless, its magic gone.

'Your father's counsellors think this room might have been how the Elite in this Compound communicated with other Compounds across the world, don't they?' I asked Ken, telling myself I'd better start calling him by his ridiculous new name. *Gideron*. The mind boggled.

'I believe so, but what do those old fools know?' he said dismissively.

'Well, even if the counsellors are wrong, at least their magical means of communication ceased at the same time as their weapons failed,' I said.

'Luckily for us.' He led the way into the small room that interested him most of all. It was empty, except for a large circular hatch cover, more than six feet in diameter, set into the floor. All attempts to open it or cut through it had failed. Ken gave the hatch a petulant kick with his boot. 'Damn, I wish I knew what lies beneath that.'

'Perhaps your father's dream: a vault full of Elite treasure,' I said, then added half-seriously, 'or perhaps it's a tunnel that leads all the way to the original home world of the Elite.'

He started to laugh, then stopped. 'You really think so?'

'No, not really.'

'So many unanswered questions,' sighed Ken. 'But hopefully we'll get some answers on our journey. Be honest, doesn't the prospect truly excite you, Jad?'

'I'm positively tingling with anticipation ... Gideron.' I suppose a small part of me – a very, *very* small part of me – *was* excited at the prospect of getting away from both Capelia and my dismal career as a jester, but in the main all I could see ahead of us was doom and disaster. My dear friend and almost brother would see to that, I just knew it.

I must say I was surprised by Tiri's reaction to my bad news: no sign of the expected flood of tears, no expressions of concern for my safety. 'Lucky you,' she said simply as she undressed in my tiny bedroom garret. She looked quite pretty in the candle-light – one of the few advantages of losing the magic Elite lights in the castle.

'What do you mean, *lucky* me?' I demanded.

She dropped her clothes onto my one and only chair and climbed into bed next to me. 'Well, you are lucky to have this wonderful opportunity to travel.'

I stared at her. 'Travel? It's a suicide mission! The chances of my returning are less than nil!'

She gave a small shrug. 'Still sounds like more fun than working in the kitchen. I've always wanted to travel.'

'Fine. Then *you* go with the Prince and I'll take your place in the kitchen. I bet I can pluck geese that aren't quite dead quite as well as you can.'

'You wouldn't last a day.' She kissed me on the nose. 'Even a couple of hours of honest hard work would kill you.'

I resented that. 'I work hard! Every day! You think being a court jester is easy?'

'I don't know. If I ever meet a real one, I'll ask him.' Sarcasm riddled the castle like a disease.

'Oh, thank you very much! You're supposed to be consoling me on my last night, not stabbing me in the heart,' I muttered.

'How do you want to be consoled?' Tiri asked me.

I told her.

'I think that can be arranged,' she said, 'but first I want to know what you're going to bring me back from your trip.'

'Hopefully, eight pints of blood in their original, non-punctured container,' I told her.

'That would be nice, of course, but it's not what I had in mind,' she replied, somewhat to my chagrin.

'So what did you have in mind?'

'Oh, any kind of loot would be nice. Preferably something in gold.'

'Tiri, this is not a looting expedition, it's a *spying* mission.'

'I thought you said it was a suicide mission.'

'It's both,' I said sourly.

'I'm sure you can fit in a bit of looting when you're not spying . . . or dying. I'd be very grateful. Like this—'

I groaned. 'I'll do my best,' I said, 'but I'm not promising anything.'

Tiri continued to console me, and very soon all my worries and anxieties about what lay ahead faded away – at least for a brief time. Later she said, 'Forget what I said about bringing me back something made of gold.'

'Are you sure?' I was touched. I'd obviously misjudged her.

'Yes. I'd prefer diamonds.'

CHAPTER THREE

'This horse must die,' I said with feeling. Once again it had stopped in front of a tree and was refusing to move, no matter how hard I dug my heels into its ribs. And once again Ken wheeled his own mount around and came trotting back along the track.

'He's playing you for the fool,' he said, sounding irritated.

'How can such a stupid animal know my profession?'

Ken came up alongside. 'He may be a dumb beast, but he's smart enough to realise you don't know what the hell you're doing. It's probably the way you sit on him. He instinctively knows you can't ride and he's taking advantage of you.'

'Sounds like every girl I've ever been involved with,' I muttered, trying to tug the wretched animal's head up.

Ken drew his sword and whacked my horse on its rump with the flat of his blade. The beast gave a whinny of protest, but immediately moved away from the tree and began to trot along the track at a fast pace. 'A trick you should remember,' said Ken with a laugh. 'It works just as well with women as it does with horses.'

'Somehow I doubt that!' I thought of Tiri. If I'd ever swatted her rump with the flat of a sword during one of our bedroom encounters, I was pretty certain I'd have been found buried upside down in the potato locker the next morning. 'Is that the technique you use with Princess Petal?'

'Can we leave her name out of this, please?' He no longer sounded amused.

'How can you leave a name like "Princess Petal" out of anything?' I asked. 'Besides, she is your bride-to-be. Eventually. When's the wedding date now?'

'Shut up, Jad,' he warned.

I decided discretion was perhaps the better part of valour when it came to discussions about the Prince's forthcoming nuptials, and shut up, though I couldn't wipe the grin from my face. The marriage between Ken and Princess Petal, from Acasia domain, had been arranged when they were both in their mid-teens, but Ken was in no hurry to claim his promised bride. The Princess was physically attractive, but insipid in the extreme, and I had a sneaking suspicion that Ken had contrived this expedition as yet another excuse to postpone the unhappy event.

It was the morning of the second day of our Great Adventure, and to say that I was saddle-sore didn't even come close.

'Your buttocks will toughen up . . . in time,' Ken had told me reassuringly, unable to hide a smug smile. He, of course, was as formidable a horseman as he was a crossbowman.

'Oh, just what I've always wanted,' I grumbled, 'tough buttocks.' It had taken an effort of will to remount the damned horse that morning. We'd spent the night in an inn, where the Prince, predictably, was treated like royalty, and I was treated . . . as usual. Still, at least I had a comfortable bed for the night and the food and drink was adequate, as was the hot bath in which I was able to soak away – if only temporarily – my aches and pains.

But from now on it would be very different: we would be camping in the woods every night. Ken maintained that as we'd be entering Vurgun later in the week, and sleeping rough while travelling through that domain, we should start getting ourselves accustomed to making camp.

I still didn't understand why we needed to start roughing it any earlier than absolutely necessary; there were plenty of decent inns in Vurgun. Ken, predictably enough, didn't see it that way. 'We must keep a low profile while in Vurgun,' he said seriously, 'my face is too well known there.'

'Your whole face or just your profile?' I muttered.

So when we left the inn that morning, we avoided the main road and took to a series of narrow tracks. Again, this was Ken's idea; I assumed it was supposed to be practice for being furtive. But thanks to my stupid horse and his penchant for pretending he couldn't go *around* trees, this choice of routes was slowing us down, and so Ken decided to return to the main road, much to my relief. He pointed out that we needed to call in at the garrison fort near the Vurgun border, to pick up supplies for our expedition, and to meet the garrison commander, who was no doubt desperately excited at the prospect of entertaining a royal visitor.

Once we were back on the road I was able to keep my untrustworthy steed a good distance from the trees on either side, and we made faster progress.

'After we leave the garrison remember that I will be Prince Kender no more,' said Ken.

'I know. Henceforth you will be Gideron Blaze, hard-bitten mercenary, and so on. How could I possibly have forgotten, Ken?'

'Jad—' he said, warningly.

'Sorry. *Gideron*. And I will no longer be Jad the Jester.'

'You want to change your name?'

'Not just my name. I want a new profession as well. I don't want to be a jester any more.'

He gave me a look of surprise. 'You don't? What do you want to be instead?'

'If I tell you, you'll just laugh.'

'That'll be a change.'

'My point exactly. I've taken to heart what you said to me a couple of days ago. I'm fed up with the constant sneering at my attempts to be a jester. I want a new identity. One that people will respect.'

'So what do you want to be now you're a grown-up?'

'An assassin.'

I will give Ken his due – he did *try* not to laugh . . . for about fifteen seconds in all. Then he guffawed so loudly he almost fell off his horse. 'An *assassin*!' he eventually managed to gasp. 'Where did you get a crazy idea like that?'

'It's not crazy. People respect assassins.'

He gulped for air for several seconds, then said, 'People *fear* assassins. And a lot of people have *contempt* for assassins ... but *respect*? I don't think so, Jad.'

'I disagree. Fear is a form of respect. As for contempt ... well, I think I'd rather people were contemptuous of me for being an assassin than for being a court jester. A bad court jester.'

'By the gods, you're serious, aren't you?' he said as he wiped his eyes.

'Very.'

'So you're just going to introduce yourself as an assassin to people we meet along the way? As in, "Hello, I'm Jad the Assassin. Mind if I share your campfire for the night?" That'll go down well.'

'Of course not. It will be more subtle than that. With your help.'

'My help?'

'Yes. You'll drop meaningful hints about my profession in passing. The odd mention of suspected links with the Guild of Assassins, but you're not sure. We'll cultivate an air of mystery about me. Am I an assassin or not? Give people something to talk about.'

'Oh, they'll talk about you, that I guarantee. Jad, you don't *look* like an assassin. You look like ... well, don't take this the wrong way but you look like a jester.'

'Perfect look for an assassin, I'd have thought. Besides, it makes more sense for Gideron, the cynical, hard-bitten mercenary, to be travelling in the company of a mysterious assassin, rather than a jester who can empty a court full of people faster than an outbreak of dysentery. Oh, and from now on call me Usborne.'

'Usborne? That's a silly name.'

'I really don't think getting into a silly names competition is a good idea, do you? You'd win hands down on that one, *Gideron.*'

After a few minutes of surly silence, Ken said, 'You know absolutely nothing about being an assassin.'

'I know enough to convince people I *might* be an assassin,' I told him. 'And I have this—' I reached into one of my saddlebags and produced an old, leather-bound book. I leaned over and handed it to him. He took it and looked at the cover, raised an eyebrow.

'*The Book of Poisons*. Where did you get this?'

'From Harius's library. This was amongst a pile of books on the medical uses of herbs.'

He handed the book back to me. 'How curious. I wonder why he had it.'

'I think that in his younger days he had an interest in all manner of unusual subjects.' I hesitated, then decided Ken might as well know the truth about Harius. 'He had an eventful life before he became a jester in your grandfather's court. He wasn't from Capelia for a start.'

'Really? I didn't know that.'

'He rarely talked about his past, but sometimes, when he was even drunker than usual, he would drop hints and tell me fragments of his life story. I tried to get him to elaborate during his more sober periods, but he'd always refuse. However, one night he let slip that he originally came from the domain of Ashtor—'

'*Ashtor!*' said Ken in an awed tone.

'—and that he'd been an officer in Lord Emminence's army.'

He looked at me in amazement. 'And he escaped with his life?'

'Yes. One of the very few. It was a lucky fluke, he told me. His wife and young son weren't so lucky. He never said so, but I think he felt guilty at surviving when they died.'

Everyone knew what happened in Ashtor. The Elite had made sure it would *never* be forgotten. Ashtor had been the last domain to rise up in open rebellion against the Elite, nearly four decades ago. The Elite had responded by razing the entire domain to the ground and slaughtering the population, man, woman and child.

Kender shook his head in wonder. 'Harius! Who would ever have thought that the old fool had such a past!'

'Harius wasn't his real name either. I never did find out what it was.'

'But why didn't you tell me about this before?'

'I'm sure you know why! He let that slip one night when he was very drunk. The next morning he made me swear to keep it a secret. If the Elite had ever found out—'

'The Elite would have reacted ruthlessly if they'd discovered we were harbouring a refugee from Ashtor, even unintentionally,' he said slowly as the implications sank in. 'My mother, my father . . . me – the Krader dynasty would have been wiped out.' The look of shock and relief on his face made me feel almost sorry for him.

'Now, with the Elite gone, it doesn't matter,' I said in a bid to cheer him up. 'And besides, I wanted to prove to you that a jester isn't necessarily what he appears to be.'

'Well, you've never convinced me as a jester anyway, but point taken. From now on you are Osbert the Assassin.'

'That's *Usborne*.'

'Right. Whatever.' He was silent for a few moments, before adding, 'Has it occurred to you that if someone takes your assassin identity seriously, you might be asked to actually murder someone?' He laughed. 'That would be really funny.'

'Absolutely – I feel an attack of the giggles coming on at the very thought.'

He leaned over and clapped me hard on the back, crying, 'At least you're getting into the spirit of the enterprise!'

The commander of the border garrison was expecting us – Lord Krader had seen to that – and so there was a guard of honour for the Prince when we arrived at the fort, which consisted of several wooden, one-storey buildings surrounded by a high, wooden stockade. After Ken had inspected the troops the Commander, a tall, saturnine-looking man in his mid-thirties called Lundor, took us to his private quarters for refreshments. On the way up, Ken finally got around to introducing me.

'Ah,' he said, 'I thought I recognised you. I saw you perform at court once.' Then he abruptly changed the subject, a diplomatic gesture for which I was very grateful.

In his quarters, where we were served wine and a selection of cold meats and cheeses by a servant, we were joined by Lundor's second-in-command, Captain Bawngrun, a big man, though only a couple of years older than Ken and me. He was clearly uncomfortable in the presence of royalty. He straightened his shoulders and stood at attention as Commander Lundor said to Ken, 'I don't mean to be discouraging, your Highness, but Captain Bawngrun has some information you should hear.'

The young Captain saluted his commanding officer, then turned to us and reported, 'I was on patrol duty yesterday and we encountered a large party of men who'd crossed over the border from Vurgun. Their leader said they were vigilantes in pursuit of a group of Elite who they believed had entered Capelia disguised as merchants. I told him we would search for this group of Elite, if it existed, but that they were trespassing on Capelia territory and that a formal complaint would be made to their Lord Vorgal.

'The vigilante leader told us Lord Vorgal was no more. He'd been overthrown in a rebellion four days ago and executed . . . as were the rest of his family.'

Ken, who'd been listening sombrely, asked, 'So who rules Vurgun now?'

'Apparently no one,' replied the Commander. 'Rival groups of rebels are fighting to gain control of the domain, but so far no one group has triumphed. According to our prisoners, all of Vurgun is riven with strife: rebels fighting each other whilst mobs of vigilantes hunt down any surviving Elite.'

'Prisoners?' asked Ken.

'The vigilantes refused my order to return to Vurgun, your Highness,' Captain Bawngrun said. 'They attacked us. We killed several of them; the remainder started to flee. We captured five of them.'

'Well done, Captain,' said Ken.

Captain Bawngrun looked both embarrassed and pleased at the same time.

'Considering the state of affairs in Vurgun, your Highness,' began the Commander, a shade hesitantly, 'perhaps you might reconsider your mission? Possibly postpone it until the situation is calmer?'

I looked hopefully at Ken, who took a swallow of wine and regarded the Commander with amusement. 'Did my father put you up to this?'

The Commander shook his head. 'No, your Highness. I immediately sent word to Lord Krader about the events in Vurgun, but I doubt if the messenger has reached him yet.'

'True. But my father had already informed you about my mission, and that I would be picking up supplies and equipment here. I'm sure in his message to you he suggested you try and dissuade me from continuing on. Am I right?'

Commander Lundor didn't reply, but his expression was one of acute discomfort.

Ken smiled at him. 'Don't worry, Commander, you did your best. I'll make sure my father knows that. But I'm determined to go on as planned. We'd heard rumours of rebellions in other domains before we'd even left the castle, but they certainly didn't deter us. Right, Jad?'

He looked at me. I gave a weak smile. 'Right, your Highness. Wild horses couldn't stop us.'

'Very well,' said the Commander with a sigh. 'Then all I can do is suggest you avoid the towns and villages.'

'That was always my intention,' Ken told him. 'Jad and I will be living rough on our journey through Vurgun.'

And probably dining on raw rabbit, I thought sourly.

'What is your planned route?' Commander Lundor enquired. 'Lord Krader didn't provide me with any details.'

'That's because I don't have a set route,' said Ken, somewhat smugly. 'We'll be playing it by ear.'

A euphemism, I felt sure, for, 'I don't really have a bloody clue what I'm doing.'

'My plan,' continued Ken, 'is to travel as far towards the centre as possible, within a time limit of about two months, gathering as much information as I can along the way.' I noted, with a sinking feeling, that Ken had made no mention of his intention to reach the Citadel. He clearly didn't want that information getting back to his father.

'Yes, your Highness,' said the Commander, perfectly concealing his true opinion: definitely a born diplomat. And he didn't even know the full extent of Ken's crazy plan. 'But perhaps some form of set route would be a good idea at this stage. You can always alter it later depending on the circumstances. You have maps, of course—?'

'Er, I did have a map but I believe I may have misplaced it . . .'

I managed not to burst out laughing.

'Then, your Highness, with your permission,' said the Commander as he rose from his chair, 'perhaps I could make a few suggestions. If you would accompany me to our map room, your Highness—'

The map room, not surprisingly, turned out to be full of maps. A huge chart showing the whole of Urba covered one entire wall. The Commander drew us over to it and began to point out a possible route through Vurgun and the domains beyond. I stared at it with interest. Urba's tubular shape had been opened out to form a flat plane that was almost a square. I noted that Capelia, a long narrow strip, was located at the centre of our end of the world. I imagined that maps produced by the map-makers of different domains would always place their respective domain in the central area; no one would care to have their own domain appear sliced in two on the top and bottom edge of a map.

Staring at the giant map, the biggest I'd ever seen, made me aware of just how huge the world was, and what a small and insignificant part of it Capelia was – and yet Capelia wasn't a small domain; I knew it ran parallel to the Wall for nearly six hundred miles and was, on average, some one hundred and thirty miles deep. Even so, it was puny when you surveyed Urba as a whole – Urba was more than eight thousand miles in length and two and half thousand miles in diameter; in this flattened presentation, Urba was nearly nine thousand miles in width ... if I remembered my lessons with Ken's tutor correctly. I tried to work out what this meant in square miles, but failed miserably. I blamed the tutor.

As the Commander pointed and spoke, Ken nodded his agreement, trying to give the impression that the Commander was merely confirming a route that Ken had already decided upon. 'So beyond Vurgun and the adjacent domain of Pelmore lies your biggest obstacle,' continued the Commander, 'the Pyman Sea.' He indicated the large body of water that stretched across nearly a quarter of the way between the top and bottom of the map. It was one of the world's four major seas. 'Finding passage on a ship may prove difficult in these unsettled times. Your best bet would be to go to the port of Persopia. It's the busiest on this side of the Sea and has, or did have, regular shipping routes to five ports on the other side.'

Ken stepped close to the map, peered at it for a couple of minutes, then authoritatively placed his forefinger on a small dot. 'Verharven. That's the port we want to go to. Almost directly opposite to Persopia and therefore the quickest voyage across the Pyman Sea.'

It was also the port most convenient for someone heading for the Citadel. Unfortunately – or fortunately, from Ken's point of view – the Citadel, rather than being dead centre, as one might expect for a world-wide command centre, was located much nearer our end of the world. It was only – *only* – some fifteen hundred miles from Capelia. Even so, it would take much longer than two months to get there; I could see this expedition turning into a life-long project – though all the signs indicated that my life wasn't going to extend very far into the future.

'Where would you go after Verharven?' asked the Commander.

'Oh, just keep heading generally inland depending on what route seems the least difficult,' said Ken blithely. 'Any suggestions would be welcome.'

And so it went on. When it was over, I was relieved to hear Ken graciously agreeing to accept a copy of the route they'd been discussing; the Commander offered to have a clerk draw it up. Getting hopelessly lost was one problem I hadn't spent much time contemplating, there being so many other potentially deadly hazards to worry about.

Back in the Commander's quarters, where I happily resumed my consumption of both the wine and the food, Ken continued, 'Of chief concern to my father and myself are the stories about the warlord Camarra. Are they true? Is he really having such success in his campaign of conquest?'

'It would seem so, your Highness,' said the Commander. 'Reports of events so far away are sketchy, but they've all been consistent. Lord Camarra appears to have conquered more than seven domains since the Day of Wonder – and that's a conservative figure. We're awaiting further reports to confirm this. Apparently he's forcing the conquered rulers of those domains to enter into an alliance with him, thus greatly expanding the size of the forces under his control. We're hearing lots of rumours that he plans to mount an attack on the Citadel.'

'That's what I heard too,' said Ken. 'What do you know about him personally?'

Commander Lundor shrugged. 'He's a ruthless and cruel man, but a brilliant military strategist. He's never lost a war and I think the Elite admired him – though, of course, they always curbed his expansive ambitions. I advise you to give him and his forces a wide berth.'

'Well,' said Ken, 'I'll take your advice under serious consideration.'

Again I managed to stifle a cynical guffaw. If Ken's intention was to try and reach the Citadel, there would be no way we could avoid encountering Camarra's ever-growing army. My sense of doom and dread intensified.

Ken continued, 'Now as soon as Jad and I have selected a few items from your stores and armoury we'll be on our way. Many thanks for your hospitality, Commander Lundor. I shall write a note to my father telling him of your invaluable help before I leave. Perhaps you can have it delivered to him . . .'

The Commander bowed his head. 'My pleasure, your Highness. But I would like to be of further service by providing you and your companion with an armed escort for at least part of your journey. Say, through the domain of Vurgun?'

It sounded a bloody good idea to me, but naturally Ken shook his head and said, 'Thank you, Commander, but Jad and I intend to travel undercover. The less attention we attract the better.'

'Very well, your Highness,' said the Commander, resigned.

Captain Bawngrun said, 'Keep a watchful eye out for vigilantes, your Highness. And some of my men have noted signs of trolls in the area.'

'Don't worry, we'll be careful,' Kender assured him.

This was news to me. 'Captain Bawngrun,' I said, 'can I ask a favour of you before we leave?'

'Yes, of course. What is it?'

'It's about my horse—'

'I told you you'd be wasting your time,' said Ken.

'At least this horse isn't coming to a dead stop in front of every tree.'

'True. This one just keeps trying to scrape you off against every tree it passes. It's like your first horse – it senses you're a useless rider. Things won't improve until you become a better rider. You've got to convince the horse you're in charge.'

'I keep trying to!'

'Yelling in its ear won't do any good. Use your spurs.'

'I don't like to. It seems too . . . drastic. Besides, the trees are starting to thin out . . .'

'So will your legs at this rate. Trust me, use the spurs on him.'

I'd picked up the spurs, on Ken's advice, back at the fort. We'd changed clothes there; he'd swapped his royal finery for the garb of a mercenary soldier. He wore a chain-mail shirt, a battered breastplate, knee-high boots and a helmet. I was dressed as I imagined an undercover assassin would: a black leather jacket, black leather cap, black leather leggings and boots. Oh, and I also had a black woollen cape. Ken told me I looked like a court jester having a very bad day.

We had a veritable arsenal of weapons. Ken now had a lance strapped to the side of his horse, along with two crossbows, one of them his own special weapon. He also had a sword and two daggers, one of them concealed in his boot. I had a sword, a dagger and a crossbow; I too tried concealing my dagger in my boot but it hurt my ankle so I stuck it back in my belt.

'Argghhh!' I cried as the damned horse rubbed me up against another tree, bashing my knee in the process. 'Right, that does it!' I dug the spurs into his sides—

Ken eventually found me about half a mile away. I'd managed to stay on the galloping horse for that far before I lost my desperate grip on the saddle-horn and fell off. I was still sitting where I landed when Ken rode up. My damned horse was a short distance away, nibbling unconcernedly on some grass.

'Are you all right?' he asked.

'Nothing's broken,' I assured him, 'though it doesn't feel like it.' I stood up to show him that I could stand up. 'Thanks for the tip about the spurs, by the way. Worked like a dream.'

'A few gentle jabs was what I meant,' he said as he dismounted. 'I didn't suggest you try and disembowel the poor beast with them.' He gave me his reins to hold and then walked over to my horse, gave it a reassuring pat and examined its sides. 'Not much blood,' he announced. 'It'll live.'

'I'm overjoyed. Let's make camp here, shall we? I don't think I can ride another yard today.'

'Yes,' he said, looking around, 'it'll be getting dark soon and this is as good a spot as any.' He led my horse, as docile as a lamb with Ken, back to where I waited. We tethered both animals and removed their saddles and our saddle-bags.

'Is it safe to make a fire?' I asked.

'I think we can risk it, unless you're afraid of attracting a bunch of trolls.'

'It's those vigilantes I'm worried about. Not to mention wild animals—'

'After the vigilantes' skirmish with the good Captain Bawngrun and his men I would imagine the survivors are still fleeing. And there are few dangerous animals in these parts.'

'I hope you're right.'

'Of course I am. Now go and collect some wood for the fire.'

I looked nervously around at the surrounding trees. 'Why me?'

'Because I outrank you.'

'Hang on a minute,' I protested, 'how come Gideron the Mercenary outranks Usborne the Assassin?'

'Those identities are only for the benefit of other people. The reality of our respective positions in society remains in force when we are alone. I am still your Prince and you are still my subject.'

'*Now* you tell me!'

Ken waved a dismissive hand at me. 'Go, subject, fetch wood. And yell if you encounter any trouble.'

'Would a high-pitched scream do instead?'

By the time I returned with an armful of dead branches and twigs the great column of the sun that stretched across the sky was starting to flicker and fade. Beyond it you could now see the roof of the world, some two and a half thousand miles above us – though of course, to the people who lived there, *we* were on the roof of the world.

'I take it from the lack of either yells or screams you saw no trolls,' said Ken.

'No, great Prince,' I said as I dumped the pile of kindling onto the ground, 'I saw nothing at all.'

'Will this sarcasm continue for long?' he asked.

'Probably. When it comes to the use of sarcasm I had a great teacher, oh glorious one. Your father.' I managed to light the kindling after only six attempts, which was rather good for me. Then I went to my saddle-bags and extracted a leather wine skin, a pipe and a large pouch of powdered dried herbs. I sat by the fire, had a large drink of red wine and then began filling the pipe's bowl with a helping from the bag of herbs.

Ken was staring at the pipe. 'What is that?' he finally asked.

'What it looks like. It's a pipe. Belonged to Harius.'

'You don't smoke.'

'It's all part of my new persona,' I said as I lit the pipe with the burning end of a twig. 'Besides, it's not tobacco, it's some sort of herb from Harius's garden. He used to smoke it all the time.'

'Have you smoked it before?'

'Er, no,' I admitted.

'It'll probably make you sick. Like the time we tried smoking tobacco when we were youngsters. Remember?'

I did, only too well. 'This isn't tobacco. Harius swore by it. You can either smoke it or mix it in food or wine. He bred this species of herb himself, he told me. I puffed on the pipe. 'It doesn't taste at all like tobacco. It's rather pleasant . . . and sweet.' I puffed away some more. A strange, soothing sensation began to spread through my head.

'Don't say I didn't warn you. I don't want you puking all over the place while you're preparing our meal.' He picked up the wine skin and took a long drink from it.

'Ah, so I'm to be the cook as well on this expedition, am I? Why am I not surprised?' I should have been annoyed but I wasn't. My mood was becoming mellower with every passing moment. I'd even stopped worrying about trolls and vigilantes. I took another deep draw on the pipe and then said, 'Do you think those vigilantes that Captain Bawngrun encountered were telling the truth about Elite entering Capelia disguised as merchants?'

'Possibly. But it might have been just a story those damned Vurguns devised to cover their intrusion into our territory. I suspect they were merely a common raiding party.'

'Even so, it make you think. I mean, could you spot an Elite in disguise?'

'Of course I could.'

'Are you sure?' I took another puff on the pipe. Now I was beginning to feel downright cheerful. Maybe it was the wine. 'Take them out of their customary black and crimson and how could you tell them apart from anyone else?'

'Simple. Because they'll still look like Elite. I could spot an Elite anywhere.'

'How? I haven't seen as many Elite close up as you have, but I've encountered enough of them to know they look just like us. Okay, they're always extremely good-looking but—'

'Their skins,' said Ken, 'they always had pale skins, yellow or light brown: I've never seen an Elite with a truly coloured complexion. No really dark brown or black Elite . . .'

'True,' I said, though that had never occurred to me before. 'But lots of people have pale complexions. Me, for example.'

Ken guffawed. '*You?* You could never pass for an Elite! You just said yourself that they're always very good-looking.'

I should have taken offence at this, but I didn't care. I was feeling no pain. 'You're missing my point,' I told him. 'Put an Elite in ordinary clothing and what you've got is a good-looking, pale, yellow or light-brown-skinned person. Nothing to automatically indicate that they're Elite. Right?'

He gave it some thought for a time and then scowled. 'Yes, I suppose so,' he admitted. Then he peered upwards and said, 'Why don't you go and collect more wood before the sun goes completely out. Then we'll eat.'

'Sure,' I said happily. I stood up, still puffing on the pipe.

'Why are you smiling in that strange way?' Ken asked me.

'What strange way?'

'You're wearing a decidedly goofy smile. It's disturbing.'

'Sorry,' I said and wandered off contentedly into the trees. I felt at peace with the world.

That didn't last long. I hadn't gone very far when something very heavy smashed into my back, between my shoulder blades. I fell forward, the breath knocked out of me. On the ground I rolled over and saw, looming over me, the unmistakeable horned form of a troll. And he was raising over his head a very large club.

CHAPTER FOUR

While I didn't really expect to survive Ken's mad adventure I didn't expect to die so early in the journey. But before the troll could bring the club down on my head, a crossbow bolt hit him in the neck and he toppled backwards with a grunt. I saw Ken running past me. A shriek told me that he'd found another target. A short time later he returned and helped me up. 'The others have run off,' he told me, 'and I don't think they'll be back. Good thing I heard them coming. You all right?'

'Oh sure. As soon as I get a new spine I'll be fine.'

'Count yourself lucky. If you weren't so tall and the troll wasn't so short he would've bashed your brains out. But at least he wiped that goofy smile off your face.'

'My pipe!' I exclaimed and began to look for it. While I was searching for it in the grass I saw Ken start to do something disgusting with the dead troll. He was cutting the bolt out of his neck. 'Ugh! What the hell are you doing?'

'What does it look like? These bolts are precious.'

I grimaced and kept searching for my pipe. I found it when I stepped on it, but luckily it didn't break. I started to head back to our camp when Ken called, 'Hey, what about the firewood?'

'No more firewood-collecting for me tonight. You do it. If you're lucky you may get to shoot another troll.'

While he went off to collect his other bolt, and hopefully some more firewood, I went back to the campfire, had another drink of red wine and relit my pipe. I needed the solace. My back felt like it had been hit by a troll wielding a large club. I slumped to the ground. The sun was now just a few streaks of light in the sky. Soon it would be completely dark.

Ken returned with a suspiciously small amount of firewood. 'Haven't you started preparing our meal yet?' he grumbled as he threw it to the ground.

'I will soon. Give me time to recuperate first.'

'By the look of you if you recuperate any further you'll be unconscious.'

I sighed, got to my feet and opened another of the saddle-bags to get the cooking implements and containers of food. Like all our supplies, they'd been provided by our friends at the border garrison fort. 'How does beef stew and biscuits sound?' I asked him.

'Depressing.'

'Good.' I set a large pot on the fire and filled it with stew. While waiting for it to heat I filled a metal cup with wine and handed it to Ken. Then I filled one for myself. I'd decided to spend the whole journey in a state of inebriation.

As we sat by the campfire and I continued to puff on my pipe I said, 'You know, I feel sort of sorry for the trolls.'

'You do?' he said, sounding surprised, 'Why? One of them just tried to kill you.'

'I know. It's just that they lead such miserable lives.'

'They're dirty, ugly, evil creatures.'

'Yes, but is it their fault they're like that? I mean, who made them that way?'

'The gods, who made everyone and everything else.'

'Yes, if the gods actually exist. You know my feelings on that subject.'

'Jad, sometimes you think too much.'

'Well, one of us has to.'

'On the basis of our long friendship, I shall ignore that insult.'

'Sorry,' I said sincerely, 'that was the wine talking. Or something.'

'More likely whatever it is you're smoking in that pipe.'

After we'd eaten and had wrapped ourselves in our cloaks to protect ourselves against the cold, I asked Ken, 'Do you really intend to travel all the way to the Citadel?'

'Indeed I do.'

'What about Lord Camarra and his army? What happens when we run into them, as seems highly likely?'

'I have a plan.'

'You do?' I wondered when he'd come up with this plan. Probably ten seconds ago. 'What is it?'

'We're mercenaries, aren't we?'

'If you say so.'

'Well then, we offer our services to Lord Camarra and join his army. Then, when I've found out all I need to know about the situation with both Camarra and the Citadel we slip away and head for home.'

'That's your plan?'

'What's wrong with it?'

I knew it was useless to try and point out the slight flaws – like our being exposed as spies and tortured to death, or being killed in a battle – and so I simply said, 'It's a marvellous plan. I think I'll try and get some sleep now.' And have hideous nightmares all night.

'Go ahead and sleep. I'll keep watch until it's time for you to take over guard duty.'

'First light tomorrow morning would be a good time for me,' I said, leaning my head against my saddle and closing my eyes.

Actually I did sleep all the way through until the morning's first light. I wondered why Ken hadn't woken me as planned. Had he taken pity on me and let me sleep while he unselfishly remained on guard duty? Well, no. When I sat up and looked at him I saw that he was in a deep sleep. Presumably he'd fallen asleep during his watch. Some professional he was turning out to be.

I got up and stretched. My back throbbed, but it could have been worse. I could be dead. Then I went and shook Ken by the shoulder. He stirred, and had the good grace to look guilty when realisation that he'd fallen asleep on guard duty dawned. But only very briefly. 'Nothing to report, your highness,' I said with a straight face. 'No sign of trolls, vigilantes or any dangerous beasties of any kind.'

He gave me a suspicious look as he got up, then he went off into the forest to relieve himself. I did the same, though I naturally went in a different direction. After breakfast – more stew and biscuits – we broke camp and resumed our journey. I was now determined to show my horse who was boss in our mutually resentful relationship and this time when he attempted to bash my leg against a tree I nudged his ribs with my spurs and he immediately desisted. He obviously remembered yesterday's painful experience. From then on he was perfectly behaved – though no less uncomfortable to ride.

The morning proved completely uneventful and we didn't see another soul. We stopped for a light lunch consisting of dried strips of beef, biscuits and a couple of apples – oh, and I had some wine, of course. The afternoon was also thankfully uneventful and that evening we made camp in a pleasant glade near a stream. The night passed peacefully. I began to lose my misgivings . . .

We'd not long left camp the following morning when we came upon across a sight that promptly caused me to lose my breakfast of beans, bacon, biscuits and an apple. And the beer I'd drunk too, unfortunately. Ken, being made of sterner stuff, simply went slightly green.

Hanging from the lower branches of a tree were five badly burned corpses; so badly burned were the bodies that it was impossible to tell whether they were male or female. On the ground, circling the trunk of the tree, were the still-smouldering ashes of what had obviously been a sizable bonfire.

When I'd finished throwing up my breakfast I heard Ken say, 'I hope they were dead before that fire was lit, but I doubt it—'

'You think they were burned alive?' I asked, horrified.

'I do. Look at how they're suspended from the branches.'

I'd been trying to avert my eyes from the atrocity, but I forced myself to look. They'd been hung from the branches with wires tied around their upper chests. The implications were horribly clear. Ken voiced my fears. He said, 'Their killers used wires, not ropes. If they'd been dead when they were strung up it wouldn't have mattered if ropes had burned through and dropped the bodies into the flames. The use of wire means they were alive when the fire was started. Their executioners wanted them to suffer as long as possible.'

'Who could do such a thing?' I asked, fighting the urge to start retching again.

'Vigilantes, most likely. We're looking at the remains of five Elite.'

'I hate the Elite as much as anybody,' I said, 'but to kill even Elite in this manner is . . . unspeakable.'

'Yes' said Ken, sombrely, 'the vigilantes appear to want to outdo the Elite in cruelty.'

I took out my pipe, filled it with Harius's magical herbs, and quickly lit it. I needed to breathe in its sweet smoke to counteract the stench of burned human flesh. The smell had taken me back to that day when, at the age of eight, I'd been forced to witness the Elite massacre of the townsmen outside the Compound. 'Let's leave this place,' I pleaded.

We rode quickly away. The contents of the pipe began to soothe my queasy stomach and my jangled nerves, but I knew the image of those five charred bodies would haunt me for some considerable time.

We rode in silence for about half an hour, then Ken said, 'What particularly disturbs me is what the vigilantes will do when they've caught and killed all the surviving Elite. They'll have the taste for blood and it won't be easily quenched. The domains should organise to stamp them out.'

'I'm afraid you're being overly optimistic, Ken,' I told him. 'If Lord Camarra's actions are any indication, cooperation between the domains is out of the question. It's going to be all-out war. Besides, it sounds as if many of the domains, like Vurgun, are falling apart.'

'You could be right,' he said gloomily.

I'd never seen Ken in such an uncharacteristically sombre mood before. He hadn't even complained about me calling him 'Ken'. I suspected he was now beginning to realise that his hope of enjoying some grand adventure had been a juvenile folly. I began to entertain the plan of trying to persuade him to return to Capelia. Perhaps now he would be more amenable to the suggestion . . .

But as I pondered just how to broach this suggestion, we ran into straight into an ambush.

They came at us from all sides out of the forest. There were about twenty of them, on horseback, a motley bunch dressed in a variety of clothing and armour but all brandishing weapons. Completely surrounded, there was nothing we could do but raise our arms in surrender. I knew immediately that they were vigilantes, possibly the same group responsible for the atrocity we'd encountered back along the trail.

A big man with a scarred face, who was presumably their leader, positioned his horse directly in front of us and made a threatening gesture with his lance. 'Who the fuck are you and what's your business in these parts?' he demanded in a tone of voice that could not, by any stretch of the imagination, be described as friendly.

Before I could start begging for mercy, Ken spoke. 'We are mercenaries, good sir. We are on our way to join the forces of Lord Camarra. Formerly we were in the service of Lord Krader of Capelia. He's a fine master but we felt our talents were being wasted in Capelia's army; it sees very little action. Also we hear there is much plunder to be won in the service of Lord Camarra.'

The leader of the vigilantes stared at us for some time, then spat on the ground and said, 'Your story has a ring of truth . . . but it could be just that: a fucking *story*. Can you prove you are not a pair of damned Elite in disguise? They bastards're everywhere and bloody cunning. But in the past week we've caught and executed over seventy of the monsters.'.

That surprised me. How could there be so many surviving Elite in Vurgun alone? I guess the vigilantes were none too fussy about establishing the true identities of those they accused of being Elite.

Ken spoke again. 'May I propose a simple test to prove we are who we say we are?'

I prayed to the gods I now hardly believed in that Ken had something clever in mind. If not, we were going to end up hanging from a tree branch over an open fire.

The vigilante leader said, 'What kind of test?'

'Have you ever known an Elite to possess any prowess with a sword?'

'No. They had no need of our weapons. They had their fucking firesticks. But I'll bet the bastards are learning how to use swords real quick now.'

'Then this is what I suggest,' continued Ken. 'Select your best swordsman to fight me. Let me demonstrate that I possess a skill with a sword that no Elite could have acquired since the day of their fall.'

The vigilante leader frowned as he considered this. He spat again on the ground. Apparently with him thinking and spitting went together. I came to the obvious conclusion that the man wasn't too bright. Whether that was good or bad for us I wasn't yet sure.

Finally he nodded. 'Very well.' He turned in his saddle and pointed at another man. 'Hortun, you're always bragging about your way with a fucking sword. You'll fight this so-called mercenary. And if you don't kill him I'll bloody kill *you*.'

Hortun was a tall, sinewy man of about thirty years. He grinned. It was both an evil grin and one that revealed he had remarkably bad teeth. 'I'll kill him, Patro. No worries.' He dismounted and drew his sword.

As Ken was also about to dismount I decided it was time to give him some invaluable advice. 'Try and win,' I whispered to him.

The nearest vigilantes backed their horses away to provide a space for the duel. I did the same, surprised that my horse so readily obeyed me. Perhaps it sensed the seriousness of the situation. Ken drew his sword and the two opponents faced each other.

The vigilante called Hortun wore a chain-mail shirt. Making high-quality chain-mail is a slow, painstaking process – each ring of the linked armour has to be laboriously bent around a metal rod – and requires great skill on the part of the armourer. Hortun's chain-mail shirt looked like it had been knitted by his mother. I took this as a good sign.

It was all over remarkably quickly. You couldn't even justify describing it as a duel: Ken made a few swift feints then unexpectedly executed a simple beat attack and lunged, driving his sword easily through Hortun's shoddy chain-mail and deep into the man's chest. Hortun looked very offended, then dropped to his knees. Ken withdrew his blade and stood back. We all quietly watched Hortun die. Blood poured both from the wound in his chest and from his mouth. He looked around imploringly at his fellow vigilantes, but they'd all suddenly adopted expressions that clearly said, 'He's nothing to do with us. We've never even seen this man before.' Then Hortun pitched forward on his face, twitched a bit and lay still. I would have felt sorry for the poor fool, but I was too occupied with being overwhelmed with relief.

Ken wiped his sword clean with a handful of grass, returned it to his scabbard and looked at the vigilante leader, Patro. 'Satisfied? Or should I butcher some more of your men before you get the point?'

'You sure know your way around a blade,' Patro admitted, 'but what about your funny-looking mate?' He looked in my direction. 'Is he as good as you?'

'My talents in despatching my enemies involve more subtle methods,' I said in a tone that I hoped sounded both sinister and enigmatic, something that's difficult to achieve when you're on the verge of a panic attack. 'But,' I added, 'I am more than competent with a sword and would be happy to give you a demonstration.' I glanced around at the surrounding vigilantes. 'So if your *second best* swordsman would care to present himself—'

There was a distinct lack of enthusiasm amongst the group to accept my invitation, thank the gods. Then their leader grinned, revealing that his teeth were as bad as the late Hortun's, and said, 'Not necessary. With your looks you're plainly not Elite.' I could have kissed him, bad teeth and all.

Ken remounted and said, 'Then we are free to continue on our journey?'

'No,' said Patro. 'You're going to join us. We need good fighters. The hunt for the fucking Elite must be stepped up. Every last one of them has got be destroyed. Our cause is fucking just!'

'I'm sure it is,' said Ken, 'but we are anxious to be on our way. We have a long way to travel. As I told you, we intend joining the army of Lord Camarra. We are anxious to share in the plunder that we hear his men are acquiring.'

'You can go when we've finished our holy mission,' said Patro. 'And don't worry, we'll make it worth your while. Plenty of plunder in our good work. Now come with us to our camp.'

Ken and I exchanged glances. He shrugged. It seemed we had no choice but to obey.

As we rode side by side, in the middle of the column of vigilantes, I said quietly to him, 'That was an impressive display you put on back there. Not that I doubted for a second that you would beat the fellow.'

'Of course you didn't,' he said dryly, 'but he had no chance. That chain-mail of his was worse than useless.'

'No pun intended, but you definitely found his weak link.' Actually I was quite pleased with my pun.

'I was also impressed by you,' he said. 'The line about your special talents was good. Thank the gods you didn't have to demonstrate them. What did you have in mind? To bore them to death with your usual court performance? Though if he'd taken you up on your offer to display your abilities with a sword they'd have all died laughing.'

'You grow more like your father every day, Ken. Clearly sarcasm runs in the royal bloodline. But tell me, do you have a plan by which we can get away from this band of fanatics?'

'Not yet, but I'm working on it.'

'I'm thrilled to hear that, Ken.'

'Now who's being sarcastic? And don't call me Ken.'

We reached their camp about an hour later. It was ramshackle affair consisting of a number of sagging tents surrounded by a half-hearted attempt at building a stockade. Only the gods knew who they expected to attack them. As we entered the camp I estimated it contained over a hundred men, including the group who'd captured us. I said in a low voice to Ken, 'Do you think any of this lot have military experience?'

'There may be several ex-members of the late Lord Vorgal's army amongst them, but only lowly troops,' he replied. 'There's no evidence of any kind of army discipline. Probably all the officers were killed in the rebellion. The rest look like a mixture of bandits and the usual scum that plague every town and village. But that doesn't make them any less dangerous – more so, in fact.'

We were told to dismount. A vigilante began to lead our horses away. 'Hey, stop!' cried Ken, grabbing the hilt of his sword.

'Calm yourself, mercenary,' said Patro, 'they're being taken to the corral to be fed and watered. You can collect your belongings later. Don't worry, everything in your saddle-bags will be as you left them. You're with us now.' Patros gestured us to accompany him, first giving us a brief guided tour of the camp, pointing out its many attractions, including the food and grog tent and the latrine, which was conveniently located immediately to the rear of the former. Then he led us to the centre, where a group of about twenty frightened and rather battered-looking people sat huddled closely together. They had no choice in this; they were joined together by a thick rope tied around each of their necks. Their hands were also tightly bound. There were several women in the group.

'Who are they?' Ken asked Patro.

'Today's catch of Elite,' he said as we walked around the group of prisoners. They followed us, their eyes terrified. None of them looked remotely like Elite to me. It was obvious what was going on. The so-called vigilantes were using the hunt for the Elite as an excuse to capture people, rob them . . . and indulge in some extremely sadistic bloodletting. As Ken had said, they were nothing but bandits and scum.

'They've confessed to being Elite?' Ken asked Patro.

'Not yet, but they will when we start questioning them,' he replied.

'You mean you'll *torture* them until they confess,' I said rashly. Patro gave me a baleful glare but didn't reply.

Ken had stopped in front of one of the prisoners. She was a young woman and despite the dirt and blood that smeared her face, she was clearly a beautiful young woman. Her oval face was olive-skinned, she had short black hair, large, piercing brown eyes and a wide mouth. It was a strong face as well as a beautiful one. She was dressed in a green robe that was ripped in several places and splattered with mud. And blood. It was obvious that she'd been severely beaten.

'Why is *she* suspected of being an Elite?' Ken asked Patro without taking his eyes from her. He seemed transfixed by the girl.

'She was found with an Elite communicator hidden in her clothing,' said Patro. 'She's Elite all right—'

'I found it lying on the ground,' said the girl, an edge of defiance still in her voice. 'I picked it up because it looked pretty. And valuable. It had jewels on it . . . that's the only reason I had it. I'm not an Elite . . . I was travelling with my father, a wine merchant. We're from Vorass.'

'Liar!' cried Patro, raising his hand to strike her.

Ken deftly blocked the vigilante leader by moving in front of him; he leaned towards the young woman. 'What's your name?' he asked her.

'Alucia,' she replied.

'Alucia,' repeated Ken. 'That's a beautiful name.'

The girl looked at Ken as if seeing him for the first time. Then I saw something in her eyes. Hope, definitely, but something else. And I became only too aware of how intensely Ken continued to stare at her.

I began to get a bad feeling.

'Don't be fooled by her pretty face,' snarled Patro to Ken, 'she's a fucking Elite and by the gods she'll confess to it when we start questioning this lot for real in the morning. She'll be screaming her guts out along with the rest of these bastards.'

Ken began to turn towards Patro. Before he could say or do anything we'd both regret, me in particular, I said hurriedly to Patro, 'Sir, we're both very thirsty—' I grabbed Ken firmly by the upper arm at the same time, hoping he'd get the message. 'Mind taking us to the grog tent? Like, right now?'

'Yeah, sure . . .' muttered Patro. 'I could do with a drink myself. Follow me.' He turned and began to walk away.

I thanked the gods he hadn't noticed the look in Ken's eyes. Still keeping a firm grip on Ken's arm, I whispered fiercely into his ear, 'Keep calm or you'll get us both killed!'

He relaxed and allowed me to walk him away from the prisoners. And the girl. And as we followed Patro, Ken turned and whispered to me, 'Jad, I'm in love.'

My remaining faith in the gods completely vanished.

CHAPTER FIVE

The swill being served up in the camp's food and grog tent proved to be uneatable – I was sure I spotted goats' testicles floating in the big pot of 'stew' – so when darkness fell I heated up some more of the food that had been provided by the border garrison. As Patro had promised, we'd been able to retrieve our saddle-bags and other gear. Nothing appeared to be missing, though I'd have bet my entire supply of Harius's special herb that our bags had been thoroughly searched. Fortunately, they contained nothing that contradicted our mercenary cover story. Okay, so one of the said mercenaries had some odd possessions, like books, but that didn't suggest anything was seriously amiss with us.

We'd set up our campfire as far away as possible from everyone else in the camp so we could talk without being overheard. But no one was paying us any attention. The self-styled vigilantes were in the process of becoming drunk on their poisonous grog, of which there was a plentiful supply. I'd had a small sampling of it earlier and still couldn't get the taste out of my mouth.

While I prepared the meal, I tried to point out to Ken that he was being somewhat unrealistic about his latest obsession, namely Alucia. Naturally, I was being subtle . . .

'—But how can you keep saying you're in love with this girl? You know nothing about her. It's ridiculous! No, it's preposterous! And how do you know she *isn't* really an Elite? If she is, then she might be casting an Elite spell over you. Which would explain your bizarre behaviour. Nothing else could.'

Ken, staring wistfully towards the centre of the camp where the pathetic captives remained huddled together, said, 'It's no

55

use arguing with me. She is no Elite. None of those poor wretches are. But Alucia is the *one*. I can feel it in my heart.' And he touched his chest as if to prove his point.

'Well, I can feel in my *head* that this is a relationship doomed from the start. Besides, you're betrothed to the scintillating Princess Petal, or have you forgotten that small detail?'

'Princess Petal is of no matter. I will never marry her. I've found my true love.'

I groaned. 'All right. Then consider this. The life-expectancy of your true love can probably be numbered in mere hours.'

Ken shook his head. 'No. That won't happen. I won't allow it.'

'Oh really? And what do you have in mind?'

'We're going to rescue her.'

I stared at him in disbelief. 'We are? *How?*'

'I'm working on that,' he said with blithe unconcern.

I wanted to throttle him. 'Have you noticed we're in a camp full of extremely nasty and heavily armed vigilantes?'

'The fact hadn't escaped my attention.'

'Good. Nor should the fact that as there's about a hundred of them and, let's see –' I mimed a quick head-count, '– only two of us. So by my rough calculations we're only outnumbered by fifty to one.'

'There are alternatives to force,' he said as he continued to look dreamily in the direction of the captives.

I took a long drink of red wine from the wine skin and said, 'That's a relief. I *think*. It all depends on what alternative you are considering.'

'I could offer to buy her.'

I hastily drank more wine and realised I would have to tread more carefully if I were to wean him from his insane intentions. This type of situation was exactly the reason his father had insisted I accompany Ken on his perilous mission. I needed to take a different approach. Sarcasm clearly wasn't working. It was time to be devious. 'An idea that has possibilities, I admit. And drawbacks. The main one being that when you produce your money-pouch full of gold coins there would be nothing to prevent them from simply slitting both our throats and taking your gold.'

He nodded. 'Good point.'

'Thank you.'

'There's another alternative. Look at how drunk they're becoming. When they all pass out, we simply sneak over to the captives, free Alucia, steal a horse for her and ride out of the camp.'

This suggestion gave me serious pause. It actually sounded plausible. But *sounding* plausible and *being* plausible are two different things. 'It might work,' I agreed, 'but there's no guarantee that they'll *all* pass out, even this ill-disciplined mob. And it would only take a few of them to stop us. Come to that, just one of them would be enough to sound the alarm and alert the others.'

'Jad, unless you come up with something better very quickly, I've just decided our plan of action tonight.' He gave me a challenging look. 'Well?'

Well, of course I couldn't. And when I finally accepted that nothing I said would divert him from this course of action, an idea occurred to me: something that just might put the balance of chance in our favour. Even though it would involve me making a considerable sacrifice.

A short time later I sauntered into the food and grog tent. There were several vigilantes present, all in various stages of inebriation, but they paid me no heed. I wandered over to the large, wooden tub that contained the atrocious brew, and which was kept topped up from barrels of the stuff lying in stacks about the tent. Whoever was responsible for producing this foul grog and charging money for it was committing a capital offence and deserved to be drowned in it. 'Can't stay away from this marvellous stuff,' I said to nobody in particular. I dipped a wooden tankard into the liquid and as I did so I emptied the contents of my sleeve into the tub. Magicians are prone to declare that there is nothing up their sleeves but there always is . . . and in this case it was my entire supply of Harius's wondrous herb.

'Well?' asked Ken when I returned to our campfire.

'We have lift-off,' I told him smugly. It was an old saying and nobody knew its origin but it seemed apt under the circumstances. 'Now we wait and see . . .'

During the next hour the previously boisterous behaviour of the drunken vigilantes began to change. The sounds of drunken brawling, the jeering and taunting at the captives and the obscene singing gradually faded. Voices could still be heard, but now they were muffled and non-threatening. There was still movement in the camp too, but it was hard to distinguish because nobody was tending the fires now, which were dying down.

'I think we can make our move soon, ' I told Ken. Despite my fears, I was now anxious to get this whole risky endeavour over with.

'I'd prefer to wait until they're all asleep,' he said.

Now *he* was being cautious, which struck me as ironic. 'That might not happen until dawn,' I told him, 'and we need to do this under the cover of darkness.'

'It's just that I don't have as much faith in your magic herb as you do.'

'Trust me.'

'This is not the time for humour, Jad,' said Ken.

I think he was being serious. Anyway, we waited for about another ten minutes. By then we couldn't even hear the sound of voices and the light from the dying fires was much dimmer. Then Ken stood up, slung his crossbow over his shoulder and drew his sword. 'Let's do it,' he said as he concealed his sword under his cloak. 'You'll have to carry all the saddle-bags. I need to be unencumbered.'

'How very convenient,' I muttered as I began to gather up the bags.

Then we began to move towards the centre of the camp. We passed sleeping figures along the way, sprawled bodies grouped around the embers of campfires. The tents we passed were also quiet, apart from the occasional snore. But just when I was beginning to think, with relief, that all the vigilantes *were* asleep, a figure suddenly emerged from the shadows and blocked our way. Ken tensed, ready to strike.

'Who are you?' asked the figure in a slurred voice as he stood in front of us, trying to see our faces. Then he said, 'I know you. You're the new recruits . . . hey, it's great to have with you with us—' Then he threw an arm around each of us and hugged us. 'Really great . . .' He let us go and staggered off into the darkness. Then we heard a thump as he collapsed onto the ground.

'What were you saying about the efficacy of my herb?' I asked Ken.

'It's probably just their ghastly liquor—'

We reached the huddled group of captives. I could sense their apprehensive eyes upon us as we stood there. Their fear practically rose up from them like an odour.

'It's all right,' I told them softly, 'we're not here to harm you. We're not vigilantes . . . just innocent travellers like you. But don't spread it around.'

'Alucia?' called Ken, much too loudly for my comfort.

'Here.'

Ken hurried in the direction of her voice. I followed more slowly, weighed down by the weight of the saddle-bags and feeling disturbingly vulnerable. I watched as Ken knelt in front of the girl, who was just a vague outline in the dim light. He laid his sword on the ground and drew his dagger. 'I'm going to cut you free,' he told her in a reassuring tone.

'I know,' she replied calmly.

How by the gods did she, I wondered? Had the same spark of love that had inflamed Ken simultaneously ignited her? Or was I just being a romantic idiot? Or, I thought with a jolt of dread, was this a sign of Elite magic? I settled on being a romantic idiot. Give her the benefit of the doubt.

While Ken was sawing through her thick bonds, a captive next to her, a man, whispered hoarsely, 'What about the rest of us? Are you going to leave us to the mercy of those barbarians?'

From his point of view it was a good question. 'Ken?' I asked.

He gave it a few moments thought, then nodded. 'Cut as many free as you can.'

I dropped the saddle-bags, drew my own dagger and began sawing through the rope that bound the man's wrists. It wasn't easy as the rope was bloody thick. 'Hurry!' urged the man.

Then, out of the corner of my eye, I saw a movement. Ken didn't notice because he was too engrossed in the freeing of his just-recently-acquired true love. 'Ken,' I said, urgently 'Behind us—'

A vigilante had appeared as if from nowhere. He was walking fast and had an axe in his hand. 'Hey,' he cried, 'what's going on here?' His voice didn't sound the least bit slurred and his movements appeared fully coordinated. Definitely not drunk, or herb befuddled, unfortunately. A lone intellectual amongst these incompetents had decided that a sober guard should be mounted on the prisoners . . .

Ken moved faster than I'd ever seen him move before. He scooped up his sword with his left hand, turned and rose, took two steps forward and skewered the man through the throat before he could have known what was happening. Ken withdrew his blade and the man fell. On the ground he made frantic gurgling sounds, but they wouldn't have carried very far. I only hoped no one else had heard his loud call of enquiry.

'Thanks, Jad,' said Ken as he returned his attention to the girl.

I similarly resumed cutting through my captive's ropes. 'Must have been a non-drinker. Let's hope he's the camp's lone teetotaller.'

'Yes, but we can't be sure of that.' Ken finished freeing the girl and helped her up. She rubbed at her chaffed wrists. 'Thank you,' she whispered to him. She swayed slightly and Ken put his hands on her shoulders to steady her. I wondered cynically if her wobble had been genuine.

'We've got to go,' Ken told me. '*Now*.'

I'd succeeded in cutting through my captive's wrist bonds. 'What about the rest of them?'

'Yes . . . what *about* us?' asked another captive plaintively.

But Ken was adamant. 'Can't take the chance of staying here any longer. We're leaving now. Come on, Jad.'

I felt bad. I handed my captive the dagger. 'Be as quiet as you can. And good luck.'

Several of them pleaded with us not to leave, but we ignored them, turning for the corral. Ken and the girl drew ahead of me, not being weighed down by the heavy saddle-bags I was carrying. I felt guilty at abandoning the rest of the captives, but at least they had a good chance of cutting themselves free now. The camp was completely still. With luck, the vigilante who'd taken us by surprise had been the only conscious one in the place. I'd noticed, again cynically, that the girl, Alucia, hadn't uttered the slightest protest at leaving her companions behind. But to be fair to her, they weren't her companions, just a bunch of similarly unlucky strangers. And in her position I wouldn't have jeopardised my unexpected chance of salvation either. I told myself to stop being cynical about her.

We reached the corral without incident. Working quietly and quickly, we saddled three horses. Or rather, Ken and the girl worked quietly and quickly, I just stood there trying to catch my breath. Those saddle-bags were bloody heavy and I was glad to put them down. The girl seemed to know her way around horses and I wasn't surprised when Ken asked if she could ride a horse, she replied, 'I ride very well.' I also said to myself, 'I'll bet you do.' But then, I have a dirty mind.

I was punished for these thoughts when I mounted the horse they'd selected. As with the previous horses I'd encountered; it clearly sensed I was no natural rider, but this particular beast reacted by trying to throw me off its back. It only quietened down when Ken grabbed the bridle from my hands and firmly established that he, unlike me, was in control. With Ken leading my horse, we made our way to the stockade's ramshackle gate. Ken slashed the rope that had held it closed, then used his horse to push it open. We were through. Easy! Behind us, the camp remained quiet. I wondered how the other captives were doing in their efforts to free themselves.

'Where do we go now?' I asked Ken.

'It doesn't matter which direction. Just as long as we can put as much distance between us those butchers as we can. Then at first light we'll get our bearings and take the route that leads us out of Vurgun the most quickly.' He handed the bridle back to me. 'I want to travel fast, so please try and stay on that damned horse.'

'I'll do my best.'

We started at a trot. My horse, amazingly, behaved itself and followed the other two horses dutifully. When they began to move faster it did too. It was all very unpleasant. Outlines of trees whizzed by in the darkness. Our speed increased. Now we were at full gallop. I did my best not to fall off; I achieved this by gripping the saddle-horn with all my strength – to hell with the bridle.

I lost all sense of time; I've no idea how long that mad, neck-break dash across the dark countryside lasted, but eventually the horses, exhausted, came to a stop, their sweat-covered sides heaving. Above us, though partially obscured by mist, the line of the sun was starting to flicker into life. We dismounted. I felt as exhausted as the horses. I also felt a little proud of the fact I hadn't fallen off.

The girl said, 'Who are you two?' She was looking with rapt attention at Ken when she asked the question so I was flattered to be even included.

'We're mercenaries,' he told her. 'I'm Gideron and he's—' He faltered and looked to me for help.

'Usborne,' I said. 'He's always forgetting my name,' I added lamely. As undercover operators we were useless.

'Oh,' she said. 'Then why were you calling each other Ken and Jad last night?'

As Ken reddened with embarrassment I amended my evaluation of our performances as undercover operators; we weren't just useless, we were shit.

'Nicknames,' I said quickly, 'those are our nicknames. Right, Ken?'

He glared at me but nodded.

'I don't believe you,' she said with a smile.

It was the first time I'd seen her smile. Despite the blood and grime on her face, it was undoubtedly a very beautiful smile.

'You're hiding something,' she said, still smiling. 'What is it?'

Ken, still blushing, stared at his feet. He said nothing. It was remarkable, In her presence he'd been reduced to a drivelling idiot. True, it hadn't been a particularly long journey for him to make, but it was still disturbing to witness.

'Look,' she said, 'you saved my life. You not only saved my life but you saved me from a manner of dying I don't want to even think about ever again. So I don't care if you don't want to share your deep, dark secret with me, but I'm curious, that's all.'

'We're not hiding anything,' I told her. 'We're mercenaries on our way to join up with the forces of Lord Camarra. Our proper names are Gideron and Usborne and we have silly nicknames.' I looked to Ken for support, but he remained fascinated with his feet. I was on my own.

She finally favoured me with a direct look. I felt honoured. Actually, I *did* feel honoured, which was annoying. I didn't want to fall under her spell like Ken had. For one thing, I had very uninteresting feet. Another more important reason was that I still suspected she might actually be an Elite. 'You don't look like a mercenary,' she said to me.

'And what does a mercenary look like?' I asked her, defensively.

'Not like you. And you don't have any scars. I've met quite a few mercenaries since I started travelling with my father and they all had scars.'

'I've got lots of scars,' I protested, 'they're just not visible. And I'm not getting undressed just to prove it to you.'

She smiled again and said, 'I'm very grateful.'

'I'm a prince.'

We both looked at Ken, who was still staring at his feet.

'What?' said the girl.

'Gideron, don't,' I said warningly. But it was no use.

'I'm Prince Kender. Son of Lord Krader of Capelia Domain.' He raised his head and looked at her. 'And I would give my life for you.'

She momentarily looked taken aback, and I didn't blame her. But she recovered quickly. 'You've already proved that. But are you really a prince?'

Ken nodded. He looked like he wanted to take her in his arms and crush her to his manly chest. Or did that look indicate a desire to ravish her on the spot? It was hard to tell. In any case he did neither, just stood there gazing at her.

'And who is he?' she asked, indicating me. 'Another prince?'

'Oh no. Jad's just my court jester.'

'Ah—' said the girl.

That single 'Ah' contained a wealth of meaning, none of which was flattering to me. I said huffily, 'I'm not *his* court jester, I'm his father's.' I'll bet that impressed her.

'Why the false identities?' she asked Ken.

'We're on a spying mission,' he told her, 'gathering information about what's happening in the world since the fall of the Elite.'

Was it my imagination or did I see her wince slightly at the mention of the Elite?

'So you're spies?' she asked. The hint of amusement in her voice definitely wasn't a product of my imagination.

I said sarcastically, looking pointedly at Ken, 'As you can see, we're masters of subterfuge.'

'Well, whatever you are, you're certainly very brave. I owe you my life and I'll never forget that.'

Ken, to whom these words were directed, visibly swelled with pride and satisfaction. I was feeling increasingly like a gooseberry. An invisible gooseberry. 'I don't want to interrupt this scene of mutual adulation,' I said, with every intention of interrupting this scene of mutual adulation, 'but apart from wanting to avoid an attack of severe vomiting I'd also like to know where the hell we are.'

The sun was growing in strength and now revealed that we were on the crest of a small hill that was shrouded in mist. It had been climbing this hill that had sapped the remaining strength of our horses. 'You're right,' said Ken, peering around. 'We must establish our position as soon as possible.' Then he pointed. 'Over there. I can see the glint of water.'

I looked where he was pointing, but could see nothing but the morning mist. 'How much water?' I asked.

'A lot,' he replied. 'It must be the Pyman Sea. Which means we're heading in the right direction and are almost out of the Vurgun domain—' He went to his horse and rummaged in one of the saddle-bags. Producing the map that the garrison commander had given us, he unrolled it and perused it thoughtfully. He looked as if he knew what he was doing. I hoped Alucia was suitably impressed by this performance. I wasn't.

'Well?' I said.

'Ahead of us lies the domain of Pelmore,' he said authoritatively, 'and by my estimation, we're within a day's ride of the port of Persopia.' He pointed to his right. 'It's in that direction.' Then he rolled up the map.

I wanted to give him a round of applause, but at the same time I wondered where we really were.

'Marvellous,' said Alucia, 'civilisation. And civilisation means I can have a hot bath.'

'Oh good,' I muttered, 'I'm glad we're getting our priorities in order.' I ignored the dirty look that Ken shot me and said, 'And speaking of priorities, I think we should have breakfast.'

Over our sausage, beans, biscuits and wine, Alucia told us how she'd been captured. Her wine merchant father, his assistant and their hired bodyguard had been killed in the vigilante attack. She'd presumed that the attackers were simply bandits, which they were, basically, but after she'd been captured they declared they were hunting Elite refugees and that they believed that she was one of them. It hadn't helped that she'd had the Elite communicator on her person.

As she'd described the death of her father, convincing tears had rolled down her cheeks, but I still had my doubts. 'Why were you stupid enough to be walking around with an Elite communicator?' I asked, tactfully.

'Jad, show Alucia some respect!' snapped Ken.

'It's all right, Ken,' she said, 'I'm happy to answer him.'

I saw Ken react when she called him 'Ken'. 'Er, Alucia—' he said.

'Yes, Ken?' she asked innocently.

He sighed. 'It doesn't matter. Go on.'

She turned to me. 'I honestly had no idea it was an Elite communicator. I found it lying in a village street. I thought it was a rich woman's compact. Except I couldn't work out how to open it. Now I know why, of course.'

'Satisfied?' Ken asked me.

'Yes,' I told him. But I lied. My doubts about her remained. I asked her, 'What are your plans now?'

'To return to Vorass,' she replied.

On hearing those words, Ken looked stricken. 'Is there a pressing reason for your return to Vorass? Family, perhaps? A lover . . . a –' He paused and swallowed before continuing, '– a husband?'

She smiled sadly at him. 'No. No husband back in Vorass. Or lover. And my father was all the family I had left.'

Ken brightened. 'Then why not stay with me? Come with us on our travels and then return to Capelia with me.'

She didn't take much time to make the decision. About three seconds flat by my reckoning. She reached over to him and held his hand. She said, 'I'd like that very much, Ken.'

Ken wore the expression of a man who'd just been handed the keys to paradise. I tried to hide my disappointment at this unwelcome turn of events. 'You'll enjoy Capelia,' I told her, 'nothing ever happens there. Unlike everywhere else in this damned world. Incidentally, how do you feel about trees?'

She gave me a puzzled look. 'Trees?'

'Ignore him,' said Ken, 'he's an idiot.'
'A *professional* idiot, Ken,' I reminded him.

CHAPTER SIX

The rest of the day passed, thank the gods I no longer believed in, without mishap. By the time we'd finished breakfast the heat of the sun had burned the mist away and ahead of us we could see the huge expanse of the Pyman Sea. It curved upwards on either side of the world and seemed to extend forever. We rode through the forests and grasslands of Pelmore until we reached the sea shore, then turned and headed along the coast towards the port of Persopia, which by then we could see slightly above us in the distance. To my amazement, Ken's guess about our location had been correct.

Persopia had been a Freetown, declared neutral by the Elite, which meant that it was not under the control of the ruler of Pelmore or anyone else, apart from the Elite, naturally. These neutral areas, of which there were many, were created mainly for trading purposes, and fighting was forbidden within their borders. However, with the Elite gone, the old rules no longer applied, as we found out when we reached the town.

During the afternoon we made a rest-stop. When the girl went off behind some sand dunes to have a pee or whatever, I had my first chance to talk to Ken alone since her arrival. We had led the horses down the beach to the water so that they could drink.

'Do you think you're doing the right thing, getting so deeply involved with this girl so quickly?' I asked him.

'Her name is *Alucia*, Jad. Try and remember that.'

'I'll try, Ken.'

'Don't call me that,' he said sharply.

I grinned at him. 'She does.'

'That's different. I'll have a word to her about it . . . eventually.'

'Sure you will. She could call you shit-face and you'd roll over on your back like a puppy. You've got it bad. "I would give my life for you"?' I shook my head in wonder. 'By the gods—'

'I can't help it. I love her.'

'You've only just met her. You don't know anything about her. Everything she's told us about herself could be a lie.'

'Why would she lie?'

'You know the answer to that.'

'She is *not* an Elite!' said Ken vehemently. 'I just know she isn't!'

'You're hardly capable of making any objective opinion concerning her,' I pointed out. 'But I am. And until I'm a hundred per cent convinced she's telling the truth about herself, then the possibility remains that she might be an Elite.'

'She is *not*!' cried Ken. He was really angry now. 'And if I hear you say anything to her I'll break your neck!'

I held up my hands. 'Calm down. I promise I'll be discreet. But I wouldn't be obeying your father's orders to keep you out of trouble if I didn't point out to you what I perceive as a potential danger.' Which sounded pompous even to me.

'Leave my father out of this! And what you describe as a "potential danger" is the woman I intend to marry!'

'In that case leaving your father out of all this is going to prove difficult for you. Seeing as he's rather keen for you to marry Princess Petal, the woman you're betrothed to.'

Ken looked thoughtful. Finally he said, 'My father will understand why I can no longer marry Princess Petal.'

'Of course he will. We both know only too well how understanding your father is. And if war breaks out between Capelia and Acasia as a result of you breaking the marriage arrangement, which as you well know, is a purely political one, he'll be even more understanding.'

He was silent. I could see I'd hit a raw nerve. And then I saw that I was being incredibly stupid. It came in a blinding flash, and it was what I'd said earlier about obeying his father's orders that provided the spark. I realised that Alucia was presenting me with the perfect opportunity to save Ken from the dangers of his mission. And in doing so I'd also save myself. I patted him on the shoulder and said, 'But if you're determined to go against your father's wishes, I'll give you my full backing.'

'You will?' he said, surprised. 'That's quite an about-turn.'

'It's in my own interests,' I said, deciding to be honest with him. 'I want you to return to Capelia. Now.'

'I can't do that,' he said with a shake of his head.

'You say you love Alucia, and I have to believe you. But do you really want to expose her to more danger? How can we follow your original plan and join up with Camarra's army with her in tow? No, if you *really* love her you'll abandon your mission and return to Capelia where she'll be safe.' And so will I, I added to myself.

Ken looked troubled. 'I hadn't really thought about that,' he said slowly. 'You're right. I was being a fool.'

Encouraged, I said, 'That's my job. But you agree with me? No more crazy ideas about trying to reach the Citadel?'

'What's that about the Citadel?'

The girl – Alucia – had returned without either of us noticing her approach.

'It's where we were headed,' I said, 'but no longer. I hope.'

'Where are we going now?' she asked.

'Back to Capelia,' Ken told her. 'Our original plans would place you in grave danger.'

She frowned. 'I appreciate your concern but I don't want you to abandon your mission just because of me. I can take care of myself.'

'We noticed that back at the vigilante camp,' I said.

She glared at me. 'That's not fair. I insist you continue with your mission. Even if it means going to the Citadel.'

Again I wondered if my suspicions were being fed by my imagination, but our mention of the Citadel seemed to have pricked her interest.

Ken looked agonised. He wanted to protect her, but at the same time he desperately wanted to keep her happy. 'How about a compromise,' he said finally. 'We'll keep travelling onwards for a time, but we won't try and join up with Camarra's forces. And we won't attempt to reach the Citadel.'

I saw a flash of fire in Alucia's eyes. Briefly her look was an imperious one. She was clearly used to getting her own way. Again I was haunted by the strong suspicion that she was an Elite. But then she smiled and said, 'All right. I agree.'

I wasn't convinced.

Persopia normally has a population of about twenty thousand people, but when we arrived in the town that evening it was evident that the population had increased. There were numerous refugees, and lots of soldiers, the latter were from many different domains, and as a result the atmosphere in the town was tense.

'So much for being a Freetown,' observed Ken as we rode through the centre.

'What do you think all these soldiers are doing here?' I asked.

'Probably looting,' said Ken. 'Persopia is a wealthy town.'

'Yes,' said Alucia, 'but they're also probably hunting for Elite. More vigilantes, but organised ones, unlike the riff-raff that captured me.'

This was confirmed by the owner of the only inn we'd found that had any vacant rooms. Well, to be accurate, it had only *one* remaining vacant room. A double. It doesn't take a genius to work out who claimed that room. The innkeeper said I could sleep in the stable. I was overjoyed. More horses. But at least I had the pleasure of a good meal of steak, potatoes and fresh bread. And a lot of red wine. The meal was served by the innkeeper and his wife, who both complained about the invasion of the town. There had so far been little outright violence, but with all the rival factions the innkeeper said gloomily it could only be a matter of time before something bad happened. The soldiers had arrested a number of people they claimed were Elite, but the innkeeper had his doubts. There were executions every day in the town's main square. I looked at Alucia as he described these grim events but her face gave nothing away.

When the happy couple, no doubt looking forward to a night of passion, soon retired to their double room, I joined the horses in the stable. I made a bed out of a pile of straw and a horse blanket. Luxury. I cursed Ken and drifted off to sleep.

Some time later I was woken by a rhythmic thumping noise coming from directly overhead. I wondered what it could be and then realised that the stable was right beneath Ken and Alucia's room. I grinned as I imagined what was happening upstairs, but as the noise continued for an inordinate amount of time I began to have different thoughts. Either Ken had acquired the sexual stamina of a god, which was news to me, or there was another explanation for the ruckus. Finally I got up and climbed the wooden stairs leading to the floor above. Perhaps I was going to make a very embarrassing mistake, but I was now convinced there was something wrong.

I knocked on the door of their room. There was a muffled response; it sounded like Ken. When I opened the door and looked inside, by the flickering light of a pair of candles I saw Ken lying bound and gagged on the floor beside the bed. I knelt beside him and searched for his dagger, but it was gone. I removed his gag and then started untying the knots of the rope. 'You took your time,' he complained, 'I've been banging my heels on the floor for bloody ages.'

'What happened?' I asked.

'Alucia happened. She hit me on the side of my head with something.'

I felt his head. There was quite a large lump there. 'You have an argument?'

'No. We came in here, we kissed, I started to undress and then everything went black.'

I picked up a heavy candlestick lying on the floor. 'She must have hit you with this. She could have killed you.'

'I wish she had,' he said mournfully as I helped him to stand.

'I find the love of my life and she does that to me. I'm heartbroken. I'll probably never recover.' Then he felt his belt and cried, 'Damn it! She's taken my purse!'

'I don't want to say "I told you so" but—'

'Then don't,' he snapped.

'Come on, let's go and look for her.'

'She could be anywhere by now.'

'I think I know where she might be.'

'You do?' Said Ken, surprised. 'Where?'

'The harbour. She seemed oddly excited when she heard our intention had been to reach the Citadel. I think that's where she's headed. And she'll need to get on a boat to do that.'

'You still think she's an Elite, don't you?'

'I would say her actions tonight reinforce my opinion.'

'I still can't believe it.'

'Yes, well, you're in love and not thinking straight. Let's go.'

We hurried down to the stable, saddled up the horses and rode quickly through the narrow, twisting streets until we reached the harbour. There were several vessels there of varying sizes, smaller fishing boats for the local waters and much bigger vessels for making the crossing to the other side of the Pyman Sea. 'Let's try this tavern,' I said, indicating the sign.

'You want a drink at a time like this?' asked Ken.

'No, I want to ask if there are any ships leaving tonight. Or early tomorrow morning.'

We tied the horses to a hitching rail and went inside. The tavern was full of rough-looking men who gave us suspicious looks as we entered. I went up to the bar and ordered two beers. I had to pay for them, seeing as Ken was now financially embarrassed. The bartender served the drinks with ill grace and I could see that extracting information was not going to be easy. So I added an extra gold coin when I paid and told him we were hoping to ship out on any vessel that was leaving shortly. Did he know of such a boat?

He took the gold coin and grunted, 'Only one. The *Black Swan*. You can't miss it. Biggest ship in the harbour; got black sails.' We thanked him, hurriedly downed our drinks and went back outside. As the barman had said, we couldn't miss the *Black Swan*. And it appeared to be making ready to leave even as we rode along the dock towards it. We dismounted and ran up the gangplank. 'We're looking for a young woman,' Ken told the first sailor we encountered. 'She may have taken passage on this ship. Dark haired. Attractive.'

He looked at us blankly and said, 'No such woman is on board.'

'Damn,' I muttered.

A man in a uniform leaned over the railing of the aft deck. He was clearly an officer. 'What's the problem?'

We repeated our query. 'We need to find this woman,' we added, 'she stole money from us. She would have boarded your ship just a short time ago.'

'No woman has taken passage with us since earlier today, and I should know, as I'm the captain,' he told us.

I sighed, disappointed. 'Well, so much for that idea,' I said.

As we thanked him and turned to leave, the captain added, 'But a young man boarded an hour ago. Good-looking young fellow.'

Ken and I exchanged a glance. 'Could be her. In disguise,' I said.

'Can we see him?' asked Ken.

The captain shook his head. 'He paid good money in gold coin for his passage. I am under obligation to protect his privacy.'

I was tempted to say that the 'young man' might be an Elite, but bit my tongue. That would not have been a wise move.

'Of course, if you were to take passage on my ship I would be obliged to accept you on board.' The captain winked at us. 'And I couldn't stop you if you were to engage the youth in conversation during the voyage, could I?'

'This is extortion, you—' began Ken angrily, but I held up a hand to stop him.

'Where are you bound?' I asked.

'Verharven.'

Ken looked pleased. Exactly where he wanted to go. And obviously where Alucia wanted to go. Ken gave me a brief smile then said to the captain, 'And how much would it cost us?'

'For the pair of you, twenty gold pieces.'

I looked helplessly at Ken. I knew Alucia had stolen all his money; all I had left was four gold pieces and some silver. 'We're buggered,' I said in a low voice.

'Not necessarily,' said Ken. He removed the glove from his right hand and pulled, with difficulty, the heavy gold and bejewelled signet ring from his middle finger. 'Good thing she didn't take this as well but I suppose she was in too much of a hurry.' He held it up for the captain to see. 'This is worth a small fortune. It should more than pay for our passage.'

'Throw it up to me,' said the captain, who caught it handily and examined it. 'It's a good piece, you're right. More than adequate for your passage.'

'I should think so,' whispered Ken bitterly to me, 'it's worth at least fifty gold pieces.'

The captain, still examining the ring, said, 'It has a royal seal on it. Where did you come by this?'

'It was a gift from Prince Kender of Capelia,' said Ken. 'I was in his service as a soldier. I saved in his life in a battle and he gave me his ring in gratitude.'

I was impressed by Ken's unusually quick thinking, though the captain didn't appear convinced. But he pocketed the ring and then said, 'Welcome aboard.'

'Go and fetch the saddle-bags and the rest of our gear,' Ken told me.

'What about the horses?'

'We'll just have to leave them. Unless you want to share a cabin with them.'

When I struggled back up the gangplank under the weight of my heavy burden, the captain said to us, 'You'll have to surrender your weapons while you're on board my ship. For all I know you may be pirates.'

'We're not pirates,' I said indignantly, 'we're mercenaries.'

He shrugged and said, 'Same difference.'

We handed over our weapons to a sailor. Ken surrendered his crossbow with extreme reluctance. 'Take good care of that,' he said as he handed it over with ill grace.

'It's a fine weapon,' said the sailor admirably.

'It should be,' Ken told him with pride, 'I made it myself.'

As the captain showed us to our cabin, Ken asked him, 'Where can we find our quarry?'

The captain shrugged. 'Come now. I'm not cooperating in any way. That's your business. But I must warn you about harming him in any way. While he's on board my ship he's under my protection. If you so much as bruise him you'll be swimming back to Persopia. And there are sharks in these waters.'

'What's he calling himself?' I asked.

'Aldran. Says he's from Marolta.'

Ken and I exchanged a meaningful look.

Our cabin turned out to be small, but reasonably comfortable. It had a tiered double bunk. Ken naturally chose the lower one. We then discussed our next move. 'Let's wait for the boat to get well under way before we start searching for her,' I suggested. 'We don't want her escaping by jumping overboard this close to shore.'

Ken stretched out on his bunk. 'Let's hope we haven't jumped ourselves. To the wrong conclusion. This Aldran could turn out to be exactly what he told the captain: a young man from Marolta.'

'No. It's all too much of a coincidence. Aldran is Alucia all right. Even the names are similar.'

He gave a long-drawn-out sigh. 'I still can't believe she did what she did to me. I thought she felt the same way about me as I do towards her.'

'She obviously has another agenda. To reach the Citadel.'

'And I still can't believe she's Elite.'

'So you keep saying. But you do realise that if she *is* Elite we'll be putting ourselves in mortal danger by not telling anyone the truth about her.'

'I don't care. I'm willing to risk it.'

'Well, good for you. I, on the other hand, am not in love with her. So, needless to say, I don't share your enthusiasm for putting my life in jeopardy on your behalf.'

'You have to. My father ordered you to. And you can't return to Capelia without me.'

'Don't remind me,' I said with a groan.

Suddenly the ship began to creak and sway. 'We're under way,' said Ken. 'This is rather exciting. I've never been on a boat this big before.'

I didn't share his excitement, but agreed, 'It can't be any worse than travelling by horse.'

We waited for about an hour then Ken climbed off his bunk. 'Right. Let's go find Alucia,' he said.

We started knocking on cabin doors. Our sixth try proved successful. We came face to face with Alucia.

She wasn't happy to see us.

CHAPTER SEVEN

She was wearing men's clothes: grey leather leggings, boots, black leather jacket and waistcoat. She'd also cropped her hair short and wore a leather cap. Instead of looking like a beautiful young woman, she now looked like a beautiful youth, which I found a bit disconcerting. When she recognised us she cried, 'No!' and tried to slam the door shut in our faces. But Ken reacted fast and pushed the door open, sending her sprawling onto her back on the cabin floor. We stepped quickly inside.

'Hello again, Alucia,' said Ken.

She also reacted fast, drawing a dagger from inside her jacket as she sprung up from the floor. I guessed it was the dagger she'd stolen from Ken. She thrust it at Ken, but he grabbed her wrist and forced her to drop it. She groaned with pain and cried, 'Let go of me, you moron!'

'Is that any way to speak to the man you're going to marry?' he asked.

'I'd never marry you . . . you *mundane*!' she spat.

Ken shoved her so that she fell back on the cabin's single bunk. I took the opportunity to pick up Ken's dagger from the floor and stuck it in my belt.

Ken stood over her. 'You really hurt me, Alucia. In more ways than one.' He touched the side of his head where she'd struck him with the candlestick.

'I obviously didn't hit you hard enough,' she snarled.

'I like the new look,' I told her, 'though you might give some serious thought to growing a moustache. And maybe a beard.' The more I studied her, the less convincing her disguise was.

'Go and shove your head up a dead bear's ass-hole,' she said.

'Maybe later. But I'd show a little contrition if I was you,' I said, 'considering what we know about you.'

'And what's that?' she asked, her eyes now wary.

'That you're an Elite.'

'I am not! That's a ridiculous accusation!'

'You certainly act like one. You just called Ken a mundane. And you seem anxious to reach the Citadel. If we were to pass on our suspicions to the captain you'd spend the rest of the voyage in chains until we reached Verharven, where you'd be handed over to whatever authorities are in charge there now. And you know what would happen to you then.'

She underwent a sudden change. The anger vanished and she now displayed a mixture of fear and cunning. You could see her trying to work out how to resume control of the situation. She even had the audacity to appear demure again. At least, *I* saw that. The gods only knew what Ken saw. She said, 'You wouldn't do that to me.' She looked to Ken for help. 'Would you?'

He said nothing, just stood there looking anguished.

'He wouldn't, but I would,' I told her coldly.

She looked at me. 'Yes, you would.'

'Are you going to admit it?' I asked. 'That you're an Elite?'

She thought it over, considering her options. Finally, she said, 'Yes, I'm an Elite. Or I *was*. We're a spent force. The Elite are no more. And I desperately want to know what happened. Which is why I want to go to the Citadel. That's where the answers are. Will you help me?'

'*Help you?*' I said incredulously. 'Why should we?'

'Because we share a common cause now. You were going to the Citadel to try and find out the answers too. Weren't you?'

'That was all Ken's idea. My big ambition is to stay alive.'

'But you are curious in spite of the danger,' she said to me, 'aren't you?'

She was right. I was curious. I nodded.

'And there's another reason for helping me to find out the

truth,' she said. 'If something so catastrophic occurred to destroy as powerful a force as the Elite, the same fate could befall the rest of you.'

She was right, of course. That possibility had already occurred to me. She sat up on the bunk, looking thoughtful. Then she came to a decision and said, 'I believe there are things you should know at this point. Things that will alter your perception of your world.'

'In what way?' I asked. I felt a surge of excitement. She was going to reveal Elite secrets!

'First, I'm going to tell you we are all in a ship. A big ship.'

'Of course we are,' said Ken, 'the *Black Swan*.'

'I'm not talking about this ship, I'm talking about Urba itself. It's one giant ship. A spaceship.'

Ken and I exchanged a puzzled look. I wondered what the hell she was talking about. I was also beginning to feel very disappointed. Instead of Elite revelations, it looked like she was going to give us nothing but Elite nonsense. I said, 'You're saying Urba is a giant ship travelling on some vast sea? Where did you get an idea like that?'

'Because it's true,' she said, 'except it's not travelling across a sea, it's travelling through space.'

I looked wonderingly at Ken again. Had she gone mad? He shrugged. 'What's space?' I asked her.

'Space is what the Universe mainly consists of. You've been taught that the Universe is solid rock, apart from worlds like Urba. A vast honeycomb of rock. That's a total lie, perpetrated by the predecessors of the Elite. It was a deliberate policy of misinformation. There were reasons for this that I'll tell you later. But in reality, space is endless. Infinite. Well, not really, but from our point of view it's as good as infinite—'

'You're saying the Universe consists of nothing but empty space?' I asked, incredulously. She *had* gone mad. 'That's a pretty ridiculous concept. The existence of Urba itself contradicts it. The world is surrounded by solid rock.'

Alucia closed her eyes and rubbed a hand across her face in a gesture of weariness. 'I knew this was going to be a difficult task.' Then she looked at us again and took a deep breath. 'I'll try again. Space isn't empty. It contains a lot of bodies called stars. These are huge balls of burning gases. Orbiting many of these stars are bodies called planets. Some of these consist mainly of gas, but many are solid. The original home of the human race was one of the latter. Humans lived on the surface of this planet, which was called Earth.'

I decided to humour her. 'People lived on the surface of a sphere? A sphere that went around a huge ball of burning gas? Surrounded by this endless emptiness you call space? Sounds very likely.' More like absolutely ludicrous, I thought.

'Not likely, perhaps, but true. Now before I continue, let me ask you a question. What keeps you on the ground here in Urba? Why don't you fly off into the sky?'

'That's simple,' replied Ken, 'because we're heavy. People, like all objects, have weight.'

'Correct again,' she said, 'but what causes weight?'

I shrugged. 'Weight is weight. There is no cause for it.'

'Wrong. You have weight because Urba is constantly rotating. You're held to the ground by something called centrifugal force. It simulates a force called gravity. Gravity was what kept the human race pinned to the surface of the Earth.'

'What's gravity?' I asked.

She gave a sigh. 'That's hard to explain. It's a natural force in the Universe, but it still hasn't been completely explained in terms of quantum mechanics. And please don't ask me to explain quantum mechanics. I'm no scientist. Anyway, you're both so ignorant it would be a waste of time—'

'That's very convenient,' I said dryly. 'You're saying that humans stayed on the surface of this sphere thanks to a mysterious force.'

'I am. You'll just have to take my word for it.'

Ken and I exchanged another glance. He looked baffled and alarmed. The love of his life was babbling complete drivel. I said to her, 'You Elite certainly believed in some weird stuff.' Then I said to Ken, 'You've had conversations with Elite in your father's court. Have you ever heard about any of this before?'

He shook his head. 'No, never,' he said.

'That's because it was kept a secret from you,' said Alucia.

'Great,' I muttered to Ken, 'she's not only Elite, she's also stark, raving mad.'

'I'm not mad, you idiot—' She stopped and rubbed her hand wearily over her face again. 'I don't expect you to accept any of this right off, but if I get the chance I'll prove it to you.'

'You're right,' I said, 'I don't believe a word of this craziness, but just for the sake of argument, what's the human race doing in Urba, which you describe as some kind of giant ship?'

'The Earth's sun, which was our local star, had become unstable. It was supposed to remain more or less unchanged for billions of years, but something changed in its core and it became steadily brighter . . . and hotter. It was predicted that human life throughout the solar system would be wiped out in just over a hundred years. So Urba was built, using material from Earth's moon . . . and Earth itself. It took forty years to construct. The idea was to use Urba to travel to another habitable planet in another star system.'

'Well, that certainly sounds plausible,' I said dryly. 'How long ago did all this supposedly take place?'

'Over thirteen hundred years ago.'

'And so Urba still hasn't reached this so-called other world?'

'Oh, Urba reached various other worlds. When it attains its maximum speed, it travels at a third of the speed of light, but none of the worlds it found were suitable. And that's when the trouble began. Well, there'd been trouble within Urba from the start, but things deteriorated when the first three worlds were discovered to be unsuitable. And so drastic action had to be taken. All of which led to the present situation. Or rather, how the situation was before we Elite were overthrown.'

I was intrigued by Alucia's fantasy in spite of myself. 'What was this drastic action?'

But Alucia yawned and said, 'No more for the time being.

I'm given you enough to digest. I know you think I'm lying about all this—'

'You've lied to us before,' I said.

'But that was when I was trying to conceal my identity from you. I have no reason to lie now. Mull over what I've told you. And consider this: the Elite ruled you for centuries, using technology that you saw as magic. Doesn't it stand to reason that we know things beyond your puny belief systems?'

'Yes, but what you told us doesn't make any sense,' I pointed out.

'Not yet, but it will. Now I'm tired. I need to sleep—' She paused. 'Unless you still intend handing me over to the captain.'

'No,' said Ken firmly. He looked at me, daring me to contradict him.

I shrugged. 'I'm not happy about it but I'll comply with Ken's wishes – at least for the time being I'll keep your secret . . . providing you don't do anything to change my mind.'

'Good,' she said, lay back on the bunk and closed her eyes. 'I'll see you later.'

'There's one just thing, Alucia,' said Ken, a little awkwardly. 'Can I have my purse back?'

'Surely,' she said and reached into her jacket. She produced the purse and handed it to Ken.

'It's all there,' she told him, 'apart from the cost of my passage and the money I spent on these clothes.'

'I believe you,' he said, without checking the contents of the purse.

'And Ken,' she added, 'I'm sorry for what I did to you. I was desperate, otherwise I would never have hurt you.'

'I believe that too,' he said, sounding as if he really did believe her.

I was speechless. Just a short time ago this woman had tried to stab him with his own dagger. It just proved the old saying: that there is no greater fool than a man in love. And Ken was turning into a champion in this particular area of foolishness.

When we returned to our cabin we both climbed onto our respective bunks; in my case 'climb' was literally the case. We were feeling tired too. It felt like a very long time since we'd last slept. 'What did you think of all that?' I asked him drowsily.

'As you say, she's an Elite and she's crazy. But I still love her.'

'So I noticed.'

'Do you think all the Elite believed in such nonsense?'

'I don't know. Maybe she's pulling some kind of trick to confuse us. But I can't see why.'

'Do you think she can be cured of this madness?'

'I don't know what I think about her. And even though you love her, Ken, don't let your guard down with her again. Be wary, Ken, be wary.'

'Jad,' said Ken.

'Yes?'

'Stop calling me Ken.'

The next morning I had changed my opinion about horses. I now loved them. As I heaved my guts over the side of the ship's railing for the third time in as many minutes I would have given anything to be back riding a horse at that moment. Horses were truly wonderful creatures and the gods were punishing me for misjudging them.

'Feeling queasy, son?' asked a sailor who was observing my discomfort with evident amusement.

I turned and gave him a baleful glare. He was a grizzled old seaman and his smile revealed several missing teeth. Probably lost them in quayside tavern brawls. He was in danger of losing several more if he didn't stop grinning at me. 'Queasy doesn't come close to describing how I feel,' I said truthfully.

'Don't worry,' he said, 'you'll soon find your sea-legs.'

'Do you have any going spare?' I asked him.

He walked away laughing. I hated him with a terrible ferocity. Just then Ken and Alucia appeared. It was obvious Ken had forgiven her for the events of last night. Nor did he appear to even care that she was Elite, our sworn enemy. And the fact that she might be barking mad had also been swept under his emotional carpet. The stupid, lovesick fool. But being lovesick was preferable to simply being sick. They both looked hale and hearty. I decided I hated them too.

'We missed you at breakfast,' said Ken.

The mention of breakfast made my stomach start to rebel again. 'Ken,' I said warningly, 'If you tell me what you actually had for breakfast I'll throw you overboard.'

With undisguised glee, he replied, 'We had bacon, sausages and eggs. All a bit greasy for my taste, but delicious nonetheless.'

And immediately I was bending over the railing again, heaving up what was left of the contents of my stomach, which wasn't much. All thought of throwing Ken overboard had gone; instead I wanted to throw myself overboard. Drowning would be better than feeling like this. I had never felt so nauseous since . . . well, I'd *never* felt this nauseous before. Then a hand was patting me on my shoulder. I realised it was Alucia's.

'You're seasick. The motion of the ship affects the inner ear,' she said quietly. 'Some of the Elite suffered similarly in air-cars. We had drugs for it. But you should visit the ship's surgeon. I'll wager he has some natural remedy which might work.'

I straightened up. 'Thank you,' I croaked, and hurried off to find the doctor. I suddenly decided that perhaps I'd misjudged her after all. I eventually succeeded in locating the doctor, who gave me a foul-tasting potion to drink and suggested I retire to my bunk until the medicine took effect. I followed his advice. I spent three or four nausea-wracked hours lying on my bunk, convinced that the doctor's remedy was anything but a remedy, when suddenly the nausea vanished and I felt my old self again.

I was sitting up in my bunk and considering venturing out on deck again for some fresh air when Ken entered the cabin. He looked very cheerful.

'Feeling better?' he asked.

'A lot better, thank you.'

'You probably won't be interested, but the captain has invited us to lunch in his cabin. Apparently it's a tradition.'

I was about to say no when I realised I was now feeling ravenously hungry. 'Sure,' I said, 'sounds great. When?'

'In an hour.'

'I'll be there.'

The captain's cabin turned out to be a spacious, well-appointed room right at the stern of the ship. He'd invited seven passengers to lunch, including Ken, Alucia and me. As we three sat down together, the captain, with a knowing smile, said, 'I'm glad to see that you three appear to have sorted out your differences.'

'Yes,' Ken told him, 'it was all a misunderstanding.'

'Oh good. But did the misunderstanding extend to you seeking a young woman when, as is clearly evident, Aldran here is a young man? Seems a misunderstanding of some major proportions.'

That put us all at a momentary loss for words. But then Alucia said, 'I'm afraid you've been the victim of a harmless act of deception, sir. I thought it safer to travel in the guise of a man. My real name is Alucia. Alucia of Vorass.'

The captain raised his eyebrows. 'You're a *woman*? My, my . . . I'd never have guessed. I congratulate you on your disguise, young lady.'

He obviously hadn't been fooled for a minute by Alucia's disguise. I guessed he was a wily old bird. He must have been in his early fifties; to have reached that advanced age suggested a keen intelligence, and the cunning of a natural survivor. He introduced himself formally for the first time: 'I am Captain Larmos. I have been the master of the *Black Swan* for eleven years. Before that I was her first mate. Now if the rest of you could introduce yourselves . . .'

Of the other four guests, all men, two were uninteresting-looking merchants in their late thirties, one was a handsome young professional soldier, a Major Sylvan, who was returning to his home domain of Storncross, and the fourth was a small, gnome-like man called Bartel who described himself as an alchemist. Ken and I used our fake names of Gideron and Usborne and our cover story of being mercenaries, late of the domain of Capelia, where we'd served in the army of Lord Krader. Major Sylvan took a particular interest in us. He'd been sent by his master, Baron Crasta, to study the differing military tactics of a number of domains; he'd been in Vurgun when the revolt had begun. He'd barely escaped with his life. I interpreted this to mean he was actually a spy, like us – though I suspected he was much better at the job than Ken and me. 'I had hoped to reach Capelia,' he said, 'but, of course, unfortunate events intervened. I understand it's a relatively peaceful domain.'

'It's downright boring,' I told him, aware of Ken stiffening with indignation on my left. 'That's why Gideron and I are hoping to join the army of Lord Camarra. We could do with a bit of excitement.'

'Lord Camarra?' said Major Sylvan. 'From what I've heard of him, you have chosen a dangerous and unpredictable master.'

'Gideron and I thrive on danger,' I said, straight-faced.

'That's fortunate. With Lord Camarra you'll be able to indulge your appetite for danger to the limit, and far beyond.' Then he directed his attention to Alucia. 'And is your attractive young lady companion a mercenary as well?'

'Not exactly,' I said. 'She's more like our mascot.' This time I sensed Alucia stiffening with indignation beside me. 'We rescued her from some vigilantes who had killed her wine merchant father in Vurgun and have more or less taken her under our wing. Admittedly, she would be less than an asset as a fighter, but she is a good cook so she'll be of some limited use.'

Alucia hissed something under her breath into my ear. It sounded obscene.

Major Sylvan now addressed Captain Larmos. 'Captain, I've

noticed you have a contingent of heavily armed marines on board. Are you expecting trouble?'

'Just a precaution,' said the captain. 'With the Elite now gone piracy is once again flourishing in the Pyman Sea . . . as it is elsewhere in Urba. Now I hated the Elite as much as anyone, but I will give them credit for keeping piracy under control.'

'Have you had any personal encounters with pirates?' Sylvan asked the captain.

'Not as yet, touch wood,' he said, rapping his knuckles on the wooden table. 'But I like to be prepared.'

'That's very reassuring,' said Major Sylvan, 'but it's unusual to find anyone with a good word to say about the Elite.'

The captain immediately looked defensive. 'I wasn't saying a good word about the Elite, sir, merely observing that in their absence piracy has returned to the seas of Urba. Though I will also take the risk of making another obvious observation that in the aftermath of the destruction of the Elite, chaos of all kinds is spreading throughout Urba.'

'Mere teething problems, sir,' said the major. 'The political and military upheavals will surely be short-lived.'

'I sincerely hope your optimistic viewpoint will be proved correct,' said the captain 'but with a warlord as ambitious and power-hungry as Lord Camarra –' and here he looked at Ken and me '– conquering domain after domain, I can't help but fear we've overcome one form of tyranny only to have it replaced by another just as ruthless.'

'I agree that Lord Camarra presents a threat at present,' said Major Sylvan, 'but I can reveal that there are plans for the formation of a union of domains to counter the threat presented by Lord Camarra. Be assured his days are number-ed.' He addressed us again. 'Perhaps you should think again before joining his cause.'

Ken and I maintained a discreet silence. Personally, I thought that the chances of any of the domains voluntarily forming a union were highly unlikely. The only way to achieve a union was by force. Which is exactly what Lord Camarra was doing.

'Well, I hope you're right,' said the captain to Major Sylvan, 'but I fear that Lord Camarra and his growing forces may be more difficult to deal with than you believe.'

The conversation paused then due to the arrival of the food – and an excellent meal it proved to be, consisting of roast beef, roast potatoes, dumplings, peas and cabbage, all accompanied by a great deal of fine red wine.

During the meal the conversation resumed, initiated by Captain Larmos, who turned to Bartel and said, 'Forgive my ignorance, sir, but I'm unfamiliar with the work of an alchemist, apart from knowing that alchemy has something to do with turning base metals into gold.'

Bartel gave a high-pitched chuckle. 'That is a goal that has no chance of ever succeeding, captain. But I am not a traditional alchemist anyway. That is just a convenient label I use. I prefer to think of myself as a scientist.'

'A scientist?' said the captain with a puzzled frown. 'I've never come across that term before, I'm sure. What is a scientist?'

I gave a slight start as I remembered that Alucia had used the same word the night before in her cabin. 'I'm no scientist,' she had said . . . What a strange coincidence.

'The word is an archaic one,' said Bartel. 'It means one who seeks after the truth by using empirical methods.'

I glanced at Alucia. She was staring at Bartel with intense interest.

The captain laughed and said, 'Empirical methods? I'm afraid you've lost me again, good sir. But perhaps you could enlighten me on a matter that intrigues me. I hear the cult of the Diggers has been revived now that the restraining hands of the Elite have been removed. Do you think there is any truth in their beliefs?'

Bartel smiled. 'Do I share their belief that we can dig our way to paradise? No sir, I most certainly do not. They are deluded fools. More than that, they are dangerous fools.'

The captain raised his eyebrows. 'Dangerous, sir? In what way?'

Bartel gave an enigmatic smile. 'I can't go into specifics, captain. I'll just say that the Diggers' desire to dig their way to the mythical paradise they call Earth may have deadly repercussions for all of Urba.'

Again I experienced a jolt of recognition. *Earth.* Another unfamiliar word that Alucia had mentioned the night before.

As Bartel refused to elaborate on his belief that the Diggers posed a threat to Urba the conversation moved on to other subjects, the main one being the increasingly dire state of the economy in these chaotic times. I noted that the two merchants contributed very little to this discussion. I thought it a little odd considering that, as a rule, all merchants had very strong opinions about the economy; usually getting them to shut up about the state of the economy was an impossible task. But I didn't really give this slight puzzle any further thought. This turned out to be a serious mistake.

CHAPTER EIGHT

After lunch, Ken, Alucia and I retired to our cabin. Ken and Alucia sat together on his bunk while I, there being no chair, sat on the floor; the status quo thus continued as usual. Alucia was annoyed with me. 'How dare you refer to me as your *mascot*,' she complained.

'Just doing my part in presenting you as an innocuous presence,' I said innocently. 'The aim was to deflect any suspicions anyone may harbour about you.'

That mollified her. A little.

'What did you think of Bartel?' I asked her.

'The man is clearly crazy,' said Ken, 'crazy as a loon.'

Alucia smiled at him. 'Crazy like me, you mean?'

'Uhhh,' said Ken as he obviously tried to find the right answer. Finally he gave up the search and said nothing.

'Bartel,' said Alucia, 'knows a lot. A hell of a lot. He's certainly aware of the danger that the Diggers represent, though he didn't spell it out.'

'What danger is that?' Ken asked, somewhat warily.

'If the Diggers manage to dig deep enough, they might just succeed in reaching the metal outer hull,' she replied. 'And if they penetrated that, which would be impossible, but let's say for the sake of argument they did, it would result in all the air in Urba spurting off into space. Every living thing in Urba would die as a result—'

'By the gods,' said Ken with a groan, 'you're back on that nonsense.'

She frowned in annoyance. 'It's *not* nonsense, you twat! Open your closed little mind and accept the truth about your world!'

'My mind is perfectly fine,' he responded, 'it's *your* mind I'm worried about.'

I raised my hands. 'Hey, hold it, you romantic fools,' I said in a placatory tone, 'let's not argue. Alucia, we have to agree to disagree. Right?'

She took a deep, calming breath. 'All right. For the time being. Until I can prove that what I say is true. Bartel clearly knows some of the truth about the reality of our situation. Perhaps he knows it all, though I don't know how.'

Again, I thought it wise to humour her. 'Could he be Elite?'

She shook her head. 'No, he's definitely not Elite. But he should be more careful about what he says because sooner or later someone will decide he *is* Elite. And we all know what will happen to him then . . .'

No one spoke for several moments until I broke the silence by saying, 'Alucia, do you have any idea at all about what happened on the Day of Wonder? Any personal theory as to how all the Elite lost their powers simultaneously, throughout Urba?'

'Why it happened I don't know, but I do know *how* it happened,' she said. 'We were victims of our own paranoia, about our technology and weapons falling into the hands of you mundanes. So everything was powered from a central source: everything from our hand weapons to the air-cars and our computers, and our entire communication system. Nothing had an independent power supply of its own. Every weapon had an individual identifying signature, so if it was seized by one of your people, it would automatically be sent a signal by a computer that would cut it off from the transmitted energy supply and render it entirely useless—'

'What are computers?' I asked, interrupting.

She waved a dismissive hand. 'I'll explain another time. Let me continue. What happened was that for some reason the entire power system was suddenly shut down. I have no idea why. It couldn't have been a malfunction because there were countless fail-safe mechanisms and back-up systems in place for such eventualities. The only answer is that someone, for some reason, deliberately shut down the whole system. I've been wracking my brains, but I can't come up with any conceivable reason for anyone to do that.'

We sat there in silence for a time. Ken looked blank as he struggled to come to terms with this revelation about the 'magical powers' of the Elite. I, on the other hand, had what I thought might be a bright idea. 'A revolt!' I said triumphantly.

'A what?' Alucia asked. 'What on Earth are you talking about?'

'A revolt,' I repeated. 'By a dissatisfied faction within the Elite. You know, a group of rebels decided to take drastic action to end Elite rule.'

Alucia gave me a cold look and said, 'No such faction existed within the Elite. There might have been disagreements from time to time, but we were a tightly knit fraternity with a common aim.'

The common aim of cruel oppression, I thought. 'Perhaps you were unaware of the existence of such a faction.'

'Impossible,' she said firmly.

'All right then, here's an alternative theory. What if just one of the Elite went, well, insane? Some mad individual decided to cut the power for some reason that made sense only to him.' Then I added pointedly, 'Or her.' If she was any indication of Elite mental stability, based on the nonsense she'd told us last night, then my theory made perfect sense.

'Out of the question. Even if such an individual *did* exist, there's no way one person could cut off the entire power system. It's not as if there's a single master switch. It would take a whole team of people acting in concert to cut the power. And somehow they would have to overcome the AIs that exist within the computer networks in the control centre below the Citadel. It would be enormously difficult to achieve.'

'And yet someone did just that,' I pointed out as I wondered what an 'AI' was. 'So someone figured out how to do it, right?'

Her shoulders sagged in defeat. 'Yes,' she admitted in a small voice. 'That's why I must reach the Citadel to find out the answer.'

Ken put a comforting arm around her. 'You haven't told us what happened to you on the Day of Wonder,' he said.

'I was travelling in an air-car over Vurgun when the power failed. The car crashed. My three companions were killed outright, but by some miracle all I suffered was some severe bruising. I hid in the woods for a time. I had some food with me, but that soon ran out. At that point I had no idea that our crash was part of a world-wide Elite catastrophe. I just thought that I and my companions had been the victims of an unfortunate accident. It was only when I left the woods, after removing my Elite uniform, and met up with some peasants, that I discovered the true situation. I told the peasants I'd been robbed and they gave me some clothes. After that I moved around, switching identities and joining up with different groups of travellers. I actually was travelling with a wine merchant from Vorass when the vigilantes attacked.'

'Thank the gods you survived,' said Ken fervently and hugged her.

The sight brought back a twinge of my seasickness. I decided another change of subject was in order. 'I've always been curious about how those air-cars of yours worked,' I said. 'How did they manage to stay in the air? Obviously not by magic.'

'They levitated and flew all over Urba by means of generated electromagnetic fields. But when the power was cut the air-cars could no longer fly ... as I found out from personal experience. As did my three friends. And so many others all over the world.' Tears welled up in her eyes.

For a few moments I felt a strong wave of sympathy for her, but then I reminded myself of whom we were talking. It prompted me to say, 'One more question, Alucia?'

'Yes?'

'Why were you Elite such absolute bastards?'

Her face reddened with anger but she didn't answer my question.

Despite the size and speed of the *Black Swan*, crossing the

Pyman Sea was going to take nearly a month. Not that I minded; now that I no longer suffered from seasickness, I found shipboard life endlessly fascinating. There was always something interesting to observe and I admired the skills of the sailors in their running of the large vessel. I was particularly impressed by the way they scampered up the rigging to impossible heights, hauling in sails or unfurling them at the captain's order. With my fear of heights, I didn't envy them in the slightest.

I did most of my wandering about the ship on my own. Ever since my 'bastard' question to Alucia, she hadn't spoken to me. Ken had gone all huffy on her behalf, and had moved into her cabin. I didn't overly mind because it meant I got to sleep in the bottom bunk. I only saw them at mealtimes, when they both went out of their way to ignore me. The only person I spent any time with was the 'scientist' Bartel. During our first conversation, he told me that since the Day of Wonder he had been travelling from one abandoned Elite Compound to another gleaning what facts about their 'science and technology' that he could. 'It's difficult,' he said, 'because most of their knowledge is locked in their dead machines and so unrecoverable.' But in some of the Compounds he had found copies of very old books, and these had proved invaluable. 'You wouldn't believe some of the things I've learned,' he said. I believed him, but when I asked him to elaborate, he went all sly. 'Not yet. I have to be sure I can trust you,' he said.

'You can trust me,' I told him, with my most trustworthy smile.

'Probably. But I have to be sure.'

I kept visiting him, and listening to his strange tales, and as a sort of friendship developed, I slowly gained his trust . . .

By contrast, several of the crew members, whose skills of seamanship I so admired, were openly hostile to me. At first I was mystified, as none of the other passengers seemed to attract this ill-feeling. Then I discovered it was simply because they didn't like the way I looked. I'd had this reaction before, but mainly from the children in Capelia, who yelled taunts at me when I walked through the town. Matters came to a head early on the evening of the fifth day of our voyage. Three crewmen cornered me near the bow. They'd obviously been overindulging, because I could smell the grog on their breaths. All three carried club-like wooden belaying pins and their intentions were clear. 'Call yourself a mercenary, do you?' sneered one of them as he kept slapping the club into the palm of his other hand. He was smaller than his two companions, but looked meaner. I was reminded of a vicious weasel. 'You look as you've never had an honest fight in your life,' he sneered, 'you look like a long, useless streak of piss.'

I smiled at them. My hope was that a charm offensive on my part would take the tension out of the situation. 'I've been called worse than that, my good fellows,' I said in a good-humoured way. 'Now let's all go and have a drink and forget about this.'

The weasel bared yellow teeth in what might have been a grin. Then he said, 'We're going to beat the living shit out of you, *mercenary*.' Then he spat on the deck in front of me. They began to close in on me. There was nowhere for me to retreat to. I was trapped.

A quick glance around had confirmed that there was no chance of any assistance arriving in the nick of time; fortunately I had something up my sleeve – literally – the dagger that I'd picked up after Ken had disarmed Alucia in her cabin. Ken was so absorbed by Alucia that its existence seemed to have slipped from his mind. Since then, I'd kept it hidden in my clothing, the captain having made it clear he didn't trust either Ken or me with weapons on board his ship. So I was able to say, with a bravado I didn't feel, 'I'm not just a mercenary, I'm also a magician. Would you like to see a little trick of mine?'

The question momentarily distracted them. 'What kind of trick?' asked the weasel.

'This trick,' I said and suddenly clapped my hands together in front of his face. The dagger appeared in my right hand as if by magic and in one quick, upward movement I sliced off the tip of his nose. He gave a howl of pain and clamped a hand over his nose as he backed away from me. Blood was already pouring out from between his fingers. I clapped my hands again and the dagger disappeared.

It had the desired effect. His two companions regarded me with fear as they backed away from me. 'My nose! He cut off my nose!' cried my victim.

'Only a bit of it,' I said, 'but I can do other tricks as well. Would any of you like to see another one?'

They all fled. I almost collapsed with relief.

After breakfast the following morning, during which I was again studiously ignored by Ken and Alucia – how much longer would this idiotic behaviour continue, I wondered? – I paid another a visit to Bartel in his cabin. On the way, all the crewmen I encountered regarded me with either fearful or wary expressions and gave me a wide berth, which amused me: obviously I'd acquired a reputation amongst the superstitious crew members after the previous night's incident.

Bartel looked pleased to see me and invited me into his cabin. There were open books on every available space, but when I asked if I was interrupting his work, he insisted I wasn't. He carefully removed some books from a chair and told me to sit down. I opened the conversation by telling him, 'You missed a good breakfast. Again.'

He moved books on top of his single bunk to one side and sat down. He was wearing a red smock, green leggings and blue boots. He looked more like a gnome than ever. A wise gnome. 'I keep forgetting about mealtimes,' he said, 'because of my work. I'm having the most exciting time of my life with these books.'

'Glad to hear it.' I decided to get straight to the point. 'You ready to trust me yet?'

He peered at me and said, 'Yes, I think I am.'

'Good. Because I have some questions I want to ask you.'

'I'm sure you do. Ask away.'

'Recently I've heard some weird rumours about Urba,' I said, 'crazy stuff . . .'

'What is the source of these rumours?' asked Bartel. 'Or rather, *who* is the source of these rumours?'

'I can't tell you. Sorry.'

Bartel smiled. 'You don't trust *me*?'

'Oh, I trust you, Bartel. But by not telling you the source of the rumours, I'm protecting you. Believe me, that knowledge would put you in terrible danger.'

'Hmmm,' he said, then, 'all right. I accept what you say. Now tell me about these rumours.'

'Don't laugh, but someone told me that Urba is a giant vessel travelling through some kind of empty void. And it's not our original home. Our original home was the surface of a sphere called Earth. And the sphere revolved around a bigger sphere of burning gas—'

Bartel didn't laugh.

I gave him a weak smile. 'Pretty crazy, right?'

'No, not crazy, though it sounds it. It's all true.'

That really wasn't the answer I'd wanted. 'Are you serious?' I asked in astonishment.

'Very,' he replied. He gestured at the books that surrounded him. 'It's fully documented.'

'But surely all that stuff is just an Elite religious belief,' I said, desperately. 'A myth, like our belief in the gods. It can't be true.'

'Oh it's true all right. Some of the books and other documents I found pre-date the existence of the Elite. I found one ancient book that actually describes in detail the construction of Urba.'

'Bloody hell,' I gasped.

He picked up a book from the bed and held it out to me. 'Read this for starters. But be careful how you handle it. It's very old.'

I took it and looked at the title: *A Short History of Planet Earth*.

I became so engrossed in both the book and further revelations from Bartel that I actually missed lunch. It was mid-afternoon when I finally emerged from his cabin, my head spinning. My head was doing a lot of spinning these days. I decided I had to talk to Alucia immediately, no matter how cross she was with me.

But before I could find her, we were attacked by pirates.

I was wandering about the deck trying to spot Alucia and Ken when I heard the lookout in the crow's nest start shouting out what was obviously some sort of warning. Of all the shipboard tasks, manning the crow's nest was the least enviable. I realised this on the second day of the voyage when the unfortunate crewman who was perched up there scanning the horizon was snatched out of the crow's nest by a dragon, which had appeared out of nowhere. The hapless lookout was carried off screaming while his shipmates and the rest of us passengers could only watch helplessly. So when the new unlucky man up there began shouting, I assumed he'd spotted another dragon. But it was nothing so trivial: when I looked in the direction he was pointing, I saw a ship approaching us. It was smaller than the *Black Swan*, but it looked faster. Then the general cry went up: 'Pirates!'

From the aft deck Captain Larmos ordered his contingent of marines to man their positions. I was jostled away from the railing as a line of men armed with crossbows quickly stretched along the entire side of the upper deck, ready to fire upon the approaching ship. Behind the first line of marines was a second line of men carrying conventional bows. They began dipping the tips of their arrows, which were wrapped with cloth, into buckets that either contained oil or some other flammable liquid. Small braziers had been put into place along the deck by crewmen. The bowmen used these to set alight the ends of their arrows to fire at the sails of the pirate ship as soon as it was within range.

'What's happening?' It was Ken, who'd appeared by my side.

'Oh, so you're talking to me again,' I said. 'I should feel flattered.'

'Shut up and tell me what's going on!'

'We're about to be attacked by pirates. But by the look of things, it should be a short, one-sided battle,' I said with certainty.

I was wrong.

'Drop your weapons and extinguish those arrows!' came a shouted order from the aft deck. Everyone turned and looked, including Ken and me. Major Sylvan was standing next to Captain Larmos, holding a dagger at his throat. It was he who'd shouted the order. Flanking him and the captain were the two 'merchants'. They were both armed with crossbows and no longer resembled merchants. Then I realised they never really had. Why hadn't I noticed that before? I remembered their unnatural silence during that first dinner on board—

The assembled contingent just stood there, unsure of what to do.

Major Sylvan repeated his order and then said, 'Captain, tell your men to do as I say or I slit your throat . . . *now*.' He pressed the blade slightly into the captain's throat. Blood began to seep from the thin flesh wound, but the captain kept silent. The pirate said, 'Captain, if your men don't follow my instructions they will all be slaughtered, but if they do obey I will spare their lives. *So tell them.*'

Ken, without turning his head, said softly to me out of the corner of his mouth, 'Do you know where the armoury is?'

'Yes,' I said. By now I knew practically every inch of the ship. 'You can reach it through the hatch behind us.'

'Do you think you can make it to the hatch?'

'Probably not. But I'll try. You want your crossbow, don't you?'

'Yes. Can you get into the armoury?'

'Ken, you know I can pick any lock.' I exaggerated but only a little; escapology *is* one of my more successful jester skills.

'Your last chance, Captain Larmos,' shouted Major Sylvan, cutting deeper into the captain's throat. '*Tell them!*'

'Do as he says,' said the captain, in a strangled voice. 'Drop your weapons. Extinguish the fire arrows.'

There was a loud clatter as dozens of crossbows fell to the deck, then the sound of sizzling as burning arrows were thrust into buckets of water. But not all the marines obeyed. One raised his crossbow and fired at one of the 'merchants'. The marine missed his target; the 'merchant' didn't. His bolt hit the marine square in the chest and he fell to the deck with a thud.

'Go now,' whispered Ken. Attention had been momentarily diverted by the felled marine, who was now dying noisily and messily on the deck. I dropped to all fours and scampered quickly to the hatchway. I was expecting to feel a bolt smash into my back any minute, but I made it undetected and dropped down as quietly as I could manage.

I was back with Ken's crossbow in just over a minute: I hadn't even had to pick the lock on the metal gate of the armoury. Someone, in their recent haste to get extra weapons, had left the gate open. I peered cautiously over the top of the hatchway. The situation hadn't changed, except that the pirate ship was much closer to our vessel. 'Here, Ken, catch!' I whispered from the hatchway. He turned quickly towards me. I tossed his crossbow to him. He caught it, turned back. One of the 'merchants' fired at Ken, but Ken had anticipated this and was already stepping to one side as he fired his own weapon. The 'merchant's' bolt missed Ken – and barely missed me – but Ken's bolt buried itself deep in the 'merchant's' chest. He grunted and dropped.

Silence followed. Then Major Sylvan, who still held his dagger at the captain's throat, smiled and said, 'Well aimed, mercenary, but I fear you've shot your bolt. Captain, order your men to kill him—'

CHAPTER NINE

'Captain, order your men to kill him—' were the last words Major Sylvan spoke, for as he started to press the dagger harder into the flesh, Ken pulled the trigger once again and the second bolt from his unique crossbow embedded itself in the pirate's throat. He dropped the dagger and grabbed at the bolt with both hands, his eyes wide with surprise. Blood spurted from between his hands. Ken fired his third bolt. This one hit the remaining 'merchant' directly in his forehead. He dropped like the dead man he now knew he was.

Major Sylvan had dropped the dagger, needing both hands in his futile attempt to stem the blood pumping rhythmically from his throat. Captain Larmos stepped behind him and pitched him over the railing of the aft deck. He landed with a loud thud on the deck below.

A cheer went up from the crew. 'To arms, men, quickly!' shouted the captain. The pirate vessel was perilously close now, and its crew had started firing arrows at us, but now the pirates really didn't stand a chance. Their ship was soon caught within a deadly rain of flaming arrows and crossbow bolts. Before long it was nothing but a burning hulk, its hapless crew either dead or floundering helplessly in the water.

After the fun was all over, Captain Larmos came over to us. He had a rough bandage tied around his injured throat, but he was all smiles. He grasped Ken by the hand and shook it over and over again. 'Sir, you not only saved my life, you saved my ship! I'll forever be indebted to you! Anything that is in my power to give you, you shall have!'

'I am happy I could be of service to you, Captain,' said Ken, trying to look modest – and failing completely.

Then the captain noticed me. 'Oh, and thank you too.'

There was no point in me trying to look modest.

Late in the afternoon I was standing at the bow of the ship watching the dolphins playfully swimming ahead of the ship, leaping out of the water, then plunging under again. I became aware of a presence standing just behind me: Alucia.

'How does it feel to be the second most popular person on the ship? Well, third if you count the ship's cook,' she said, putting her hands on the rail beside me.

'So now you're talking to me again as well,' I said. 'My cup runs over.'

'The question is, how do you feel about talking to *me*? I know you hate me.'

I considered my answer before I spoke. 'It's not so much you I hate personally, it's what you represent.'

'I can't help what I am . . . or what I was.'

'What you were? No, I think you still *are* what you were. If that makes any sense.'

'I've begun to realise you're more intelligent than you look,' she said.

'I'd take that as a compliment, if it was one. Which I doubt it was. In fact, I'm sure it wasn't.'

'Believe me, it was a compliment. And because you're intelligent, it's important we become allies. Not friends. That would be impossible. But we do need to become allies.'

'You have an ally in Ken.'

'I have a lover in Ken.'

'When you're not trying to kill him.'

'That's all in the past. I realise now he genuinely loves me.'

'And how do you feel about him?'

'I'm very fond of him.'

'That's not exactly the same.'

'True, but we're not discussing Ken, we're discussing you. I need you as an ally because I need your help to find out what went wrong on that day, that day you people so callously call the Day of Wonder.'

'Well, from the viewpoint of "us people", something went very right on the Day of Wonder. It meant the end of Elite rule over us. And I'm certainly not going to help you somehow restore it. I won't be your ally.'

'There's no way Elite rule will ever be restored in Urba,' she said with conviction.

'Isn't there? There must still be thousands of Elite alive in the Citadel.'

She shook her head. 'I very much doubt it. If there were, they would have solved the problem by now and restored the power. Some catastrophe occurred both within the Citadel and the control centre that cut off the power and probably killed most, if not all, the Elite who were there. And as I said to you before, this catastrophe, whatever its nature, probably presents a threat to the whole of Urba. To *your* people. That's why you and I must put aside our differences and join forces. I just wish I could convince you I'm telling you the truth about Urba. I wish I could convince you I'm not crazy.'

I said quietly, 'I learned something this morning, from Bartel. I believe you. I believe everything you told Ken and me about the true nature of Urba.'

She stared at me with wide eyes. 'You do?'

'Yes. Bartel has all these old books that he found in various Elite Compounds. His descriptions of what's in them backs up everything you said. I have no choice but to accept that all I was taught about the world was wrong—'

'You didn't tell him about me, did you?' she asked, looking anxious.

'Don't worry. I didn't mention you at all. I just told him I'd heard these weird rumours about Urba from someone.'

'Good.'

'I read one of the books myself. *A Short History of Planet Earth*. Fascinating. But I've got to admit I'm having a lot of trouble taking it all in. I keep thinking I'm having some kind of strange dream.'

'That's to be expected. Your entire world view has been turned inside-out. Literally, in a sense.'

'And there's so much I still don't know,' I said. 'A lot of what I read in that book went entirely over my head.'

Alucia placed her hand on my forearm. I felt an odd tingle at her touch. 'Then I shall be your teacher,' she said. 'Whatever you want to know. I'll do my best to explain it all to you. By the time we reach the Citadel you'll know as much as any Elite.'

I didn't want to be reminded of our ultimate destination. Nor did I welcome the thought of becoming anything like an Elite. I said, 'While I agree with you that I'm more intelligent than I look – strangely enough, though, you're the only person who's ever noticed that – I doubt I'm going to learn enough to be of any help to you.'

'We'll see,' she said. 'And as a first step in your education, ask me a question.'

'I've got so many questions it's hard to pick just one.'

'Well, make a start. Anywhere.'

'Okay. The gods. They don't exist, do they?'

'No. We invented them.'

'You invented them? The Elite invented the gods?'

'Yes. Who do you think gave them those stupid names? "Maurice the god of War"? "Beryl the goddess of Fertility"? "Ethel the goddess of Good Housekeeping"? Good grief. We invented them at the same time as we invented this pseudo-medieval society you inhabit. Except we didn't call ourselves Elite back then. That came later.'

'Why did you invent the gods?' I asked.

'We wanted a nice, bland, safe religion to replace the existing religions like Christianity, Islam and Judaism, the three big monotheistic religions: they all tended to produce dangerous fundamentalists. Especially Christianity and Islam. And there were seriously disruptive schisms within the religions themselves. They were one of the main causes of catastrophic conflict in Urba, just as they had been back on Earth. But let's go back to the beginning . . . I've already told you both how Earth's local star became unstable and the great project that was Urba was undertaken. An entire self-contained world capable of carrying most of the worlds' populations out of the solar system—'

'Worlds?' I interrupted. 'There was more than one?'

'Oh yes, by that time there were colonies established on Earth's moon, on a planet called Mars and on the moons of Jupiter and Saturn. There were also several space habitats, like Urba but much smaller.'

'You mentioned Urba was used to transport *most* of the human race,' I said. 'Didn't everyone leave?'

'No. Quite a lot refused to leave for various reasons – thought they'd take their chances in their own homes. Human nature is a funny thing. Which is why everything eventually turned sour in Urba.'

'Sour? How so?'

'We imported all our problems from Earth: interracial tensions, political differences . . . and of course, those all-important religious differences. Urba had been deliberately made as big as possible to give every nation plenty of space, but even so, it became a pressure cooker of conflicting differences. Humanity is naturally aggressive, particularly the male half of the species. Wars between the nations broke out—'

'I read about nations in that history book,' I said. 'They were like big domains.'

'Exactly. Urba was originally divided up into nation states, reproducing the division of people on Earth. Anyway, the wars got increasingly bad. In theory, seriously destructive weapons were prohibited in Urba, but soon they were being manufactured in every state. It began to look like by the time an inhabitable planet was found there wouldn't be anyone left alive to inhabit it. So this great social engineering project was devised by the technocrats who ran the ship—'

'Technocrats?' I was getting a little punch-drunk from all these unfamiliar terms.

'Scientists and technicians. A class remote from the general population, just as it had always been on Earth. Most people were positively hostile to science; they'd been like that for centuries. Yet at the same time, they needed what science and technology provided. But on board Urba the two groups had grown ever further apart over the years. The masses considered scientists and technology necessary evils, but evils all the same. The scientists and technicians thought the masses ignorant and superstitious fools; they considered themselves to be . . . an elite.'

'Aha!' I said.

'Aha indeed,' said Alucia. 'Anyway, the technocrats who operated Urba decided that drastic action was called for if disaster was to be averted. They proposed a radical act of social engineering on a massive scale: nothing less than the total deconstruction of Urba's various nation states. And the deconstruction was carried out all the way down to the smallest social unit, the family. Communities and families were broken up and scattered all over Urba. The domains were formed: small, easy-to-control feudal states. It took four generations to achieve this, even with the mind-controlling drugs that were used to help the process along. But within two hundred years, Urba's social structure had been totally homogenised. Traditional religions, political movements, national boundaries and individual languages had been completely wiped out. Ango, based on a useful polyglot language called English, already most people's second language, became the mandatory universal language. All forms of sophisticated technology were banned; from then on it remained solely in the hands of the ruling technocrats, who now openly called themselves the Elite.'

'So you deliberately reduced us to a primitive condition?' I said, going over these points in my mind.

'Yes – but why a medieval fantasy world was chosen for the basis of this new society has always been something of a puzzle to me. Probably some technocrat had read *The Lord of the Rings* one too many times—'

'*Lord of the Rings?*' I asked.

'A book written on Earth a long time ago. Three books, actually. Tried to read them once, but never got through the first volume. Dreadful stuff. Actually, it's more likely the decision was made by some committee of sociologists.'

'What's a sociologist?'

'They used to be a kind of pseudo-scientist. They don't exist any more.'

'What happened to them?'

'We exterminated them. Best thing the Elite ever did in my opinion. Anyway, the transformation of Urba stopped all the major conflicts; it saved the world. We subsequently encouraged lots of minor wars as a way of siphoning off humanity's natural aggression, but a war of total destruction was avoided.'

'By the Elite reducing the bulk of the ship's population to slavery.'

Alucia looked pained, even a little guilty. 'That wasn't the original plan. But I'm afraid that was the eventual result.'

'Why? I asked you before, and I'm asking now: why did the Elite become such cruel bastards? And don't get all offended again,' I added as I saw anger begin to blaze in her eyes. 'You *know* the Elite behaved like total shits towards us *mundanes* for centuries. I'm not accusing you personally – for all I know, you spent your life trying to stop them. But you have to admit the Elite as a group carried out some major atrocities. So why?'

I thought she was going to erupt, but then the anger faded from her eyes and her shoulders slumped. It occurred to me that this might be all an act, but I decided to give her the benefit of the doubt – for the time being. She leaned against the railing and stared at the water. 'Seen from your point of view I can understand your perception of the Elite's actions. And since I've been forced to live amongst you commoners now for some time, my own perception of us has been forced to change. But we never thought of ourselves as evil—'

'But you were,' I said, uncompromisingly. 'So why did you become that way?'

'I suppose it all comes down to power,' she said slowly. 'There's an old saying, "Power corrupts; absolute power corrupts absolutely." And we had absolute power over you people.'

I thought about it, then nodded. 'You certainly did.'

She said nothing.

'And there's another thing I don't understand,' I said. 'How did your predecessors get the entire population of Urba to capitulate? I mean, you said the nations had weapons and obviously your technowhatevers—'

'Technocrats,' she said dully.

'Right. Your technocrats would have been greatly outnumbered. So how did they impose their will on the bulk of Urba's population?'

'Simple. They switched the sun off.'

I stared at her as my mouth gaped open. 'They ... *what*?'

She pointed upwards to the flickering column of the fading sun. 'They switched the sun off. Some of the nation states remained resistant for months, but eventually they all capitulated.'

'But that's impossible,' I said. 'You can't just switch off the sun!'

'You're still thinking in terms of your old world view,' she said. 'Urba's sun is not a natural phenomenon, it's man-made. The sun is a tube of plasma gases contained within a powerful electromagnetic field and stimulated to extreme temperatures by high-intensity lasers. It's modulated by *those* gizmos—' She pointed upwards again.

I shaded my eyes and looked into the distance ahead of us to where she was pointing. It was one of the spherical Beads of the Gods that punctuated the column of the sun. 'One of the Beads of the Gods,' I said.

'No. That huge object, one of many that float in an area of zero gravity along the length of the sun, is both an amplifier and a modulator. It, together with the others, ensures that the temperature of the sun varies from region to region. The fluctuations in temperature are necessary to create an artificial weather system within Urba, along with the air-recycling systems and the giant seas; they're also vital. The "Beads" also maintain the electromagnetic cocoon that contains the sun.' She pushed herself away from the railing, turned and pointed at the Wall behind us, the Wall that Capelia nestled against. 'There are giant fusion reactors behind what your people call the Walls of the Gods,' she said. 'They power the sun. They also power the giant air-recycling units that lie behind the circle of huge holes in the Walls that surround the sun generators. And behind your Wall they also power the great engines that drive Urba through space. Your Wall is towards the stern of the ship. Since leaving the last planetary system we investigated nearly twenty-five years ago, Urba is still accelerating—'

'Again, I have absolutely no idea what you're talking about,' I said. 'I did warn you—'

'I know, I know . . . it's not your fault. I've never done this before. I'm obviously not a natural teacher. I've just got to be patient and start you off with the basics.'

'Okay, so what's a fusion reactor?'

'Jesus Christ,' she muttered. She turned and leaned against the railing again. 'This is going to be hard work.'

I wondered who this Jesus Christ woman was, but decided not to ask just yet. One question at a time . . .

'A fusion reactor uses a process like the one that occurs naturally in stars – *real* suns – to produce energy,' she said. 'The reactors provide all the power for Urba.'

I was none the wiser. 'But you said that someone had cut off the power in Urba. How is it that the sun is still functioning?'

'Separate systems. Same energy source, but separate systems. The system that powered all of the Elite's various equipment was put into operation much later. That's the one that's been shut down. The one that actually runs Urba is operating as normal.'

'Ah,' I said.

'Next?'

But while I was thinking which of my myriad questions to pose next, we were interrupted by the arrival of Captain

Larmos's steward, a thin, dark-skinned man the same age as the captain.

'Excuse me, Sir Usborne, sir,' he said in an agreeably deferential manner, 'the captain has invited you to join him at a celebratory party he's holding in his quarters. If that would be convenient.'

'Yes, it certainly is,' I said. I needed a break from Alucia's torrent of information. It was making my head hurt.

'Am I invited too?' asked Alucia.

'If Sir Usborne so wishes, of course, madam,' said the steward.

'Yes, I do,' I said. 'By the way, you don't have to call me sir. I'm not a knight.'

'Yes sir. So how would sir like to be addressed?'

I thought for a few moments and said, 'As one Lucky Bastard.'

As we followed the steward, a number of crewmen smiled warmly at me: a big contrast to the reception I'd received from them before the pirate attack and its happy outcome. 'You must be enjoying this adulation,' Alucia said. 'I know Ken is.'

'Like I said, we were lucky. But then Ken is a damned good shot with that crossbow of his. I used to complain about the amount of time he spent on the archery range, but now I thank the gods that he did so.'

'Those would be the gods you now know definitely don't exist?'

'The very same.'

CHAPTER TEN

hen we arrived in the captain's stateroom, Ken was already there. He gave me a suspicious look when I entered with Alucia, then drew me to one side and whispered angrily, 'You haven't been insulting Alucia again, have you?'

'On the contrary. We've been having a pleasant discussion.'

'About what?' he demanded.

'My education.'

'Your what?'

'My education. I've got some bad news for you. Everything she's told us about Urba is true. We are in a giant vessel travelling through an endless void.'

He stared at me as if I'd gone mad. 'You've gone mad,' he told me.

While I was wondering how to convince him, I was rescued again by the steward, who pressed a goblet of red wine into my hand. I drank most of the wine in one gulp. Captain Larmos began banging a knife blade against the side of his goblet to attract the attention of the crowd. Judging from his flushed face and his bloodshot eyes, he'd started the celebrations much earlier – not that I blamed him. He'd come closer to death than anyone would be comfortable with.

'Quiet, everybody!' cried the captain. 'I want to salute our two guests of honour, Gideron and Usborne! Without their timely intervention today, especially Gideron's prowess with his wonderful crossbow, this ship would have fallen into the hands of the pirates and I'd probably be dead by now. Let us show our appreciation!' He put down his goblet and began to clap his hands. Everyone else quickly followed his example, and there were several cries of 'Hurrah!'

As the applause began to die down, the captain came over to us. 'I'm still shocked that Major Sylvan was the pirate leader,' he said, not for the first time. 'I've always considered myself a good judge of character. And to think I suspected you two of being pirates—' He shook his head in wonder. 'I must be getting old.'

'The major fooled us all,' said Ken. 'I certainly accepted his every word at face value.'

'I thought he was a spy,' I said. Everyone looked at me. 'But I didn't spot him as a pirate,' I added hastily. 'And in retrospect, there was something odd about those two fake merchants: I noticed it when I first met them but stupidly I didn't pursue my suspicions.'

'My companion can be very perceptive,' Ken told the captain. Then he looked at me. 'Except when it comes to women.'

'You're mad,' said Ken in his irritatingly matter-of-fact way.

We were in Alucia's cabin, or rather, *their* cabin. They were sitting side by side on the lower bunk while I was perched, as usual, on the floor. We were all drunk after the excesses of the captain's celebratory party.

'Most of what Alucia has told us about Urba has been verified by the alchemist, Bartel,' I pointed out.

'That loony elf?' snorted Ken. 'He's mad too.' He picked up one on the bottles we'd liberated from the captain's stateroom on our way out and took a long swig of red wine.

I automatically followed suit, then said, 'He has evidence. Books. Lots of books he's found in the Compounds.'

'Elite forgeries. The alchemist is mad, like you. You should both be locked up.'

'Hey, hang on,' I protested. 'What about Alucia? You know she believes exactly the same; she's told you so. But I haven't heard you suggesting she be locked up.'

'That's different. Alucia may be crazy but I love her. I'm

willing to overlook her insanity for the sake of true love. And I have faith that the power of our love will eventually bring her to her senses.'

Funnily enough, this didn't go down well with Alucia.

Ken slept in our cabin that night, which meant I was required to use the top bunk again. He and Alucia, after a great deal of arguing, were no longer speaking. At this rate no one on the entire ship would be talking to anyone else by the time we reached Verharven. I was sure it was just a temporary hiccough in their relationship, but it was annoying. Before I finally fell asleep I tried to come to terms with all that I had learned that day; I got another headache from attempting to comprehend a universe that was the exact opposite to the one I'd been taught about all my life. I still couldn't fully accept this new concept, but my whole belief system was definitely being seriously undermined.

But there was another worry that kept me awake: the suspicion that I was being manipulated by Alucia. I still didn't like her – she was undeniably beautiful, but she was an Elite, after all, and I didn't believe leopards could change their spots. And the ease with which she appealed to my vanity unsettled me. Of course, *I* know I'm highly intelligent but, as I'd told her, no one else had ever noticed this quality about me. Why had she? Was she being genuine in her assessment or was it mere flattery? And am I such a fool that I could be so susceptible to mere flattery? Well, who isn't?

I slept uneasily.

We docked at Verharven some three weeks later; there had been no more unpleasant incidents, other than an attack by a kraken. Fortunately it hadn't been a very big kraken, and the marines and crew were able to drive it away.

Unlike Persopia, Verharven was not a Freetown; it was part of the domain of Cruzave that was ruled, still, by the warlord Zielon, a man with a very bad reputation. As soon as we'd docked, a contingent of the warlord's soldiers boarded the

Black Swan and searched the ship thoroughly. The officer in charge told the captain they were looking for Elite stowaways. They also questioned the passengers and crew. The captain personally vouched for Ken, Alucia and me, which was a big help. I was worried about Bartel, but when I checked on him, all his books had been packed away out of sight in a large trunk. 'I may be eccentric but I'm no fool,' he told me. 'I'll be fine. And perhaps our paths will cross again someday.'

When the time came for us to disembark, Captain Larmos again thanked us warmly for our help in defeating the pirates, and not only did he give Ken his precious signet ring back, but he also handed us a small purse of gold coins. Ken protested that we didn't need it, but the captain insisted. 'You're mercenaries. And mercenaries always need money. Verharven is an expensive town. So please take it. It's the least I can do after what you did for me.'

Ken was about to protest again so I quickly took the purse, offering our sincere thanks.

The crew cheered us as we started down the gangplank, even the sailor whose nose I'd surgically altered. I was a little sad to be leaving the *Black Swan*. I'd enjoyed my first sea voyage, seasickness, violence, pirates and the kraken aside.

Like Persopia, Verharven was full of soldiers and there was an oppressive air of tension – but the reasons for the uneasy atmosphere were different here. There was the usual hunt for suspected Elite survivors, but the main source of wariness was Lord Zielon: he was keeping an iron grip over the city to avoid any chance of rebellion within his domain. Lord Camarra's rapidly expanding campaign of conquest was more than mere rumour these days; although, in reality, the nearest of Camarra's forces were still far away, not only from Cruzave's borders but from the neighbouring domains, I got the impression that the average Verharven inhabitant expected Lord Camarra to pitch up any moment.

Under the circumstances we thought it wise not to mention our destination to anyone. We also thought it wise to get out of the city as soon as possible, which we did as soon as we'd bought horses, supplies and various items of essential equipment. Our cover story to the soldiers manning the city gate was that we were on our way to Vorasss, to help defend it against Lord Camarra. That tale, and a sizeable bribe, got us out of Verharven without any trouble.

We rode fast, quickly leaving the main road and seeking out an obscure trail so we could avoid even the villages. Over the last three weeks, the relationship between Ken and Alucia had run hot and cold: they'd make up, become inseparable (and unbearable) for a time, and then Ken would invariably say something to antagonise her and once again they'd no longer be talking to each other. Right now the relationship was in one of its cold stages: the atmosphere between them had remained frosty all day and when we made camp for the night in a secluded glade in a small forest, the chill was positively tangible.

While I roasted a chicken on a spit over the fire the pair of them practised synchronised sulking. They were sitting as far apart as they could get without moving to different domains. I was both amused and annoyed by the situation.

Finally, as I poured myself a mug of red wine, I said, 'As sickening as I find it to watch you two indulge in displays of public foreplay, I would prefer that, nauseating as it is, to this childish behaviour.' Alas, my subtle attempt at counselling fell on deaf ears.

We ate the chicken, accompanied by fresh bread and apples that we'd bought in Verharven, in silence. But afterwards Alucia did start talking, though only to me.

'You know,' she said, 'I've been thinking about your theory. You might be right.'

'I had a theory?' I asked, puzzled.

'Your theory about a rebellion within the Citadel.'

'Oh, *that* theory. But you said all the Elite were in perfect harmony. A rebellion was out of the question.'

'I'm not talking about a rebellious faction amongst the human Elite, I'm talking about the AIs.'

'Ah, yes. You mentioned them before. What are they?'

'Artificial Intelligences. Self-aware machines.'

I was on my third mug of wine and my brain was in no condition to grapple with yet another of Alucia's mind-boggling concepts. 'Machines that can think? How is that possible?'

'I'll try and explain—'

A snort of derision was Ken's invaluable contribution to the conversation. We both ignored him.

'The AIs are not simply machines,' Alucia continued, 'they're highly advanced computer systems.'

I took another swallow of wine and asked her again what a computer system was. She didn't answer. From the light of the fire I could see the expression on Alucia's face. She looked desolate. I had a sudden insight into how alone she must be feeling. It was said that before the Elite invaded Urba and imposed the universal language, Ango, throughout the world, each domain had its own language, which meant a visitor to a different domain wouldn't understand what anyone there was saying, nor would the inhabitants be able to understand anything the visitor said. I realised that Alucia must be feeling like such a visitor. We couldn't understand her language. She was completely alone, cut off from her own kind . . . who were now almost all dead. For the first time since I'd learned she was an Elite, I felt real sympathy for her.

I decided to make an effort on her behalf. 'It really would help if you could explain to us what a computer system is.'

She nodded, smiling slightly. 'Yes, of course it would. A computer is basically a machine that does calculations. But *lots* of calculations and very, very fast.'

'Right, got it,' I said encouragingly.

'Good. Now, from that essentially simplistic function computers can be made to perform a wide variety of actions. Computers control every aspect of Urba's environment, for example. They also control the rest of the ship's operations, like navigation and propulsion – where we're heading and the power to get us there. Urba couldn't exist without them. Computers are incredibly smart; so smart that they can mimic perfectly human intelligence. You can conduct a conversation with a computer and convince yourself you're communicating with another intelligent being, though in reality you're conducting a conversation with a simulation of another intelligent being.'

She was losing me again. 'But you said these AI computers *are* intelligent beings—'

'Because the AIs are a more advanced generation of computers. They are not simply infinitely sophisticated calculating machines. They are something more. They contain organic material: synthetic neural systems similar to those in the human brain. They really are intelligent, self-aware entities, like human beings, but vastly more intelligent than us. And they control most of the other computer systems in Urba, all those that are involved in the running of the ship.'

'I see,' I said, which I did, sort of. Well, no, I didn't really, but I bluffed anyway. 'But they can't act independently, can they? I mean, they're under the control of the Elite? Or rather, they were—'

'Built into the core of their beings are strict rules that ensure they must obey human beings,' said Alucia. 'But at the same time they were designed to possess a certain degree of independence, otherwise their efficiency would have been seriously constricted.'

I saw at last, I think, the point she was trying to make. 'Are you saying you believe these intelligent machines might have rebelled against the Elite?'

'I'm saying it's a remote possibility. I don't know how or why, but I have to consider it.'

'Have they ever tried anything like this before?' I asked.

'Over a hundred years ago an AI went mentally unstable. It displayed all the symptoms of classic human neurological failure. It became schizophrenic. Insane. It had to be deactivated – a difficult process as the AI definitely didn't *want* to be deactivated. The scientists said there had been some freak degeneration of the AI's organic tissue. They couldn't really explain it, but they did give assurances it couldn't happen again.'

'But you think it might have?'

'I don't know. It's hard to believe that all the AIs could suffer some kind of mental breakdown simultaneously, but at the moment I'm desperate for any kind of explanation for what happened within the Citadel.'

I excused myself then, having an urgent need to pee after all the wine I'd drunk. As I entered the edge of the woods I heard a sound behind me. I turned. It was Ken.

'What do you think you're doing?' he demanded. He sounded annoyed.

'I'm taking a piss,' I said.

'You know what I mean. Pretending to believe all that Elite rubbish that Alucia keeps coming out with. What are you playing at?'

I tried not to laugh. He was actually jealous. 'You think I'm humouring her in order to get into her pants? Not so, I assure you. I actually believe what she says.'

'You can't possibly! The idea that Urba is inside some giant sailing ship floating on some infinite sea called "space" is . . . it's absurd!'

'Well, that's not exactly an accurate description of the true situation, Ken. You should open your ears as well as your eyes. I admit it's hard to accept her version of the Universe, but sooner or later you'll have no choice.'

'Never! And just stay away from her,' he warned and stomped back towards the camp. As I stood there emptying my bladder I contemplated just how difficult obeying his demand would be, seeing as there were just the three of us.

When I woke up the next morning I wasn't too surprised to see that Alucia and Ken were both under the same sleeping blanket. Obviously yet another reconciliation had taken place during the night. My main reaction was one of relief. At least the childish period of non-speaking was over. Again. Yet at the same time I felt a small twinge of regret that they were back together. I didn't want to examine too closely the reasons behind *that* reaction.

When they woke they were *definitely* back in full lovey-dovey mode, but as I cooked breakfast, I kept reminding myself that this had to be better than the previous day's chill. I wondered if Ken's ridiculous jealousy had prompted him to swallow his pride and apologise to Alucia . . .

After our usual breakfast, we discussed our route for the day, then reviewed our long-term plans. Ken unrolled the map of Urba that the Capelia border garrison commander had given him, using small stones to keep it flat on the ground, and we all studied it. 'Two more days' riding and we'll be out of Cruzave,' said Ken. 'We can either head in that direction –' he pointed at the map '– and enter Tascoli Domain, or go that way and travel through the domain of Faldor. It doesn't matter which. Both routes will take us closer to the Citadel . . . and to Lord Camarra's ever-expanding territories.'

'Faldor?' asked Alucia, sounding excited. 'Are we near that domain?'

Ken pointed at the map again. 'It's right there. See.'

'We must go there,' said Alucia firmly.

'Why?' I asked.

'There's something in the Faldor Elite Compound that would be invaluable to us,' she said. 'Believe me.'

'There can't be,' said Ken. 'All the Compounds have been ransacked.'

'That's right,' I agreed. 'There'll be nothing of value left in any of the Compounds by now. Anything that's moveable will have been removed. Except for a few books, perhaps, and only a scholar like Bartel recognises their importance.'

'If my memory isn't playing tricks on me, I guarantee that the thing we need will still be within the Faldor Compound. Or rather, far beneath it. Several Compounds were built over existing installations and these each contain a Sprite. No one but an Elite could gain access to it, but very few Elite these days ever bothered to learn how to operate a Sprite. I was one of the rare exceptions, even though I had to endure being constantly called a throwback at school. So I'm pretty sure it will still be there.' She was so excited she actually clapped her hands with glee.

'What's a "Sprite"?' I asked.

'You'll see, you'll see!' she said with an excited laugh.

I was mystified. 'Okay, I presume a "Sprite" is some sort of Elite machine, but how can it work? As you've explained to us, the power to all Elite devices has been cut.'

'I'm not saying anything else about the Sprite. I might be completely mistaken about there being a Sprite under the Faldor Compound. I don't think I am, but I don't want to get your hopes up only to have them dashed.'

'What hopes?' I asked, exasperated. 'At least you could give us a clue about what we should be hopeful about.'

'All I'll say at this stage is that a Sprite is a ship like Urba, but much, much smaller—'

Ken groaned. 'Here we go again.'

Alucia gave him an exasperated look. Then she picked up the map and said to him, 'I'm going to make one more attempt to show you the reality of our situation –' she picked up the map from the ground, '– so please refrain from any sarcastic comments for the time being. Or else.' She carefully formed a tube out of the map. 'This is how Urba looks in reality, right?' she said, holding the parchment tube up so that Ken could see through it.

Ken made a grunt of assent.

'Right,' said Alucia, 'except that what you see is only a section of the giant spaceship that contains Urba—'

Ken made another grunting sound. It was different from his last grunt; Alucia gave him a withering look. She went on, 'Urba extends much further at both ends than what you see here.' She stuck one end of the tube under his nose. 'That's the Capelia end of the world. Without the wall, of course. It's actually located towards the stern of the great ship. Beyond your Wall, as I've already explained to Jad, there are huge fusion reactors which power the sun and the air-recycling system, and also generate the power for the giant engines at the stern—'

I'm sure he was trying hard not to, but Ken couldn't resist letting loose a small, but pointed, snort of derision. Alucia paused and simply stared at him. Fearing I was about to witness the beginning of another wearying period of hostility between them, I quickly interjected, 'What about the opposite Wall? The one towards the bow?'

Alucia said, talking directly to me, 'There are other fusion reactors in the bow, which also provide energy for the sun and air-recycling units, and a number of smaller engines. The bow section also contains huge, sealed compartments that are off-limits to us. They will only open automatically when a suitable planet is found . . .'

She stopped again. Not because of another derogatory sound effect from Ken but because a large shadow had suddenly fallen over our small camp. We all looked up in time to see a dragon making a pass over us. It was a big dragon.

CHAPTER ELEVEN

'**S**hit!' exclaimed Ken and drew his sword, at the same time making a dash for his crossbow. I just stood there, frozen to the spot. The dragon made a sharp turn and came back towards us in what was practically a dive. The wicked-looking claws on its hind legs were fully extended. Alucia tugged urgently on my arm. 'We've got to get into the trees!' she shouted. Then she ran towards the horses.

She'd galvanised me back into life. I started to follow her. Ken had reached his crossbow. He scooped it up and aimed it one-handed as the dragon made its attack. He fired all three bolts in quick succession, and all three hit the dragon: two in the chest and one in the stomach. Even I could have hit a target that big . . . and that close. The dragon gave a shriek, though whether one of pain or just sheer anger it was impossible to tell. It veered off, climbed a short distance and then began to make another turn.

Alucia and I had reached the horses. We untied them and quickly mounted. Ken had sheathed his sword and was desperately trying to rewind the crossbow's windlass.

'No time for that, Ken!' Alucia shouted at him. 'We've got to get under cover, fast!'

Ken – for once – listened to her. He ran over to us and jumped on his own mount, which was shaking in terror: the horses were as frightened as I was. I glanced over my shoulder as we made for the trees. The dragon was making another killer swoop towards us; it appeared Ken's bolts had simply annoyed it. I'd never seen such a large dragon before. I didn't even know they could grow that big . . .

As we made it to the forest edge and plunged on into the

darkness, I heard the dragon shriek again, followed by the snapping of branches. It had obviously not pulled out of its dive in time and had hit the top of the trees.

'Keep going!' cried Alucia, a little redundantly, I thought: nothing would have forced me to stop at that point in my flight.

My horse needed no such urging either, but Ken yelled, 'But I need to stop and reload!'

'Not yet!' responded Alucia breathlessly. She had my full support.

We rode on as fast as we could, ducking under branches and swerving around brambles, until finally, when we had ridden deep into the woods, Alucia raised her hand to signal we should stop.

As Ken immediately returned his attention to resetting and rearming his crossbow, Alucia said urgently, 'Listen!'

I listened. Behind us I could hear more sounds of snapping branches. Then something fell with a crash. I realised it was a small tree. Then I heard another tree smashing through the undergrowth.

'It's following us through the woods!' cried Alucia, in astonishment. 'On *foot*!'

'Can they do that?' I asked in amazement.

'This one apparently can,' she replied. 'It's a big son of a bitch. Let's keep going.'

'Hang on,' said Ken, 'I need a few more seconds—'

We waited impatiently as he finished reloading his weapon. Another tree went crashing down – and not that far away, from the sound of it. 'Right, I'm ready,' said Ken at last. We continued on through the woods . . .

But we hadn't gone much further when suddenly we ran out of trees. Stretching ahead of us was nothing but clear grassland. There was another small copse in the distance, but we had no chance of reaching it before the dragon reached us. And once it had smashed its way through the woods behind us it would take to the air again—

'It's bright idea time,' I said, failing to keep the panic out of my voice. 'Anyone got any?'

Ken pulled his horse up and turned, raising his crossbow. 'I'll aim for a vital spot. Any suggestions?' he asked, looking at Alucia.

'You could try for one of its eyes,' she said doubtfully, 'but it would be a very difficult shot.'

Another tree was felled and then, a short time later, the dragon emerged from the wood. It was walking on all fours, its huge wings folded along its sides. It stopped when it saw us. I'd swear it was grinning at us. Then the dragon began to extend its wings. Ken raised the crossbow to his shoulder. Took aim. The dragon was about thirty yards from us, ready to launch itself at us. I couldn't see how Ken could possibly hit one of its eyes. I could barely make them out.

'Wait!' cried Alucia before Ken could fire. 'I'm going to try something very stupid.'

She then dismounted, which I thought was very stupid indeed. And when she started to walk towards the still stationary dragon, I thought her stupidity had progressed rapidly through idiocy to utter madness.

'What the hell are you doing?' cried Ken, who clearly shared my opinion of her actions.

'Shush!' she warned him as she continued to walk towards the dragon. The dragon, its huge wings now fully extended, cocked its head like a giant bird as she approached. It too appeared puzzled by what she was doing.

She halted about ten yards in front of the dragon, then she suddenly shouted at it: '*Klaatu barada nikto!*'

The dragon flinched, then shrieked at her. Alucia stood her ground, then shouted at it again, the same incomprehensible words: '*Klaatu barada nikto!*'

The dragon's reaction this time was to flap its mighty wings and start to move towards Alucia.

'We're doomed,' I said quietly.

Then, to my astonishment, rather than attacking Alucia, the dragon launched itself into the air. Beating its wings furiously it rapidly rose above us. It gave another shriek of annoyance, and then flew off. We watched as it quickly became a small dot in the distant sky. Then it disappeared completely from sight.

Alucia walked, a little unsteadily, back towards Ken and me. Ken dismounted, hurried to her and hugged her. I noticed her face was very pale. I guessed mine was as well.

'How in the world did you do that?' Ken demanded, a little in awe. 'What did you say to it?'

'I told it to piss off,' she said, and gave a shaky laugh.

'But *how*?' I asked.

'I took a gamble it would remember one of the key commands it had been taught in the training pens when it was a youngster,' she said. 'And the gamble paid off.'

'Thank the gods it did!' I exclaimed.

She looked at me and smiled. 'The gods you no longer believe in?'

'Yes, they just won't go away. But what language was that?'

'Old Hollywood,' she replied.

'What's that?'

'An Elite joke.'

She and Ken remounted. Their horses, I hasten to point out. My relief at not becoming dragon fodder had made me feel quite giddy. 'What now?' I asked.

'We should return to the camp and collect our belongings,' said Alucia, with supreme common sense. I'd forgotten we even had belongings.

The ride back through the woods to our camp was much easier, thanks to the wide trail the dragon had left behind it when it smashed through the trees. On the way I rode up beside Alucia and asked, 'Why did you bring such ferocious animals from the home world?'

'We didn't. Dragons never existed on Earth. They were mythical creatures. And if they had, they wouldn't have been able to fly like our friend just did. They would have been too heavy in Earth's gravity. But Urba's centrifugal force only generates three quarters of an Earth G.'

I gave her a typically blank look, then asked, 'If they didn't come from Earth where did they come from?'

'We created them. By that I mean the Elite did. Don't ask me how; there's no way you could understand the answer – not yet, anyway.'

That was undoubtedly true so instead I said, 'Why?'

She shrugged. 'Partly for set dressing, like all the other mythical creatures in Urba: the sea serpents, griffins, trolls, krakens, gnomes, elves and so on.'

'Set dressing? What's that supposed to mean?'

'Background colour for this medieval fantasy theme park my predecessors established within Urba. But the dragons were also chosen as a symbol for the Elite: to strike even more terror into the hearts of the yokels.'

'By yokels you mean us?' I asked.

'Hey, don't blame me,' she said, 'all these decisions were made long before my time. Naturally I don't regard you and Ken as yokels.'

'Really?'

'Cross my heart and hope to die.'

We collected everything we'd left behind when we'd fled our camp and continued on our journey, stopping for lunch beside a stream. After we'd eaten Ken and Alucia wandered off together to look for a place to bathe where they'd be out of my sight. It didn't take much imagination to work out what they intended to get up to, and unfortunately I have a very good imagination.

Not for the first time the image of Alucia stark naked arose, unbidden, in my mind. I chided myself for having erotic thoughts about Ken's woman. I then chided myself even more strongly for having erotic thoughts about an Elite woman. The Elite had been the epitome of evil for so long, the persecutors of humanity. But it was becoming increasingly difficult for me to think of Alucia as an Elite; the more time I spent with her, the more human she seemed. I knew I might be deluding myself about her, and that I really shouldn't trust her, but I couldn't help it.

Having nothing better to do, and to take my mind off what Alucia and Ken were probably doing at that very moment, I decided to go fishing. I rooted around in the saddle-bags until I found the coiled line and hooks that I'd brought along. The stream turned out to be teeming and before very long I'd caught three large trout, which pleased me. At least *I* was making myself useful, unlike my companions – who returned after about an hour, looking cleaner, and distinctly flushed.

As the stream flowed in the general direction in which we were headed, we followed it for the rest of the day, until it was time to make camp again. It was getting dark as I started preparing the fish for our meal.

And then we heard the distinct sound of bells tinkling. Somebody was approaching us.

We'd had enough surprises; we all made a grab for the nearest weapon to hand, Ken inevitably picking up his trusty crossbow, and we waited apprehensively. As we stared in the direction of the sounds, Alucia said, 'They can't be bandits. What bandits in their right minds would announce their arrival with the ringing of bells?'

'Very confident bandits?' I said.

The tinkling sound grew louder. Then, out of the gloom, came a garishly painted caravan, drawn by two large white horses. The horses were the source of the sound; their bridles and harnesses were festooned with small bells.

'Somehow I don't think this is a bandit attack,' I said.

'Once again my faith in your acute intelligence is confirmed,' said Alucia, with a degree of sarcasm that I thought was completely unwarranted.

The horses came to a halt and the occupants of the caravan alighted. There were six of them, four men and two women, and their clothing was as glaringly colourful as their caravan. They carried no weapons, or none that were visible. One of their number stepped forward. He was a large, very fat man with an absurdly big white moustache that curled upwards at its ends. He raised a hand in greeting and said, in a loud, booming voice, 'Friends, we come in peace. We mean you no harm. We are nothing but a band of poor travelling players. We saw the light of your campfire and were drawn to it in the hope that we might throw ourselves on your goodwill and mercy and acquire some sustenance. We have fallen on hard times in these perilous days and are presently destitute. If you are bandits I assure you we have nothing worth stealing.'

We all lowered our weapons. Ken said, 'We're not bandits. We're professional soldiers on our way to offer our services to Lord Camarra.'

'Then, unlike us, you will have no trouble in finding gainful employment,' said the fat man. 'From where we have just fled there is nothing but warfare. But to address our most pressing problem of the moment, can you spare us any food? We have, as I said, no money, but in return for a meal we will entertain you.'

Ken and I exchanged a look. Apart from the fish I'd caught, we had plenty of supplies that we'd bought in Verharven. I nodded to Ken and he nodded to me in turn. Then he said to the fat man, 'You're welcome to share our food and our campfire.'

The fat man beamed. 'May the gods bless you for your kindness, young sirs!'

'Hey, don't I get a vote in this transaction?' demanded Alucia.

Ken and I looked at her. She looked annoyed. 'You have an objection, Alucia?' Ken asked, politely.

After a long pause she finally shook her head. 'No, I guess not.' But she still didn't look happy.

'Well then,' said Ken to the fat man, 'you and your companions make yourselves as comfortable as you can.'

As our unexpected guests sat down around the campfire, and I added more wood to it, the fat man introduced himself and his companions. His name was Parelli, but I didn't pay any attention to the others, apart from the younger of the two women. She was called Juliet: an odd name, yet it was strangely familiar to me. She was also very pretty. She had long blonde hair and couldn't have been older than seventeen or eighteen. And when she caught me staring at her I was gratified, not to mention thrilled, when she gave me a smile that was quite enchanting.

Preparing a meal for nine people presented me with a bit of a problem, so I took the easy way out and made a very large stew, the principal ingredient of which was the trout I'd caught. While I worked, without any help from either Ken or Alucia, of course – the art of cooking apparently not being part of the latter's vast range of Elite knowledge – Parelli described how they'd becoming refugees.

'It is sheer chaos in the lands to which you are travelling,' he told us. 'War is everywhere. It's certainly not a place for people in our profession: our unique talents are in no demand at all. And it is mainly the fault of the man to whom you intend offering your own talents, Lord Camarra. More and more domains fall under his control. The warlords either join him or face certain annihilation.'

As I chopped up vegetables and added them to the very large cooking pot which the players had produced as their contribution to the meal, I said, 'You should head for the domain where Gideron and I last served: Capelia. It's very peaceful. Nothing there but trees. Lots and lots of trees. It lies at the end of the world, a long way from here.' I pointed in the general direction of Capelia. At least, I *hoped* I was pointing in Capelia's general direction.

But Parelli said sombrely, 'I fear that eventually, if Lord Camarra continues with his campaign of conquests, no domain in Urba, no matter how remote, will be safe from *him*. Clearly his ambition is to conquer the entire world.'

The players may have run out of food, but they still had a plentiful supply of wine and by the time we'd finished the meal – which, in all modesty, turned out remarkably well – the mood around the campfire had become quite merry. Then, after a loud burp, Parelli got to his feet and said, 'Now it is time for us to repay your hospitality. With your permission we shall perform our famous version of a play called *Hamlet*—'

'Ah,' I said, 'by Shakespeare.'

Parelli regarded me with astonishment. 'You are familiar with the works of William Shakespeare?' he asked me. 'You're young, a mercenary soldier – but forgive me, dear sir, I mean no offence.'

'None taken,' I said. 'But before I took up soldiering, I was in show business myself.'

'Really? How fascinating! Were you an actor?'

'Well, no. More of an all-round entertainer.' I paid no attention to Ken's snigger and continued, 'Anyway my mentor had a book called *The Plays of William Shakespeare* in his library, and I dipped into it occasionally. But it was written in a very strange type of Ango and I found much of it difficult to understand.'

'Ah, yes,' said Parelli. 'Shakespeare wrote those plays a very long time ago, so they're written in very archaic form of the language. Scholars believe Shakespeare lived well before the invasion of the Elite. The domains he mentions in his plays no longer exist—'

'How very true,' said Alucia. We all looked at her, but she said nothing more. In my opinion she'd already said too much; perhaps she realised that herself. Maybe she'd drunk too much wine. I know I had.

Parelli went on, '*Hamlet*, for example, is set in a domain called Denmark, which can't be found on any map. And *Julius Caesar* takes place in another very old domain called Rome. No trace of that remains either. Of course, some scholars claim that Shakespeare's plays are all sheer fantasies, set in a world that never existed.'

I glanced at Alucia but wisely this time she kept her mouth closed.

'If I remember correctly,' I said, '*Hamlet* is a very long play.'

'You are quite correct, young sir,' said Parelli, 'if you kept strictly to the written text it would last over four hours—'

A groan escaped from Ken's lips.

'—but,' continued Parelli, 'we have abbreviated the text somewhat for our version.'

In the event, their version of *Hamlet* lasted barely half an hour. The language had also been modernised, and I actually understood every word. They'd also included lots of jokes and slapstick. All in all, it was very enjoyable version of the play – I was particularly impressed with Juliet's portrayal of Ophelia, Hamlet's sister. My enjoyment of her performance had absolutely nothing to do with her costume, a gown that in a certain light was practically diaphanous.

After the play I invited her to go for a walk with me along the stream. We'd both consumed a fair amount of wine and one thing led to another – namely, getting out of our clothes, for a start. It did occur to me, somewhat cynically, that her enthusiastic response to my advances might have been a part of the players' payment for our hospitality, but I didn't care. You don't look a gift horse in the mouth . . . if I can be forgiven for connecting this crude equine analogy to such a blissful encounter. I blamed the wine. Again.

I was sad to see them leave the following morning when our two parties went our separate ways, but the memory of the previous night provided me with ample compensation.

'From the expression on your face you had an enjoyable time last night,' said Alucia as we rode off.

'I have no idea what you're talking about,' I told her.

'Hah,' she said.

CHAPTER TWELVE

It took us a further six days of travelling before we entered Faldor, and another two days to reach the capital, Tureas. But once there, Alucia had a disappointing setback: the Elite Compound was heavily guarded by soldiers and we could see no way of getting into the place. The town was in a dangerous state, and no place for strangers; we were regarded with suspicion by everyone we encountered. Both Ken and I decided it would be best to continue on, despite Alucia's protestations.

'There's a Sprite under that Compound,' said Alucia angrily as we rode out of the town, 'I just know it.'

'It might help if you'd tell us what you want to do with this "Sprite",' I told her. 'And I'm still not even clear what a "Sprite" is. Care to illuminate us?'

But she refused to say anything else.

Later that night, after we'd made camp, eaten a meal and drunk a fair amount of wine, she became maudlin, changed her mind and began to explain why she was so desperate to get her hands on a 'Sprite'.

'They're spaceships,' she told us. 'There are a number of them stashed in various locations throughout Urba, as well as a fleet of them in a huge space dock near the control centre. They were once used for surveying planetary systems . . . back when the Elite showed any interest in such matters. I'm one of the few who actually learned how to operate a Sprite in recent years . . . like I said, I'm a sort of throwback. I've been outside Urba in a Sprite on three occasions . . . amazing experience . . . nothing like it—'

'That I can believe,' muttered Ken darkly.

Confused, I said, 'But you told me the whole point of Urba was to locate a new world. A new home for the human race.'

'That was the original intention,' sighed Alucia, and drank some more wine. 'But the Elite became insular over the centuries . . . they lost interest in searching for a new world. I hate to admit it, but they had everything they wanted right here in Urba.'

'Power, you mean. Power over the rest of us. The power to treat us like shit.'

'You're justified in your opinion,' Alucia admitted, 'but it wasn't like that in the beginning . . . it was all done with the best of intentions—' She refilled her cup with wine; she was becoming quite drunk. And depressed. 'Anyway, I was probably being a fool when I thought we could reach the Sprite under the Faldor Compound. With the power cut off we'd have to climb all the way down to the docking bay . . . a bloody long climb . . . and that's assuming the hatches could be opened manually . . .' She drank more wine.

'Amongst the multitude of things I don't understand,' I told her, 'and when I use the word "multitude", believe me I'm not exaggerating – why was it so important to you that we reach this Sprite vessel?'

'Obvious, isn't it? We could use it to fly outside Urba . . . we'd reach the control centre, and the Citadel, in minutes rather than weeks . . . find out what the fuck went wrong—'

'You wanted *us* to go with you *outside* Urba?' I exclaimed. The very idea left me weak in the knees.

'Sure. No problem. Like I said, it's a great experience . . . You would have loved it . . . But hey . . . probably wasn't even a Sprite down there anyway . . .'

Good, I thought.

She passed out shortly afterwards.

Ken and I regarded her sleeping form and then he said to me, 'Do you really believe any of this stuff?'

'Yes, I do. I have to. And eventually so will you.'

'Never! I think it's all a load of Elite bollocks. I mean, I do love her and everything, but she's talking complete balls. She's still following some Elite pack of lies for some reason.'

'And I still think you're completely wrong,' I told him. 'Sooner or later you're going to have to accept the truth.'

'I think it's *you* who's going to have to accept the truth,' said Ken smugly.

Just a couple of days later, as we were about to stop for lunch, we were startled by a loud rumbling sound, the source of which was somewhere ahead of us. 'It sounded like thunder,' said Ken, 'but there's no sign of any storm.'

We rode on until we reached the top of a hill, from where we saw an amazing sight. In the valley below us was a large pit at least a mile in diameter and very deep. Several hundred people were at work within it. Around the edges of the pit was a large encampment.

'Diggers!' exclaimed Alucia, a note of fear in her voice.

Diggers: the religious cult who believed they could dig their way through to paradise.

As we continued to watch, we heard the sound of a shrill siren. It was clearly a warning signal, because the people in the pit began to scatter and take cover wherever they could. A short time later there was a loud rumble and smoke rose to form a cloud in the centre of pit.

'Gunpowder!' cried Alucia. 'Those blind fools are using gunpowder!'

I knew what gunpowder was – most people did, even if they didn't make it themselves. It was a mixture of certain common ingredients, like charcoal and saltpetre, and, apparently, urine, which could be ignited to create an explosive force. The Elite had strictly banned its use, under punishment of death. The Elite had banned *many* things under punishment of death.

Alucia, in a shocked voice, said, 'If the fools keep going at this rate they might actually succeed blowing a hole through the ship's outer hull!'

'And then what would happen?' I asked her.

She looked at me as if I'd asked a really stupid question –

which I had. 'I told you before, you idiot: the entire atmosphere would escape from Urba into space and all life in Urba will end.'

'Oh, yes,' I said, 'I forgot. Er, just how thick is Urba's hull?'

'On average, the rock base is over a mile thick throughout most of Urba, and the exterior is covered by a sheath of dense alloys. I thought it would be impossible for the Diggers to penetrate the outer hull even if they ever succeeded in reaching it, but their use of explosives changes all that. We're all in terrible danger!'

'Not good,' I said.

'That's the understatement of the century,' she said sourly.

'I don't know what you two are getting so worried about,' said Ken. 'Everyone knows the rock goes on for practically forever. It will take them ages to reach another world.'

'Jesus Christ!' muttered Alucia. There was that name again.

'What should we do?' I asked her. 'Somehow I don't think going down there and asking them politely to stop digging would work.'

'Well, we've got to do *something*,' she said. 'Otherwise we'll all be trying to breathe in a vacuum. And believe me, it can't be done.'

'Uh oh,' said Ken, 'don't look now but we're about to have company.'

A column of riders was coming up the hill towards us; I counted about twenty of them. 'Shouldn't be any problem,' I said. 'We'll just tell them we're harmless travellers passing through . . . Let me do the talking.'

The horsemen, all seriously armed, formed a circle around us. I raised a hand in friendly greeting. 'Hello friends,' I said, 'that's a pretty impressive hole you've got down there in the valley.'

'We're glad you like it,' said their spokesman, a pale, thin-faced man with a wispy beard, 'because you'll soon be helping us dig it.'

I smiled. 'I don't think so. We have urgent business elsewhere.'

'Not any more,' said the Digger. 'Our High Priest, His Holiness Driscarla, has decreed that all able-bodied people will take part in our great Holy Mission to reach Paradise.'

'That's complete and utter nonsense!' exclaimed Alucia angrily, not exactly helping the situation. 'There's no way you morons can dig your way to Paradise. All you'll succeed in reaching is an airless void that will kill you all!'

The previously pale face of the Digger spokesman went red with anger. He pointed an accusing finger at Alucia. 'That's blasphemy, woman!' he proclaimed. 'By rights you should be put to death for uttering those lies. But we need as many people as possible to serve the Holy Cause, so your death will be postponed until we have attained our goal.' Then he ordered his minions, 'Disarm them!'

Ken reacted by raising his crossbow and for a moment I thought he would start firing and get us all killed. But he saw the hopelessness of our position and lowered the weapon. We were all stripped of anything even remotely useful.

'You will now accompany us,' said Pale-face, 'and start work immediately.'

Ken raised himself up to his full height on his saddle. 'That's out of the question.' He pulled off his glove to reveal his royal signet ring. 'I am Prince Kender of Capelia. I don't dig *holes*.'

Pale-face said, 'Your previous status no longer matters. The old world is gone. Our Holy Mission is all that matters now. You will dig . . . or you will be flogged into submission until you do. Now come with us . . .'

We were taken down to the camp beside the pit and told to dismount. Our horses were led away, along with our belongings. They removed Ken's breastplate, took our cloaks and even removed our watches. Then we were handed tools – I got a pick-axe – and large wicker baskets to strap to our backs, and then forced down into the pit towards an overseer. I saw that the overseers carried whips. This was some religion.

Once we were in the pit we were split up and Alucia was led away to join the women's brigade. She gave us a forlorn wave as she went. My heart sank.

The work was simple, if back-breaking. After each explosion, we had to break up the loosened rock with our pick-axes and carry it up the sides of the pit in the baskets. Very soon every muscle in my body was on fire from the effort.

'Well,' I said to Ken on one occasion as we struggled up the slope, 'what's it like to go from being royalty to slave in a matter of moments?'

Ken didn't answer.

When night fell, Ken and I were taken to a large dormitory-tent full of men. Alucia was presumably in a women's tent somewhere nearby. The Diggers clearly practised strict segregation between men and women. In the tent we were fed some tasteless gruel and told to get some sleep. The bunks, not surprisingly, were hard and uncomfortable. Even so, I knew I would sleep well after the day's exertions. Before I did fall asleep, I asked Ken, in a bunk next to me, 'Well, have you got any bright ideas on how we're going to get out of this mess?'

He still didn't answer. I guessed he wasn't talking to me. Again.

This torture went on, day after day. I soon realised my body was not going to be able to take this punishment for very long: I was beginning to lose weight. Whatever was in the gruel had the nutritional value of stewed grass, which it probably was. Every morning there were unmoving bodies of men on the bunks, those who'd died during the night. It struck me as odd that the Diggers, who said they needed able-bodied people to do complete their Holy Mission, worked these people to death.

But death soon became an attractive prospect. I consoled myself with the thought that when the Diggers achieved their objective and dug their way out of Urba, they'd all die along with the rest of us. I tried sharing this cheering thought with Ken but he still wasn't talking to me.

And then, after we'd endured this hell for nearly two weeks, something happened.

An army happened.

It was about ten o'clock in the morning and Ken and I had just hauled another load of rubble up the slope of the ever-deepening pit. My load, typically, felt like it weighed a couple of tons by the time we'd reached the top. And then suddenly there was all this shouting and the clanging of steel on steel and we saw this great mass of armed men wash through the camp. The Diggers' militia didn't stand a chance against the invading force and it was all over fairly quickly.

Then the place was swarming with soldiers in black uniforms and chain-mail, all ordering everyone to stop work. Ken and I were more than happy to oblige, and immediately dropped our burdens.

Then a group of men who looked important – their black uniforms had a lot of silver on display – rode into the camp. Their leader, a cruel-looking type with a pointy black beard streaked with grey, announced he was Lord Megus of the Thoran Domain, and that he had joined forces with Lord Camarra, who wanted the digging halted. The Diggers' cult had been outlawed as of now; the cult leaders and their supporters would be punished. As for the rest of us, we were free to go. However Lord Megus made it clear it would be in the best interests of the men amongst the captive army of slaves if they chose to join up with Lord Camarra's forces.

As that had been our intention all along, Ken and I had no problem with the 'suggestion'.

While Ken went off to find Alucia, I watched as Lord Megus's men dealt with the leaders of the Diggers: they were summarily hung from a hastily erected scaffold. His Holiness, Driscarla – an elderly man with the face of a fanatic – was amongst them. He went to his death promising everlasting doom to his executioners. I can't say I felt the least bit sorry for him.

Ken finally returned with Alucia in tow. I was shocked at how bad she looked: thin and clearly exhausted, but at least she was alive.

And soon after that, our fortunes took yet another turn for the worse.

Alucia went distinctly pale when she saw Lord Megus. She tried to hide her face, unsuccessfully: as Lord Megus rode by us, he spotted her. Reining in his horse, he pointed at her and cried, 'You!' in a threatening voice. 'Alosa!' Then he gave a chilling smile. 'The gods have truly favoured me on this day!'

'You've mistaken me for someone else, your lordship,' she said, though she looked shaken to the core.

'Yes,' said Ken, helpfully, 'her name isn't Alosa, it's Alucia.'

'Whether it's Alosa or Alucia,' said Lord Megus, 'she's still an Elite. And one I know only too well.'

'She's not an Elite,' protested Ken, 'she's an old friend of mine. I've known her for years.'

'In that case, you must be an Elite as well,' said Lord Megus. 'And no doubt so is your companion.' Now he was pointing at me. Oh, fucking great.

One of his officers spoke up. 'I've never seen an Elite with features like that before.' He indicated me.

I felt mildly insulted at this – but, under the circumstances, not too insulted.

'No matter. Even if he isn't Elite he's clearly in collusion with them. Arrest all three. I'll decide their fates later.' He smiled his evil smile at Alucia again. 'Be assured, Alosa, that your death will not be an easy one.'

We were quickly bundled away into one of the now empty dormitory-tents and chained up. When the soldiers had gone Ken and I both looked at Alucia. 'Is there something you'd like to share with us?' I asked her.

She took a deep breath. 'I was stationed in Thoran for some time, so I saw quite a lot of Lord Megus. It was a case of extreme mutual dislike from the start. I was promoted to leader of the Elite contingent and he didn't like having his military ambitions vetoed by someone he saw as a mere girl—'

'That's more than apparent,' said Ken. 'He clearly hates you.'

Alucia looked at the ground. 'There's something else . . . something you're not going to like.'

'There's a surprise.' We waited.

'When he kept ignoring the curbs imposed upon his conquests I had his oldest son executed.'

Neither Ken nor I said anything.

She raised her head and looked at us. 'You've got to understand the situation,' she said imploringly. 'I had no choice. I had to follow orders.'

'Well,' I said, 'it certainly explains why you're not his favourite person.' As a mood-lightener, my comment was far from successful.

'I'm only sorry I've dragged you two into all this,' she said.

'Hey,' said Ken, 'the very fact that we've been travelling around with somebody we both know is an Elite is a capital offence just about everywhere it seems. We would have both been fucked anyway.'

'Perhaps . . . but I fear the punishment may be more severe for you both because of my history with Lord Megus.'

She was certainly right about that. It was nightfall when Lord Megus entered the tent, flanked by two soldiers. 'After much thought,' he said cheerfully, 'I've decided on the manner of your execution. Tomorrow morning all three of you will be hung, drawn and quartered. Have a good night.' And with that he left. Smiling.

CHAPTER THIRTEEN

An uneasy silence followed Lord Megus's departure from the tent. Finally I said, 'I've heard the term before, but what exactly does being hung, drawn and quartered actually involve?'

'Maybe it's better if you don't know,' said Alucia.

'Well, I'm going to find out first-hand tomorrow morning, so you might as well tell me now.'

Ken said sombrely, 'First they hang you by the neck until you've almost choked to death, then they cut you down, slice open your belly and draw out your intestines with hooks, slowly. Then they burn your intestines in front of you. After that they lop off your arms and legs and then your head.'

I thought about it for a time and then said, 'I wish you hadn't told me that.'

'You wanted to know,' said Alucia.

'We've got to escape,' said Ken. 'Jad, can you pick the locks on these chains?'

'I could, if I had my set of lock-picks. But they were taken when we were searched on our arrival.'

'Can't you use something else?'

'Possibly. Alucia, do you have a hairpin?'

'Do I look as if I've got a hairpin, you twat?'

I tried to think of an alternative. And failed.

I've had better nights.

At daybreak Lord Megus entered our tent, again flanked by two guards. Here we go, I thought grimly. The start of what was going to be a long, gruesome and extremely painful death. I mentally cursed Ken, and his father, for getting me involved in this stupid enterprise from the start. I cursed Alucia for good measure too. But then I noticed that Lord Megus wasn't smiling, which I thought was odd. In fact, he looked positively unhappy. Odder still. He should have been rubbing his hands with expectant glee.

'I've received new orders from Lord Camarra,' he said with ill grace. 'Any Elite uncovered by my forces must be transported to his camp as quickly as possible. He's laying siege to the Citadel. The orders are very explicit, so I have no choice but to obey them. You leave immediately. My only hope is that the fate you suffer at Lord Camarra's hands will be more prolonged and painful than that which I'd planned for you this morning.'

He left, glaring. The two guards remained behind and began to unshackle us. I said to one of them, 'Any chance of us having breakfast before we leave?'

We didn't get any breakfast. Instead, we were shoved into a dirty, smelly cage on the back of a wagon. It was clear that the previous occupant, or occupants, had been obliged to use the straw covering the floor as a toilet. I got the distinct impression that this was going to be a very long and unpleasant journey.

'Look on the bright side,' said Alucia as the wagon began to trundle out of the Digger camp with its escort of six mounted soldiers and an officer. 'At least we weren't hung, drawn and quartered this morning.'

'Ah, but what fate awaits us in Lord Camarra's camp?' I asked. 'As Lord Megus so fervently hopes, Camarra may have something even worse in store for us.'

'I don't know,' she said. 'There was something odd about his treatment of the Diggers. Something that doesn't add up.'

'What do you mean?'

'Well, it's as if Lord Camarra was aware of the danger of what they were doing. That suggests to me he knows that Urba is a giant spaceship.'

'Oh, not that nonsense again!' scoffed Ken, pulling tentatively on one of the chains that manacled him to the bars of the cage. Did he, I wondered, think he could snap it with brute force? I'd looked carefully around the cage but there was nothing in it that I could use as a lock-pick.

'If Camarra does know the truth about Urba, there's only one way he could have found out about it,' continued Alucia, as if Ken hadn't spoken, 'and that's from an Elite. And he obviously also needs Elite advice for his attack on the Citadel.'

'You think he's in collusion with some surviving Elite?' I asked.

'Who knows? But I'm sure "collusion" is the wrong term. Captivity and torture are sure to be a more accurate description.'

'But,' I said, 'if he already has some Elite in captivity, why would he need more?'

'Because he doesn't have them any longer,' said Alucia. 'They've either escaped . . . or they've been tortured to death. And we're the replacements.'

That certainly cast a pall over the proceedings. We all fell into a state of gloomy silence as the day dragged on. As we expected, it was a bitterly uncomfortable ride, and matters weren't improved when we got drenched in a sudden downpour, which made the straw in the cage smell even worse. But at least we were able to quench our thirst. Around noon, we stopped for what was laughably described as lunch: a few pieces of gristly meat and mouldy bread. The soldiers laughed at the expressions on our faces as we forced down this meal. Even the gruel supplied by the Diggers hadn't tasted this bad.

'We have to escape,' said Ken as we resumed our journey. We hoped the noise from the wagon wheels concealed our voices from our captors.

'I don't fancy our chances,' I told him, looking around our cage.

'Neither do I,' agreed Alucia.

'We'll wait until nightfall,' said Ken. 'Some opportunity is sure to present itself when they let us out to relieve ourselves.'

'Somehow, I don't think we're going to be let out of this cage until we reach our destination,' I said seriously.

'But they'll have to let us out occasionally,' he said, 'for reasons of hygiene.'

'I doubt it,' I said. 'Not from the smell in this cage. Haven't you even looked at the floor?'

Both of them looked at me, aghast. 'That's *revolting*!' exclaimed Alucia.

'Yeah, you can say that again. But I don't think our hosts give a shit about our comfort ... if you'll pardon the expression.'

The horrible journey in the wagon took for ever; it wasn't long before we were in an even worse state than we'd been in the Digger camp. We continued to lose weight, we became covered with sores and all three of us stank like trolls. The nights were particularly bad: we had neither cloaks nor blankets and had to huddle together for warmth.

'At this rate we're never going to survive long enough to reach Camarra's camp,' groaned Ken as we tried to force down the virtually uneatable rations our tormentors laughingly referred to as 'lunch'.

'True,' agreed Alucia weakly. Then she said, more brightly, 'And that gives me an idea ...'

I watched apathetically as she called one of the guards to come over to our cage.

'What is it, you Elite cow?' he snarled as he approached the bars.

'Is it true that Lord Camarra has given you and your companions orders to deliver us to his camp?' she asked.

'Yeah. So what?'

'So what will his reaction be if you deliver us to him dead?'

'Uhhh—' he said as he considered the question. He frowned and then went off to confer with his companions.

Alucia's scheme worked. Our diet instantly improved. And during the rest of the journey we were regularly doused with buckets of water. We were even allowed, one at a time and in chains, to get out of the cage for brief periods of exercise. We began to regain our health and some of our strength. It wasn't freedom, but at least we were still alive.

At long last Lord Camarra's huge encampment hove into view. How long the journey had lasted, I had no idea. We'd lost all track of time. Beyond the encampment, in the distance, rose the great, glittering tower of the Citadel. As our wagon passed through the gate in the stockade that surrounded the entire camp, Alucia said to us, 'If, by good fortune, Camarra requires our cooperation, let me do all the talking. You just keep quiet and act like typical Elite.'

'And how do we do that?' Ken asked her.

'Just act superior,' she told him. 'For you, Ken, that should come naturally. Jad might find it more difficult; just shut up and look arrogant.'

As we were dragged through the camp, we were watched by soldiers who had emerged from their tents to stare at us with a mixture of curiosity and hostility. When we finally came to a halt, we were released from the cage, our manacles were removed and then we were escorted into a large, heavily guarded tent. Inside, it was a revelation. It was luxuriously furnished and there was the sweet smell of incense in the air. We were met by attractive female servants who were polite and expressed sympathy at our wretched appearance. It might have been an act, but I for one felt grateful.

They told us that Lord Camarra regretted our treatment during the journey to his camp; now he wanted us to be made as comfortable as possible. He would see us once we had washed and eaten. After hot baths – hot baths! I was beginning to think I'd never be clean again! – and fresh clothing, we were taken to another section of the tent that contained a long table laden with a variety of foods and pitchers of wine. At one end of the table stood a throne-like chair. There were three other chairs that were obviously meant for us.

'I smell a rat,' I whispered to Ken as we sat down at the table.

'So do I,' he muttered out of the corner of his mouth.

'Just the make the most of this while we can,' said Alucia, helping herself to a serving of cold chicken. 'But don't overeat. In our condition that would make us ill.'

Our small but delicious repast consumed, we waited anxiously for the arrival of Lord Camarra. When he finally made an appearance I was taken aback. He wasn't at all what I was expecting. He was a lot younger than the image I'd built up in my imagination; I was expecting another version of Lord Megus. But Lord Camarra was a tall man, aged about thirty, with a handsome face framed by a long mane of blond hair. No beard. He was wearing a shirt of gold chain-mail over a black robe. Most unexpected of all was the small white dog he was carrying under one arm. The overriding impression I got from him was one of effeteness. It was all a bit of a shock.

He greeted us each in turn, shaking our hands, then took his place at the head of the table. One of the female servants placed a gold goblet of wine in front of him before refilling our own pewter goblets.

'My apologies again for the wretched method of your transport here,' he told us in a richly toned voice. 'That was Lord Megus's idea. I gather there is some bad feeling between him and one of you.' He looked pointedly at Alucia. 'But you'll be pleased to know your entire escort party has already been put to death.'

Then he looked at me. 'No offence,' he said, 'but you don't look like an Elite.'

'I'm sort of a throwback,' I told him, remembering Alucia's use of the term.

'Really? So am I . . . in a manner of speaking.' He poured some of his wine into an empty gold dish in front of him, then he put the little white dog onto the table. The dog lapped up the wine noisily. 'I'll get straight to the point,' he said. 'I have a serious problem.'

That was pretty obvious, I thought to myself: he's a megalomaniac who carries a small white dog around with him.

'It involves the Citadel,' he continued. 'I'm in the process of laying siege to it. I've breached the outer wall and sent in a force of some fifteen hundred men. The problem is that none of them have returned. Not a single one. Not even a messenger or a runner to explain what happened. I was hoping that you Elite could enlighten me.'

Alucia said to him, 'It seems evident to me that you've already had some recent close contact with Elite. You appear to be fully aware of the true nature of Urba.'

'That Urba is actually a giant vessel travelling through a void called space? Yes, indeed,' he said affably.

'You seem to have no difficulty in accepting this revelation,' Alucia told him.

He shrugged. 'I've always suspected this world was not what it seemed; when my captured Elite told me that the true reality was the opposite to what we had all been taught, it came as no profound surprise to me. But then, I am no ordinary person . . . I consider myself to be more like a god. But unfortunately I've misplaced my tame Elite. Very careless of me, I know. I had them accompany the force I sent into the Citadel and so they too never returned. Which I why I need you three as replacements. What I want from you is cooperation. I want to know what threat lies within the Citadel. I want to know the nature of the secret weapon that can overcome a force of fifteen hundred of my men. Now, hopefully you will cooperate freely or, I'm afraid, I will use more drastic methods to extract the information from you.'

He drank from his goblet again, and then poured more wine into the dish for his dog. 'So,' he said, 'what is the answer?'

Alucia, Ken and I exchanged blank looks. Then Alucia exclaimed, 'I . . . *we* . . . swear we have no idea. The bulk of the Citadel's defences are on the perimeter walls. And presumably, without any power source, those defences are inert. No one ever imagined that an invasion force could ever penetrate the Citadel's outer defences. We Elite reigned supreme. It would have been unthinkable. Besides, the Citadel itself would be without any power. There can't be any working defence system within the Citadel itself . . . even if such a thing existed. And I know for a fact that it doesn't.'

After about a half a minute of deep thought, Lord Camarra said, 'So it appears we have a mystery on our hands, because *something* neutralised, or perhaps even destroyed, my entire force.'

'But we can't tell you what it is,' said Alucia, 'because we haven't any knowledge of what it could possibly be.'

'For the time being I'll give you the benefit of the doubt,' he said. 'My tame Elite told me that the Citadel is linked with a control centre located partly on the outer hull of the vessel. Could it be that is still activated? By a separate power supply?'

'I honestly don't know,' Alucia told him. 'I've never been in that installation. It was the domain of a small number of specialised technicians. And AIs.'

'Ah, yes. Those intelligent machines I was told about. Fascinating. Would they possess separate power sources?'

Alucia frowned. 'I assume they would.' Then she told him of her theory about the AIs, and how one of them had turned rogue a century ago. She wondered aloud whether the AIs could be responsible for cutting off the Elite's power throughout Urba. 'But what their motivation would be I have no idea. Or even how they managed to do it; there were so many safeguards built into them.'

'Well, in the next few days you'll have ample opportunity to test your theory,' said Lord Camarra. 'I'm sending another force into the Citadel and you three will accompany it. And this time I'm taking the precaution of maintaining a direct line of communication between my force and the outer wall. Messengers will constantly ride back and forth reporting on events inside the Citadel.'

'Fine,' said Alucia, without much enthusiasm, an attitude I shared. 'But can I ask you why the Citadel is so important to you?'

'My intention is to somehow restore the power. With the power of the Elite in my hands, there will be nothing to stop my conquest of all of Urba. And of the entire ship itself and all that implies . . . Who knows, I may become the conqueror of other worlds beside Urba. I would enjoy that greatly.'

He picked up the dog and rose to his feet. 'In the meantime, relax, and enjoy yourselves. Regain your full strength. You'll be leaving the day after tomorrow. And please don't fail me.' Then he paused and looked down at Alucia. 'Incidentally, I found it intriguing that you, the woman, did all the talking while your two male companions said virtually nothing at all.'

'Well, Lord Camarra,' I said, 'you know what women are like when it comes to talking. You can't shut them up for love or money. And that especially applies to Elite women.'

Lord Camarra gave us a knowing smile and left.

We were escorted to another, much smaller tent, but this too was luxuriously furnished, and included three large beds. There were tables with bowls of fruit and more pitchers of wine on them. One of the guards told us these were to be our living quarters for the time being.

Once we were alone I threw myself onto one of the beds. It was remarkably soft.

'So what was your impression of our dear Lord Camarra?' I asked the others as I popped a grape into my mouth.

'Not what I was expecting,' Alucia said as she sat on one of the other beds. Ken sat beside her.

'Same here,' I said.

'I think he was on his best behaviour,' she said. 'He's decided to try and win our cooperation instead of forcing us to do what he wants. My guess is that most of his "tame" Elite died during interrogation. We mustn't underestimate him.'

'The man's barking mad,' said Ken. 'Like his stupid little dog.'

I turned to Ken and asked, 'Do you still not believe anything you've been told about Urba after tonight's conversation?'

'No,' relied Ken, 'I've been completely converted. I now believe everything about Urba being a giant vessel.'

Alucia and I looked at each other in surprise. 'You do?' she asked him.

Ken laughed. 'No, of course not. I was just joking. Like I

said, the man is barking mad. He's swallowed all that Elite garbage.' Then he said to Alucia, 'Nothing personal, darling.'

'Isn't love grand,' I said.

Fortunately both of them were too exhausted to indulge in any amorous activities once the candles had been extinguished. I was able to drift off into a much-needed deep sleep.

The next day and the following night passed only too quickly, and then our life of luxury was over. On the second morning we dressed in the travelling clothes that had been provided for us and prepared for our next plunge into the unknown.

CHAPTER FOURTEEN

At least this time we got breakfast before we left. We were given horses but, of course, no weapons. Then as we waited on our horses, a big man in expensive-looking chain-mail rode up to us; he looked like he was used to authority. He was. 'I am Baron Darmon, Lord Camarra's third-in-command,' he told us. I wondered what had happened to Camarra's second-in-command. 'I'm in charge of this assault on the Citadel. You are to ride with me at the head of the column. I warn all three of you that if you attempt to escape, death will be swift.' Obviously a man of few words.

We followed him to the head of the column of mounted soldiers; I estimated there were some two thousand men. It took time to assemble the column and it was nearly noon before the force was ready to move.

As we rode out of the camp behind Baron Darmon I observed to Ken that even after losing fifteen hundred men in the Citadel, Lord Camarra still seemed to possess an inordinately large army. 'It must number in the tens of thousands.'

'I agree,' said Ken, 'and this must be just a small portion of the men who have joined his cause after his conquest of so many domains.'

'True,' I said.

Ken continued, 'But even with this large force I'd feel happier if I knew just what awaited us in the Citadel.'

'So would I,' said Alucia. 'There's something not right about all this. I have a premonition of doom.'

'I have those all the time,' I told her cheerfully.

After we'd ridden about half a mile, I said happily to Ken,

'You know, I think I'm finally getting the hang of this horse riding business—'

'No, you're not,' he replied firmly.

The great tower of the Citadel loomed in the distance throughout the day. It provided me with something of interest to look at, because the land we were travelling through was flat and featureless. To me, the Citadel resembled a giant penis constructed of polished steel and black glass. Perhaps it was meant to. I mentioned this to Alucia. She laughed and said, 'Yes, it's the ultimate phallic symbol. All three thousand feet of it.'

The distance between Lord Camarra's main camp and the outer wall of the Citadel was only about fifteen miles, but it took us several hours to reach it because the large column of troops moved slowly. The light was beginning to fade by the time we arrived at the smaller camp based just outside the breach in the wall. During the journey, Baron Darmon had broken his silence long enough to tell us proudly that the breach had been achieved by a combination of siege engines and gunpowder. 'So much for your much vaunted impregnable wall, you Elite scum,' he sneered.

As we neared the wall, the commander of the siege force rode up to meet the Baron. He had nothing to report. Nobody had emerged from the Citadel and there was no sign of life beyond the wall.

Alucia, staring up at the Citadel, said, rather sadly, 'The Citadel should be ablaze with lights. Now it looks like some kind of giant mausoleum.'

Overhearing her words, the siege commander looked at her curiously and said, 'The lights of the Citadel *have* blazed on one occasion since we've been here, madam—'

Baron Darmon cut in angrily, 'Pay her no heed, captain. She's another of Lord Camarra's damned pet Elite. When she's served her purpose she'll be put to death, along with her companions.'

The siege commander nodded in understanding and started to turn away from us.

'Wait!' cried Alucia. 'When did you see the Citadel light up?'

After debating with himself briefly on whether he should talk further to an Elite, the commander couldn't resist saying to her, 'On the night when our first invasion force entered the Citadel . . . and fell victim to Elite trickery.'

'Don't worry, captain,' Baron Darmon assured him, 'at the first sign of any further trickery on the part of the Elite, I shall cut this one into pieces myself.'

The Baron ordered his men to make camp outside the wall. His intention was to enter the Citadel the next morning. We three spent a miserable, sleepless night huddled around a feeble fire and surrounded by sullen soldiers who looked at us as if they'd like nothing better than to hang, draw and quarter us themselves. Very, very slowly.

'I don't understand it,' Alucia had said quietly as we ate a revolting meal of cold beans. 'For the Citadel to become illuminated, the power would have had to be restored.'

'Maybe your Elite colleagues are still alive in there,' I suggested, 'and they turned the power back on in order to deal with Lord Camarra's invading force.'

She shook her head. 'No. That just doesn't make sense. If that were the case, the Elite would have solved the problem of the power cut ages ago. There's got to be another explanation.'

I wasn't so sure, but I didn't say anything else. I couldn't shake off the disturbing suspicion that Alucia was still holding something back from us.

At daybreak Baron Darmon gave orders for the invasion to begin. The army, including us, roused itself and got ready. Being at the front of the column, and defenceless, I was becoming increasingly nervous. I was also hungry. No one had offered us any breakfast. Didn't any of these fools realise that breakfast was the most important meal of the day?

We moved through the breach in the outer wall. It was very

large and Alucia observed that Camarra's men had destroyed the rows of defence towers on the wall on either side for some distance as a precaution. 'Wise move,' she commented, 'because if the power had been restored even briefly, the entire force, along with the camp, would have been annihilated . . .'

Beyond the wall, the landscape was like the grounds of the Elite Compound back in Capelia, except on a much larger scale. There were extensive gardens, lakes and a number of wooded areas. There was no sign of life and an eerie silence prevailed, broken only by the clink of horses' harnesses as the large force of men moved towards the Citadel itself. It took us over an hour's ride to reach the Citadel from the outer wall, which was now a distant smudge. You could barely make out the wide gap through which the column had passed.

The previous night Baron Darmon had quizzed us on the best way to enter the Citadel; Alucia had revealed that there were any number of available entrances; gaining access would be no problem. It was what lay within that was the trouble.

When we finally reached the towering Citadel, the Baron called a halt while he deliberated on a plan of action. I thought it rather late in the day to be only now addressing the question of tactics. My opinion of him as a professional soldier, as opposed to my already set opinion of his bullying tyranny, dropped considerably. He finally decided on a pincer movement: his men would completely surround the Citadel, then half would enter the building while the remainder of his force would remain outside, held back in reserve.

While part of the army carried out the encircling man-oeuvre, Ken, Alucia and I dismounted and waited on a wide patio area outside one of the large entrances. Staring up at the vast structure of shining metal and dark blue glass made me dizzy.

'Makes our castle look like a peasant's hut,' said Ken, clearly impressed.

I turned my attention elsewhere. Looking at the large number of mounted troops waiting for their next orders, I realised I hadn't noticed any visible indication that a similarly large force had recently been in the same area. Then, as a nearby horse deposited a large amount of dung on the ground, a thought occurred to me. Before I had time to voice it, though, the Baron returned and dismounted. An officer shouted orders and the troops also dismounted.

'You can do the honours,' Baron Darmon told us. 'We'll be right behind you.' I didn't find this remotely reassuring.

'Before we enter, sir, may I ask you a question?' I said.

'What is it?' he snapped, giving me a fierce glare.

'Lord Camarra's previous force was on horseback, weren't they? Like yours?'

'Yes. What of it?'

'What happened to their horses? Did they return, riderless, to the encampment, perhaps?'

The Baron shot an enquiring look to one of his officers standing nearby. The man shrugged and said to him, 'I understand some did, sir. Not many. About thirty.'

'Then what happened to the rest of them?' I asked.

'It's a good question, sir,' said the officer. 'And there's no sign of the elephants either.'

'Elephants?' I asked.

'There were ten armoured war elephants with the invading force,' said the officer, a little nervously as he noted the Baron's growing displeasure.

'That's not important at the moment,' said the Baron dismissively. 'Stop your stalling. We go inside. *Now*.'

Closely followed by the Baron and the first wave of his men, the three of us walked through the entrance, into a large hall of intimidating dimensions. Great vaulted ceilings of glass and steel soared above us. In the centre of the seemingly endless expanse of marble floor was a pool of water in which stood a sculpture that had a vaguely human form. As we walked towards it Alucia said, 'When the power was on, that projected a fountain of water some hundreds of feet into the air—'

Behind us I could hear the clanging of steel spurs on marble as the horde of troops followed us into the vast space. When we eventually reached the edge of the pool, Alucia turned to the Baron and said, 'Let me explain to you the basic layout of the Citadel –' she pointed upwards '– the Tower itself contains mainly recreational facilities, along with extensive living quarters; it has theatres, gymnasiums, cinemas, restaurants, art galleries ... arenas ... and other attractions ... oh, and air-car maintenance facilities attached to the landing pads.'

I was aware of Alucia's voice faltering slightly at one point. What wasn't she telling us? I glanced at the Baron. He wore the expression of someone who had no idea of what she was talking about. I knew the feeling only too well.

She went on, 'The living quarters can cater for five thousand people. Individual apartments ... and dormitories for certain personnel ...'

Her voice faltered again. I wondered who the hell these 'certain personnel' had been.

Now she pointed downwards. 'The functional parts of the Citadel lie beneath our feet and extend downwards for many levels. They contain the communications centre, research laboratories, automatic factories, medical facilities ... armouries ...'

With the latter word the Baron's face finally lit up. 'Armouries?' he said eagerly. Finally, a word he could understand.

'They contain nothing of interest to you, Baron Darmon,' she told him. 'Without any power the weapons are all useless.'

'Damn,' he said, looking disappointed. Then he said, 'Where are your people likely to be hiding?'

She shrugged. 'I don't know. If there are any Elite left in the Citadel they could be anywhere.'

'How do we move from level to level?' he demanded.

'Follow me,' she said as she led us all towards an archway on the opposite side of the great hall. I glanced behind me and saw that the room was so huge that it easily accommodated Baron Darmon's entire force – a lot of men – just like Lord Camarra's previous invasion force. But where were *they*? So far there was no visible indication they'd ever existed. And where were the Elite? And, the most pressing question of all, where were all those bloody horses? Not to mention the elephants.

We went through the archway into a much smaller but still intimidating space. There were two large, ornate staircases leading upwards. There were also several glass tubes that disappeared into the ceiling. In the tubes, at ground level, were some sort of vehicles. Pointing to the tubes, Alucia said to Baron Darmon, 'Those are elevators . . . when they're functioning . . . that travel to the upper levels. Those –' she pointed at metal doors set in one of the walls '– are also elevators. For the lower levels. Next to them are stairs leading down as well—'

The Baron began to give orders to his officers, which resulted in two large parties of men breaking off from the main body and ascending the two staircases. Then he ordered Alucia to lead us down.

We followed Alucia to the stairs beside the non-functioning lifting devices. It looked dark down there, but Lord Darmon had come prepared. Many of his men began lighting torches. Then we started our descent.

We arrived at the next floor into some sort of hub area from which corridors radiated in all directions. 'Kitchens and food storage facilities mainly,' said Alucia. More soldiers branched off to search the floor.

As we continued down, more patrols would be dispersed at each level, but so far no one had found a trace of any other living thing.

We had just reached the seventh level below the hall when the lights suddenly came on: lights everywhere, illuminating the corridors, the stairs . . . they were so bright they dazzled the eyes. For a few moments everyone was frozen with surprise, then the Baron turned on Alucia, grabbed her by the arms and shook her violently. 'What is this? What Elite trickery is this?' he demanded angrily.

'I don't know!' she cried. 'The power has been restored but I don't know how or why!'

Then, from far below us, came a thunderous sound. It was

as if the gods were smashing their way through the rock between the worlds. The floor shook. This went on for a minute or so, then it ceased and an eerie silence followed.

But not for long—

Somewhere men started yelling, but the yells quickly turned into screams. As we all peered around in confusion and anxiety, I saw something come scuttling towards us along the ceiling. It was like a cross between a scorpion and a centipede: it had several legs and two large pincers and a tail that arched over its back. It was about seven feet in length, matt-black in colour, and it moved very fast. It dropped on top of one of Baron Darmon's nearby soldiers, scooped him up and ran off with him. Then I saw *lots* of the scorpion-things coming across the ceiling . . . and even more scuttling across the floor. The soldiers never stood a chance. They stabbed at the scorpion-things with their swords and spears, but nothing made any difference: each soldier was quickly, efficiently, snatched up and carried away, screaming, by one of the creatures.

The terrified Baron grabbed Alucia by the throat and slammed her against a wall next to the door of one of the lifting devices.

'What Elite treachery is this?' he screamed, but as she couldn't breathe, she couldn't answer. Ken hit the Baron very hard on the back of his neck and he collapsed.

Alucia, gasping for breath, cried out, 'Whatever you do, don't pick up any discarded weapon!' She turned and started punching a button beside the door. A short time later it slid open. 'Quick! Inside!'

We hurriedly entered what appeared to be a small, square room. She pressed one of several buttons on a wall and the door slid shut just as one of the scorpion-things came scuttling towards us. She pressed another of the buttons and I felt the small 'room' begin to descend. Surely this was the wrong direction—?

'Shouldn't we be going up?' I asked her, my heart pounding with fear.

'Not yet.' Alucia sounded surprisingly calm.

'What were those devilish things?' Ken asked.

'I have no idea,' she replied. 'I've never seen anything like them before.'

We hadn't gone far when the 'room' stopped descending. The door opened and Alucia cautiously looked outside. 'Coast is clear . . . so far,' she reported. 'Come on.'

We followed her along a corridor until she stopped at a door and pressed more buttons. The door slid open, we entered a narrow room lined with lockers and Alucia shut the door behind us. 'One of the smaller armouries,' she explained as she opened a locker. She took out three belts on which hung short scabbards containing devices with handles. Each belt was also fitted with a box-like device. She handed two of the belts to Ken and me. 'Put these on,' she instructed as she put the third around her own waist. We followed suit. Then she drew her own device from its scabbard. 'Now that the power has been restored these will rapidly charge up. These are HTE guns; that stands for High Temperature Electron guns. That's because they fire a beam of high temperature electrons. They're heavy because of the necessary shielding. Simply aim at your target and press the red button on the inside of the handle . . . keep firing and when they no longer work, replace them in their holsters like this—' She pointed at the box-like device on her belt. 'These will rapidly recharge them.'

I drew my own weapon and examined it. As she'd said, it was heavy. I asked her, suspiciously, 'Are you sure you don't know what those creatures are?'

'No, I don't,' she said firmly. 'But I don't think they're *creatures* as such. I believe they're machines – but machines of a kind I've never seen before. I also believe that whoever is behind them is the person who's restored the power.'

'Then your Elite friends must be behind all this,' I insisted as I put my new weapon back in its scabbard. 'Who else could do that? And those machine creatures must be something new the Elite have devised. A new type of weapon—'

She shook her head. 'No, I don't believe it.'

'Then what's your explanation?'

'I don't have one. Not yet, at least.'

Just then the room shook as the loud crashing, grinding sound resumed. It was much closer now. And it kept going—

'I suppose you don't know what that is either?' I asked her loudly over the din.

She shook her head again before saying, 'But whatever it is we can't stay here. We're going to have to take our chances topside with those creatures—' She drew her weapon again, opened the door and looked out cautiously. 'Coast still clear. Follow me—'

Ken and I followed suit as we stepped out into the corridor behind her. The floor shook alarmingly as the terrible crashing sound grew ever louder I couldn't even begin to imagine the source of such a sound. We returned to the 'elevator', got in and waited for Alucia to press a button; this time we began to rise. My gorge rose along with it. I wasn't looking forward to what we'd be walking into . . .

'Will these weapons be of any use against those things?' Ken asked her.

'I hope so,' she said, 'otherwise . . .' She shrugged.

CHAPTER FIFTEEN

The elevator came to a halt. 'Once more into the breach . . .' Alucia said softly.

Shakespeare again I thought, as the door slid open— It was like stepping into the midst of a particularly bad day in hell. The black scorpion-things were everywhere. They were streaming towards the stairs; each one of them carried a soldier, like ants carrying plunder from a picnic. Many of their victims were still alive and continued to struggle and scream in their grip while others, motionless, were clearly already dead.

The scorpion-things ignored us as we walked amongst them, but their living victims didn't. The men begged for help as they passed us, but there was nothing we could do. We reached the great hall unmolested. The creatures were pouring into it through the entrance; I saw one of the creatures carrying a bloody section of a horse. I now had an answer to the mystery of the missing horses . . . along with everything else.

As we entered the main hall, I noticed that the fountain was now working. It was a spectacular sight and in different circumstances I would have stopped to admire it. Our luck had held so far, but we'd just hit its limit: halfway across the great hall we attracted the attention of those scorpion-things that weren't preoccupied with carrying victims. As they began to converge on us, Alucia cried, 'Now or never,' and aimed her weapon at the nearest of them.

It worked: spectacularly. The creature – or whatever it was – exploded in a flash of flame, sending fragments in all directions.

Ken and I were quick to follow Alucia's lead; as we took aim and fired, two more of the scorpion-things exploded. We kept firing until we'd destroyed all those that had been intent on taking us.

We went outside to more carnage: the black monsters were no longer overpowering Camarra's men and carrying them off; they were dismembering them on the spot. But we did see that a number of the soldiers were retreating on horseback towards the distant breach in the wall, well out of reach of the creatures.

We fought our way through the mêlée, blasting as many of the creatures as we could. 'How long before these weapons need recharging?' I called to Alucia.

'Not for ages!' she called back.

We were past the worst of the one-sided battle when there came a loud crashing sound from behind us. We looked back towards the Citadel. Through a dust cloud we could see that a large section of the Citadel wall had collapsed outwards. Through the gaping hole something very big was emerging: a bigger version of the scorpion-things. A *much* bigger version. It had to be over a hundred feet in length. And apart from its vast size, it possessed another unique feature. Its raised, scorpion-like tail suddenly unleashed a blast of flame from its tip that was focused like a beam; it swept through the battleground, incinerating men and creatures alike. Even though we were some distance from it I could feel the intense heat.

'Run!' cried Ken, unnecessarily.

We ran. I looked back to see a second similar creature emerge from the Citadel, and then a third. A beam of fire passed over us, catching several riders and their horses far ahead of us.

'We're not going to make it!' I cried.

'This way!' yelled Ken and veered suddenly to the left, heading for one of the lakes. The three of us jumped into the water – fortunately, it was quite deep.

'Get under the water!' Ken ordered. I need no urging. I took a large breath and went as deep as I could, and stayed under as long as I could, until, finally, my lungs crying out for air, I had to return to the surface. My head broke the water just in time for me to see one of the giant creatures passing right by the lake. With its collection of multiple legs it was able to move incredibly fast. I saw several more of the creatures had emerged from the Citadel before I took another deep breath and submerged again.

When I surfaced again, a couple of minutes later by my reckoning, all the creatures had passed by the lake, and were moving at high speed towards the breach in the wall. One passed through it as I watched. At least no more were appearing out of the Citadel. There was smoke everywhere and the acrid smell of burning in the air. A nearby wood was ablaze.

'I think it's safe to get out now,' gasped Ken, breaking the surface himself next to Alucia.

We dragged ourselves out of the water and all three of us lay gasping on the grassy bank beside the lake for a few minutes. When we'd caught our breath, we got to our feet and surveyed the scene. It was ghastly. Everywhere you looked were the charred and dismembered bodies of soldiers and horses.

'Are you going to tell me those things aren't the Elite's secret weapons?' I accused Alucia.

'I most certainly am,' she said. 'They aren't Elite technology. I really have never seen them before in my life.'

'They came out of the Citadel, which means they were constructed within it. That spells Elite technology to me.'

She gave me a condescending look. 'Haven't you realised the obvious yet?'

'Which is?' I demanded.

'Urba has been invaded. By aliens.'

'Aliens?' I said incredulously. 'What are you talking about? What do you mean by aliens?'

'Foreign beings. *Non-human* beings.'

'How can there be such creatures?'

'Because they've come from outside Urba,' she replied.

'So where would they have come from?' I asked.

'I have no idea, but think about it,' she said. 'An alien

invasion explains everything that has happened recently. The sudden loss of power and the subsequent fall of the Elite ... the whole picture suddenly makes sense.'

'Look,' interrupted Ken, 'can we save your crackpot theories for later? Right now we've got to concentrate on staying alive. So let's make some decisions about what we do next.'

'You're right,' said Alucia. 'What do you suggest?'

'First, let's put as much distance between us and the Citadel as possible.'

'That's obvious.' Alucia nodded.

'The problem,' said Ken, 'is that the only way out of here is through that hole in the wall. And that's where the creatures went.'

'True,' she agreed, 'but being behind them is probably the safest place to be right now.'

So we headed for the breach in the wall. I was still clutching the Elite hand-weapon, which was dripping wet from our unexpected swim. 'Will these things still work after being immersed in water?' I asked her.

'Of course,' she replied dismissively. 'They're Elite. But I suggest you put them back in their holsters for the time being. They'll recharge.'

Along the way we kept a wary eye out for the smaller versions of the scorpion-things; those few that did try to attack us were dealt with easily. Alucia pointed out: 'Those things must have been used as initial shock troops by the aliens to take over and defend the Citadel, but they seem to be expendable now that their big brothers have been unleashed.'

'You really think that some kind of foreign beings are behind all this?' I asked her.

'Yes, I do. They must have entered from outside via the control centre on the outer hull of the ship. That gave them access to the Citadel. Somehow they've taken over the AIs and the entire computer system.'

'Why?'

'Obviously to invade Urba. They want this world. If their intention was to simply destroy it, that could easily have been done by other means. A few nuclear missiles aimed at the hull, or even conventional missiles directed at the sections containing the fusion reactors, and Urba would cease to exist. Instead they appear to want to capture the place intact – except first they want to eradicate us ... cleanse Urba of all human occupation. Hence their rather crude method of utilising these giant death machines.'

'They don't seem very crude to me,' Ken complained.

'Well, they are,' she told him. 'Another alternative is that they simply want to conquer humanity. Don't ask me why. I'm still puzzled as to why they carried all those soldiers away into the depths of the Citadel.

'And another thing that puzzles me is how we managed to encounter this alien ship. Or ships. We aren't near any planetary system. The chances of Urba accidentally bumping into alien vessels in deep space are literally astronomical.'

We trudged on through the blackened landscape. What had been, just a short time ago, a beautiful Elite garden was now unrecognisable – as were the victims of the giant scorpion-things we kept coming across. The intense heat from the fire beams had turned both humans and horses into grotesque caricatures. I kept glancing nervously back towards the Citadel, hoping I wouldn't see more of the creatures emerging from it. We'd be right in their path.

Finally we reached the breach in the wall, now even larger, thanks to the passage of the giant creatures – I still couldn't think of them as machines though I knew Alucia was probably right about their true nature. Beyond lay the smoking ruins of the encampment. The siege machines had been reduced to piles of smouldering wood. All the tents had been destroyed and there was the familiar sight and smell of scores of charred bodies, both human and equine. Of the creatures themselves, there was no sign.

Alucia wandered around the outskirts of the burned-out encampment, staring at the ground. 'The tracks are too confused to tell how many of them there are,' she said. 'Did anyone manage to count them?'

'I didn't,' I said. 'I had other things on my mind. Like trying not to breathe underwater.'

'Same with me,' said Ken.

'We'd better not linger here,' said Alucia. She pointed back in the direction of the Citadel. 'The aliens could be producing more of these things even as we speak.'

'So where do we go?'

'Let's go back to Lord Camarra's camp,' she suggested.

I pointed at the column of black smoke rising from the distant camp. 'Why bother?' I asked. 'It's obviously been attacked by the creatures. By now it's probably nothing but a pile of ashes.'

'Because we might be able to salvage something from amongst the ruins,' said Alucia. 'There's certainly nothing left to find here, but the main camp is much bigger. There's a better chance of scavenging something useful. Like food.'

'True,' said Ken, 'but we'll never get there unless we can find some horses—'

'Ha! We'll be lucky,' I said. 'Any animal that survived that carnage will have fled to the other end of the world by now.'

'You're overestimating the intelligence of your average horse,' he replied. 'They're stupid. I'm sure we'll find some still in the vicinity.'

'So let's go and look,' said Alucia.

He was proven right about the horses. We hadn't gone far when we came across one grazing placidly; within an hour all three of us had mounts.

Our arrival at the main camp was much as we had expected. It was totally devastated, the posts of the stockade now charcoaled stubs, still smouldering; every tent had been incinerated and, inevitably, the ground was littered with the twisted, charred remains of human bodies. 'I don't think we're going to find anything salvageable here,' I said as we rode into the camp, the horses nervous and reluctant to go any further. I had every sympathy with them: the smell was awful.

'I wonder how many managed to escape,' said Alucia. 'More importantly, I wonder if Lord Camarra did—'

Ken said, 'Keep a lookout for a corpse holding a small, charred dog.' Then he brought his horse to a halt, dismounted and started to rummage around in the debris, producing, with a flourish, a sword and a dagger. Both weapons were blackened, but when Ken began rubbing at them with a cloth he revealed shining metal; they were both quite serviceable underneath the layer of soot.

'I feel much better now,' he said as he slipped them into his belt and remounted.

'A lot of good they'll do you against those machines,' Alucia told him.

'Would your Elite weapons do any better?' he asked her.

'No,' she admitted. 'They're effective against the smaller machines, but I don't think they'd touch the big ones; they're too heavily armoured. What we need is an air-car-mounted beam-cannon.'

'Which are kind of in short supply these days,' I pointed out.

She stared at me. 'Oh, Jesus Christ,' she whispered.

She'd gone white. She leaned forward in her saddle and covered her face with her hands. 'I am so fucking *stupid*!'

'What's the matter?' Ken asked her.

'Air-cars,' she wailed, 'back at the Citadel. Lots of them. On the upper levels. We should have gone and got one. Stupid, stupid ... STUPID!'

'But there was no time,' I said, conciliatorily. 'We would never have made it. The place was crawling with those smaller scorpion-things and the bigger things were in the process of demolishing the foundations.'

'We should have *tried*,' she cried.

'Well, it's too late now,' Ken told her.

Our search for food in the burned-out ruins of the camp proved futile, though Ken did find, half-covered by the charred body of its previous owner, a damaged crossbow that he reckoned he could repair. 'If I can get it working I can shoot some small game, like a rabbit, and then we get to eat.' He turned to Alucia. 'I'm presuming our hand-weapons aren't much good for shooting down small animals?'

'No. There'd be nothing left of them to eat.'

Ken also found a short dagger that he was able to conceal inside one of his boots.

We discussed our next move. 'I suggest we head back to Faldor,' said Alucia. 'I need to get to that Sprite ship which I'm sure is docked under the Compound there. With the power restored we'll be able to reach it.'

'It will take us several weeks to get there,' Ken pointed out. 'And we have no supplies.'

'We *have* to get there,' Alucia insisted. 'That ship could be our salvation. You'll just have to shoot a lot of rabbits on the way.'

We rode hard for the couple of remaining hours of daylight, constantly on the lookout for the giant killing machines. Finally, as it started to get dark, and with the horses exhausted, we stopped and made camp in a small wood – not that it was much of a camp, consisting as it did of just a fire. We'd found a stream along the way so at least we weren't thirsty, but we were all very, very hungry. As Ken worked on trying to repair the crossbow, we kept asking him how close to success he was until he finally lost his temper and told us both to shut up or he'd throw the damn thing on the fire.

Despite having neither bedding nor cloak, I quickly fell asleep on the hard ground. I awoke thinking I was being bitten on the neck by an insect. But it was no insect, it was the point of a dagger—

There were four of them, and one of them, alas, was Lord Camarra. Like his men he was looking very much the worse for wear. His face bore scorch marks, most of his hair was gone and his former finery was in soot-covered tatters. He'd been lucky to escape with his life. But, unluckily for us, he had . . . somehow.

'When we spotted your fire,' he told us as his men disarmed us, 'I thought it might belong to survivors from my army who'd managed to escape the attack on my camp by those

Elite fire-creatures. But finding you three here is even better. I'm hungry for vengeance and the gods have delivered you into my hands.'

I noticed that he no longer had his small dog. I wondered what pissed him off the most, losing his army or his dog?

'Those things aren't Elite creations,' Alucia told him. 'They're some kind of alien machines. Urba has been invaded by—'

Camarra kicked Alucia hard in her side, causing her to grunt with pain. 'Shut up!' he commanded. 'No more of your Elite lies! You led my men into a trap. You knew all along what lay in wait for them within the Citadel.'

'If the creatures are part of an Elite counter-attack,' I said, 'then what the hell are we doing hiding out here in the wilderness like you?' One of his men, in imitation of his master, kicked me in the ribs as well. This, I realised, was going to be a one-sided conversation.

Camarra was holding one of the Elite weapons that had been taken from us. 'You've restored your Elite power, haven't you? And this will prove it.' He aimed the weapon at a nearby tree and fired. The tree burst into flames. 'See!' he said triumphantly. 'I knew it! You and your fire-creatures are spreading out across the lands in an attempt to regain your old Elite supremacy!'

'That's not what's happening at all!' protested Alucia. 'You must understand the truth of the situation—'

'I understand perfectly the truth of the situation,' he said as he bent down, grabbed Alucia by the neck and hauled her to her feet. He put the Elite weapon to the side of her head. 'You and I are going for a walk into the woods where I shall reprimand you. An act that requires some degree of privacy—'

At his words, Ken also jumped to his feet. 'If you touch her—!' he said, moving towards Camarra and Alucia. But he stopped when one of Camarra's men pointed an Elite hand-weapon at him.

'Sit back down on the ground, your hands on your head,' he ordered. Ken did so.

Camarra said to his men, 'Don't hesitate to kill either of them if they give you the slightest trouble. But I'd like to find them both alive when I return as I'd prefer to make their deaths as long-drawn-out as possible.' Then, with his hand around Alucia's neck, he marched off into the trees. They were soon out of sight.

Ken and I sat there impotently while Camarra's three men kept their weapons trained on us. Two had our Elite hand-weapons, while the third aimed a crossbow.

I don't know how many minutes passed until, suddenly, from the woods, came a scream. It distracted all of us ... except Ken. Moving as fast as he had back in the vigilante camp, he pulled the small dagger from his boot and flung it at the nearest of Camarra's men. The dagger hit the man in the throat. Ken was on his feet and had grabbed his victim even as the remaining two were beginning to react. One fired his Elite weapon, but by that time Ken had swung the body of the dying man round and he caught the blast instead. Ken, now in possession of the dead man's weapon, fired back. The other man screamed as he burst into flames. The third man, with the crossbow, fired wildly and missed. He dropped the crossbow, turned and ran. He didn't get very far.

Moving like a paralysed snail, I finally stood up and stared at the three smoking corpses. It had all happened so quickly. Ken tossed me one of the Elite weapons; somehow, I managed to catch it.

'Come on!' he cried. 'We've got to find Alucia!'

CHAPTER SIXTEEN

We charged off into the woods, and thanks to the light from the still-burning tree we soon found Alucia. She was lying on her back on the ground, naked and covered with blood. There was no sign of Camarra.

'By the gods, she's dead!' screamed Ken. 'The bastard's murdered her!'

'I'm not dead, you clown,' said Alucia, raising herself up on her elbows, 'and the blood's not mine, it's Camarra's. I stabbed him with his own dagger while he was trying to rape me.'

'He raped you?' cried Ken. He knelt down beside her and tried to hug her. 'I swear by the gods I will not rest until your honour has been avenged!'

She gave him a shove that sent him falling on his backside. 'I lost my honour a long time ago, so don't go losing any sleep over it on my account.' She got to her feet. 'Though being almost raped by Camarra was, needless to say, a far from enjoyable experience, it did allow me to stab him while he was so preoccupied with what he was doing. Somewhat clumsily, in my biased opinion. So instead of indulging in all these dramatics, shouldn't you be looking for the bastard? He can't have got very far. I cut him deeply.'

Ken was a little dazed by her cold reaction, but then he rallied. 'You're right! I'll find the bastard and finish the job.' He was about to charge off again into the woods when he paused and asked, 'Er, which way did he go?'

Alucia pointed at the ground. 'Just follow the trail of blood.'

'Of course!' He was about to do just that when he paused again and said, 'Does he still have that Elite weapon?'

Alucia held out her hand. She had the weapon. 'I grabbed it from him after I stabbed him. All he has is a sword. And a dagger protruding from his side.'

'Splendid!' said Ken, and this time he did disappear off between the trees in a mad rush.

As I helped Alucia pick up her clothes, while trying, not terribly successfully, not to look at her naked body, she said, 'What happened to the other three?'

'Ken killed them,' I told her. 'All by himself. But I did give him moral support. From a sitting position, admittedly.'

She wiped much of the blood from her body with a handful of leaves, while I still tried to avoid looking at her, then started to dress. 'He may be a fool but he does have his uses,' she said tonelessly.

I presumed she was acting oddly because of the ordeal of what she'd just experienced. 'You're in a state of shock,' I told her.

She stopped dressing and looked at me. 'No. More like a state of guilt.'

'Guilt?' I asked, puzzled.

'I can't complain about being raped. Well, semi-raped in this case. I've done worse to others myself.'

'You have?' I said, shocked.

'Things happened in the Citadel you wouldn't want to know about. Things I now feel guilty about.' She didn't elaborate. 'And now I'm even feeling guilty about Ken, which is funny.'

'Why?'

'I know you're not stupid, so you must know that I don't love him. I've just been using him, as I'm sure you've suspected all along.'

I didn't know what to say, even though I knew she was right.

'I'm weary of the sham, I admit,' she said, in the same blank tone of voice, 'but it has to continue. And you know only too well what I really am. I've done many things that I'm no longer proud of. But I *am* an Elite, and I can't change that.'

'But Ken really does love you,' I said, a little plaintively.

'Yes, perhaps he does. But the relationship has no future.'
She gave a bleak smile. 'On top of everything else, there's the
age difference.' She resumed dressing.

'Age difference?'

'I'm over three hundred years old, Jad. Oh, my actual body
is as young as it looks, but my mind is very old. The process
involved is one I've undergone many times, like all Elite.' She
finished dressing. 'Life's a bitch and then you don't die. At
least, that used to be the case. Now, of course, it will be
different. I'll age and die just like you mundanes.' She sighed.
'Come on, let's return to the camp.'

As I followed her, I tried to come to terms with what she'd
told me. I thought there was nothing left to learn about the
Elite and the true nature of things, nothing that would surprise
me now . . . but the idea that she was *three hundred years old*
had completely shaken me. I simply didn't believe her. And
what exactly were those events in the Citadel that she now felt
guilty about? Did they, I wondered grimly, involve the
mysterious 'disappearances' of young women from the
domains? Did I want to know the answer?

Back at the camp, the air was filled with the now overly
familiar smell of burned human flesh. I thought about burying
the three corpses, but decided I couldn't be bothered. We
wouldn't be staying here much longer anyway.

'I trust you won't repeat anything I've told you to Ken,'
Alucia said. 'Let him keep his illusions about me awhile
longer.'

'While he's still of some use to you, you mean?'

'Yes,' she said bluntly.

'You'll end up destroying him.'

'No, it won't come to that. He'll be devastated for a time,
but he'll survive. After all, he possesses a vital survival quality.'

'What's that?'

'A male ego.'

*

Eventually Ken returned, his face grim. 'I couldn't find Camarra,' he told us. 'He got away somehow.'

'But that's impossible,' said Alucia, 'I stabbed him really deeply. And all that blood he was losing . . . you must have missed him in the dark.'

'I searched everywhere,' insisted Ken. 'Checked under every damned bush. He's nowhere to be found.'

It was only then that we noticed that one of their horses was missing. 'He must have doubled back here while we were gone,' said Ken, 'the cunning bastard.'

'Cunning bastard?' she exploded. 'No, he has to be a bloody *supernatural* bastard!'

Ken went to her and hugged her. 'Are you all right?' he asked, his voice full of concern.

She replied stiffly, 'I'm perfectly fine. Now let's get out of here—'

We had grilled rabbit for breakfast. Provided with a working crossbow, courtesy of one of Camarra's three dead soldiers, Ken was able to abandon the one he'd been trying to repair. Early the next morning, when we'd set up a fresh camp far from the one Camarra and his men had desecrated, he set out on a hunt and soon returned with two freshly killed rabbits. Naturally it fell to me to skin and cook them, but we were all hungry and they were delicious.

Alucia's mask was now firmly back in place. She was being overly affectionate towards Ken, to a degree that seemed patently false to me, but which he lapped up like a grateful – happy – puppy. But then, he didn't know what I knew. And he wouldn't have believed a word of it anyway. I'm not sure I did either, to be perfectly honest.

We'd been keeping a lookout for Lord Camarra, but there'd been no sign of him. Alucia was certain he would have bled to death by now, but I wasn't so sure. However, we did see evidence of the continued activities of the alien machines. In any direction we looked there were distant columns of smoke, obviously the results of attacks on towns and villages. I asked

Alucia if she thought that the machines were being directly operated by the foreign beings she believed in – these *aliens*.

'I mean, are the actual creatures inside the machines?' I tried to expand my question.

'I seriously doubt it,' she replied. 'Too dangerous for them. The machines are being operated by some other method. Possibly they're following pre-set programmes, but I think it's more likely they're being remote-controlled. My guess is that they're under the direct control of the AIs, but I can't be sure of that yet. But I definitely believe that the machines are the reason why the power has been restored throughout Urba—'

'You do? Why?'

'Because the aliens are using our own energy system to provide power for their machines. And that has interesting implications . . .'

I wondered aloud if Alucia thought their form reflected the actual form of the foreign invaders: were they a species of intelligent insects?

'I could be wrong,' she said, after giving it some thought, 'but my gut feeling is that the shape of their machines is a psychological contrivance. It's as if the aliens know of the instinctive revulsion most humans have towards insects. That also suggests that this is no chance encounter. This invasion is the result of a long-term plan. They've been studying us for some considerable time. But just when, and how, they encountered Urba I have no idea.'

Our own long-term plan was to follow Alucia's suggestion and return to the domain of Faldor. Though I thought it a thin chance, she was still pinning all her hopes on finding a 'Sprite' ship beneath the Elite Compound. Not only was she not completely positive that there *was* a ship beneath the Faldor Compound in Tureas, it was likely that the Compound, along with the rest of the town, had by now been destroyed by one of the alien machines. But as a detour to Faldor as we headed back towards the Pyman Sea wouldn't take us too long, Ken and I had decided to go along with her plan.

Two mornings later, Ken returned from yet another rabbit-hunting expedition without any rabbits but wearing an enigmatic expression. 'Come with me,' he said to us mysteriously. 'I have something to show you.'

We followed him into the woods, through some particularly dense undergrowth; progress was hard work. 'This had better be worth it,' I complained.

Finally we reached his secret: hidden in the middle of the woods was a crashed Elite air-car, complete with its original crew of three.

The bodies, still dressed in the traditional black and crimson Elite uniforms, were in a bad state of decomposition; by now they were really little more than skeletons. One had been thrown clear of the vehicle after it had hit the ground while the other two had remained in their seats. But the air-car itself, its fall partly cushioned by the thick canopy of branches it had plunged through, appeared relatively undamaged, apart from its landing struts, which were badly bent.

As an excited Alucia began to examine the external damage to the vehicle, I asked her, 'Do you think it's flyable?'

'I don't know yet. It might be—' She unceremoniously dumped the other two bodies out of the air-car and seated herself at the controls. With the power restored, there were lights flashing on the control panel. She started pressing buttons and explained she was running a series of system checks. Her face was flushed when she said happily, 'Yes, I think I can get this into the air again. It's crippled but I think it will fly! Get in . . .'

Ken and I climbed in and sat in two of the seats behind her. We watched as she pressed several switches, gripped a pair of levers that were mounted on a movable base and pulled back hard on them. The air-car shuddered as its engine gave a tortured whine. Then the vehicle began to slowly rise into the air in a series of jerky movements. It stopped and for a moment or two I thought it was going to fall back to the ground, but then it continued its rise. Branches snapped as it rose up through the trees. Then it was above the forest canopy.

It continued to rise and I began to feel giddy as well as nervous.

Then it stopped. 'Damn,' said Alucia. 'This is as high as it will go. That's not good . . . but it's better than nothing.'

Actually I felt relieved. I figured we were some sixty-five feet above the ground. That was high enough for me. I was certain Ken agreed because he'd gone slightly green, even though he was doing a pretty good job of looking blasé.

'Now let's see if it's capable of any speed,' said Alucia, punching another button. The air-car suddenly lurched forward and dipped. For a moment I thought we were falling and my stomach did a flip-flop. I was glad it was empty. But we weren't falling. The air-car was moving forward in a series of lurching movements, much like a lame horse, though a lame horse would have moved faster. 'Damn it,' said Alucia.

'Is this as fast as it will go?' Ken asked her.

'I'm afraid so. I'm no engineer but I'm going to have to try and fiddle with the engine . . . We need to get more height and more speed, otherwise we're going to be sitting ducks in this thing. On the plus side, the car's electron-beam-cannon seems to be still in full working order . . .'

She guided the air-car back to what passed for our camp and set it down on the ground with a bone-jarring bump. The horses, all tethered to trees, reacted with alarm.

We all got out of the air-car; I for one was glad to be back on solid ground again. While Alucia opened a panel at the rear of the vehicle and peered into it with a puzzled frown, Ken said, 'I might as well have another try at shooting us some breakfast.'

'Go ahead,' said Alucia, distractedly. 'This may take some time.'

'Is there anything I can do?' I asked her as Ken headed off back into the woods.

She looked at me and said, 'You can tell me you don't believe I'm a complete shit.'

I knew what she was referring to. Since that night she'd been attacked by Camarra we hadn't discussed what she'd said to me immediately afterwards. 'Sorry,' I said, 'can't do that in all sincerity right now.'

She nodded. 'That's understandable. Considering what I told you about my feelings for Ken.'

'It's not just that. It's those other things you said. About feeling guilty over what you've done to people in the past. You'd been practically raped by Camarra and you said you'd done worse things yourself. What, exactly, and to whom?'

She stood there looking at me for a time and then she said, 'I was raving. I'd been severely traumatised and I was babbling.'

I didn't believe her. 'Tell me about the "disappeared".'

She frowned. 'The "disappeared"?'

'All those young women that have vanished over the years. We all know the Elite were responsible. What happened to them?'

Again she was silent for a time. Then, 'Okay, I'll tell you the truth. The Elite are – were – sterile. We took them for breeding purposes. Their children were trained to become new Elite. But don't worry, the abducted young people were well cared for.'

Oh sure they were, I thought cynically. 'And what was all that stuff about you being over three hundred years old?'

'Like I said, I was raving. I was hysterical. You can't really believe I'm that old, can you?'

'I'm not sure I know what to believe about you.'

She smiled, walked over to me and kissed me on my cheek. 'That's exactly how I want it to be with you.'

She went back to the air-car, climbed into it, rummaged about for a while and then got out holding a toolbox. She produced a hammer from the box and began whacking furiously with it at something inside the engine housing.

'Should you be doing that?' I asked. 'I would have thought the mechanism was pretty sensitive.'

'The crash knocked the engine out of alignment. I'm trying to force it back into its original position. I might just be able to restore the vital contacts to give us full power. But like I said, I'm no engineer. But these vehicles are tough babies, and simply constructed. They're basically just large electromagnets with jet thrusters attached. I doubt if I'll cause any more damage than it's already suffered . . . and I might just improve matters. It's worth a shot.'

I watched until finally she closed the engine housing and replaced the toolbox inside the car. 'Now the moment of truth. You'd better stay on the ground just in case something goes seriously wrong.'

I didn't need any further encouragement. I watched anxiously as she switched on the power. The air-car rose shakily into the air. It kept rising. It reached about a hundred and fifty feet, then started to move forward. Even to my inexperienced eyes, it clearly had more speed than before. Alucia circled round the camp, then landed. She climbed out. 'Still far from perfect, but it's definitely performing better than before.'

About fifteen minutes later Ken returned, carrying a rabbit. 'All I could find this morning,' he said apologetically.

After breakfast, we unsaddled the horses and tried to convey to them that they were free now. They didn't get the message. So we got into the air-car and flew off, leaving the horses behind, neighing disconsolately.

'They'll be fine,' said Ken. I wasn't so sure. I never thought I'd feel guilty over bloody horses.

As we flew on in the direction of Faldor, my initial nervousness at being in the air faded away and I began to enjoy the experience. In fact I began to find the experience of flying downright exhilarating – even when we were caught in a sudden downpour of rain. But Alucia did something with the control panel and a transparent canopy slid up from the rear of the car and covered us. I thought it was made of glass, but when I tapped it with my finger it didn't feel like glass.

'Plastic,' said Alucia.

'Oh, plastic,' I said. 'Of course it is.'

It occurred to me that the sight of the air-car was going to cause consternation amongst those on the ground if it were spotted. It would look like the Elite definitely were back in power. I was soon proved right when we overflew a group of people who, I presumed, were refugees fleeing the alien killer machines. Some were on horseback, but most were on foot. The majority scattered in panic at the sight of us, but a few brave souls made a stand and crossbow bolts whizzed towards us. A few actually hit the air-car. Alucia tried to climb to a higher altitude, but couldn't get the vehicle to go above what I estimated to be about two hundred feet – still well within crossbow range.

'Idiots,' muttered Alucia. 'We're on a mission to save their stupid hides and they're trying to kill us.'

'We're on a rescue mission?' I said, surprised. That was news to me.

Then, instead of flying on, away from the danger, Alucia made a tight turn and put the air-car in a dive towards the small group on the ground who hadn't fled.

'What are you doing?' I cried.

'Watch this,' she replied. She pressed buttons and a small picture of the ground appeared on the control panel. There were two lines that intersected on the centre of the image. She pressed another button and the next thing I knew there was a large, fiery explosion on the ground, very close to the group of people firing at us. This time they did flee in all directions.

I was shocked. So was Ken. 'You're trying to kill them!' he accused her.

'Some rescue mission this is,' I added.

As the air-car hovered over the spot where the refugees had been, Alucia said, 'I wasn't trying to kill them. If I had been trying, they'd all be dead by now. I was just putting a scare into them with the car's beam-cannon.'

'Why?' I asked. 'We could have simply flown away.'

'You two aren't very observant,' she replied. 'Right – the coast is clear now.' She put the air-car down, with the inevitable bump, on the ground. 'Now look around and tell me what you see.'

'Lots of bundles dropped by terrified people as they ran away,' I said.

'Yes, so what?' Ken asked her.

She sighed impatiently. 'And what are some of those bundles certain to contain?'

'Ah,' I said as I realised what she was talking about. 'Food!'

'Brilliant!' she said sarcastically. 'I'm getting tired of living on a diet of rabbit alone, so go and quickly check them out before some of those foolhardy idiots recover their courage and return.'

Ken and I did as she'd instructed and returned to the car with a variety of foodstuffs. 'I'm not sure I feel right about this,' I said as we stacked our prizes into the vehicle. 'Stealing food from refugees.'

'It's all in a good cause,' said Alucia as we rose into the air again.

'I know, I know,' I muttered, 'we're on a rescue mission. But who or what exactly are we going to rescue?'

'If all goes to plan,' she replied, 'the entire world. Or what's left of it.'

'Oh, is that all?' I said. 'I'm relieved to hear we're not intending to be too ambitious.'

Alucia laughed. I got the distinct impression she was enjoying herself. Firing at those helpless people on the ground must have reminded her of the good old days. Once an Elite, always an Elite. I would have to keep reminding myself of that.

CHAPTER SEVENTEEN

That afternoon we saw a thick cloud of black smoke start to rise up from about twenty miles away to our left. 'We've caught up with at least one of our friends,' said Alucia. 'Another town's under attack, but the attack appears to have just begun. Let's go and check it out.'

'Is that wise?' I asked her as she sent the air-car veering towards the column of smoke. 'The machine creature is sure to see us.'

'Can't be helped. I need to know if the car's beam-cannon has any effect on them.'

'I can tell you now,' said Ken, 'that their fire-beam will definitely have an effect on *us*.'

'I'll be careful,' Alucia promised. We both shuddered.

On the way to the stricken town we passed over many groups of people, but they paid us no attention. What they were fleeing from was clearly more terrifying than an Elite air-car.

The burning town came into view – and so did its attacker: one of the huge, black machine-creatures. It was emerging from the ruins of the town with the obvious intent of killing as many of the departing residents as it could. We saw the deadly beam of fire being emitted from its curved tail and watched as the sweeping beam claimed several victims. Alucia had raised the crippled air-car to its maximum altitude as she circled around the killer machine, but even from that height, which was far too low for my liking, the thing on the ground appeared enormous as it scuttled swiftly along on its sets of multiple legs. I reckoned it to be well over a hundred feet in length.

'Hang on,' warned Alucia, 'we're going in—'

We went into a dive, approaching the thing from its right side. She activated the beam-cannon and instantly there was a large explosion on the surface of one of the central segments of the creature. The thing immediately stopped moving; it remained stationary as we passed over it and for a few glorious moments I thought we had inflicted terminal damage. But when I looked back I saw it begin to move again. It was turning towards us.

Whatever it used for eyes had found us. 'We're in trouble!' I cried as I watched the tip of the great, curving tail beginning to target us. It was glowing red.

'I know,' said Alucia, adding, 'shit!' Then she warned us to hang on—

The air-car began to zigzag while simultaneously rising as fast as it could. The tip of the scorpion-thing's tail unleashed its beam of fire, but it missed, passing the car some few yards to our right. I could feel the heat from it through the canopy, which had begun to blister. The car shuddered and kept shuddering as Alucia put it into a tight turn. I thought it was going to fall to pieces – or simply just fall out of the sky.

To my increased alarm so did Alucia, because she yelled, 'This wreck is in no shape for much in the way of fancy manoeuvres so one more might be the end for us!'

The air-car was now on the right side of the killer machine. Keeping track of us, it was turning very rapidly. *We're doomed*, I told myself yet again. It was becoming a familiar mantra.

Then I realised what Alucia had in mind. She was speeding towards the burning town. And the next thing I knew we were enveloped in thick, black smoke – but we were hidden from the killer machine.

Through the smoke I heard Alucia say grimly, 'Let's just hope the damned thing only uses visual sensors and isn't equipped with bloody radar!'

I didn't know what *bloody radar* was, but I knew from the way she said it that *bloody radar* was not good news for us.

But we were lucky: we flew on through the black smoke without suddenly being burned to a crisp. All around us was the total blackness of the smoke. Then suddenly we were flying in bright sunlight again and the burning town was behind us. And so, thank the gods, was the alien machine.

'Thank Christ,' said Alucia. 'For a time there I didn't think we were going to make it. It was a close call.'

Ken said, diplomatically, 'Maybe attacking that creature wasn't such a good idea.'

'Well, I think it was worth a try,' said Alucia. 'And now we know more about the nature of the damned things.'

'Like what?' I asked. 'That they're invulnerable to Elite weaponry?'

'Not invulnerable,' she replied. 'The beam-cannon definitely penetrated the thing's armour and caused some damage, but not serious damage. Didn't even slow it down. But it means that if there's a vital weak spot, we can hit it. Of course, we'd have to find that weak spot first.'

'You're not thinking of returning for another attempt, are you?' I asked nervously.

'Of course not. Next stop is Faldor. In the meantime, let's eat. I'm famished.' She turned away from the controls and looked expectantly at us. 'So what gourmet treats do we have in the way of food?'

I regarded her with alarm. 'Shouldn't you concentrate on flying this thing?'

'Relax. There's no need. It's on automatic now, and locked on course for the Compound at Tureas. With the power restored throughout Urba I can link up with the world-wide navigational system. Unless there's an engine malfunction, I won't have to do another thing until we reach the Compound. So let's eat!'

'That's fine,' I said, though only partially reassured, 'but before we eat there's another problem that needs solving.'

She frowned at me. 'What's that?'

'Er, is there a toilet in this thing?'

*

There wasn't. Alucia folded the canopy back into its recess and I was obliged to take a piss over the side of the car. Very elegant.

None of us was surprised when we reached Tureas to find that it was in ruins. Smoke still rose from the remains of the charred buildings. The hilltop castle that had previously dominated the city had been flattened. It was as if one of the alien machines had walked right through it. There was no sign of life amongst the ruins. Apparently any survivors had long fled.

Alucia guided the air-car towards the Elite Compound, located, as was the usual custom, beyond the outskirts of the city. We hovered over it. The Compound hadn't escaped the attention of the alien machine either. Its walls had been shattered and its central building subjected to the machine's heat-beam. Not much remained.

'Looks like our journey here was a waste of time,' said Ken.

'Not necessarily,' replied Alucia. 'Access to the underground installation may still be possible.'

She set the air-car down on a section of blackened lawn near the ruins of the Compound's central building. We got out. Despite the place appearing deserted, all three of us had drawn our Elite hand-weapons. We entered the burned-out building, moving gingerly in case we caused the few walls still standing to collapse on us. Alucia paused while she orientated herself, then she pointed. 'The entrance to the below-ground facilities should be over there—'

We followed her to a pile of rubble, where she stopped and groaned. 'Shit. It's under all that.'

'Like I said before,' said Ken, 'a wasted journey. We'll never shift that lot. So let's head back to Capelia.'

I agreed with him. Capelia now seemed like heaven to me. And it would be, compared to this bleak wasteland. But I also knew that sooner or later the alien war machines would reach it. And then what would we do? I had a terrible image of Capelia's vast forests all ablaze.

'Don't be so quick to give up,' Alucia told him curtly, 'there is a way to solve this problem. Come on, back to the car.'

We did as we were ordered, Ken and I exchanging puzzled glances on the way.

'You two wait here,' she told us as she climbed into the car. As the vehicle rose into the air and hovered over the ruins of the building, I realised what she had in mind.

Alucia fired the car's beam-cannon at the large pile of rubble. There was a deafening blast as a fireball shot upwards. The ground shook and several of the remaining walls collapsed.

She landed the air-car next to us and got out. 'We'd better wait a little while until everything cools down,' she said pragmatically.

After fifteen minutes she declared it safe and we re-entered the ruins. The blast had removed the large pile of rubble from above the entrance to the underground section, though a layer of debris still covered it. We began to clear what remained by hand, a painful task as the small pieces of rubble were still hot to the touch.

So engrossed were we with what we were doing we weren't aware of the impending danger until it was almost too late. As usual, it was Ken's natural-born warrior instincts that saved us from disaster: he suddenly leapt to his feet and cried, 'We're under attack!'

I quickly stood and looked around. A group of about a dozen armed men were converging upon us from all sides. They must have been attracted to the Compound by the sound of the explosion. The nearest of them was less than twenty feet away when Ken drew his weapon and began firing. Two of our nearest would-be attackers fell burning to the ground. Alucia and I also drew our weapons and started firing.

Before long only five of the men remained alive; they – wisely – turned and ran. Alucia took aim at one of them, but Ken pushed her arm and she missed.

'Let them go,' Ken told her angrily. I had never seen him display any anger towards Alucia before and I was surprised.

'Why?' she demanded, equally angry. 'They intended killing us.'

'Because killing an enemy with one of these things –' he waved the Elite weapon in front of her face '– makes me feel sick. It's not clean, like a sword or a spear or a crossbow bolt.'

'These weapons you despise just saved our lives,' she told him, still angry.

'I know that,' he replied, 'but I just don't like using them. And those five who ran away no longer presented a threat to us. There was no need to kill them.'

'They could return with reinforcements.'

'No, I don't think so. Not after they saw what happened to their companions here—'

She held up her weapon. 'Yes, thanks to *these*.' She shook her head. 'You know what you are, Ken? A hypocrite, that's what. You think it's perfectly all right to kill someone with a crossbow bolt – which is far from a pleasant way to die – but you consider using one of these weapons unethical. That's ridiculous! Killing someone is always an ugly business, no matter what method you use.'

'At least I don't kill in cold blood,' he snapped back.

I was finding this exchange interesting. Was Ken finally becoming aware of Alucia's true nature? Even so, I decided it was time I intervened. I said, 'As entertaining as this lovers' spat is, I think we should get on with what we came here to do.'

They looked at me. Both their faces were still flushed with anger. Then Alucia nodded. 'Jad is right. This argument is a waste of time. Let's keep on digging . . . but stay alert for any more unwelcome visitors.'

Ken gave a grunt of assent and we resumed removing the remaining pieces of debris from the entrance. Eventually we uncovered the large door that had collapsed across the entrance to the stairwell that led to the underground section. Ken used his sword to prise the door to one side, providing us with access to the stairs. He peered down into the opening and said, 'I can see light down there.'

'That's not surprising,' said Alucia. 'When the power was restored, the lights would have come back on automatically. There should be lights on the stairs too, but I guess they were knocked out when the building was destroyed.'

She started down the stairs, but Ken and I hesitated and scanned the Compound one last time. It remained deserted; there was no sign of the five survivors from our attackers returning with reinforcements. Then we followed Alucia down the darkened stairs. I couldn't help wondering when I'd see daylight again.

At the bottom we entered a room that was identical to the one beneath the Compound building at Capelia – but where the one in Capelia had been dark and inert, this room was brightly lit and all its mysterious devices hummed with life. Numerous screens flickered with countless dots of light.

'What is this place?' I asked Alucia.

'The Compound's nerve centre,' she replied. 'It's both a communications centre and a monitoring centre. This is where we would be constantly gathering information about the local inhabitants. Of course, what went on in the castle would have been the main source of interest to us. The discussions between the local warlord and the members of his court, his advisors, his army commanders and so on.'

'How was that done?' I asked, both fascinated and appalled.

She pointed at the devices with the flickering screens. 'They would have been linked to the many miniature cameras and microphones hidden throughout the castle. The homes of various leading citizens would have been similarly bugged. Everything that was said or done by anyone of interest to us was recorded.'

I reeled at the implications of this. 'This went on throughout the world?' I asked her.

She nodded. 'It was standard procedure everywhere.'

I thought of the number of times in Lord Krader's court when the Elite had been discussed in less than flattering terms; I myself had not been slow to contribute my own opinions – that they were a loathsome plague infecting the whole human race was one of my milder descriptions, as far as I could remember. I said, 'But the Compound at Capelia was rarely occupied by any Elite—'

'It didn't matter,' Alucia told me. 'Everything would have been recorded automatically and checked later. Basically, it was done for intelligence-gathering, but –' she hesitated '– but I have to admit that much of the material was used for entertainment purposes.'

'Charming,' I muttered darkly. I looked at Ken. He was clearly having the same bitter reaction as me. Then I thought of Harius and his deadly secret. Presumably the Elite hadn't bothered to secrete their devices in the living quarters of the court jester, otherwise we'd have all been in serious trouble. That is: dead. I had another reason for being relieved that the jester's quarters weren't being monitored. The idea of a bunch of Elite laughing themselves sick at the sight of my bouts of love-making with Tiri definitely didn't appeal to me.

Ken and I followed Alucia into another room that was also familiar to us: it was a replica of the small room under the Capelia Compound with the large, mysterious circular hatch in the middle of the floor. Like the one in Capelia it was about six feet in diameter.

Ken stared at the hatch and said what I was thinking: 'Just like the one in the Elite Compound back in Capelia.'

'What?' exclaimed Alucia. 'You have a Sprite facility in Capelia? Why didn't you tell me?'

'Because I had no idea what it was,' he replied. 'We never managed to open the hatch.'

'No, of course not,' she said, 'it was a stupid question. Sorry.' She touched a button near the doorway. A panel slid open in the wall to reveal a row of flashing lights and a large metal wheel. She began pressing a number of buttons next to the row of lights. As she did so she said, 'Prepare yourself, gentlemen, because very soon your lives are about to totally change for ever.'

The hatch suddenly made a clicking sound and swung upwards on a huge hinge. Ken and I stared down at what had been revealed; it was rather disappointing. All we saw was a tubular metal room some ten feet deep. The floor of the room contained a smaller hatch. Set flush in one side of the room was a ladder. Not exactly a soul-shattering sight, I said to Alucia, adding, '*That* is going to totally change my life?'

'This is only the start,' she replied. 'Climb down inside.'

I gestured to Ken that he could go first. He sighed and began to climb down the ladder. I followed. Alucia came after me. When all three of us were on the floor of the room, I asked what we were supposed to do next.

'Nothing,' she said, 'just enjoy the ride.' She pressed one of several glowing buttons on the tube wall and I was taken by surprise when the floor of the tube began to descend. My stomach lurched as the rate of descent grew faster. 'We're in another *elevator*!' I exclaimed, absurdly proud that I'd remembered the correct term.

'Yes,' said Alucia, 'but this one is going down a *very* long way.'

'So where exactly are we going?' Ken asked.

'To the Sprite dock facility on the outer hull,' she replied.

'Right,' he said, as if that meant anything to him. But it did to me. I began to feel scared. Well, more scared than usual, which, on this trip, was saying something.

After what felt like ages we finally slowed down and came to a halt.

'We've arrived,' said Alucia, unnecessarily. She bent down and turned the wheel on the centre of the small hatch in the floor. The hatch swung downwards. 'Follow me,' she said and lowered herself through the open hatchway. When she'd disappeared I looked at Ken. He gave a helpless shrug. I looked down through the hatchway and a saw a ladder leading down into another tubular room the same size as the elevator. Alucia was already at the bottom. She looked up at me and said, 'Come on, quickly, you two. And shut the hatch behind you. Turn the wheel until you hear a loud click.'

'I'll do it,' Ken said. 'You go first.'

As I climbed down the ladder and joined Alucia on the floor

of the tube, I saw that there was a door set in one side. We waited while Ken did as she'd instructed and sealed the hatch above him, then, as Ken climbed down to join us, Alucia began to punch buttons beside the door. 'We're in an airlock,' she told us. The door slid open and she stepped out.

I followed her through with Ken behind me. Then I gave a gasp of amazement—

CHAPTER EIGHTEEN

We were in a very large, brightly lit and very long room that was entirely white – such a gleaming white it was dazzling. Filling almost the entire room was some kind of . . . *thing*. As I stared at it, I realised it had to be a vehicle of some sort. My first impression was that it resembled a giant crossbow bolt or dart. One end came to a rounded point while the other, wider, end had an array of fletchings or fins. It too was gleaming white and its surface appeared to be some sort of a ceramic material rather than metal. At a rough estimate I put its length at about one hundred and ninety feet. Something about it suggested coiled power. Tremendous power.

'What *is* it?' I asked Alucia in awe, my voice almost a whisper.

'That, Jad, is a "Sprite". A spaceship. A very versatile vehicle capable of travelling both through space and through the atmosphere of a planet. Once they were regularly used to explore first-hand the worlds of the planetary systems that Urba encountered. Now such worlds are simply checked by robot drones controlled by the AIs . . . pah!' She sounded disgusted. 'As I told you, the Elite became completely inward-looking. Ships like this have been virtually ignored for over a century and a half, except by rare individuals like me, who expressed an interest in learning how to operate them – and who also had an interest in what lay beyond the hull of Urba . . .

'The Sprites are also weapons platforms. They were to be our first line of defence if we ever encountered a hostile alien civilisation. But as the centuries passed and the most complex life form we ever discovered on a world was the equivalent of an earthworm, that possibility became increasingly unlikely—'

I squeaked and jumped as something that looked like a large metallic spider scuttled passed me and disappeared under the vehicle. 'What the fuck was *that*?' I cried as I pulled the Elite hand-weapon from its holster.

Alucia laughed and said, 'Relax. Put the gun away. It's just a servo-mech. A maintenance robot. There are lots of them about in here. They keep the Sprite in tip-top working order. Or at least they do when the power is on—'

My nerves still jangling, I slipped the weapon back in its holster, then I glanced at Ken. He was staring at the awe-inspiring vehicle with an unreadable expression on his face. I suspected that his firmly held belief system about the true nature of the world was starting to give way at its foundations.

'How many of these –' I groped for the term she'd used '– these *spaceships* are there?'

'Over a thousand. Most are in the central dock near the control centre, but there are others scattered at various locations throughout Urba. Once it was mandatory to have an experienced Sprite pilot on constant duty in every Compound that had a ship docked below it but that was another custom that slowly withered away and was eventually abandoned. And now we . . . or rather, *we the Elite*, have paid the price for our lack of vigilance.'

'And so has the rest of the world,' I said.

'True,' she said, 'so let's see if we can do something to put things right before it's too late for everyone.'

'What do you plan to do?'

'Attack whatever's attacking us,' she said simply. 'We can take off as soon as I prime the ship . . .' She led the way to a glassed-off area at the far end of the long room. We passed through two sets of doors – another airlock – and entered a room full of the usual mysterious Elite devices. 'The control room,' said Alucia. Then she pointed to another doorway. 'Through there are living quarters, including a kitchen, bathroom, toilets and so on. Take advantage of the facilities while you can.'

Both Ken and I had need of the toilets. Alucia showed us the way, then left us to our own devices.

'What do you think?' I asked Ken as we stood side by side at the urinals.

'Very clean,' he replied. 'We're probably the first people to take a piss in here for hundreds of years.'

'You know what I mean. Alucia plans to take us outside of Urba. How do you feel about that?'

'More Elite madness.'

'You don't believe yet that it's going to happen?'

He didn't answer.

We returned to the area that Alucia had called the 'control room'. Through the glass wall I could see a hatch open on the side of the vehicle near its nose with a ladder extended down from it.

'We're all primed and ready to go,' Alucia told us.

'I'm not getting into that thing,' said Ken.

Alucia and I both turned and looked at him. He glared back at us defiantly.

'I'm having nothing more to do with Elite magic,' he said, taking his weapon from its holster and throwing it away. It bounced heavily on the floor. 'It's poisoning my soul.'

'Ken,' said Alucia quietly, 'this ship isn't Elite magic. It isn't even Elite technology. It's *old* technology, created by your ancestors. Who knows, if *my* ancestors hadn't turned most of Urba into a fucking medieval theme park, you might have become a pilot of one of these ships instead of becoming a—' She didn't continue.

'Your words make no sense to me, Alucia,' Ken said, 'and I refuse to enter that satanic machine.'

Alucia glared at him. Then she said, 'You want to see your entire home domain of Capelia scorched to a cinder? Your family horribly killed?'

'No, of course not.'

'Then forget all this "satanic machine" crap and get on board the fucking spaceship.'

'No,' said Ken, 'I won't.' He sounded adamant. I'd heard him use that tone of voice before. Ken could be really stubborn when he wanted to be.

Alucia looked at me. 'Can't you talk some sense into him?' she asked.

'I've never succeeded in doing that in the past,' I told her, 'so I doubt he's going to start taking my advice now.'

'No one could convince me to get inside that *thing*,' said Ken.

I realised then that Ken was scared. That seriously shook me. I'd never seen him scared before. I was witnessing yet another previously undoubted certainty having the props kicked out from under it. Put Ken up against a group of armed men, or a dragon or anything else, and he was fearless, but the idea of boarding this Elite vehicle clearly genuinely terrified him.

I myself found the prospect of a voyage outside Urba in this *spaceship* an unnerving one, but at the same time I was being pulled by a strong curiosity to see what lay beyond. So, after some thought, I made a suggestion to Alucia: 'Why can't Ken stay here while we go and do whatever is we have to do outside?'

Alucia looked dubious. 'I suppose he could. The problem is, there's no guarantee we'll be coming back. I have no idea what we'll be facing out there.'

I sincerely wished she hadn't said that. My curiosity began to pall.

'Okay,' she said to Ken, 'you stay here while Jad and I take the Sprite out to attack the aliens. If we can. And I thought you were a man of courage. Instead you're letting a woman and a court jester do your fighting for you.'

'Hey—' I began.

'Sorry,' she said, 'no insult intended.'

I wasn't mollified by the apology, but then I noticed that

Ken was now looking indecisive. The aspersions she'd cast on his manhood had hit home.

He took a deep breath. 'All right, I'll come with you two—'

Alucia stopped him there with a kiss. 'I knew you wouldn't let me down!' She smiled.

Ken looked far from happy as we boarded the vehicle. The air in the cabin, which contained eight seats, had a musty odour to it. I wondered how many years it had been since anyone had been inside the thing. Same as the toilet, I supposed. Two of the seats were at the front of the cabin and faced a wide, curving window and a control panel that made the one in the air-car look childishly simple by comparison. Alucia sat in one of the front seats and indicated we should sit in the two seats immediately behind her. She instructed us on how to strap ourselves securely into the seats. Then she threw a couple of switches on the control panel and it lit up with a large number of coloured lights. Six screens like the one on the air-car also began to glow. Four of them displayed images like the dials of clocks. Alucia kept throwing switches and pressing buttons. A small mechanical whine came from somewhere and I noticed the air becoming noticeably fresher.

Eventually she said, 'All systems are go. We can get moving now.'

'All systems are go.' It was an old saying that no one had known the origin of.

'A word of warning,' said Alucia. 'Once we leave Urba we're going to be in a state of what's called near-zero gravity. What that means is that your bodies won't have any weight. Or hardly any, anyway. You may feel strange, even nauseous, but you'll get used to it. Eventually—'

I was so nervous I was already feeling nauseous. I glanced at Ken. He looked nauseous too.

'Here we go,' said Alucia, sounding pleased.

The vehicle shuddered and there was the sound of whooshing air, followed by an eerie silence. I looked down through the curve of the window at my side and saw that the vehicle was descending through the floor of the room. Two great doors had swung open beneath it. My stomach felt like it had surged into my throat . . . and stayed there. The sensation was similar to when we made the speedy descent down the tube in the elevator, but much more acute. I began to feel woozy—

Then, looking up through the window in the front of the vehicle, I saw the room that had housed the Sprite rapidly recede. It soon became a brightly lit oblong surrounded by grey metal, growing smaller as I watched. Then the doors swung shut, cutting off the light.

Alucia said, 'I'm now going to flip the Sprite over . . . so get ready to be amazed.'

The great mass of metal that was the exterior of Urba swung round until it was 'below' the vehicle; 'above' us we could now see what appeared to be countless points of bright lights set against a background of complete blackness. The points of lights were moving across the window at quite a fast rate; they made me dizzy just to look at them.

'Gentlemen,' said Alucia, 'I give you . . . the Universe!'

'I think I'm going to throw up,' said Ken. I knew how he felt.

'The Universe often has that affect on people,' she said.

'What are all those lights?' I asked her.

'Stars,' she replied. 'Those balls of fire I told you about.'

'But they're all moving,' I said.

'No. We're moving. We're still moving relative to Urba's rate of rotation. But if you wait a couple of minutes while I brake the Sprite, you'll see the Universe as it really is—'

While she worked the vehicle's controls I glanced again at Ken. He had his eyes shut.

Looking 'down' at Urba I could see that our vehicle was turning. Then I felt a pressure as my body was pushed against the harness of straps holding me into my seat. At the same time I saw that the surface of Urba had begun to move. It was turning beneath us.

'We're slowing down, no longer moving relative to Urba's rate of rotation,' explained Alucia. 'Now look at the stars again.'

I thought I just about grasped what she was talking about. I looked through the window again and watched the points of light slowly became stationary. They were an impressive sight. But they all looked very small to me – how could any of them have been home to the human race?

'In reality they're huge,' Alucia told me, 'much bigger than Urba. But they're a very, very long way away from us.'

'Ken,' I said, 'open your eyes and take a look. It's incredible.'

He opened his eyes and looked through the window. 'Yes, marvellous,' he muttered, 'we're in the middle of nowhere and I feel sick.'

'You'll get used to being in near-zero gravity,' Alucia assured him. 'It just takes some time. Different people react differently.'

'Still think that all that Alucia has ever told us is a pile of Elite bullshit?' I was being cruel, considering how shaken Ken was, but I couldn't help it. I was in a strange state of mind myself.

'Shut the fuck up.'

Well, at least it was an honest answer. I asked Alucia, 'Just how big are the stars?'

'Millions of miles in diameter,' she replied. 'Some are much bigger than others. Of course, what you're seeing is just a small part of the Universe. Just a small section of our own galaxy—'

'Galaxy?'

'A cluster of about one hundred billion stars. And it's estimated that there are about one hundred billion galaxies in the Universe.'

My already woozy head swam at the enormity of the concept. It was too much to take in.

'A lot of the stars have planetary systems,' she continued, 'but unfortunately, Earth-type planets appear to be rare.' And for Ken's benefit she added, 'Earth, as I've told you, was the home planet for the human race—'

Ken made one of his noncommittal grunts.

'When Urba left the planetary system that included Earth, its original target was a star called 55 Cancri in the Cancer constellation, forty-one light years from Earth. Gas giants had been discovered in orbit around 55 Cancri, but at orbits that suggested that its planetary system was similar to the one that orbited our sun. Alas, after a journey that had taken more than a hundred and thirty years, the result was disappointment. There were rocky planets similar to Earth in orbit around 55 Cancri, but all three of them were incapable of supporting life. So the search for a suitable planet had to continue ... And we've been searching ever since. In theory. But as I've said, the Elite's enthusiasm for finding a replacement Earth began to wane centuries ago. Now we just go through the motions, or we did, leaving the search to the AIs—'

'Why does take so long to travel from star to star?' I asked.

'Because of the vast distances involved. I told you that the star called 55 Cancri was forty-one light years from Earth. What that means is it takes light that long to travel that far. Do you understand?'

I tried getting my head round it; I was having great difficulty. 'I always just presumed that light travelled instantaneously,' I said.

'Oh no.' She was sounding more and more like a teacher. 'It travels at around one hundred and eighty-six thousand miles a second. That means in one year it travels nearly six million million miles. So that should give you some idea of the distances involved.'

'Yeah,' I said doubtfully. My head was *really* hurting now – as usual, when I listened to one of Alucia's lectures.

'Now Urba, several years after it leaves a planetary system, can reach, eventually, a maximum speed a third of that of light, which is pretty good going. But it still takes the ship between one and two centuries to travel from one planetary system to the next. So you see the problem ...'

'Yeah.' That I *could* understand.

'Many years ago, back on Earth, there was talk of developing a faster-than-light drive. Lots of theories were thrown around and on paper it seemed possible, but nothing ever came of it. So even travelling at a third of the speed of light, Urba was basically just dawdling through space.'

'Dawdling? Uh huh, if you say so,' I said.

She returned her attention to the controls. 'Now let me show you an overview of Urba,' she said. 'You'll feel some pressure as the ship accelerates.'

'Fine,' I said, worriedly. I looked at Ken. His expression was grim. 'How are you feeling now?' I asked him solicitously. 'Any better?'

'No,' he replied.

I decided to leave it at that – then suddenly I was pushed back into my seat. My body felt incredibly heavy and to my alarm I discovered I couldn't lift either of my arms.

'Arghhh!' cried Ken, echoing my own thoughts.

'What's going on?' I shouted.

'Just the effects of the acceleration I warned you about,' she replied. 'Relax, both of you. It won't last long.'

My body got heavier by the moment. The flesh of my face felt like it was being peeled back—

'Arghhh!' cried Ken again. I looked at him, and saw that the flesh on his face was being pulled back too. It was actually rippling.

'I don't like this!' I cried to Alucia.

'I said relax. You're both young and healthy. Your hearts will easily cope with the strain.'

While I pondered uneasily on *those* words, the pressure on my body continued to increase. It all seemed to last for a very long time before, to my immense relief, the pressure began to ease up. Then it stopped. I gasped for breath—

'See?' said Alucia. 'Nothing to worry about. Now, take a look at this . . .'

She was turning the vehicle and the next thing I knew, I could see all of Urba through the window.

'There it is,' she said, 'your world in its entirety. What do you think?'

I had to admit to myself that I was vaguely disappointed by

the sight. Urba resembled nothing more than a very thick metal cigar, rounded at one end and blunt at the other. I found it difficult to accept that this featureless-looking object contained the entire world that I had grown up in. 'It looks so small,' I said weakly. I realised I was beginning to feel strangely numb. My brain was having trouble coping with it all.

'But it *is* big,' said Alucia, 'it's over nine thousand miles long. It just looks small from this distance.'

'Uh-huh.' It was all I could manage. I wondered when I was going to wake up in my bed.

'See where it bulges at one end?' she asked. 'That's the stern, where the main fusion drive is housed. A giant electromagnetic field extends out around the stern for hundreds of thousands of miles. It acts as a vast scoop, drawing in cosmic dust as Urba moves through space. The dust serves as fuel for the fusion reactors.'

'Uh-huh.' I needed a stiff drink really badly.

'Urba is still accelerating, though slowly,' Alucia continued. 'It will be at least another ten years before she reaches her maximum velocity . . .'

I looked at Ken. He was doing his best to ignore Urba. Still trying to deny the obvious truth, I guessed. I didn't blame him. But then he suddenly pointed over Alucia's shoulder and asked, 'What the hell is *that*?'

CHAPTER NINETEEN

Alucia and I both stared at what Ken was pointing at. It was like a giant black egg blotting out a section of the stars as it moved through the void.

'What *is* it?' I asked her.

'I'm not sure yet, but I have a strong suspicion that we may have found our aliens,' she said. 'But the weird thing is that it's not registering on the ship's radar. And it's fucking *huge*. I was expecting to find a ship out here, but nothing that big! It's the size of a small planet.'

'Could it be a planet?' I asked. 'Or is that a stupid question?'

'It's a stupid question, Jad,' she told me as she furiously punched at buttons on the control panel. 'You don't find planets alone out here in deep space far from the nearest star. No, my guess is that a vehicle that large is another generation ship like Urba. The question is, how did it manage to encounter us? The chances of that happening are ... well, literally astronomical. It's simply impossible.'

'But there it is,' I said.

'Yes. I can't argue with you on that one. There it is ... Ah, I'm getting a visual close-up on it at last. Take a look.'

I tried leaning forward to look, but the harness prevented me from getting a clear view of the screen she was pointing towards. So I tried loosening the straps ... with the result that I released the harness completely and found myself starting to float up out of my seat. 'What's happening?' I cried in alarm.

'By the gods,' I heard Ken groan as I continued to float upwards, 'I don't believe this—'

Alucia twisted round in her seat and grabbed me by the arm.

'Sorry. I should have warned you about this. It's one of the effects of zero gravity.'

'Now you tell me,' I said as she pulled me down. First I grabbed hold of the back of her seat, then the harness on my seat and, after an awkward struggle, managed to strap myself back into it. I saw that Ken had screwed his eyes shut again.

'I did warn you two before we left the docking bay that your bodies wouldn't have any weight,' said Alucia.

'Well I didn't think you meant it *literally*,' I griped.

'What else can weightless mean except weightless . . . Oh, it doesn't matter. I'll describe to you what I can see on the visual close-up of the alien vessel.'

'Please do,' I muttered.

'Well, the image isn't very good quality, even with computer enhancement. The object is too far away, and it's also moving in relation to Urba's rate of rotation, as we were. But I am picking up some detail. The surface of the hull is very pitted, which suggests that it's even older than Urba; I'd say it's been travelling through space for a very, very long time – much longer than us. And some of the hull damage is quite serious. The vessel has obviously suffered some major meteor hits. Repairs have been carried out, but from what I can see, they appear to be somewhat rudimentary. All very interesting—'

'Why? What does that tell you?' I asked.

'First, that this vessel is close to falling apart. If it's the alien equivalent of a generation ship, its search for a new world has been fruitless, just as ours has been. Which is probably why they've invaded Urba. They're desperate for a new home. And somehow they've managed to come across another generation ship – ours – that's still in perfect working order. And that leads me to another interesting area of speculation.'

'Which is?'

'If the aliens have taken control of the AIs, which I'm pretty convinced they have, it would be a simple matter to destroy all human life by altering the environment in some radical way. But they haven't done that. They clearly don't want to damage Urba's delicate environmental balance. Which suggests they have similar metabolisms to us. They may not *look* human but they must be very much like us.'

'So that means they can be easily killed,' said Ken.

I was relieved that Ken was at last taking an interest in what was going on. It was a good sign. I'd been beginning to worry that the experience of going outside of Urba in the Sprite had pushed him over some mental edge.

'Well, I wouldn't be so optimistic as to say that they can be *easily* killed,' said Alucia, 'but yes, I would say they're just as vulnerable as we are. Of course, I could be completely wrong about everything. I still can't understand how they could have found us. It doesn't make any sense.'

'Didn't you say they must have been following us for some years?' I asked her.

'Yes, I did,' she said. 'Their invasion has all the hallmarks of a long-term plan.'

'How long since Urba last visited other worlds?' I asked tentatively, convinced that my idea would turn out to be another stupid one.

'Relatively recently . . . nearly a quarter of a century ago. Why do you—?' She paused and exclaimed, 'Oh shit!' She turned and looked at me over her shoulder. 'I see what you're getting at. Why didn't I think of that? Jad, you are definitely smarter than you look!'

I couldn't help glowing with pleasure at the compliment.

'That wouldn't be difficult,' muttered Ken, which took the gloss off the moment.

'The survey of the system was carried out by robot probes controlled by the AIs,' she said excitedly. 'They reported finding no habitable planets. I should be able to access the records . . . Hang on.'

After about a minute she announced, 'Got it! Yes, the system consisted of four gas giants and two small rocky planets. The latter were in orbit too close to the system's star to support life—' She fell into silence as she continued to scan the information that was unfolding on one of the screens. Finally she said, 'Aha . . . here's something. An anomaly was detected in the system – or rather, outside it: an object that might have been a small planet or a large asteroid, in orbit way beyond the rest of the planetary system. The AIs intended to send a probe to investigate, but the decision was overridden by an Elite technician on the basis that even if it was a planet, it was too far from the star to support life. Good God.'

She turned and looked at me again. 'This supports your theory. Those stupid fools should have investigated the object. It's quite likely it was that alien starship right there. It must have been lying dormant, emitting no transmissions across the electromagnetic spectrum. They would have known Urba was coming towards the system years before it arrived. Urba's engines, being used to slow the ship down, would have been like a nuclear beacon in space. God knows how long the alien ship had been in orbit outside of that system. Maybe that system had been their last hope and they'd given up. Maybe their failing engines weren't capable of taking them all the way to another system. But along comes Urba and the aliens are given fresh hope. Their clapped-out ship was capable of following Urba for nearly twenty-five years while they made their plans to invade . . . yes!' She nodded vigorously. 'It all makes sense! It's no longer due to an almost impossible chance encounter in space, but because two different generation ships were attracted by the same potential prize. It's still a huge coincidence, that such an event happened within such a relatively short time frame, but definitely possible . . . *Fuck and damn!*' She punched more buttons.

'What's the matter?' I asked.

'I just made a serious error,' she said grimly. 'I've corrected it but—' She shook her head in dismay.

Her reaction worried me. The error was apparently a bad one – but what was it?

'So what are you going to do now?' asked Ken. 'Attack the alien vessel?'

'No. At least, not yet. The ship may still have an effective defence system that would simply reduce us to radioactive dust as we approached. Before we risk that fate, our main priority should be the aliens' point of entry into Urba, which has to be the control centre on the hull and lies above the Citadel . . . or below it, depending on your point of view.' She turned back to the control panel. 'We're going back down to the surface of Urba. There'll be more uncomfortable G-forces to endure as we accelerate . . . sorry. But time is now of the essence.'

I braced myself as the ship began to speed back towards Urba. Even though I knew what to expect this time, the pressure on my body was an extremely unpleasant and draining experience. Soon the hull of Urba filled the window; it looked like we were going to crash right into it, but then the ship began to slow down and instead of being pinned against my seat, I was forced against the restraining harness. The ship turned and then we were skimming over Urba's rotating hull.

'It will take me a little time to manoeuvre the ship back into a position relative to Urba's rate of rotation,' Alucia told us. We nodded, as if we understood what she was talking about.

When it appeared Urba was no longer rotating below us, Alucia said, 'Right, now it's time I told you two the bad news.'

'Is it worse than being reduced to radioactive dust, whatever that might be?' I asked.

'It comes to the same thing, really,' she said. 'When I accessed the records of the exploration of that planetary system, I alerted the AIs to our presence. My mistake. I should have thought of it earlier. Anyway . . . the AIs know we're out here. And if they know, so do the aliens.'

'You mean they know we're heading towards them right now?' I asked anxiously.

'No. As soon as I realised my mistake I immediately shut down the link between the ship's computer and the central system. But that doesn't mean they aren't taking precautions against the likelihood of our imminent appearance in their vicinity.'

'Right,' I said, suddenly feeling very exposed.

'What sort of weapons do you have on this infernal machine?' Ken asked her.

'You name it and we've got it,' she told him, 'electron-beam-cannons, long range, high-intensity lasers, missiles with high-explosive warheads. No nuclear missiles, unfortunately. They were banned back when the Sprite was constructed. Then again, even if there was one on board, I couldn't use it against the control centre.'

'Why not?' I asked, as if I understood what she was talking about.

'Because it wouldn't just destroy the control centre, it would vaporise a very large section of Urba's hull. But it would be handy to have one to use against the alien ship—' She broke off and fiddled with the controls, then announced, 'Control centre is dead ahead. I'm taking us up for an overview of the situation.'

The Sprite lifted rapidly away from Urba's hull and once again I was pushed back into my seat. But this time is was only briefly, before the vehicle levelled out.

'Take a look,' she told us. Ken and I peered down through the window as the Sprite circled the control centre, which protruded from the hull like the circular flat top of a barrel. I guessed it was over a mile in diameter. There were windows around its rim. But it was what was on top of the control centre that drew my attention. They looked like large, black beetles. I counted eight of them. They were positioned around a circular construction that rose from the middle of the control centre.

'What are those things?' I asked Alucia.

'At a guess, I'd say they were alien shuttle-craft,' she replied. 'And that thing in the middle is a large docking bay the aliens have built . . .' She began to stare intently at the screens on the console. 'These fuckers don't show up on radar either. With the AIs corrupted by the aliens, any Elite technicians working in the control centre would have been taken completely by surprise. The aliens blasted a hole through the centre's shielding that would have caused an atmospheric blow-out, killing everyone inside. Except they would been *outside* when they died, sucked out through the hole. But that still leaves a lot of questions unanswered. Like—'

Before she could continue, we saw one of the beetle-shaped objects lift off from the control centre.

Alucia said tersely, 'Here comes the welcoming party. Hang onto your privates, boys. The fun is about to start.'

As the alien craft continued to rise, somewhat sluggishly, I thought, Alucia sent the Sprite speeding towards it. My stomach lurched. Then I saw a red beam shoot from the nose of the Sprite, straight into the top of the alien vessel. It promptly blew up, becoming a rapidly expanding cloud of glowing debris.

'Well, *that's* encouraging,' Alucia murmured.

'Good shooting,' Ken told her. He sounded more like his old self.

The Sprite continued in its dive towards the control centre. She fired the beam-cannon again, raking it over the cluster of beetle-like vehicles; wherever it touched them, they exploded.

'Their shielding is shit!' said Alucia, sounding delighted. The Sprite pulled out of its dive and we skimmed over the centre, narrowly avoiding the spreading debris, and then its nose was pointing at the stars. Once again I was slammed back into my seat. This was becoming a habit. I checked Ken. His face was now flushed with excitement. Nothing like a battle – any kind of battle – to bring Ken back to normal, or what passed for normal with him.

And then we were diving 'down' towards the centre again. 'Time to give them some of their own medicine,' said Alucia. The Sprite shuddered and I saw two blurred objects with fiery tails shoot ahead of us.

'Missiles,' she explained just as the objects hit the circular structure in the middle of the control centre. There was a massive explosion. Though there was no sound, I felt the shock wave rock the Sprite. Alucia pulled out of the dive immediately and we were heading back towards the stars. 'Going to be a lot of shit flying around,' she said.

She was right. When we started circling the area at a safe distance I could see a great geyser of wreckage shooting out below us from the control centre. The alien structure had vanished, as had a large portion of the roof of the centre.

Ken was impressed; I knew because he was making sounds of amazement. Firing his crossbow was never going to be the same for him from now onwards. It was the end of an era.

Alucia was peering intently at one of her screens.

'See anything?' I asked.

'You mean aliens?' she said, and gave a dry chuckle. 'I think I'm probably seeing bits and pieces of aliens, but it's hard to tell. There are definitely some clouds of blood globules among the debris . . . and the blood is red, which tells us something.'

'It does? What?'

But she was already aiming the Sprite at the control centre again. 'Two more to finish the job,' she said. We did a short dive and she fired off another couple of missiles. These vanished through the huge hole in the roof and there was a pause before a brilliant flash of light erupted through the hole. The blast made the hole even bigger.

'Was that wise?' I asked her as we headed back 'up' again. 'That explosion could have penetrated the hull.'

'No chance of that,' she assured me. 'I was just making sure everything was cleared out on every level of the control centre. My intention was to destroy the AIs along with everything else. They were located on the lower levels—'

'The AIs?' I said, alarmed. 'But I thought you said they controlled Urba's entire environment. Like the sun . . . the air recycling—'

'Relax. Those tasks will be automatically taken over by back-up systems located in different parts of Urba. My theory is that aliens were using the AIs to operate their war machines.'

'I hope you're right.'

'So do I,' she said.

I realised we were still climbing. 'Where are we going now?'

'We've got four missiles left. I don't intend to waste them.'

A short time later I saw her next target in the window: the dark mass of the alien ship in the distance. Not that I could actually see the thing, only its outline against the stars it blotted out with its presence. From this angle it appeared perfectly circular.

Alucia said, 'I'm firing from here. I don't want to get any closer to the mothership, just to be on the safe side—'

That was just fine with me. The Sprite shuddered again as the missiles were launched. 'Will they reach the thing from this distance?' I asked her.

'Sure. Their rocket motors will give out about halfway there, but the missiles will keep on travelling at the same speed until they reach the target. Except I don't think they will. The ship must have some kind of defence system.'

We waited, Alucia glued to one of her screens. Then, even from that distance, I saw red flashes near the centre of the black, sinister-looking mass. 'Did the missiles hit the ship?' I asked Alucia. 'Or were they destroyed?'

'They hit the ship,' said Alucia.

'Yes!' cried Ken, in triumph.

'No defence system,' said Alucia, sounding mystified. 'Not even an automatic one for protection against meteors.'

'Does Urba have one?'

'We did have: strategically placed beam-cannons around the hull programmed to destroy any object approaching of a size capable of causing serious damage. It used a whole range of detection systems as well as radar, so it should have spotted any approaching alien shuttle-craft—'

'So what happened to this system?'

'The AIs must have neutralised it.' Then she said thoughtfully, 'If our theory is right and the alien ship was in the vicinity of that planetary system for a very long period, it would explain all the damage to their hull. It kept being hit by local debris. The question is, why didn't they use their defence system?'

She was silent for a time, then said, 'Unless they were reserving their dwindling energy resources. That would explain why they're depending on Urba's restored power system to operate their war machines.'

'Do you think you've caused them fatal damage?' Ken asked her.

'No. Those four missiles couldn't seriously affect a ship of that size,' she said. 'But they probably caused major damage to a large area. Certainly appears so on the visual monitor. I can see signs of atmospheric emissions. Must have penetrated the hull. It can't be as thick as Urba's.'

'But if you've blown a hole in their hull,' I said excitedly, 'then surely they'll lose all of their air, right?'

Alucia straightened up and shook her head. 'We can't take that for granted. No guarantee that their ship's internal structure is like Urba's. Instead of being basically hollow, it might be honeycombed with separate compartments.'

'If they don't have a defence system, why don't we attack?' asked Ken, his bloodlust obviously fired up. 'You may be out of missiles, but you've got other weapons.'

'Not a good idea,' said Alucia. 'I saw something else on the monitor: what looks like several of their shuttle-craft being deployed. Picking off a few of them when they're sitting ducks is one thing, but going up against a bunch of the bastards is a different kettle of fish. Time to head for home.'

'But we can't leave this area undefended!' I protested. 'If we leave they'll simply send more ships and set up a new base here.'

'They'd have a lot of difficulty in doing that,' she replied. The Sprite had already turned and was speeding away. 'There's nothing in the control centre now but molten slag, which must extend down several levels. I've basically sealed them off from access to Urba. There are probably aliens still in the Citadel but they should be helpless—'

'You *hope*,' I said.

'Yeah,' she admitted, 'I *hope* so. But it would be best not to underestimate these bastards.'

'What if they find another way to enter Urba?' I asked her.

She didn't answer for a time. Then she said, 'There's no equivalent to the control centre in terms of providing large-scale access into Urba. Any alternative attempt would require a massive engineering operation, and I don't think the aliens have the resources for that.'

'You *hope*,' I repeated.

'Shut up, Jad.'

A short time later she slowed the Sprite. 'We're there,' she said, and flipped the ship over onto its back so that we were now looking 'up' at Urba's hull. I searched in vain for any sign of the doors to the docking bay we'd departed from.

'Are you sure?' I asked her. 'I can't see anything.'

'We're definitely in the right place,' she said. 'I'm transmitting the signal to reopen the bay doors—'

But nothing happened.

'Shit,' she muttered.

CHAPTER TWENTY

'**A**re you sure we're in the right place?' I asked.

'Yes, of course we are,' she told me huffily. 'The on-board computer wouldn't make such a mistake.'

'It wouldn't?' It seemed to me that computers were about as reliable as horses.

'No,' she said as she moved the ship closer to Urba's hull. 'See?' she said, triumphantly. 'You can see the outline of the doors now . . .'

I had to admit she was right.

'So why aren't they opening?' asked Ken.

'I don't *know*,' she said in exasperation and banged her fist on the console.

'By blowing up the control centre and everything in it,' I said, moving cautiously into dangerous territory, 'you didn't by any chance cut off the power again?'

'No, impossible,' she said firmly. 'Destroying the AIs wouldn't have cut off the power. Like I told you, their functions would have been taken over by back-up systems located elsewhere, which would have included maintaining the power supply. The power was cut before because the aliens deliberately cut it—'

'Then what's going on?' I asked.

'Bloody hell!' she exploded. 'I don't bloody know! How many times do I have to tell you two cretins that fundamental truth?' She unbuckled her harness and started to float out of her seat. She kicked her legs and passed over our heads, grabbing at hand-holds in the ceiling of the cabin that I hadn't noticed before. I've never seen her this angry, I thought, as I ducked my head to avoid being knocked unconscious by one of her flailing boots. 'Come on you two, follow me,' she ordered peremptorily.

I didn't hesitate in unstrapping my harness but, as I started to float upwards, I saw that Ken had no intention of moving.

'Hey,' I said to him, 'it's not as bad as it looks. In fact, it's kind of fun.' I reached over and started to undo his harness. He tried to resist, until Alucia said, in a voice of cold steel, 'Hurry up, you two or I'll leave you in here to rot.'

Ken finally let me help him out of his harness and together we made awkward progress towards Alucia. She was floating beside a door at the rear of the cabin.

'I guess it's your day for new experiences,' she said angrily, as we advanced slowly towards her.

'And what's our next new experience?' I asked, a little fearfully.

'Space walking,' she said. 'Unfortunately, it's a new experience for me too. I've never done it before. Except in a simulation tank.'

As was still so often the case, I had no idea what she was talking about. 'What's space walking?'

'I'll break it to you as gently as I can,' she said. I began to feel seriously scared as a result. 'We can get back into the docking bay through an emergency hatch which can be manually opened.'

'That's good,' I said.

'In theory,' she said. 'The problem is, we have to leave the Sprite to reach it.'

'Go outside?' I said. I have a mind as sharp as a steel trap. Nothing blindingly obvious ever escapes me. 'But surely we'd die!'

She nodded. 'Indeed. That's why we'll be wearing these—' She pressed a button beside the door and it slid open. At first I thought there were two rows of people standing beyond it, then I realised they were suits, empty suits, standing there rigid, like suits of armour, except they were made of some kind of stiff, white material instead of metal.

'What are those?' I asked.

'Space suits,' she answered. 'Getting all three of us into the bloody things should only take a couple of hours. At least.'

'We're going *outside*?' said Ken. Ken not being as sharp as me, the gold coin had only just dropped.

'Afraid so,' said Alucia. She manoeuvred herself through the doorway and began to unhook one of the suits from the wall. 'No choice.'

'I'm not going outside!' Ken protested, his voice rising in alarm. 'I'm not going into that endless void!'

'Swallow your misgivings about your journey,' I told him, repeating his own words to me before we started this mad expedition, 'you're about to go on a grand adventure.' Then I clapped him hard on his back, an action that sent him tumbling across the cabin. I enjoyed doing that, but in truth I was probably just as scared as he was.

'Stop playing around and help me with this damn thing,' said Alucia as she pushed the suit through the doorway. 'This is no time for games.'

I helped her get the suit through into the cabin. She began to dismantle it, starting at its waist. 'Exactly how old are these suits?' I asked her.

'Don't ask,' she replied, frowning as she concentrated on her task.

'I wish you'd stop saying that to me.'

'Saying what?' she said, distracted.

'Don't ask.'

'What?'

'Exactly. I'll try again. How old are these suits?'

'Very old, but don't worry. They would have been maintained by the servo-mechs, kept in perfect working order, just like everything else in the Sprite.'

I wondered who maintained the servo-mechs as I went to fetch Ken, who was now floating helplessly near the control console and beginning to make the sounds of someone who was becoming very annoyed.

She was right about the amount of time it took to get the three of us into the suits. It proved to be an awkward, exhausting struggle before I was fully sealed in mine. It would have been hard enough in normal circumstances but in conditions of weightlessness, it was nearly impossible.

Alucia had carefully explained to us how to operate the keypad situated on the left forearm of the suits that activated the air supply, the radio, the temperature and various other doubtless useful functions. The latter included the simple controls for the small gas thrusters built into the suits. I experienced a moment of panic when Alucia locked my helmet into place, but the air supply came on immediately and I calmed down. Ken looked similarly panicked when Alucia helped him on with his, but he too managed to keep his alarm under control, like the warrior he was.

Alucia had also explained, at length, what the space walk to the emergency hatch would entail, before dropping into the lecture the information that the Sprite's airlock was too small for all three of us in our suits. I naturally asked her what an airlock was – I knew we'd been through one earlier, but I hadn't stopped then for a technical evaluation; now I just wanted to delay the moment of leaving the safety of our nice, comfortable Sprite.

It all made sense, I think. But what it *meant* was that she and Ken would go together first and I would have to follow on my own. I was less than pleased at the prospect, but I had to accept that Ken needed her assistance more than I did – I suppose I should have been proud.

The airlock was a circular chamber located at the end of the corridor where the suits were stored; once Alucia was sure I knew how to operate it myself, she and Ken entered and the curving door slid shut. Shortly afterwards a red light began to glow on a panel on the wall beside the door. I was already feeling cut-off and alone. Holding onto a support handle in the wall I waited, floating—

It may have been just a short time later, but it felt like years before I heard a series of indistinct sounds through the thick metal door. Then the red light went out and a green one began to shine. It was my turn now. I breathed deeply and pressed the button that opened the door, then pulled myself into the now empty airlock.

The top of the circular chamber was just slightly higher than the top of my helmet. I pressed the button on the control panel that closed the door, then, following Alucia's instructions, I pressed the button that vented the air out of the chamber. When the needle in the dial on the panel registered zero I knew it was now safe to open the upper hatch. I reached up and turned the wheel, and opened the hatch.

All I could see was Urba's hull 'above' me. Keeping a firm grip on the hatch's inner wheel with my left hand, to prevent myself from drifting out of the airlock, I pulled the end of the tether out of the reel attached to the side of the suit; reaching out of the hatchway, I managed to clip the metal catch on the end of the tether onto the metal ring that ran around the hatchway on the Sprite's outer hull. Once I was positive I was firmly secured, I took another deep breath and pulled myself out through the hatchway and into the void.

I was overwhelmed by several sensations at once. Ever since the Sprite had left Urba and we'd become weightless, the feeling that my stomach was surging up into my throat had stayed with me, though by now I was sort of used to it. This was different. As I looked around, I was seized by a violent sensation of vertigo. There was nothingness in three directions: it was like being suspended over a bottomless pit while, at the same time, seemingly suspended 'above' me was the vast, looming bulk of Urba. It was so big, the curving hull looked completely flat. I tried to fight the irrational fear that it was going to fall on me. I shut my eyes and drifted aimlessly. 'Whatever you do,' Alucia had told Ken and me, 'try not to throw up in your helmet.' Now I knew why she'd warned us, but it was easier said than done.

As I struggled to keep whatever was left in my stomach down where it belonged, I forced my eyes open and looked towards Alucia and Ken. They were about twenty-five yards away, upside down in relationship to me, their feet on Urba's hull. Alucia was looking 'down' at me and waving.

Then I heard her voice in my helmet: 'Jad, are you all right?'

'Oh, I'm fine,' I told her, 'apart from being terrified and feeling horribly sick. Other than that, it's a breeze.'

'Just keep looking at us and ignore everything else,' she advised me.

Simple. Why hadn't I thought of that?

'Now do as I told you and activate your thrusters system,' she said.

I pressed the relevant button on my suit's forearm control panel and immediately I was moving under power towards Urba's outer surface. My tether to the Sprite automatically unreeled from the side of my suit. I heard Alucia's voice again: 'Aim yourself towards us! Press the "S" button to increase the power in your starboard thrusters.' I did as she said. My course changed. I was now heading straight towards them. More or less.

'Okay, cut your power!' instructed Alucia. Using her own thrusters, she lifted – or dropped – away from Urba's hull to intercept me. It was a huge relief when she grabbed me and guided me towards Ken.

As the surface of the hull grew closer, she turned me over so that my feet were pointed at it. Alucia had told us that the soles of the suits' boots were powerfully magnetised, so I wasn't surprised when I felt a tug towards the hull's surface. 'Like I said before, Urba also has a gravitational field,' she said, back in lecture mode, 'but not a very large one. It would be different if Urba were a solid body rather than being mainly hollow: there's not enough mass to generate a gravity field of any use. We need the magnetised boots to overcome the outward force being exerted on us by Urba's rate of rotation.' I wondered whether any of this would ever make perfect sense to me . . .

I was now 'standing' beside Ken on the hull; 'above' us was the Sprite, now appearing upside-down. My vertigo got worse. I concentrated on not throwing up. 'Ken, how are you doing?' I asked him over the radio.

'Doing my best not to throw up,' he replied.

Alucia came to rest next to us on the hull. 'The emergency hatch,' she said, pointing at a circular door nearby. She made her way over to it, bent down and began trying to turn the wheel at its centre – without success. 'Damn thing is stuck,' she finally grunted. Her efforts had dislodged her magnetised boots from the hull and her legs were now floating free. She hung onto the wheel and managed to get her boots reattached to the hull. As Ken and I made our ungainly way towards her, I began to worry about what would happen if we couldn't get the hatch open. We'd be stuck out here on the outer hull—

'Okay, both of you get a grip on the wheel,' she told us. 'Turn it to the left . . . all together now.'

The wheel refused to budge. My feelings of anxiety increased.

'Keep trying,' said Alucia, breathlessly. I wondered what would happen when our air ran out—

And then, to my intense relief, the wheel began to turn. Soon the hatch was open and bright light was spilling out through it – which meant that the power hadn't been cut off again.

'Ken, you go first,' Alucia said, 'and remember, once you're inside and on the floor of the docking bay, you'll be subject to Urba centrifugal force again.'

Ken disappeared headfirst through the hatchway, assisted by Alucia. Then it was my turn. Even though I thought I was expecting it, the sensation of weight when I'd pulled myself 'up' onto the floor of the docking bay caught me by surprise. All of a sudden 'up' had become 'down' again. But at last the constant feeling of nausea was fading away.

Once we'd unclipped our tethers from our suits and pushed them out, she sealed the hatch. While I looked around, trying to get my bearings, Alucia, moving as fast as her suit would permit, rushed the length of what I soon recognised as the long docking bay, into the control room. Before long I heard a whooshing sound as air was released into the docking bay, filling the vacuum.

Then Alucia's voice came over our helmet radios: 'Right, you can remove your helmets now—'

Ken and I helped each other; as we joined Alucia in the control room I asked, 'What about the Sprite? Are you just going to leave it outside?'

'I suspect I don't have much choice,' she said as she moved across to a console and started pressing buttons. Peering at a screen, she said, 'It looks like the docking bay's computer system is refusing to communicate with the Sprite's computer system.'

'Why?'

'God knows—' She massaged the sides of her head with her hands. She looked very tired, which was understandable. 'Just give me a fucking break,' she said wearily, then gave me a quick smile of apology. 'Sorry. But I really haven't got a clue what the problem is right now. And I've got a pounding headache so any serious thinking is out of the question for the time being.'

'I'm starving,' announced Ken.

I realised that I was feeling extremely hungry too, now that the weightlessness nausea had passed. 'Would there be any food down here?' I asked.

'In the kitchen facility,' she replied. 'Fresh food stocks would have been automatically maintained by the servo-mechs. Any frozen food would have been spoiled when the power was cut, but there should be dried food and canned stuff that's safe to eat. But let's get out of these suits first.'

It took much less time to get out of the suits than it had to put them on; it helped a great deal that we were no longer in a weightless environment. Then Alucia led us into a kitchen that was all pristine whiteness. How different it was, I thought, to the kitchen in Lord Krader's castle; it was hard to even think of this sterile box as a kitchen. Thinking of the castle kitchen reminded me of Tiri who, I guiltily realised, I hadn't thought about for some considerable time. I didn't care to speculate why.

Alucia started searching through storage lockers and produced tins of stew, casseroles and curries. She emptied the contents of some of the tins into bowls and put them into a big oblong metal box. She called it a microwave oven, but it didn't look like any oven I'd ever seen.

Nor did it cook like any oven I'd ever seen! The food was ready to eat within a few minutes. She removed the steaming bowls from the oven with the aid of a pair of thick mittens and then we sat down at a table and dug in. I wasn't sure about some of the ingredients, or the taste, but food is food and at that point I would have eaten anything.

While we ate, Alucia said, 'There's a small dormitory down here as well. I don't know about you two but I'm going to bed as soon as I finish this. I'm shattered.'

Neither Ken nor I was feeling particularly tired, so we said we'd join her later. Before she left she earned my undying gratitude by finding a bottle of red wine and two glasses.

We drank the first glass of wine in silence. Then, as I refilled our glasses, I said to him, 'It's been quite a day. Or night. Or whatever.'

He looked at me and said simply, 'Yes, it has been.'

'How do you feel?'

He took a large swallow of wine and said, 'Better, now that we're out of that infernal machine and back in the world where you can tell the difference between up and down.'

I took a large swallow myself. I could feel tension growing between us. 'And how do you feel about everything we saw when we were . . . outside?'

'My senses took a serious battering,' Ken admitted. 'My mind is still reeling from it all.'

'But you finally accept that everything Alucia has been telling us is the truth?' I persisted. 'About Urba and everything else?'

He gave a bleak smile. 'I have no choice now, do I?'

I was encouraged by his reply. I'd been worried that he would try and explain it all away as some kind of Elite magic spell that had been worked upon his mind. 'Good,' I said.

'And once I'd got over the initial shock,' Ken continued, 'I found it very exciting. The way Alucia blasted the shit out of those alien bastards was tremendous. Serves them right for trying to invade us.'

I couldn't help smiling. Give Ken an enemy to focus on and he was back to his old self, despite having his whole world turned inside out. But then he said, in a serious tone, 'I know I behaved badly at times, Jad. Like when I refused to get on board the vehicle . . . and at other times during the journey outside.'

'Hey, I understand,' I told him. 'I was terrified the whole time myself.'

His expression became cold and I immediately realised I'd said the wrong thing. The air of tension increased. 'I wasn't scared,' he said stiffly. 'I was never scared. I was just . . . confused.'

I didn't know how to react to that. 'Confused . . . right,' was all I said.

'The point is,' he said, 'that I don't want you talking about my behaviour when we return to Capelia.'

'Of course I wouldn't dream—'

'Because if you did I'd be *extremely* displeased.'

I can be pretty thick on occasion, but I could *hear* the italics in Ken's voice – and I can always recognise a threat when I hear one. I said, in a tone positively dripping with sincerity, 'Ken, you know you can trust me. I swear I won't tell a soul.'

He gave me a long, lingering look and finally said, 'Good.' He poured another glass.

So did I. I really needed it.

To get the conversation on safer – well, slightly safer – ground, I said, 'Speaking of returning to Capelia, do you still intend taking Alucia back with us and marrying her?'

To my surprise, he looked completely taken aback by my question. 'Of course I do. Why would you think I've changed my mind?'

I picked my words carefully. 'Well, things seem a bit strained between you two now. I mean, there was that argument you had with her after the attack in the Compound . . . and since then . . . well—' I shrugged and said no more.

'That's all in the past,' he said firmly. 'Of course I still love her, and I *am* going to marry her.'

'Fine,' I said, thinking he was as crazy as ever. But then, I knew things about Alucia that he didn't. And I wondered how she felt about marrying Ken now. She would only do it if it were to her advantage; the question was, did she still need Ken? Or me, come to that. I wished I could explain all this to Ken, but I knew that it would be useless to even attempt it. Instead I topped up our glasses and prayed to the gods I certainly didn't believe in that everything would turn out right in the end.

Some hope.

CHAPTER TWENTY-ONE

The fortuitous discovery of a whole locker full of bottles of wine helped abate the tension between us even more. Once again I was reminded that the Elite had enjoyed their luxuries, even in a functional setting like the docking bay. By the time we'd started on our third bottle, we getting quite merry, the mental and physical shocks we'd so recently experienced almost forgotten. It was just like old times. When we'd finished the fourth bottle we'd wisely decided not to open a fifth and left the kitchen to find the dormitory. By that time exhaustion had caught up with us, not to mention the alcohol.

In the dormitory Alucia was sprawled, in her underwear, on one of the lower bunks. She was obviously in a deep sleep. I was half expecting Ken to crawl in next to her, which I didn't think was a good idea, but instead he climbed up to the bunk above. I collapsed on an adjacent lower bunk and rapidly passed out. I slept well, apart from a nightmare that briefly startled me awake: in the nightmare, I was falling helplessly through the endless void of space, and I knew that I would be falling through the blackness for ever—

When I woke again, I'd no idea how long I'd slept. I sat up and looked around. There was no sign of Alucia, but Ken was still asleep in the upper bunk. My mouth felt awful and I was very thirsty. I also had a terrible headache. I got up, deciding to leave Ken asleep. After a necessary visit to the toilet and bathroom facility, I went off to find Alucia.

She was in the control room, bent over a computer console; as I approached, she looked round and grimaced. I held up a hand. 'You don't have to say it. And I feel as bad as I undoubtedly look.'

'I could tell by the empty wine bottles in the kitchen that you and Ken had a party after I went to bed,' she said. 'Serves you right.'

'Yeah, yeah—' I noticed then that there was a half-full cup of coffee on top of the console. I knew it was coffee because it smelled like coffee. It was a great smell. I gestured at the cup and said, 'Is there any more of that?'

'There's a coffee machine in the kitchen,' she said, returning her attention to the screen. 'I'd show you how it works but I'm busy. However, it's very simple to use and I'm quite sure someone as bright as you will be able to figure it out.'

'Thanks,' I muttered, and headed for the kitchen, where I easily tracked down the aforementioned coffee machine. I was beginning to wonder if the Elite had machines for *everything*. It took me about twenty minutes to succeed in filling a cup with hot coffee; when I returned, Alucia was still in the same hunched position as when I'd left her.

'That took you less time than I expected,' she said without looking up.

'I'm even brighter than you think,' I said as I sat down in a chair in front of another console. I moved my chair closer to hers. 'How long was I out?' I asked.

'Over ten hours,' she replied. 'I presume Ken is still sleeping it off.'

'He was when I left the dormitory,' I told her. 'I've lost all track of time. How long is it since we left the surface? And what's the time now?'

'We left the surface nearly thirty hours ago. It's now Tuesday and it's just past midnight.'

'Midnight? I could have sworn it was morning.'

'Your body clock is out of whack. Being down here where there's no day or night is the main reason – that, and our little jaunt into space. All very disorientating.'

'It certainly is,' I said. I wanted to ask if she'd found out anything important, but there was something else I wanted to discuss with her first, before Ken woke and joined us.

'Alucia, before Ken and I got drunk last night . . . well,

whatever time it was ... we discussed you, amongst other things.'

'Good choice. I make an excellent topic of conversation,' she said, her attention still on the console's screen.

'Do you realise he still intends taking you back to Capelia with him? And he still intends marrying you.'

'How sweet.'

'Yeah,' I said, 'very sweet. The question is, what are *your* plans – assuming we survive whatever awaits us back on the surface. Do you still intend marrying him?'

She gave a slight shrug of her shoulders. 'It remains an option.'

'An option? Is that all?'

'Don't get all morally superior on me. I told you how I really felt about Ken. Nothing's changed. Besides, I have another reason for going to Capelia now quite apart from seeking a safe sanctuary.'

'You have?'

'That Sprite ship sitting below the Elite Compound in your hometown.'

'Ah, yes,' I said, remembering.

She stopped staring at the screen and turned to face me. 'What do you feel about it?'

'The Sprite ship?' I asked, puzzled.

'No, you idiot. The idea of me returning to Capelia with you and Ken.'

Completely at a loss, I said, 'What have *I* got to do with anything?'

'Come on, Jad. I know how you feel about me, even if you haven't fully admitted it to yourself yet.'

I sat there stunned. 'How I feel about you,' I repeated

'Yes, it's pretty obvious. It's been obvious for some time. You're obsessed with me. Even though you know what I am ... or rather, *was*. So what are you going to do about it?'

I sat there frozen, just staring at her. She stared back at me, her expression serious. My heart pounded. I knew she was right—

What might have happened next I don't know, because I heard the airlock door open and Ken say, 'What are you two looking so serious about?'

I turned, startled, as he walked into the control room. 'Uh,' I said, 'we were just discussing the Sprite ship underneath the Compound in Capelia—'

Ken went to Alucia, put a proprietorial hand on her shoulder, leaned down and kissed her on her offered lips. I felt a sharp pang of resentment. Then he straightened up and said, 'We have a perfectly good Sprite right outside.'

'And that's where it's going to remain,' said Alucia. 'There's no way I can get it back into the docking bay. The bay's computer system still refuses to admit it, for reasons I still can't fathom. I have a theory; I just can't prove it yet.'

'How come?' asked Ken, then noticed our cups. 'Is that coffee?'

'It is indeed,' said Alucia. 'Want some?'

Ken grinned. 'Yes, but I'd like a cup of coffee too.'

Alucia laughed and stood up. 'Come on; I'll make you one.'

Seething with emotions I had yet to identify, though jealousy was definitely prominent amongst them, I picked up my own cup and followed them as they headed for the kitchen. They were acting as if everything that had occurred between them the previous day hadn't happened. The problem was, I knew that Alucia *was* acting.

As they stood together at the coffee machine, Ken draped his arm around her shoulders while she made him a cup of coffee. I sat at the table and watched, still seething. Her words of only a few moments ago kept running through my mind. She was right. I was obsessed with her; had been for a long time. And the obsession had increased over that time, despite everything I now knew about her past. And I hadn't fully admitted it to myself until that moment. But I couldn't help thinking, knowing her as I did – or as I *thought* I did – that she might be using me in much the same way she was using Ken. At the same time, the possibility didn't seem to be that important. I was simply consumed with an overpowering need for her—

I broke into my own riotous thoughts and asked, 'So what's your theory about the Sprite problem?' Part of me genuinely wanted to know the answer, but the question was mainly prompted by a desire to interrupt the game of happy couples she and Ken were playing.

She stopped giggling at some private joke they were sharing and looked at me. 'Just let me finish with this and then I'll tell you what I think.' Then she had the audacity to wink at me!

When the coffee was brewed, they sat down together on the opposite side of the table to me. 'Okay,' said Alucia briskly, 'this is pure speculation but it's possible it's all to do with me making the mistake of downloading the records of the exploration of the last planetary system into the Sprite's computer. Apart from alerting the AIs to our presence, I might also have provided them with the opportunity to insert a virus into the Sprite's computer. And now the docking bay system thinks the Sprite is tainted and doesn't want anything to do with it.'

'What's a virus?' I asked.

She sighed. 'Think of a computer virus as a very small bug, except that it consists of information rather than solid matter. A bug basically buggers up a computer. Understand?'

'Would it make you feel better if I said I did?' I asked.

'A lot better.'

'Then I do.'

'Me too,' said Ken, feeling left out.

'Okay,' said Alucia, 'I'll pretend I believe you both and continue. I've isolated one of the docking bay's computers from the rest of the system and established a link with the main computer on the Sprite to try and discover just what the bug that's corrupted it was designed to do. But so far no luck. The computer here is still trying to find out—

'Somehow, the aliens corrupted the AIs in the same way. My theory is that when Urba entered that last planetary system twenty-five years ago and sent out the robot probes to survey the planets, the aliens captured one of the probes for a brief period, inserted their bugs, and then released it. It's not uncommon for probes to malfunction or lose contact with Urba for various reasons when they're exploring a system. The probe returned to Urba and its data was downloaded by the AIs and the alien bugs invaded their systems. The result: the AIs were now working for the aliens, though no Elite technician was aware of what had happened. And don't ask me how the aliens achieved this. Their computer technology must be superior to ours.'

'You're saying this happened twenty-five years ago?' I asked.

'That's my theory. I can't see any other opportunity the aliens had to gain access to the AIs.'

'Twenty-five years,' I said, puzzled. 'Why did they wait this long before taking action against us?'

'I don't know for sure,' she replied. 'Maybe it took them that long to analyse everything about the human inhabitants and their society and devise a plan of attack. Maybe it took them years to design and build their war machines. Then again, maybe they're really *slow* when it comes to doing anything—'

I frowned. 'What do you mean?'

'It's another of my theories. I could be talking complete bollocks, but I've got this feeling they live at much slower rate than human beings. That means their perception of time wouldn't be the same as ours.'

I gave her my blank look, which I was becoming pretty adept at. In return, she put on her look of exasperation, which she was even more accomplished at, as she wore it while trying to explain something to me. Or Ken.

'Well, let's say that they march, or rather, crawl, to the rhythm of a different drummer than we do. Do you understand?'

'Sort of,' I said. This time it was true. 'You're saying they don't move at the same rate as we do.'

She nodded gratefully. 'Or think as fast . . . or *live* as fast. To them, humans must be racing around like actors in a piece of speeded-up vid footage.'

'Right,' I said, encouragingly. Once again I hadn't a damn

clue what she was talking about: speeded-up vid footage? Sometimes I wondered if we were even the same species . . .

She sighed again. 'Okay, useless analogy. But you get my general drift?'

'The aliens are slower than us.'

'Right. It explains something that puzzled me during our attack on the control centre. When I stupidly accessed the central computer system, the AIs would have instantly alerted the aliens to the fact that a ship had been launched from Urba and that it presented a potential threat, yet when we reached the centre, the alien ships were just sitting there. The logical tactic would have been to place the ships in a protective formation above the centre. Maybe that's what the aliens planned to do, but they hadn't got around to doing it. Same with the alien mothership. No defences had been activated by the time we fired on it. If I'm right, it gives us a real advantage in dealing with them.'

'You mean,' said Ken, 'that in a face-to-face fight their reflexes would make them useless as opponents?'

Alucia smiled at him and squeezed his arm. 'Exactly!' She was reacting as if he'd just said something amazingly profound, whereas in truth all that had happened was that he'd finally caught up with the gist of the conversation. May the gods give me strength, I thought sourly.

'The problem is, though,' said Alucia, 'the opportunity to confront them face-to-face might never arise. And their machines, as we know, are *not* slow.'

'What effect do you think destroying the AIs has had on their killer machines?' I asked.

'I'm not sure,' she admitted. 'Ideally, if they were under the direct control of the AIs, they've been completely deactivated. But if their on-board computers were acting independently, then they're still functioning as before. Let's hope the latter isn't the case.'

'Yes, let's,' I agreed.

'But we won't know until we return to the surface and find out at first hand,' she said, ignoring my sarcasm.

'Do we have to? I was rather hoping I could spend the rest of my life down here. Or at least until the food and wine run out. It's quiet down here ... and peaceful.' Actually, I was only half-joking.

'We're going to have to go back upstairs sooner or later,' she said. 'Might as well be sooner.' She yawned suddenly. 'Sorry. I've been up for hours working while you two party animals slept it off. I'm going to grab a few hours' more sleep before we leave. But first I'm going to have a shower—'

'Shower?' Ken interjected.

'Yes, a shower. It involves taking your clothes off and getting wet. You'd love it.' She sniffed at him and made a face. 'And you could certainly do with one.' She stood up and pulled on his arm. 'Come on ... we'll have a shower together.'

After a token display of reluctance, Ken allowed himself to be led out of the kitchen. He flashed me a quick grin as they left. It didn't improve my mood.

'Damn it,' I muttered to myself, and proceeded to wallow in self-pity for a time, then I got up and made myself another cup of coffee, which I took back to the table, sat down and wallowed in self-pity again. Then I began thinking about food.

About half an hour later I finally sat down with a bowl full of steaming – something or other. The first two attempts had resulted in bowls full of incinerated food; I'd obviously made a mistake with the controls on the Elite oven. The third attempt had produced something that looked and smelled edible, so I was feeling pretty proud of myself.

I was waiting for it to cool down before I began eating when I heard the sound: a persistent, high-pitched beeping. I wondered idly what it was. At first I tried to ignore it, but it seemed to possess an urgent quality. It was probably just my imagination but ...

I got up from the table and walked through to the control room. The beeping got louder; it was coming from the computer that Alucia had been working on. I went over to it and looked at the screen. The word WARNING in big red letters was flashing on and off in time with the beeping.

I have, as noted before, a mind like a steel trap. It only took me several seconds to realise that WARNING spelled TROUBLE. I ran as fast as I could to the dormitory and bathroom facilities; the dorm was empty. I started to panic – well, to panic even more – when I heard the sound of running water coming from the bathroom. I threw the door open and rushed inside. The room was full of steam. Alucia and Ken were both naked under the 'shower'. In normal circumstances, their activity would have both embarrassed me and made me very envious. But these were not normal circumstances.

Ken naturally reacted angrily to my unexpected entrance, shouting, 'Jad, what the hell do you think—'

I cut him off sharply, crying, 'Alucia, that computer you were working on – it's flashing a warning sign and beeping! I think there's something seriously wrong somewhere!'

Alucia gracefully disengaged herself from Ken and ran past me, pausing only to grab a towel from a wall rack. Ken, his expression murderous, stepped out from under the spray of water and said to me, 'Jad, if this is one of your "jokes", I'll kill you.'

I handed him a towel. 'No joke, Ken,' I told him. 'I only wish it were.'

By the time we reached the control room, Alucia was already furiously punching at buttons. She looked grim. And beautiful. The towel was loosely tied around her waist and her small but perfectly formed breasts drew my eyes like a magnet. But I looked away as I asked, 'Is it serious?'

She wiped wet hair from her eyes with one hand, still punching buttons with the other. 'Couldn't be any more bloody serious,' she said. 'Ken, go and grab our clothes and weapons. We don't have much time.'

'What's happened?' he asked.

'Don't just stand there,' she snapped at him, 'get our gear! Hurry!'

This time Ken obeyed, and ran out of the control room while Alucia kept staring at the screen. Then she shook her head and said softly, 'Shit.' She looked at me. 'I don't think we're going to make it.'

CHAPTER TWENTY-TWO

'What's going on?' I asked, a solid lump of cold fear forming in my stomach.

She didn't answer, but headed straight for the airlock. I followed her through the docking bay to the door that led to the elevator. She had turned the wheel on the door and it swung open as Ken appeared at the run, his arms clutching a bundle of clothing and weapons. As he ran, the towel tied around his waist came adrift and fell to the floor. He stopped, bent down and tried to pick it up—

'Leave it!' commanded Alucia. 'No time!' She shoved me through the doorway and into the chamber. 'Open the hatch to the elevator, quickly!'

I scurried up the short ladder and did as ordered, then pushed the hatch open and climbed through. I looked back down. Ken, encumbered by his gear, was climbing the ladder with difficulty. Alucia was already sealing the chamber door. I reached down and relieved Ken of his burden; he climbed, naked, into the elevator, closely followed by Alucia. Her towel was still tied precariously around her waist. Despite the obvious urgency of the situation, I couldn't help feeling stirred: she was an incredibly beautiful woman.

Oblivious to my prurient thoughts, Alucia slammed the hatch shut, sealed it and then frantically jabbed at two buttons on the wall of the elevator. Immediately we began to rise. Fast.

'Will you please tell me what the problem is?' I asked as she and Ken sorted through the clothing on the floor and started dressing.

'It's all my fault,' she said, her expression grim, 'I should have anticipated something like this.'

'Something like *what*?' I asked, exasperated. Exasperated and very scared.

'The bug in the Sprite inserted by the AIs,' she said, as she pulled on her leggings. 'It was a booby-trap. A fail-safe plan by them in case they failed to take over direct control of the Sprite. The computer in the docking bay finally deciphered its purpose—'

'A booby-trap?' I definitely didn't like the sound of that. 'What kind of booby-trap?'

'A big one,' she said, unhelpfully.

I gave a start as a loud clanging came from below the floor. Then my ears popped. 'What was that?'

'Just an emergency buffer hatch closing,' said Alucia, 'one of many that will close after we've passed them. *If* we pass them.'

I was going to ask her again about the nature of the danger we faced when the floor suddenly jumped and we were all sent flying off-balance. We collapsed in a heap together. Then came a sound of thunder so loud that I thought my eardrums were about to burst. At the same time the lights in the elevator flickered and dimmed to near darkness. And then we began to rapidly descend. The rapid descent became a fall. I was convinced we were about to die.

I wasn't alone in this. 'May the gods save us!' I heard Ken cry.

But we didn't die. The floor stopped falling beneath us and we slowed to a gentle stop as the lights in the tube returned to their full strength. Then we began ascending again.

'Jesus Christ . . . we actually made it,' sighed Alucia. She was lying on her back, across Ken's legs, and I was lying on top of her. She was still naked from the waist up. I realised I had a serious erection; whether it was due to my intimate facial contact with the bare flesh between her breasts or as a reaction to the close brush with death I didn't know. Perhaps it was a combination of the two.

'Would you get the fuck off me,' growled Ken from the bottom of the heap.

We untangled ourselves and got unsteadily to our feet.

Alucia said wonderingly, 'The hatches below us maintained their integrity. A bloody miracle.'

'Are you going to explain what just happened,' I asked, 'or do I have to strangle you?' I gave what I hoped was a menacing glare.

She smiled and resumed dressing. Ken was doing the same. He said, 'Yes, Alucia, tell us what made that hell of a noise.'

'A small fusion reactor going over the top and beyond,' she said.

'Perhaps you'd be kind enough to translate into plain Ango, please,' I said.

'The bug the AIs planted in the Sprite's computer system caused the ship's power source to self-destruct,' she told us. 'The explosion has no doubt completely destroyed the docking bay area. The damage would have been far worse if the Sprite had been *in* the docking bay. Even so, we're lucky to have survived.'

I felt a chill spread through me. 'The AIs, or the aliens, were taking a serious risk, weren't they?' I asked. 'They might have blown a hole right through the hull.'

She shook her head. 'No. The blast wouldn't have penetrated all the way to the interior. The aim was to destroy the Sprite, the docking bay and everyone who happened to be in either location.'

'Devious bastards,' muttered Ken.

'Yes,' she agreed. She'd finished dressing now and was putting on her weapons belt. I did the same.

I frowned as something unpleasant occurred to me. 'Alucia, can you be certain that the new computer systems running Urba now haven't been infected with any kind of alien bug?'

'The new systems would only have been activated when the AIs were destroyed so I'm ninety-nine per cent certain they're completely clean,' she said.

'But not a hundred per cent certain?' I said.

'No,' she admitted.

We stayed in the basement area of what remained of the Elite building until daylight. Then, weapons at the ready, we cautiously went up the stairs and climbed out through the opening we'd cleared. The Compound appeared deserted. The bodies of our would-be attackers still lay where they'd fallen. All was eerily silent.

Constantly scanning the area as we moved, we headed for the air-car. There we got proof that no one had entered the Compound since our one-sided fight with the group of armed scavengers. The car hadn't been damaged during our absence and our supplies of food inside were undisturbed. We boarded the vehicle and Alucia soon had it rising into the air.

'Where do we go now?' I asked her.

'We look for the nearest alien machine,' she replied.

As the air-car sped through the sky I stared around. I was seeing the world differently now I knew the great curves of the landscape rising up on either side in the distance were the interior of a vast man-made cylinder speeding through a limitless void. I shivered. My world had suddenly become fragile, a vulnerable thing despite its size.

During the next few hours we passed over several groups of people travelling along the roads and tracks. They stopped and stared up at us; I could imagine what they were thinking when they saw an Elite air-car flying over their heads: a mixture of fear, confusion and anger. I wished we could land and ask if they'd seen any of the alien scorpion-machines, but that would have been suicidal.

It was around noon when we first spotted a scorpion-thing: it was in a lake. Only its upper section and its great tail were visible. At first it was completely stationary, but as we circled above it, at what I hoped was a safe distance, it began to stir, apparently reacting to our presence. I felt a stab of fear as the deadly tip of that great tail pointed in our direction, but nothing happened. Though it continued its feeble movement, it remained where it was.

'It looks as if it's stuck,' observed Ken.

'There's definitely something seriously wrong with it,' said

Alucia. 'If it were functioning properly, it wouldn't have blundered into that lake. A good sign, I'd say.'

'What should we do?' I asked her.

'This.' She put the air-car into a slow dive towards the alien machine. My stomach lurched. As we dropped dangerously near the machine, she fired the beam-cannon. The beam hit the tail near the tip; there was an explosion and the end of the tail sheared neatly off and toppled into the water, quickly sinking from sight. Then we were rising again.

'Even it manages to get out of the lake, which I sincerely doubt it's capable of doing,' she said, 'it will no longer be a threat to anyone.'

I wasn't so sure about that, but as I looked back at the machine its struggles became even weaker.

We flew on at speed and soon the lake and its crippled alien inhabitant were far behind us. Alucia said, 'Now let's see if we can find another of the bastards. We've got to make sure that wasn't just a one-off event—'

It took us an hour to find another of the giant killing machines. This one was moving erratically through a forest. As we hovered some distance away, it soon became obvious that the thing was walking in a tight circle, blindly crashing into trees as it moved.

Alucia gave a whoop of delight. 'One fucked-up machine doesn't prove anything,' she said cheerfully, 'but *two* fucked-up machines changes everything! It's beginning to look as if our attack worked like a dream: the machines have been neutralised.'

'They still looks dangerous to me,' I observed gloomily. We passed directly over the stricken scorpion-thing for the second time. Its tail didn't even acknowledge our close proximity. Alucia started firing the beam-cannon down into the thick woods below. Flames were soon visible as both trees and underbrush caught fire. I quickly caught on to Alucia's plan; before long the awkwardly moving alien machine was surrounded by fire. As we watched, it kept colliding with burning trees that fell either on top of it or under it. Its progress was rapidly slowed. Then, a few minutes later, it came to a dead stop in the centre of the raging forest fire. Its legs gave way and it collapsed.

Alucia kept the air-car circling high above the inferno. Even so, my eyes began to stream as we were subjected to hot air and smoke. 'How much longer are we going to remain here?' I asked her.

'Not much longer,' she replied, sending the air-car diving towards the inferno. As she fired the beam-cannon at the stricken machine, it blew apart; the force of the massive explosion severely buffeted the air-car. I felt sick all over again.

'Now we can go,' she said with a triumphant grin as we rose again and began to speed away from the blazing forest.

'It's as I hoped,' she told us. 'The aliens were using the AIs to directly control the war-machines. With the AIs and the control centre no more, the machines are on their own, and they lack enough on-board intelligence to act independently of their masters. They still pose a threat, but nothing like as before. They can be picked off one by one.'

We encountered a third scorpion-thing late in the afternoon. It had partly fallen into a large ditch, but this time it was no accidental mishap: it was surrounded by a large number of soldiers who were attacking it with catapults, burning oil and anything else they could lay their hands on. It was obvious by the other deep ditches dug in the vicinity that a trap had been laid for the blundering machine.

Those on the ground were too occupied to notice our hovering air-car as we watched their actions. 'Someone has shown initiative in getting such a large group of men organised so quickly,' observed Alucia.

'They must be remnants of Lord Camarra's army,' said Ken. 'No other forces would be in the area. Perhaps Camarra himself is responsible—'

'Camarra is dead by now,' said Alucia quickly. 'He must be.'

'Then maybe the man behind this counter-attack is Lord

Megus,' I said, 'which, from my point of view, is even worse.'
His penchant for hanging, drawing and quartering had stuck
in my mind like a thorn.

'Only if we fall into his hands again,' she said, 'which we
won't. In the meantime, it doesn't matter *who* is organising the
resistance, just as long as *someone* is.'

We continued to watch the activity on the ground as the
scorpion-thing was slowly but systematically destroyed. Occasionally it fired the deadly beam from its tail, but it didn't
appear able to aim, so the ray went harmlessly into the sky.
After a time I suggested we move away before we were
spotted; I didn't fancy being a target for their pot-shots at us –
nor did I relish being hit by accident by the alien monstrosity.

But scarcely had I finished my plea than the pit was rocked
by an explosion. As we stared down, we saw one of the
catapults fire an object at the machine that exploded when it
impacted against its side.

'An explosive device,' murmured Alucia, almost admiringly.
'Humanity's discovered how to make bombs again. Amazing
how quickly the old skills of mass destruction are relearned
. . . We might as well go now. The outcome is inevitable. Like
death and taxes.'

She sent the air-car speeding forward again.

'Now what?' Ken asked.

She shrugged. 'Find a secure place to make camp and then
discuss what our next move should be.'

That sounded good to me. I was starving. 'And what do you
think our next move should be?' I asked her.

She glanced at me. 'Return to the Citadel and see if we can
find out what the remaining aliens are up to.'

I immediately lost my appetite.

We made our camp on the top of a densely wooded hill. There
were none of the alien war machines in sight and we hadn't
sighted any armed human forces for several hours, so we felt
reasonably secure. Over a meal of heated beans and cold,

heavily spiced sausage, washed down with warm beer, Alucia repeated her desire to return to the Citadel.

Ken was adamant that we should head back towards Capelia, while our luck still held.

'I agree with Ken,' I told her. 'We've been pretty lucky so far. Going back to the Citadel would be seriously pushing that luck. The machines aren't much of a threat any more and they're being taken care of.'

'But they're just one threat,' she said, practically. 'The real threat is still out there. We're the only ones who really know what's going on. People probably think the same as Lord Camarra did: that the machines are some Elite secret weapon. They have no idea there are aliens out there; it's up to us to find out as much about the aliens as we can.'

'What are you suggesting?' I asked. 'That we try and *capture* one of them?'

'I don't know,' she said, 'we'll just have to play it by ear and see what develops.'

'Play it by ear?' I said. 'Well, my ears are already picking up a serious message. It says – get the hell out of here while we can.'

'As I'm with Jad on this,' said Ken, 'it's two to one against you. So you lose. We go to Capelia.'

She smiled at him. 'It's a bit late in the day for you to discover the democratic process, your royal highness.'

Ken frowned. 'Democratic process? What's that?'

'Something that was denied to your people a long time ago, my pretty young Prince. Which means that you two do as *I* say. I'm sure you're more familiar with the workings of dictatorship than that of democracy, *your highness*.'

'What?' said Ken.

She remained adamant, delivering her trump card: she was the only one who could operate the air-car, and therefore she was the one who would decide in which direction it would go. I had to admit she had a good point. I mean, she could tell Ken and me that we were en route to Capelia when we were actually heading towards the Citadel and neither of us would be any the wiser until we got there.

We were trumped.

Ken continued trying to persuade her to see sense after we'd all turned in for the night but pretty soon his heated whisperings turned to heated sounds of another kind. I tried to deafen my ears, but it was no use.

Finally all was quiet and I began to drift off. Then I felt fingers on my lips and I came fully awake with a start. 'Wha—?' I began.

'Shush,' I heard Alucia whisper in my ear, 'it's me. Don't make a sound.' She took hold of my hand, gave it a tug. In the feeble light of the dying campfire I got up and quietly went with her into the trees. When we were a fair distance from the camp she stopped and turned to me. 'It's time we had a talk,' she said softly.

'What about Ken?' I said. 'When he wakes and finds you gone—'

'He won't wake,' she assured me, 'he's in a deep sleep. After all, he's had a very eventful and stressful day.'

'Haven't we all?' I said.

She moved closer. 'And it's not over yet.'

'What do you want to talk about?' I asked as my heart began to beat alarmingly fast. 'To convince me that your desire to return to the Citadel isn't sheer folly?'

'Desire is the subject of our discussion, true, but it doesn't concern the Citadel,' she said. Then her lips were on mine. We kissed for a very long time, her tongue fiercely probing my mouth. I threw myself into the kiss enthusiastically; the next thing I knew, we were on the ground, frantically removing each other's clothing. What followed was more like a fight to the death than an act of lovemaking—

But as I entered her, a small voice in the back of my mind reminded me I was entering territory that had only been recently vacated by Ken, my best friend, my Prince – but I squashed that small voice like a bug. I also squashed the thought that I might be having sex with a woman who was over three hundred years old.

Her body thrashed beneath me as I thrust violently into her; one of us was moaning loudly. I think it was me . . .

Then she suddenly went completely still. For a moment I thought I might have hurt her, but she whispered urgently, 'Listen! Do you hear anything?'

'No.' All I could hear was the pounding of blood in my ears.

'It sounded like the jingle of a horse's harness,' she said.

'I can't hear a thing,' I said, anxious to the point of desperation to continue what we'd begun. Then I heard a faint clink of metal too. 'Shit,' I muttered. 'You're right. Horses, and more than one of them.'

CHAPTER TWENTY-THREE

We quickly disengaged ourselves – to put it politely – and frantically gathered up our clothes. I was torn between fear and utter, *cosmic* disappointment. Clutching our clothing, we started to run back towards the camp, until an unwelcome thought trickled into my otherwise occupied brain. I grabbed Alucia by the arm and pulled her to a halt.

'Wait,' I said, 'we've got to get dressed—'

'No time! Those horses are *close*.' She tried to pull free of my grip.

'You want to explain to Ken why we're both naked?'

'Oh shit . . . but hurry!'

In the darkness we struggled to dress. Alucia was right about how close our unwelcome visitors were. Now I could hear the familiar snorting of horses and the whisper of human voices; it sounded like they had us surrounded. Carrying our boots, we hurried to the camp.

'I'll load the air-car,' I told her, 'you go and get Ken.' I was already throwing our gear and supplies haphazardly into the air-car.

Alucia woke Ken and quickly filled him in on our possibly unwelcome visitors. He was instantly on his feet, Elite weapon in one hand and a crossbow in the other. He looked eager for a fight.

'No!' said Alucia urgently. 'We don't know how many there are; we've got to go.' She started pulling him towards the air-car. I'd already climbed into it, wishing desperately I knew how to operate the thing.

With a show of reluctance, Ken allowed himself to be led by Alucia to the car.

'Hurry up, you moron!' I cried in exasperation. 'We're surrounded!' The sounds were growing louder. Our visitors had given up on stealth.

At last Ken climbed into the car. Alucia sat herself at the controls. The air-car began to rise –

– just as mounted troops emerged from the trees all around us. They wore the black and silver uniforms of Lord Megus's men. All were carrying crossbows. 'Duck!' I yelled as we and the air-car became the target for a swarm of bolts. Several thudded into the vehicle; others whizzed just over our heads as all three of us ducked down. Then Ken stood up and fired both his crossbow and the Elite weapon. I remained crouching, so I didn't see what happened, but from the screams below us he'd evidently got a result with both weapons. The air-car continued to rise, somewhat jerkily. I heard more bolts thud into it and held my breath. But we kept going upwards then forward, until, eventually, Alucia declared us out of range.

I risked a look over the side of the car, which was bristling with bolts, and saw the dark shapes of several scores of mounted soldiers in the woods behind us. 'Set the whole place alight with your damned beam-cannon!' Ken shouted at Alucia. 'Fry every last one of the bastards!' – this from the man I'd heard only recently admonish Alucia for her cold-blooded use of Elite weaponry.

'Can't risk doing that,' Alucia replied. 'From the way this clapped-out heap is handling I think we've sustained further damage. Best to put as much distance between us and them as possible.'

These words cheered my heart – the words about getting far away, that is, not the words that suggested that the air-car might fall out of the sky at any moment. 'Where in hell did they suddenly spring from?' I asked. 'There was nobody in sight before we made camp.'

'We were spotted earlier in the day, weren't we?' said Alucia. 'By those troops we flew over.'

'Yes, but we must have travelled more than fifty miles since then,' I pointed out. 'They couldn't have possibly caught up with us so quickly, not on horseback.'

'Different group of soldiers,' she said. 'They'd been informed of our course by the previous group, who estimated how far we would have travelled by nightfall and knew roughly in which vicinity we'd probably make camp. The local group were ordered to make a search . . . and they found us.'

'But *how* were the local forces told about us?' asked Ken.

'After we'd taken off back then,' said Alucia, 'I spotted an officer talking into an Elite communicator. One like I had when I was caught by those vigilante bandits—'

'You're saying those troops were *Elite?*' I interrupted, aghast.

'No, you idiot,' she said, 'it means that Lord Megus's forces are now utilising Elite technology. Not a good development: that definitely does not bode well for us all.'

The rest of the night was spent in uncomfortable silence. Once again most of my thoughts were occupied with images of that grisly process known as hanging, drawing and quartering. The rest of the time I dwelt bitterly on the unfairness of Fate: to be so rudely interrupted while enjoying what promised to have been one of the high points of my entire life was almost unbearable.

Daylight arrived and we still hadn't fallen out of the sky. But my relief was short-lived.

'Jad,' said Ken in a tone of voice I knew spelled bad news, 'there are a couple of things we need to discuss.'

I looked at him. He was regarding me with an expression I also knew from experience spelled bad news. 'What are they?'

'Is my recollection correct that back at the camp you called me a *moron?*'

'Did I?' I said, feigning innocence. 'I honestly don't remember. If I did I apologise humbly. Heat of the moment and all that.'

'Apology accepted,' he replied. 'Now perhaps you could explain why you're wearing Alucia's jacket.'

I looked down. My long, bony arms protruded quite a long way from the sleeves of the leather jacket I was wearing – a jacket I now realised was uncomfortably tight across my back. A jacket I now saw was very short on me. In panic, I looked quickly at Alucia.

She quickly looked away.

I looked at Ken. He looked at me. With narrowed eyes. 'Well?' he said, coldly.

I shrugged – which wasn't easy to do in such a tight-fitting jacket. 'Well, in all the confusion I must have snatched it up by mistake,' I said. 'I didn't even notice it didn't fit until you mentioned it. I've had other things on my mind since we took off.' Yes, indeed. Being hung, drawn and quartered, and the memory of Alucia's writhing body beneath me . . . Even Ken would have to admit both counted as major distractions.

Ken looked at me for a long time. Then he nodded, and said, almost to himself, 'Yes, that's the only possible explanation.'

Whew, I said to myself. Thank the gods, I thought, that Ken found the very idea of Alucia and me together completely absurd; the thought of us getting sexually involved was unthinkable. I took off Alucia's jacket and handed it to her, then sorted through the various articles of clothing strewn about on the deck of the air-car and found my own jacket.

'That's better,' I said with a guileless smile as I put it on.

'Notice anything unusual about the land we're flying over now?' Alucia asked us some hours later.

We looked down at farmlands, fields of wheat, barley and corn. Fields with grazing sheep and cows. Burned-out farm buildings. No people. This whole area had been ravaged by the alien machines. 'No,' answered Ken and I in unison.

'The crops and the farm animals have been left untouched,' she pointed out. 'The machines have only targeted humans and their buildings. Which bears out my theory.'

'Which theory was that?' I asked. 'You have so many theories I've kind of lost track.'

'That the aim of the aliens was to conquer Urba, leaving all the food resources as intact as possible,' she said. 'The aliens are running out of everything. They're hungry.'

We'd set down earlier by a stream near some woods, to have lunch and to give Alucia the opportunity to check out the fresh damage to the air-car.

'Looks like a porcupine,' I'd commented as I walked around the vehicle. There were about thirty bolts protruding from the so-called armoured shell of the car. Alucia had opened the panel at the rear and was peering at the mechanism within as if she knew what she was looking at. Ken wandered down to the stream. I stood next to Alucia and scanned our surroundings. I felt a little nervous. We hadn't seen a soul, but after the events of last night that no longer meant anything.

'None of the bolts have penetrated the drive's housing,' she said, head still inside the panel, 'but one or more of them might have buggered up the fibre optics leading from the controls. I'd have to dismantle the whole air-car to find out what the problem is, and there's no way I can do that. We're just going to have to hope that this thing gets us as far as the Citadel.'

'Why not try and make it to Capelia instead?' I asked.

'We'd never make it.' She withdrew her head from the rear of the car. 'Citadel's our best hope.'

'What good would it do us to be stranded there?'

'We won't be. Remember there are plenty of air-cars on the Citadel's upper levels.'

She was right. I'd forgotten about that.

By then Ken was in the stream and splashing water on his face. It was a hot day. Even though he was a good distance away I kept my voice low as I said, 'About last night—'

She looked at me with unreadable eyes. 'Yes?'

'Well, uh . . . I was having a really good time,' I told her lamely, 'before events took a sudden turn for the worse.'

'I'm glad to hear it.'

'Yes, well . . . did you too? Have a good time, I mean. With me.'

'It was certainly interesting,' she said, her tone infuriatingly blank.

I began to feel annoyed. 'Are you playing some sort of perverse game with me, Alucia?'

Her eyes widened with pretended surprise. 'Why would you say that, Jad?'

'Never mind,' I said, and walked away from her. Women!

Ken was returning from the stream, dripping water as he came. He saw the expression my face and said, 'What's up?'

'This bloody air-car, hopefully,' I muttered.

As nightfall approached we looked for another suitable landing place. We still hadn't seen any sign of human life though we did spot a dragon high above us; the sight of our Elite air-car caused it to fly off at speed. We set down for the night on another hill, but this one was treeless. It seemed very unlikely that we would have any unwelcome guests during the night, but as an added precaution we agreed not to light a fire. That meant no cooked food. Worse still, we'd run out of beer. And wine.

Again, after we'd bedded down, I was obliged to listen to Alucia and Ken being intimate with each other. But this time there was no subsequent visit from Alucia. Why wasn't I surprised?

We took off early next morning, after an unappetising breakfast of cold beans and stale bread. Alucia estimated that if the air-car held out, we'd reach the Citadel that afternoon. I noticed we were moving even slower than before.

Alucia's estimation turned out to be correct; it wasn't long before we saw the great tower of the Citadel looming in the distance, although we didn't appear to be getting any closer to it. 'At least it's still standing,' said Alucia, hopefully.

All three of us kept a lookout for any activity, human or otherwise, on the ground, but we saw nothing. Even so I was feeling increasingly nervous. That old familiar sense of dread was back, with a vengeance.

I also felt hot. I looked up at the long column of the sun overhead. Was it brighter than usual, or was that just my imagination at work? I was reminded of what Alucia had said, about how the pre-Elite had brought all of Urba to its knees, and suddenly I felt cold. 'Why do you think it's so hot today?' I asked her.

'Because it's a hot day here,' she said, giving me a look that suggested I'd asked her one of my more stupid questions.

'That's a really stupid question, Jad,' said Ken.

'Alucia, tell me again how the sun works,' I said. 'It's made up of hot gases held in place by some invisible energy force, right?'

'More or less.'

'So you think the heat today is perfectly normal?' I asked.

'Yes,' she said, a little impatiently. 'Jad, is there a point to all this?'

'You told me that the Elite once shut the sun off.'

'That was a long time ago. And it wasn't the Elite, but their predecessors, the technocrats.'

'But the Elite retained the power to control the sun?'

'Yes,' she admitted. 'So?'

'So what if the aliens now control the sun? What if they've begun using it as a weapon against us?'

She laughed, then told me to relax. 'The aliens are no longer in control of anything in Urba now,' she said.

'But they did have that power?'

'In theory, yes. Before I blew up the control centre. And the AIs.'

'But what,' I said earnestly, 'if the computers that have replaced the AIs have been infected by a similar bug that caused the Sprite to blow itself up?'

A shadow passed over her face. She frowned. 'You're suggesting some sort of self-destruct order placed in the system that would come on line if the invasion attempt failed?'

'I am?'

She kept frowning. 'A sort of "If I can't have you, no one will" approach to the situation?' She seemed to be talking to herself now rather than to me. 'Not very logical, but a very human thing to do. Which would mean the aliens are more like us psychologically than I thought—' Then she shook herself and said, 'But it's very unlikely, if not impossible, that they had the time to do anything along those lines. Like I told you before, I'm ninety-nine per cent certain that the new system that's kicked in is a virgin when it comes to potential alien contamination.' She gave me a reassuring smile that failed to convince. 'No, Jad, an interesting idea, but I wouldn't waste time worrying about it.'

But I noticed that afterwards she kept casting surreptitious glances towards the sun.

We arrived at the outer wall of the Citadel and flew over the burned-out remains of Camarra's siege encampment, then Alucia guided the air-car in a slow circuit as we scanned the vast grounds between the wall and the central tower for any sign of the alien war machines. There wasn't any.

There were, however, plenty of charred bodies, of men and horses, and the shattered remains of the several smaller scorpion-things that we ourselves had destroyed.

We started to ascend as Alucia attempted to reach one of the Citadel's landing platforms, but it began to look as if our air-car had finally given up.

'The car isn't capable of absorbing enough of the transmitted energy to fully power our electromagnetic field generator,' Alucia said through gritted teeth. 'And those landing pads are designed for fully operational air-cars—' She fought with the controls, almost willing the vehicle along as we inched upwards, slowly, to one of the lowest landing pads. After what felt like hours we landed on it with a bump. I was quite sure the air-car had breathed its last. We sat there expectantly for a time, weapons at the ready, waiting for something to happen. Nothing did.

Then we climbed out of the vehicle. I looked around. The landing pad was a semi-circular ledge protruding from the side of the tower, like the pouting lower lip of a giant. There was a large open doorway in the wall of the tower. We all stared warily towards it, but still nothing emerged. All was silent. As Alucia had promised, there were other cars parked on the pad; I prayed to the gods I had never really believed in that they were all in fully working order, in case we needed to make a speedy getaway.

Ken, carrying both his crossbow and his hand-gun, moved towards the doorway; I turned my attention to the other direction and walked to the edge of the landing pad. A thin railing was all that stood between me and a sheer drop of about three hundred feet. I stared across the grounds towards the distant outer wall. Alucia joined me.

'You expecting to see an army rolling towards us?' she asked, half-seriously.

'I don't know what to expect any more,' I said, which was an honest answer.

'Not much chance of Lord Megus's forces turning up here so soon, or anyone else's,' she said. 'Besides, everybody thinks the Elite have regained control here.'

'Even if they do, I don't believe the Elite carry the same air of omnipotence any more,' I said. 'Not since the Day of Wonder. Look at the way Megus's men attacked an Elite air-car.'

'True,' she said, 'but a force approaching the outer wall at any point other than the breach created by Camarra's army are in for a reminder of how deadly the Elite were.'

'Why?'

'Because with the power restored, the automatic defences have been reactivated.'

'Oh,' I said. That hadn't occurred to me. 'How come they didn't fire on us?'

'They wouldn't fire on an Elite air-car, you twit.'

'Nothing beyond that doorway but a big room containing a few air-cars,' said Ken, coming up behind us. 'What are you looking at?'

'Just admiring the view,' I said. Then something far away in the grounds caught my eye, an object moving near the middle of a large area that was different from the rest of the gardens.

There were long stretches of flat grass, bounded on both sides by shrubs and trees. Each one ended in a circular area of a different kind of grass. Obstacles lay in front of each of the latter; pits of sand and small lakes. I couldn't make out the details of the object from this distance, but it was red in colour, and moving slowly along one of the stretches of grass. I pointed towards it as I said to Alucia, 'What's that?'

'Oh,' she said dismissively, 'that's just an automatic lawn mower. It's mowing the golf course.'

'It's mowing the what?'

She sighed. 'The golf course. A course on which you play golf.'

'What's *golf*?' asked Ken before I could.

'Golf is a game. You play it by hitting a ball down the fairway with a club until you reach the green. Then you use a different club to try and get the ball into a small hole on the green. See those flagpoles? They mark the positions of the holes in the greens. The aim is to complete the course using as few club strokes as possible.'

'Why?' asked Ken.

'Why what?' she asked him.

'Why go to all that bother? What was the point of it?'

'No point. You did it just for the sheer fun of it all. And it was supposed to relax you.'

'And did it?' I asked her. 'Relax you?'

'No. The few times I played golf I became anything but relaxed.'

Ken and I exchanged a glance. 'You Elite really were weird,' I told her.

She sighed again. 'Tell me about it.' She turned from the railing. 'Come on. Let's go and look for aliens.'

I immediately decided I'd prefer to learn how to play golf.

CHAPTER TWENTY-FOUR

Weapons at the ready, we went through the doorway and into the large room that Ken had already scouted out. As he'd said, it contained a number of air-cars. On the walls were tools of all descriptions. A couple of those spider-like machines I'd seen in the Sprite's docking bay were standing immobile by one of the tool racks.

'This is a hangar,' said Alucia. 'Air-cars are both stored here and repaired.' She led the way to a pair of closed doors at the rear of the room and regarded them doubtfully.

'Elevator,' she said. 'It would take us all the way to the lower levels, but I don't think that's a good idea. No telling what nasty surprise we might be facing when the doors open. Be best if we proceed down on foot. Carefully.'

'Definitely the better option,' said Ken.

'In my opinion,' I said, 'the best option would be to get into one of the fully working air-cars and get as far away from the Citadel as possible.'

'No,' said Ken, 'let's see this through.' I don't know when it had happened, but Ken had switched sides and was now backing Alucia on this mission of utter foolhardiness. I guess his blood-lust was up again or something. Maybe he wanted an alien head to hang in his father's trophy room. If the aliens *had* heads, that is . . .

'Actually, Jad has a point,' said Alucia.

My hopes leapt upward. At last, someone was taking my advice seriously – the gods were surely in a state of shock. 'We leave?'

'No,' she said, 'we take one of the air-cars down to ground level.'

My hopes sank again. The laughter of the gods rang in my ears.

We walked back onto the landing pad, where Alucia selected a car at random. A short time later we touched down on the ground, right in front of the gaping hole in the side of the Citadel from where the alien war machines had made their exit. We surveyed the hole. I expected another of the monstrous scorpion-things to emerge at any moment – but I consoled myself with the thought that there were no sounds at all and we would have heard it coming. It was silent. It was also dark. It was as if we were at the mouth of some sinister cavern, a cavern that led downwards to only the gods knew where. Except there wouldn't be any gods at the end of this cavern—

'I have an idea,' said Alucia, with a distinctly forced brightness.

'We flee now?' I asked. An optimist to the last.

'No. We take the air-car inside. Into the hole. Go down as far as we can. We'll have the advantage of the car's firepower—'

'That makes sense,' said Ken.

'No it doesn't,' I said, to no avail.

The air-car lifted a couple of yards from the ground and moved slowly towards the gaping maw. Then we were inside the Citadel, in a landscape of utter devastation. My stomach fluttered nervously. The huge hole led downwards at a sharp angle, shattered masonry and twisted metal on all sides. There were still no sounds apart from the reassuring hum of our own air-car. No signs of any movement either, thank the gods. We kept descending.

'How far down do you think this goes?' I asked Alucia.

She shrugged. 'Don't know. Depends on what level they set up their base.'

Peering over the side of the car, Ken said, 'I see some lights flickering down there somewhere.'

Alucia surprised me by laughing. 'So there's light at the end of the tunnel?' she said and laughed again.

I failed to see what was funny.

We kept going down until, as we passed another floor level, Alucia stopped the air-car's descent and manoeuvred it out of the hole and over a section of sloping floor.

'Making a temporary detour,' she said. The vehicle touched gently down.

'What's the problem?' I asked as I looked around. We were sitting on what remained of some sort of concourse from which radiated several wide corridors. Lights shone feebly in some of the corridors.

Alucia was already climbing out of the air-car. 'There's an armoury on this level that contains something that will come in handy. Very handy. Come on, Ken, I'm going to need help.'

'What about me?' I asked plaintively as Ken followed her out of the car.

'Stay here and guard the vehicle,' she told me over her shoulder. 'Yell if there's trouble. We should be able to hear you.'

'Oh sure,' I told her, 'that's if I have *time* to yell.'

The pair of them disappeared into one of the corridors. The sound of their footsteps died away. I sat there uneasily in the subsequent silence. After a time I decided I'd feel less vulnerable moving about, rather than just doing my imitation of a sitting duck. I got out of the car, Elite weapon in my hand. I moved warily across the sloping floor to the edge of the huge hole and stared down into it. Like Ken, I could see an intermittent glow at the bottom of it, but I couldn't tell how far away the bottom actually was. Then a large chunk of the floor fell away from the edge close to where I was standing and I hurriedly stepped back. Some time later I heard the debris land at the bottom of the hole. It made a distant crashing sound that echoed hollowly.

I realised that I'd done the equivalent of announcing to whatever was down there that we were up here. Stupid.

I went, very quietly, back to the air-car. I climbed into it and sat there, very quietly. Eventually I heard Alucia and Ken returning along the corridor; when they emerged onto the concourse, I saw that Alucia was lugging two metal cylinders that looked heavy and Ken was weighed down with three mysterious packs. They set down their burdens beside the air-car.

'What is this stuff?'

'Our secret weapon,' replied Alucia. 'Anything happen while we were gone? I thought I heard a sound.'

'No. Nothing happened,' I lied.

'Good. Come and put one of these things on.' She was opening up the packs. She produced what appeared to be a suit, made of a flexible grey material. The helmet was transparent and attached to the front of the suit were two canisters that I assumed, correctly, as it turned out, was some sort of breathing unit.

'Why do we have to wear these?' I asked.

'They're anti-contamination suits,' she said. 'If we use the poison gas in those cylinders we'll need the suits to stay alive. Satisfied?'

'Completely,' I said, taking the suit from her. It took some time to don the loose-fitting suits, following Alucia's instructions; the helmets hung loosely from the back of our necks as she said we didn't need them yet.

After loading the cylinders into the car, we lifted off and drifted over to the hole, then began our descent again. There was still a glow of light at the bottom of the hole, but the flickering had stopped. I thought that odd. I wondered, somewhat guiltily, if I should mention the chunk of debris falling into the hole – not that I'd pushed it or dropped it deliberately, or anything. I decided against it.

'Jesus Christ!' exclaimed Alucia.

There was that name again. We'd emerged out of the bottom hole into a vast, cavernous space. Judging from her reaction, Alucia obviously was caught by complete surprise. Extending from the edge of the hole was a ramp of metal lattice-work that went all the way down to the floor. The whole area below us was dimly lit, but there was enough light to provide a fair degree of visibility in all directions. What particularly caught my attention were several sections of the alien killer machines lying around. There were other large machines, also in sections, that I hadn't seen before. Scattered around everywhere was a variety of equipment, and lots of huge metal containers. There were also a large number of the smaller scorpion-things that had originally attacked Lord Camarra's forces. To my relief, nothing appeared to be moving.

'Christ, the lousy shits have been busy down here,' said Alucia, disgustedly. 'They've combined at least three levels and extended them. Built themselves a bloody factory. Part of this was the genetic laboratory complex ... the bastards have wiped out an irreplaceable genetic library—'

'No sign of any aliens,' said Ken, sounding disappointed.

'Thank the gods for small mercies,' I muttered. I couldn't help wondering if my accidental dislodging of that section of masonry had served to alert them, and as a result they were all in hiding. I again considered passing on this piece of possibly important information to the others, but I continued to hold my tongue.

Big mistake.

The car continued to descend.

'A strong smell of ozone in the air,' commented Alucia. 'There's been some kind of electrical activity here only recently.'

Ken sniffed and said, 'To me it smells like an unwashed codpiece.' His powers of description were always unique.

We hovered above one of the unfinished scorpion-things as Alucia peered closely at it. 'They transported the machines from their mothership in sections and assembled them here,' she said. 'Impressive.'

The uncompleted monster was surrounded by all manner of mysterious smaller machines. 'Looks as if they were in the process of putting this one together when they got interrupted,' observed Ken. 'Probably when you blew up the control centre.'

'Yes,' said Alucia, slowly. 'But this one looks different from the others we saw. It has modifications.'

She moved the air-car over to one of the large, unfamiliar machines. As I looked down at it, I tried to make sense of the disassembled sections. I decided that once all the pieces had been put together, it would have looked like one of the sea creatures that the sailors caught for sport during our journey on the *Black Swan* – they'd called it a manta ray. I presumed the long tail section would have served the same deadly function as the tails on the other machines.

'It doesn't have any legs,' I said observantly.

'It's a flying machine,' said Alucia. 'These were to be the next stage of their invasion. Only three here so far. I guess our attack on the control centre and the AIs also cut off their delivery system.'

She sent the air-car moving on. Ken, eyes narrowed as he scanned the area reported, 'Still no sign of any movement.'

'It's possible there are no actual aliens in here,' said Alucia. 'All this could have been done by their robot machines under the supervision of the AIs.'

'Glad to hear it,' I said, sincerely.

We hovered over a circular structure some twenty yards in diameter. 'A new hatch system, courtesy of the aliens,' said Alucia. 'Big enough to transfer all this stuff down from the surface of Urba. But it looks as if it's automatically sealed itself. Probably happened when those missiles detonated deep under the control centre.'

'Are those what I think they are?' asked Ken.

I looked in the direction he was pointing: large heaps of what looked like armour and clothing, close to the hatchway.

'Let's take a closer look,' said Alucia, taking us down again. To my alarm, she set us down on the floor, next to one of the heaps of clothing.

'Is this wise?' I asked. 'I mean, landing? We'd be safer staying in the air.'

'I don't believe we're in any danger, Jad. There don't appear to be any aliens here and all their machines are now inert.' She and Ken started to climb out of the car.

'Uh, maybe there's something I should mention to you,' I muttered.

She paused and said, 'What?'

'Oh, nothing important.' I took a deep breath and followed them. We went over to the nearest enormous pile. It did indeed consist of clothing, chain-mail shirts and leggings, breastplates, helmets, boots and gauntlets. The clothing was all in shreds and stained with blood. We stared at the huge heap in silence for a while, until Alucia said, 'I would guess all these belonged to Lord Camarra's missing soldiers—'

'Not just them,' said Ken. He bent down and pulled a black and scarlet tunic from out of the pile. He held it up. It was very familiar: an Elite tunic. It was also in shreds. I glanced at Alucia. Her face was expressionless.

Ken bent down again and rummaged further through the edge of the heap. 'There're more of them in here.' He pulled out another Elite tunic, displayed it briefly, and threw it back on the pile contemptuously.

I looked at the other mountainous heaps of clothing. If you added up all the Elite who'd been in the Citadel, together with the two armies Camarra had sent in here, you were dealing with several thousands of people. So . . .

'So where are all the bodies?' I asked aloud.

'I think I know,' said Alucia.

Then I noticed something really strange. 'Look at this,' I said, walking over to what appeared to be a large heap of horseshoes. It *was* a large heap of horseshoes.

'What do you make of it?' I asked as the others joined me. 'What happened to all the horses?'

Alucia said, 'The same thing that happened to all the bodies of the people. They were transported back to the alien mother ship.'

'Why?' I asked.

'Work it out for yourself,' she said curtly and walked off.

We kept exploring the area, but there was no sign of life,

human or alien. I paused by a curious-looking machine which stood about nine feet tall: it consisted of four large jointed legs from which was suspended an egg-shaped metal body. There was an egg-shaped section of black glass set in the front of the body. Standing on my toes, I tried to see through the glass but couldn't. Four flexible metal arms extended from the sides of the body, ending in big, claw-like appendages. I guessed it was some kind of worker machine used to construct the bigger machines.

I headed back towards Alucia and Ken. 'Can we go now?' I called out.

They both looked in my direction. Then they both pointed their guns in my direction. For one dreadful moment I thought they were going to shoot me. 'Hey, what the f—?' I began in alarm.

'Behind you!' yelled Ken.

I looked over my shoulder. The machine I'd been examining had come to life; it was slowly turning to me.

'Shoot it, Jad,' cried Alucia, 'you're the closest!'

I stood frozen to the spot as the machine began to walk towards me.

'Shoot,' yelled Ken, 'we can't – you're in our line of fire!'

I finally unfroze and fired, but the Elite gun appeared to have no effect on the machine. It just kept coming. I fired again, aiming this time at the section of black glass, which shattered, then there was an eruption of fire from the machine's interior. Something *alive* inside the egg-shaped body of the machine made a low-pitched wailing sound. I turned and ran.

I put on a burst of speed. Alucia and Ken had already reached the air-car; I practically threw myself in as it began to rise. I looked back at the burning machine, which walked blindly into the side of one of the big machine sections and fell over. Then the dim lighting in the place began to get even dimmer.

I heard Ken say, in an alarmed voice, 'What the hell is happening?'

'The place is beginning to wake up,' Alucia replied tersely. 'I was wrong. There are still aliens here. We've walked into a trap.'

As the car rose higher, another of the four-legged machines appeared from behind one of the nearby giant containers. Ken and I simultaneously opened fire. 'Aim for that black glass!' I cried, and sighed in relief when the same thing happened: the glass, or whatever it was, shattered and our beams ignited the interior. Again came that strange, unsettling wailing sound – then a third appeared.

The nose of the air-car dipped as Alucia activated the vehicle's beam-cannon, blasting the machine into fiery fragments. She fired again; a blinding flash was followed by a very satisfactory explosion. When my eyes had adjusted to the sudden glare I saw that one of the containers was ablaze.

Alucia kept firing; soon there were fires everywhere. The glow of the flames from two of the vast heaps of clothing lit up much of the area below, but there was no sign of any more of the four-legged machines – or anything else, thankfully.

'Hang on,' Alucia warned, 'we're getting out of here. Fast.'

We sped towards the hole in the ceiling. We didn't make it.

Something slammed into the rear of the car and there was an explosion. After that it was all confused. The car came down with a bone-jarring impact and tipped over on its side, skidding along the floor. That's when we parted company and I was suddenly freewheeling through the air, this time on a solo flight.

I slammed face-down onto the floor, stunned and winded. I could neither move, nor draw breath. As I lay there helpless, vainly struggling to breathe, a puddle of something warm and wet was forming around my face: blood. My blood.

All was silent for a time; I don't know how long because I lost consciousness. Then I heard Alucia's voice: 'Jad? Ken? Are you still alive?'

I tried to answer but I still couldn't breathe. Then I heard Ken say in a strained voice, 'I'm alive, but I can see Jad and he's not moving. He might be dead—'

I'm not dead, I silently protested, *I just can't breathe—*

'What about you?' Ken called to Alucia.

'Banged up my ribs and my knees,' she called back, 'otherwise I'm fine. Can you see anything else in the vicinity?'

A pause and then Ken replied, 'No, nothing.'

Then I heard someone coming towards me. Friend or foe, I wondered? A hand gripped me and turned me over on my back. Ken's face loomed into view. Blood trickled from cuts on his forehead and face. 'He's alive!' he called to Alucia, then he tried to sit me up. At long last I managed to draw in a breath through my mouth. Then I looked down and saw that the front of my suit was covered in blood.

'Where's all this blood coming from?' I croaked, still breathless.

'Your nose,' said Ken. 'It's squashed flat. Anything else broken?'

'My nose?' I gasped. I touched my nose tentatively. It *was* flat. I sucked in more air through my mouth and experimentally moved my limbs; they worked, but my chest felt very painful. The breathing apparatus might have broken some ribs when I hit the floor. Then I saw Alucia limping towards us. Like Ken, her face was covered in blood.

When she reached us, she and Ken helped me to stand. I looked around and saw, some distance away, the air-car, which lay on its side in a crumpled heap. 'What happened?' I wheezed. 'What hit us?'

'Some sort of missile,' said Alucia, as she looked about us apprehensively. 'Fortunately not a big one, otherwise we wouldn't be having this conversation. We've got to get those cylinders out of the car. You two still got your guns?'

Neither Ken nor I had. Alucia's was in her holster. She drew it as we staggered over to the wrecked vehicle, then handed it to Ken. 'You see anything moving at all, you shoot it,' she told him.

'Would I do anything else?' he replied grimly.

'Help me,' she ordered as she began to drag one of the metal cylinders out; despite the pain in my chest, which was growing worse by the moment, I grabbed the other one and hauled it out.

We were both startled by the sound of Ken firing the weapon, but we could see nothing.

'Thought I saw something moving out there,' Ken explained.

I expected to see another of the four-legged machines, but there was nothing in sight.

'We've got to get away from the air-car!' said Alucia urgently, and made for one of the huge alien containers; we'd barely reached it where was an explosion behind us. I looked back and saw that the air-car was burning. 'Another missile,' said Alucia redundantly. We took cover behind the container.

Ken announced he could see nothing. 'Where the hell are those missiles coming from?'

'Just fire blindly,' Alucia told him as she slumped with her back against the container.

Ken fired again. And this time he got a result: that weird sound again, a cross between a moan and a scream.

'You hit an alien?' I asked Ken eagerly as Alucia and I quickly moved to peer out from our cover.

'I hit *something*,' said Ken, 'but I can't see what.'

About twenty yards away something was burning but I couldn't make it out, until I saw, briefly, a slowly writhing shape outlined by the flames. It was the source of the strange, chilling sounds.

I looked at Alucia. 'What is it?'

'An alien,' she replied, her expression rapt as she stared at whatever it was we were staring at.

Ken said, 'But I can't see it!'

'No,' she said, 'you can't.'

Astonished, I said, 'Are you saying it's *invisible*?'

'No. I'm just saying you can't see it.'

'There's a difference?'

'Yes.'

The flames died away. So did the awful sounds. I could now make out a shapeless mound and some twisted metal.

'Ken, keep firing,' ordered Alucia.

She returned her attention to the cylinders.

'What's happening?' I asked.

'We're being rushed by the aliens – albeit a very *slow* rush, but a deadly one nonetheless. They haven't registered our new position yet, but they will. We can't stay here much longer.'

Ken kept firing, but there were no more horrible sounds so I presumed he hadn't hit anything else.

A thought occurred to me. 'Why don't we attempt to communicate with them?'

'How do you suggest we do that?' she asked. 'Wave a white flag?'

Ken laughed and said, 'I *am* communicating with them. I'm shooting at them! You can't give anybody a more direct message than that. I just wish I could *see* the bloody things! I keep seeing things moving out of the corner of my eye, but when I look directly at them there's nothing there.'

'So aim out of the corner of your eye,' Alucia told him.

He fired again. 'Aha,' he cried, 'got another of the bastards.' And to confirm his words, that awful, low-pitched moaning sound echoed around us.

'Their equivalent of screaming,' said Alucia.

'I remember now what you said about these creatures being slower than us,' he said to Alucia. 'Why don't we just keep firing at random until we've wiped them all out?'

The container shuddered violently as something slammed into the other side of it and a sheet of flame rose upwards. We were almost thrown off our feet by the force of the explosion.

'That's one reason,' said Alucia. 'The second is that we don't know how many of them there are. And the third reason is that we have a much better weapon at our disposal than the one you're holding. But first we've got to get away from here. They've found us again.'

She picked up one of the cylinders. I picked up the other one, trying to ignore the pain in my chest that was definitely growing worse by the minute. The effort of lifting the cylinder caused black spots to dance before my eyes. We moved away from the container, which was now on fire, and headed to the hole.

'We put some distance between us and them,' panted Alucia, 'then take cover again—'

'Good plan,' said Ken, 'but what if there are more aliens ahead of us?'

'Then we'll soon find out.'

We kept moving, Ken firing at invisible targets as we went. He didn't hit anything.

'Over there,' said Alucia finally, pointing at a large, black apparatus that resembled the central section of a giant armadillo shell with a cluster of metal tubes protruding from each end. I couldn't begin to imagine its function, but it didn't do badly as a cover – at least, remembering what Ken had said, I *hoped* we were behind it rather than in front.

'Now it's time,' she said. She patted the cylinder she'd set down in front of her. 'This contains a gas called CGN, very lethal. Breathe it and you're dead. Let even a tiny droplet touch your skin and you're dead—'

Ken and I looked at each other. Neither of us said anything.

'But don't worry,' she went on, 'these suits will give us full protection. And the gas becomes harmless after thirty minutes, which is good news for us because the air supply and recycling units on these suits are only good for about fifty minutes.

'After we've released the gas we return as fast as we can to the hole and climb up the ramp to the next level. In theory the suit material is impenetrable, but take care during the climb anyway.'

'Where do we go once we get onto the next level?' I asked. 'There's no way we can reach the hole in the level above that one.'

'We won't have to. There are other means of access from that level onwards: stairs, a clever invention which the Elite can't claim the credit for.'

'Oh. Stairs. Right.' I'd forgotten all about stairs.

'Now,' she continued, 'we put on our helmets, like this, and seal them, like this—'

We followed her example; she checked the seals and, her voice muffled now, pronounced them secure. Then she showed us how to switch on the suits' air systems.

'Next,' she said—

'Duck!' yelled Ken.

We all ducked, just as something whooshed overhead and exploded as it hit a wall some distance away. The problem was that the missile, which it presumably was – look how au fait I was getting with all this new stuff – had come at us from an angle, not from the other side of what we were 'sheltering' behind. We were exposed.

'Shit,' said Alucia, 'let's move.'

I grabbed one of the gas cylinders, Alucia picked up the other one and we moved off again, Ken firing fruitlessly in the general direction of the missile's source.

We'd gone about fifteen yards when Alucia, panting, said, 'Okay, this'll do. We've got to release the gas fast.'

I put down my cylinder with relief; my chest felt like it had been kicked by a horse. Several times.

'What if the aliens are wearing suits like this with their own air supply?' Ken asked her.

'No reason they should be,' she said, 'but if they are we're fucked.' She squatted next to one of the cylinders and used a key of some kind to unlock the valve mechanism, then she turned the handle on the valve. There was a hissing sound. I don't know what I was expecting to see – a cloud of ominous-looking vapour, perhaps – but there was no visible evidence of anything happening. The second cylinder got the same treatment, then she stood up and said, 'That's it.'

I waited expectantly. Nothing.

'Let's go,' said Alucia.

Leaving the cylinders where they lay, we headed for the ramp, less than forty yards away. But we hadn't gone very far when it started: the same awful sound as before, but this time from several sources. A chorus of low-pitched wailing grew louder and louder, echoing throughout the whole area.

We stopped and listened as the nightmarish wailing continued from all around us. I couldn't stop shuddering; I knew I would be hearing this sound in my dreams for a long time to come . . .

I heard Alucia, in her muffled voice, say, 'I guess this proves they aren't wearing self-contained suits after all.'

The grisly death-agony chorus began to fade away, thank the gods; we started moving again, as fast as we could. I, for one, couldn't wait to get out of the place.

That is, if we *could*.

CHAPTER TWENTY-FIVE

I was beginning to feel more than a little drunk. The tavern was crowded and the air in the big room was becoming uncomfortably warm. The rising temperature only increased my thirst and I gestured to one of the serving girls for another round of beers.

Alucia shook her head. 'No more for me just yet; I haven't finished this one.' She indicated the large pewter mug on the table in front of her. She spoke in an unnaturally low voice because she was pretending to be a man again. With her hair shaved to a stubble and a smear of charcoal on her cheeks and chin to suggest the beginnings of a beard, she looked to me to be a beautiful young woman with close-cropped hair and smears of charcoal on her face. But then, I was biased. So far her disguise seemed to have been effective as far as other people were concerned. Maybe it was the fake scar running down her left cheek.

All three of us were in disguise: Ken and I had reverted to our mercenary cover, no longer on our way to join Lord Camarra's army; now our story was that we were deserters *from* Camarra's army. Originality was not our strong point. However, with my newly acquired broken nose, I felt I looked more the part than I had previously.

We were in Tarantio, Parthus Domain's central town. Though it lay well beyond the range of the alien war machines and had escaped invasion, it had since been swamped by refugees from the affected areas, as had so many other domains. Of course, no one but us knew the true origin of the machines; most people believed it had been a last ditch effort by the Elite to re-conquer Urba; that had been enough to renew the hunt for Elite survivors, so Alucia had to be particularly careful. This time, though, there was not the slightest danger that I would betray her out of pique.

Despite the flood of refugees, many of them actual deserting soldiers and thus heavily armed, Parthus remained relatively stable, politically speaking. Its ruler, Warlord Heider, had managed to keep control after ruthlessly putting down one short-lived revolt. With the threat of the killer machines now neutralised, the big fear on everyone's mind, and no doubt on Heider's, was that Lord Megus, who had apparently stepped into Camarra's boots, would carry on with Camarra's plan of world conquest. However it was generally understood that Megus was still occupied with reorganising the remnants of Camarra's scattered forces, along with his own, and had yet to begin his military campaign.

It was to pick up information like this that we had stopped at Tarantio – that, and the rare opportunity to sit in a warm tavern, eat hot food and get drunk. The serving girl returned and deposited three fresh mugs of beer on the table, an action that involved her displaying a spectacular amount of cleavage. I found the sight immensely cheering.

'I told you I didn't want another beer,' muttered Alucia when the girl had left.

'Don't worry, I'll drink it,' I assured her, my eyes still on the departing girl. She was a very shapely young thing. I looked at Ken. He too was watching her progress through the crowded room. His eyes were hooded, which I knew from experience meant that he was as drunk as I was. Then he rose unsteadily from his chair.

'Got to use the latrine,' he announced far too loudly.

'Can you repeat that?' I said. 'I don't think they heard you in the castle.'

'As a jester you're as piss-poor as ever,' he told me and lurched off, but I noted that instead of heading for the door that led outside to the latrine, he was on a course to intercept our serving girl. Bastard.

'Will you be returning to your old job when you get back to Capelia?' asked Alucia.

I looked at her. It wasn't easy because I was having trouble focusing. 'What?' I said, stupidly.

'Your old job. As court jester. Remember? Isn't that what you used to do?'

I considered her words, which also wasn't an easy task in my current condition. 'Oh yes,' I said, 'it was.' It all seemed so long ago now.

'So? Will you pick up where you left off?'

'I don't know,' I said truthfully. I really hadn't given the matter any thought. 'Doesn't really appeal to me any more.' I leaned over the table. 'To be honest,' I said in a conspiratorial whisper that, like Ken's latrine proclamation, could probably be heard by everyone in the room, 'I wasn't a very good jester.'

'Really? You amaze me.'

I gave her a suspicious look. Her expression was serious, but she didn't fool me. 'You're laughing at me, aren't you?' I said accusingly.

'Someone has to.'

'Hmmphh,' I snorted and leaned back in my chair, my feelings ruffled. I began to suspect I was drunker than I'd thought. I turned my attention to Ken. It took a while to locate him, but then I spotted him by the bar. He was chatting to the serving girl. She was smiling.

'How much for the boy?'

The voice, a rough, low baritone, took me by surprise. I turned my head and saw, when I'd refocused my eyes, a large man with a large red beard looming over our table.

'Pardon?' I said.

'I asked you how much the boy would cost,' said the large man.

I frowned as I tried to understand what the hell he was talking about. Then it finally occurred to me that he was referring to Alucia. 'Oh,' I said, 'he's not a—' I stopped because Alucia had kicked me sharply in the shin.

'He's not a what?' asked the man.

I was at a loss, but Alucia said firmly, 'I'm not for sale.'

Without turning to look at her, he said, 'I wasn't talking to you.' He kept his gaze on me. 'So, how much for ten minutes out back with the boy?'

'Hmmm,' I said slowly, 'let me think.' Then, 'How about one silver piece?'

Alucia kicked me again under the table. It was beginning to bruise.

'Are you kidding?' said the large man. 'What's he got? A gold-plated arsehole? I'll give you half a silver piece.'

'Done!' I said and offered him my hand. He shook it and grinned.

Alucia kicked me again. 'Are you mad?' she demanded angrily. I grinned at her.

The big man began to turn towards her. She looked alarmed. I said to him, 'But there's just one thing you should know—'

He turned back to me. 'What?'

He leaned down as I gestured and whispered something into his ear. 'Eurrkk!' he exclaimed. He straightened up, said curtly, 'The deal's off,' and hurried away.

Alucia, looking relieved, was staring at me. 'What did you say to him?'

'I told him that the last time I buggered you I got a nasty disease that could only be treated by having a red-hot wire inserted up my urethra.'

'Thank you.'

I shrugged. 'It was the least I could do. Of course, there was always the danger that he was someone who'd *enjoy* having a red-hot wire inserted up his urethra.'

'True,' she agreed, and picked up her mug of beer. She took a long drink. Then she said, 'You bastard.'

I laughed. 'Speaking of bastards—' I looked for Ken. There was now no sign of him. No sign of the serving girl either. I pointed this out to Alucia. She didn't show any concern.

'So what?' she said.

'So the love of your life is off somewhere making all sorts of squishy noises with a gorgeous serving girl and you don't care? As great romances go, yours and Ken's would drive minstrels to cut their wrists.'

'Ken is right about you. As a jester you really are piss-poor.'

'Aren't you at least worried that he might pick up a nasty disease?'

'If he does, then having a red-hot wire thrust up his urethra will be the least of his worries.'

'Underneath your cold exterior you're just a big softie,' I told her.

She grunted.

I drank more beer, burped noisily and refocused my eyes on her. 'You asked me if I intend to resume my less than glittering career as a court jester when we reach Capelia—'

'I did.'

'So what about you? What are you going to do in Capelia?'

'Marry Ken. Become part of the domain's ruling family. It's a role I was born to play.'

'Yeah,' I slurred, 'but like you say, it will be just a role. You're just like one of those travelling players we met, acting all the time. What will you be really doing?'

'If you're lucky I might be doing *you* . . . when Ken isn't watching.'

'That isn't funny.' I said. 'You know how I feel about you.'

'*You* don't even know how you feel about me. And please don't start becoming the maudlin drunk. It's boring.'

'Right. Point taken.' I drank more beer. 'But seriously—'

She rolled her eyes upwards until only the whites showed. It was a scary sight, and even sobered me up a little. 'Please don't do that,' I said.

Her eyes returned to normal.

'When I used the word "seriously",' I told her, 'I wasn't referring to us, but to you and Capelia. Or rather, you and Ken's family.'

'Go on.'

'I don't believe that his esteemed parents, either Lord Krader or Lady Kalina, are going to be thrilled when Ken turns up at the castle gate with you as his bride-to-be.'

'Oh? And why not?'

'Ken is their only son and they tend to be overly protective of him. No woman will ever be good enough for their beloved Prince Ken in their eyes.'

'I'll overcome any initial animosity they may feel towards me,' she said, confidently. 'I can be very beguiling, you know.' She fluttered her eyelids at me.

'Take it easy, *boy*, or you'll attract more rough trade,' I cautioned. 'I know only too well how beguiling you can be. But you have another obstacle in your grand plan to marry Ken. He's already betrothed. To Princess Petal—'

Alucia looked taken aback. '*Princess Petal?* What kind of a stupid name is that?'

'It is a pretty stupid name, isn't it? Blame her parents, they're rulers of the Arcalia domain. The same parents who came to an arrangement with Ken's parents years ago. Ken and Petal are to marry, sooner or later. And both domains take this sort of thing very seriously. As you would know, as the Elite probably started the custom.'

'Yes,' said Alucia slowly.

'Surely Ken has already mentioned his arranged marriage to you?'

'No, he hasn't. I am quite certain I would remember a name like *Princess Petal*.'

'Well, that's the situation. How are you going to handle it?'

She stared pensively into the middle distance for a time, then said, 'I'm not sure yet, but I'll think of something. Anyway, I'll have Ken on my side. If he insists on marrying me, there's not much his parents can do to stop us.'

'Don't be too sure about that. You haven't met them yet.'

'I'll deal with the problem somehow. Anyway, It's all purely academic at this point. First we have to actually reach Capelia.'

It had been nine days since we'd left the Citadel; we'd used an air-car and travelled mostly by night. By day we'd hidden our vehicle as completely as possible, then either made camp nearby and remained there all day or, if it seemed safe, travelled into the nearest village or town to acquire both fresh food and, hopefully, information. Our decision to extend our visit to Tarantio into the night was an exception to our usual routine, but its attractions were hard to resist after all our trials and tribulations. The thought of a real bed, even for just a night, was enough to overcome our hard-won natural caution.

After we'd released the gas and, hopefully, wiped out all the aliens, we'd succeeded in climbing the ramp of metal lattice-work without tearing open our protective suits on the way, which was nice. From that level we climbed some stairs to the next one, where Alucia said it was now safe to get out of the suits – not that we had much choice, as she also told us that our air was about to run out. Despite her assurances, I removed my helmet and waited to die a horrible death. When I didn't I felt pretty relieved.

'Told you so,' she said.

Alucia led us to another armoury, where we replaced our missing hand-weapons. She filled a backpack with an assortment of objects that I assumed were all deadly in one way or another; Ken was rather upset at not having the chance to examine all these new weapons.

Next stop was an infirmary that was full of mysterious-looking equipment. She 'scanned' Ken and me, and then herself, and announced that none of us had suffered any internal injuries. I was relieved to learn that my ribs were intact, despite the fact that they felt like a dragon had fallen on me; she assured me – rather callously, I felt – that it was nothing more than bruising. My broken nose was definitely broken.

'I'm sorry, but I don't know how to set a broken nose,' she said.

Ken stared around the room and said, 'Surely there must be a magical device in here that cures broken noses.'

'Probably,' she replied, 'but I have no idea what it would look like.'

After applying lotions to our cuts and bruises she gave me a supply of painkillers. I took two of them and almost immediately my ribs, and my nose, began to feel much better. *All* my various aches and pains rapidly vanished. Ken reported a similar reaction when he took two of the tablets as well. Though grateful, I couldn't help feeling resentful that such medical knowledge had been withheld from the bulk of Urba's population for so long.

By that time we were all feeling very hungry and began looking for food. We didn't find any.

We searched everywhere, one level after another, but every kitchen and food storeroom had been scoured clean of anything edible. As we stood in yet another larder that had been thoroughly ransacked, Ken said, 'Someone was bloody hungry.'

'Yes,' said Alucia, 'they're definitely short of food on that mothership of theirs. Which explains where all the bodies went. The horses too.'

I looked at her in horror. 'Are you saying what I think you're saying?'

She nodded calmly. 'I am.'

'I don't know what either of you are saying,' said Ken. 'What about the bodies?'

'She's saying the aliens used them for food,' I told him.

Ken looked at both of us. 'You're joking,' he said, looking sick to his stomach.

'Nope,' said Alucia. 'The bodies would have been transported back to the their mothership and processed. Looks like they're really short of protein. And there were an awful lot of bodies here. At least two and a half thousand Elite in the Citadel when the aliens struck, and more than double that number again when you add Camarra's forces.'

'By the gods,' said Ken, 'they're *cannibals*.'

'Not by their reckoning,' said Alucia. 'They're not eating

their own species, they're eating human beings. We obviously don't count as equals in their eyes. We're just fodder.'

'Even so,' said Ken, 'it's still *barbaric*.'

'Well, it does suggest a certain desperation on their part,' she said. 'I would guess it's more like a stopgap measure. I guess their plan, once they'd got a secure hold on a major slice of Urba's territory, was probably to start harvesting crops and livestock. But now that's gone down the tubes, they're in a bad way: if they're really in such a desperate position, it means they're on their last legs. And they're also clearly suffering from an energy shortage too. They had to depend on Urba's energy supply to power their war machines. I'd say they're close to the end.'

'Is that a good thing for us?' I asked. 'Or a bad thing?'

'I would say it's a good thing,' she said. 'But there's a slim chance they may be capable of one rash last act.'

'You really think so?' Ken asked. He still looked rather shaken.

'It's a remote possibility. Highly unlikely, in my opinion, but just to be on the safe side we should launch another attack on their mothership. Finish them off, just in case they do have one last dying kick left in them. But for that I need access to another Sprite ship.'

'You believe there's one under the Compound in Capelia?' he said.

She smiled at him. 'I do indeed, my darling. Capelia . . . my new home.'

Ken smiled back at her. I cringed and stifled a groan.

'I remember you mentioned that the bulk of the Sprite fleet was located in a large docking facility,' I said. 'Couldn't we go there for another Sprite?'

She shook her head. 'No. You could only reach the docking area via the control room. It was forty miles away from the centre and linked by a transport system under the surface of the hull. The aliens would have ensured the spaceport was sealed off when they took over. It's certainly sealed off now after our attack.'

'So it has to be Capelia?'

'It has to be Capelia. There are other Sprites in other locations, but I'm not sure where. I know for sure there's one in Capelia, so getting there is now our top priority.'

'Well, right now our top priority is finding something to eat,' I said. 'I'm famished.'

'There's food in our abandoned car,' Ken pointed out.

'So let's go,' said Alucia.

We made our way back to the landing platform, making the occasional detour for Alucia to show us some feature of the Citadel that she thought of particular interest, like the Council Room, where the Elite's ruling body regularly met to make the decisions that affected all of Urba's population. It was a circular room that could seat some hundred people. The room itself was spectacular, its curving walls panelled with sheets of gold and silver and its domed ceiling constructed of a glass-like substance coloured a deep blue. The carpeting was blood-red; the furnishings were luxurious.

At the centre of the floor was a dais on which stood a large, black leather chair – the Council Leader's seat, said Alucia as we walked down a sloping, red-carpeted aisle.

'The Council Leader was the ruler of the Elite?' I asked.

'No. We didn't have a ruler, not as you know the meaning of the word. The position of Council Leader was a temporary one, lasting only a year. The Leader was selected at random from the Council Members. And a new body of Members was elected every five years. We were really big on the democratic process.'

'But not as far as we were concerned,' I said. 'The low life. Us mundanes, as you so charmingly referred to us.'

'True,' she admitted.

'You ever serve on the Council?' I asked her.

'Indeed I did.' Alucia stepped onto the dais and sat down in the high-backed, black leather chair. 'I even served a term as the Council Leader. Great fun. Power is so addictive. But,' she added with a laugh, 'I didn't get to hold and stroke a white cat on my lap.'

'An Elite joke?' I ventured.

'No, much, much older than the Elite.'

'I don't get it,' said Ken.

'That makes two of us,' I told him. 'And I know all about telling jokes that people don't get.'

'I'm not talking about the joke,' said Ken, looking at Alucia with a puzzled frown. 'I don't understand how you could have been both a Council Member and Leader. Surely you're not old enough to have done all that?'

Alucia glanced at me. She'd made a serious slip in front of Ken. She said lightly, 'I'm a little older than I look.'

'How old?' he asked. It sounded like a serious question. He clearly wasn't going to let her gloss over the subject of her age. And I was curious to know the answer myself. Had she actually been telling me the truth when she'd told me she was a three-hundred-year-old personality in a new, young body?

'How old do I look?' she asked Ken.

He gave a slight shrug. 'I don't know . . . about the same age as Jad and me. Twenty-three. Maybe younger—'

'I'm older than you. I'm twenty-seven. Nearly twenty-eight. Elite youth treatments keep us looking young. Or they did. Without them I'll eventually look my age. Does that bother you?'

He considered her question. Then he said, 'No. Not at all.'

She smiled at him. The smile looked a little forced to me. 'I'm glad to hear it,' she said. 'But then it's not as if I'm old enough to be your mother.'

Ken laughed and said, 'Now that *would* be a problem.'

I kept my face blank while I wondered how he'd feel about the possibility that she was old enough to be his great great great-and-so-on grandmother. Then I wondered how *I* felt about the possibility—

Time for a change of subject, I decided. I looked about the Elite Council Room and said, 'I know I'm probably being foolish, but I keep feeling we're being watched. How can we be sure there aren't more aliens lurking about in the Citadel? After all, the things are invisible.'

'They're weren't invisible,' said Alucia, 'we just couldn't—'

'I know,' I interrupted, 'we just couldn't see them. That still makes them invisible as far as I'm concerned.'

'Think of it as very sophisticated camouflage,' she said. 'They were wearing devices that created some sort of field of visual distortion. They weren't naturally invisible.'

'If something's there that you can't see, then it's invisible,' I persisted. 'And that means there could be aliens in this very room.'

Ken immediately drew his weapon and looked about warily. 'You really think so?' he asked.

'Yes,' I said.

'I don't,' said Alucia, 'because I don't think the aliens' camouflage devices are one hundred per cent effective. They worked downstairs because of the poor light. And even there Ken kept spotting them in his peripheral vision when he was acting as lookout for us. In here the lighting is too bright.'

'Perhaps,' I said doubtfully, 'but that's just your theory. You don't know any of this for sure.'

'My theories have usually proved correct,' she said. 'I was right about the aliens living at a slower rate than us.'

'Yes, they were definitely slow,' I said, 'except for the aliens operating those four-legged machines. *They* weren't slow.'

'I think those machines acted as augmenting devices for the aliens inside them. Sped up their mental and physical processes somehow. The ones not inside a machine were perceiving reality at the aliens' natural rate. But one thing bothers me about that: I can't figure out how they managed to react to our arrival so quickly.'

'Oh?' I said, innocently.

'Yes. They'd stopped whatever they'd been doing, turned off most of the lights and activated their camouflage devices. Considering the evident slowness of their perceptions and equally slow subsequent reactions, it's as if they knew we were coming well in advance.'

'A mystery,' I said, nodding. Then, 'What do you think they were trying to do down there?'

'You willing to consider another of my theories?'

'Sure,' I said graciously. I could be gracious as I'd avoided having to admit my part in our near-annihilation.

'I think they were trying construct the remaining war machines, while at the same time modifying them so that they would be under the direct control of the aliens. The aliens would have been actually operating them from inside. And like the four-legged machines, the modified bigger machines would be designed to augment the aliens' response time. Bring them up to our speed, so to speak. No need for the AIs. If they'd succeeded, they would have presented a considerable threat.

'That's the reason I doubt we're going to encounter any aliens in any other part of the Citadel. They needed every available "man" to complete their crucial task down in their base.'

It sounded logical to me and I was reassured. Ken must have been too because he holstered his weapon.

Another of our detours was to a small room that was literally full of treasure. Its unlocked cabinets and drawers contained huge amounts of silver and gold coins, small gold bars and precious stones. Ken and I stared in awe at this incredible display of wealth. Alucia affected an air of nonchalance.

'You could buy half of Urba with all this,' said Ken softly.

'That's what we used it for,' said Alucia. 'We didn't just use force to influence the warlords; we bribed them as well when it suited us. Naturally, such riches meant nothing to the Elite. We had no personal use for gold or silver. Anyway, help yourself.'

We looked at her in astonishment. 'You mean it?' asked Ken.

'Of course,' she replied. 'Who cares about it now? Just don't be greedy. You don't want to weigh yourselves down with gold—'

I tentatively picked up a handful of gold coins and put them in my pockets. So did Ken. Then I picked up another handful and pocketed those too. It was hard to stop, but I knew she was right. I turned my attention to a drawer full of diamonds and selected several large stones. 'I promised Tiri I'd bring her back some diamonds, if I could,' I explained.

'Tiri?' asked Alucia.

'She's Jad's pretty little kitchen maid,' said Ken with a touch of disdain. 'Provides him with treats from the kitchen during the day and provides him other treats in his bed at night. Eh, Jad?' He leered at me.

I gave him a dirty look, but held my tongue.

'You haven't mentioned her before, Jad,' said Alucia, playfully. 'Why have you been keeping her a secret?'

'I believe he's ashamed of her,' said Ken. 'After all, she's a mere kitchen maid, and Jad has always had ideas above his station.'

'I am *not* ashamed of Tiri!' I protested.

'I'm sure you're not,' said Alucia. There was a definite gleam in her eye. 'I'm sure she's delightful. And Tiri is such a lovely name.'

It's certainly a better name than Princess Petal, I thought, glowering at Ken. Our exchange was interrupted by a rumbling: Ken's stomach.

He grimaced and said, 'I'm bloody starving. Let's find some food.'

'But there's so much more I want to show to you,' said Alucia. 'There are so many wonders here in the Citadel. Like the virtual reality suites. Enter one of those and you can become part of a simulation so real you believe you're back on Earth, centuries ago. You can travel to any part of the planet. And there are the viewing theatres. We have complete libraries of every holographic production ever made, and a vast collection of vid-copies of the old two-dimensional movies, right back to the twentieth century, when the cinema began. You could see what life was like on Earth over several centuries.' She looked at us expectantly.

'Some other time perhaps,' said Ken offhandedly. 'Right now food is our number one priority.'

'Yes,' I agreed. 'It all sounds really interesting but I'm starving too.'

'Philistines,' muttered Alucia. 'I was going to introduce you to one of the sex simulation suites too. Would have blown your little minds out of their cod-pieces but—'

Ken and I exchanged a look. 'What's a sex suite?' asked Ken.

'Food!' I reminded him firmly.

He nodded. Reluctantly. 'Yes. Food. Let's head back to the landing platform.'

'Philistines,' muttered Alucia again.

I was pretty certain it was an insult.

CHAPTER TWENTY-SIX

A shadow fell across our table. I looked up, expecting to see the big man with the beard again. Had he decided that buggering Alucia was worth the risk of enduring the red-hot wire treatment? But it wasn't him, it was a different big man, with a different beard. And this one looked like he'd been travelling hard. His face was covered with grime and his clothing and boots were splattered with mud.

'I need a word with you two,' he said.

'The boy's not for sale,' I told him.

He frowned at me. 'What?'

'I said, the boy's not for rent. Not even for a quickie behind the latrine.'

'What the hell are you talking about?' he asked me. 'I'm not interested in fucking your companion. Or you, for that matter. Particularly not you.'

'Then what do you want?' I said, feeling affronted.

'I hear that you're deserters from Lord Camarra's army. Is that true?'

I glanced at Alucia, but couldn't read anything helpful in her neutral expression. I said cautiously, 'What interest would that be to you?'

'Because I'm a deserter from Lord Camarra's army too,' he said. 'Or what remained of it after that Elite attack with their devil machines.'

Damn, I thought, don't tell me this idiot wants to share reminiscences about the jolly times had by all in the service of the insane Camarra. Or did he have an ulterior motive in approaching us?

'You are?' I said. 'Good for you. There must be a lot of us about now that Camarra's dead.'

'That's what I wanted to talk to you about. Lord Camarra isn't dead.'

'Yes he is,' said Alucia firmly. 'I know that for a fact.'

He turned towards her. 'You see him die?'

'Well, no,' she admitted, 'but I know he's dead.'

'The gods provide you with the gift of second sight, boy?'

Once again I was amazed that anyone could be fooled by Alucia's feeble impersonation of a male.

'No,' she told the man, 'they didn't. But a friend of mine saw him mortally wounded.'

'He was badly wounded, yes. But he survived—'

Alucia shook her head. 'He couldn't have. It's impossible.'

'But he did, boy. And now he's trying to marshal the remains of his forces. If he succeeds in defeating Lord Megus, he will once again be the dominant power in Urba. He's not a man to be stopped.' The man turned back to me. 'That's why I thought you should be warned. We deserters face an unenviable fate if we should fall into Camarra's hands. I suggest you travel as far away as you can. That's what me and my companions intend to do. Good luck.' And with that dire warning ringing in our ears, he turned and headed back towards the bar.

I looked at Alucia. All the colour had drained from her face. 'It can't be true,' she whispered, 'I killed him.'

I took a long drink of beer, put the mug back on the table and said, 'Perhaps you didn't. He had enough strength to ride off on his horse after you'd stabbed him. Perhaps, against all the odds, he did survive. And that soldier seemed pretty certain of his facts.'

Alucia didn't answer. She just sat there, obviously lost in thought. Her silence stretched on. Minutes passed. I looked around the bar but there was still no sign of Ken, or his serving girl. They were either still at it, or Ken had passed out drunk somewhere. I finished my beer and gestured to another of the girls. She wasn't as pretty as the missing one, but I ordered another beer from her and asked Alucia if she wanted anything. I had to ask her twice before she abruptly snapped out of her trance.

'Yes. I'll have a brandy,' she said. 'A big one.'

While we waited for the girl to fetch our drinks, Alucia lapsed back into silence. I assumed she was thinking of the night Camarra had raped her and she'd stabbed him. Finally I said, 'Cheer up. If we're lucky Camarra and Megus will fight each other to a stalemate. And if we're really lucky, both will get killed in the process.'

She regarded me with a solemn expression. 'Or Camarra will defeat Megus. Which will not be good for all concerned.'

'True. But it would be the same if Megus defeats Camarra. One power-crazy warlord is much the same as another.'

'No. It wouldn't be the same. Camarra is the more dangerous. And he knows too much.'

The serving girl returned with our drinks. I paid her and added a generous tip. She might not be as pretty as Ken's prize but I wasn't feeling fussy. She rewarded me with a smile full of promise – or was that the alcohol feeding my fantasies? Either way, I was determined to pursue the possibility later. Then it occurred to me that at this rate of serving-girl attrition, the landlord would have to start serving all the drinks himself.

'Pretty girl,' said Alucia and took a large gulp of brandy. Almost immediately the colour began to return to her face.

'Was she? I hadn't noticed.'

This made her smile, which I was glad to see. Then she looked around the room and said, 'I see that my beloved fiancé is still conspicuous by his absence.'

I lifted my fresh mug of beer and poured about a third of it down my throat. Then I said to her, 'You don't sound exactly bothered.'

'I told you before, it doesn't upset me in the least.'

I waggled my eyebrows at her in what I hoped was a playfully suggestive way, though only the gods knew what I looked like – probably a deranged troll. 'While the cat's away, why don't we two mice play?' I said.

She nodded. 'Sure. Let's rent a room.'

'What? You're joking!'

'No. I'm being serious.'

She certainly sounded serious, but I'd drunk so much it was hard to tell. I peered suspiciously at her. Actually, at *both* of her. I was having trouble focusing again. 'Well, *I* was joking,' I said.

'You were? That's disappointing. You really don't want go upstairs with me and ravish me for the rest of the night? Or to be more realistic, to ravish me until you pass out from your excessive alcoholic intake?'

'I'd love to ravish you for any amount of time,' I said sincerely.

'A period longer than a minute would be good,' she said with another smile.

'I think I can manage that. Maybe even two minutes. Three, tops. Let's not get carried away.'

'Best offer I've had so far tonight.'

All thoughts of the serving girl had fled my befuddled brain. Then I remembered the only other offer Alucia had had tonight. A gloomy thought struck me.

'So? Shall we go see the landlord about a room?' she asked.

'The place is probably full,' I said.

'Jad, we're rich. I'm sure the landlord will suddenly discover he has an empty room if we wave enough gold under his nose.'

And he did.

Any guilty feelings I may have had about the previous occupants of our room, who had no doubt been tossed unceremoniously into the street by a landlord suddenly faced with a persuasive quantity of gold, rapidly disappeared once I was alone with Alucia. In the romantic light shed by several flickering candles, I slowly undressed her on the large bed.

'Hey,' I murmured, 'you sure are a funny-looking boy.'

She laughed, and slowly undressed me. As the old, obscure saying goes: it was more fun than a box full of fluffy ducklings. As was what followed between us . . . Unlike our frantic and rudely interrupted coupling near the campsite, this time we made love slowly, almost languidly. The pleasure was intense, even through the haze of alcohol.

Afterwards I lay beside her, sighed and said, 'Maybe I was wrong about the gods. Maybe they do exist after all.'

'You flatter me,' she murmured.

'Actually I was flattering myself. Though I did miss the element of excitement from our previous act of intimacy,' I said.

'Oh?'

'Oh yes, being almost trampled to death by a horde of horsemen while making love adds a certain zest to the whole experience, don't you find?'

'True. Perhaps we should spend the rest of the night downstairs in the stables. Try and recreate that unique atmosphere.' She sat up and reached for the jug of wine that was sitting on a rickety little table by her side of the bed. The wine was courtesy of the landlord. With what we'd paid him for a one-night stay in the room, he could probably buy himself an entire vineyard. When I'd handed him his more than tidy sum of gold, he'd winked at me and whispered, 'Like the boys, do you? Lean that way myself. Fancy a threesome?' I'd politely declined his kind offer, suppressing a shudder of revulsion at the same time. The landlord was a very fat and very hairy man, and fifty years old if he was a day.

I watched Alucia pour herself a mug of wine, admiring her body. It was a boyish body, I supposed, if, amongst other things, you ignored her breasts. I couldn't, and didn't. Now unencumbered by the length of bandage with which she'd bound them under her shirt, they positively rejoiced in their freedom. I felt like rejoicing too. She looked over sternly and said, 'I'm not sure if you should have any more to drink.'

I sat up too. 'Just a small amount,' I pleaded. 'I'm thirsty.'

'All right, but if you fall asleep I'm going to kick you out the door without your clothes.' She poured some wine into the other mug and handed it to me. I drank it eagerly.

She leaned against me and put her arm around me. 'Tell me something, Jad,' she said softly.

'Anything,' I said, 'anything at all.'

'When you did your act back in Capelia . . . you know, your court jester routine, did you wear the full outfit?'

'The full outfit?' I asked, puzzled.

'You know: the garishly coloured costume with the droopy, three-pointed hat, and the bells hanging from the pointy bits, and the funny shoes with bells on their toes—'

'Uh, yes,' I admitted reluctantly. This was not the sort of question you expect to be asked by a woman you've just made passionate love to. 'It's a tradition. People expect it.'

'And you had no choice in the matter.'

'Err, no.'

'Don't you feel a utter and complete cretin when you have to go and face people dressed like that?'

'Err, yes.'

She traced a line down the side of my face with a fingertip. My skin tingled. 'I'm sure you look very cute in your costume, Jad.'

'"Cute" is not helping,' I said, a little bitterly. Well, a *lot* bitterly.

She put her lips to my ears and whispered, 'I want you to promise me something.'

'Oh, yes?' I said, warily.

'I want you to promise me that when we get to Capelia, and we get the opportunity, you'll make love to me in your jester's costume.'

I jerked my head round in surprise and stared at her. 'You want me to do *what*?'

She grinned. 'You heard me. The thought excites me. It's what used to be called a turn-on.'

'It's what I call weird. You're one weird lady.'

'Guilty as charged. But you like me anyway.'

'I . . . I love you, Alucia.'

The mischievous grin vanished from her face like a light being turned off and she turned her face away and withdrew her arm from under me. 'You don't know what you're saying,' she said in a monotone.

'I do. And I mean it.'

She wrapped her arms around her chest and hugged herself. 'I've told you before, you don't know me. Not the real me. So when you say you love me you're just fooling yourself.'

'I think I'm aware of what you *used* to be.'

'No. You have no idea. No idea at all.'

I put my hand on her shoulder. She felt cold. She stiffened at my touch, but at least she didn't shrug herself free of my hand. Then I couldn't help myself: I had to ask the question. 'Are you really over three hundred years old?' When it came to inappropriate questions shortly after making love, I had her beaten hands-down.

'Would it matter to you if I were?' She was still facing away from me.

'Well, I am often attracted to older women,' I said, 'though women three hundred years older than me is pushing it a bit.'

She turned to me and I saw the hint of a smile on her face. Once again the sight gladdened me.

'So? Is it true?' I asked.

'Yes and no,' she replied, helpfully.

'I really do find those sort of answers very annoying. Let's start with the "yes" part.'

'Yes, I have gone through several regenerations. Aspects of my personality extend back over three hundred years.'

'Wow,' I said, which was the best I could do.

'This body, like many of the bodies of the Elite, was grown in a laboratory, a laboratory that no longer exists, thanks to the aliens,' said Alucia. She ran her hands down herself. 'This body is a clone of my original body.'

'A clone?' I said. The word, like so much of her vocabulary, meant nothing to me.

'The new body was *based* on my original body, like a cutting from a plant. In theory, a clone should be identical to the original, but they never are. Copies of *anything* are never exactly the same as the original. With clones, small changes occur and accumulate in the growing process of each new body. And the same applies to my personality. As you said, but meaning something else entirely, I'm not the person I used to be. Every time my personality was stored in a computer and then down-loaded into a fresh, blank body, I changed. I have memories of my original life, but I'm no longer that person. Switching bodies isn't like changing into new clothes. The new body itself alters you – what with hormones and countless other factors. I may have some memories stretching back over three hundred years, but I really am, in essence, a twenty-three-year-old woman.' She frowned at me. 'Do you understand?'

'I think so,' I said. 'You certainly act and sound like a twenty-three-year-old woman. And feel like one – for which I'm truly grateful. Especially after what we've just been doing on this bed—'

She smiled again, this time a genuine grin. 'Good. And we've only just begun.'

'Uh, I don't think I have the energy right now,' I said in alarm. 'I'm really feeling kind of drained.'

Her smile became mischievous again. 'I know some tricks that should restore your energy level – I'm sure they're not in your little Tiri's repertoire of bedroom antics.'

Alucia was definitely right about that.

I lost track of the time, but I guess it was an hour or more before a combination of physical exhaustion and alcohol plunged me into a deep sleep. At some point I became aware that Alucia seemed to be talking to someone in the room. Her voice wasn't more than a murmur, but there was a note of anxiety in her tone. Had Ken discovered us? I tried to fight my way back to full consciousness, but even with the threat of certain death hanging over me if Ken had found us naked in bed together, I couldn't will my eyes to open. I lost the battle and sank back down into alcoholic oblivion. At another point I felt her lips press softly against mine, and a drop of water splash on my cheek. Then, once again, sleep claimed me—

When I awoke fully, the room was flooded with bright daylight and I was alone. That didn't surprise me. I assumed Alucia had risen earlier and gone in search of Ken. I lay there, my head pounding painfully with each heartbeat. My mouth was dry and I felt vaguely ill. In the harsh daylight, the room no longer looked romantic: on the contrary, it was little more than a hovel, and the mattress felt as if it was stuffed with gravel. And yet, despite all this, I was suffused with a glow of well-being, which was all due to Alucia. I had no idea where our relationship was going, but I couldn't wait to see her again, even if, inevitably, it was in the company of Ken.

Ken. Something of a major obstacle in any future I might have with Alucia.

Then I remembered half-waking during the night to the sound of her talking to someone. Who had she been talking to? It couldn't have been Ken or he'd have dragged me out of the bed and given me a fatal beating. Had it been a dream? I decided it was.

First things first. I got out of bed and checked to see if there was any wine left in the jug. There was. I drank it and waited. If I didn't throw up, there was a good chance I'd start to feel a little better.

I didn't throw up, and after a while I felt slightly better, enough to dress and go downstairs, where I found Ken sitting alone at a table. There was a mug of beer in front of him. He didn't look well. There were a few other people seated about the room. None of them looked well either. Feeling both nervous and guilty, I sat down opposite Ken and said, 'Good morning.'

He grunted. That was good. The fact that he hadn't leapt up and tried to strangle me was a fair indication that he didn't know what his fiancée and I had been up to last night.

'You look terrible,' I told him helpfully.

'So do you,' he grunted.

A serving girl appeared through a doorway and came over to our table. I didn't recognise her. Fresh blood. Must have been a member of the day shift. 'Can I get you anything, soldier?' she asked me. 'Drink? Breakfast?'

My stomach heaved. I fought it into submission and held up a hand. 'No breakfast. Don't even tell me what breakfast consists of. Just a mug of beer, thanks.'

When she'd gone, I made a show of looking around, then, as casually as possible, I asked, 'Where's Alucia?'

'Haven't seen her since last night. Haven't you seen her this morning?'

I shook my head quickly. 'No. Last time I saw her was in here last night. She left to look for you. I take it she didn't find you.'

'No. I wonder where she is.'

So did I. 'You have an enjoyable time with that beautiful serving girl?' I asked him.

He looked at me with haunted eyes. 'Yes, I did. Now I feel awful. I don't know what got into me.'

'More to the point,' I said, 'what got into her?'

He didn't laugh, much less smile. The haunted look remained in place. I still had that old touch when it came to creating boundless mirth. The new girl returned with my beer, set it down on the table and left.

'Was she angry with me?' Ken asked.

My brain wasn't working properly yet. I said, 'Why ask me? You spent the night with her.'

'Who?'

'The serving girl.'

'I'm talking about Alucia, you idiot!' he snapped. 'Was she angry after I went off with that girl?'

'Well, she wasn't happy,' I said. Which was true. But Ken wasn't the source of her unhappiness.

'What did she say about me?'

Now that was a difficult one to answer. My brain was in no shape for creativity.

'Umm . . . she said she hoped you didn't catch a disease off the girl.'

He grunted again. 'She assured me she was clean. So did the

landlord. If either of them were lying, I'll come back and gut them.'

I was confused. 'What has the landlord got to do with it?'

'Had to pay him. For the girl.'

'Oh,' I said, understanding finally dawning. It had certainly been a profitable night for our hospitable tavern keeper.

'What else did she say?'

'Not a lot.'

'You must have talked about something after I left, apart from the possibility of me catching the pox.'

'Well . . . we talked about Capelia, your parents . . . your betrothal to Princess Petal—'

I realised my error when I saw his eyes suddenly blaze with anger. 'You told her about Princess Petal?' he exploded. 'You stupid fool! Why did you do that?'

'Because I assumed you'd already told her,' I protested, clapping my hands to my ringing head. 'And anyway, she would have found out pretty damn quickly after we reached Capelia. How exactly did you expect to keep the fact that you are supposed to marry another woman a secret from her?'

His anger subsided, but not much. 'You shouldn't have told her. No wonder she's mad at me.'

'Oh, so it's all my fault now, is it?' I said with a sneer. 'Typical. The gods forbid you should accept the blame for any of your own actions, no, shift the fault onto someone else. Spoken like a true Prince.'

His eyes grew cold. 'Yes, I'm a Prince. *Your* Prince. Your lord and master, and you'd do well not to forget that, *jester*.' His voice was as cold as his eyes.

'Only in Capelia, your *highness*,' I told him, in a tone as icy as his own. 'And perhaps I won't go back there. Maybe I'll go somewhere else instead. Like Alucia probably has.'

His face, which had been growing ever more flushed, now began to drain of all colour. He stared at me in shock. 'Is that what she's done? Has she abandoned me?' He gripped my wrists painfully. 'What do you know? Tell

'I don't know anything,' I said, pulli

'Then why did you say that?' he demanded. 'Why did you say she's gone?'

'I have no idea,' I said as I rubbed my wrist. 'She's not here, is she? It just popped into my head.' Which it had. There was a falling sensation in the pit of my stomach. Had Alucia really left us? More to reassure myself than Ken, I said to him, 'She's probably just gone for a walk. She'll be back, don't worry.' I picked up my untouched mug of beer and drank some of it.

'I hope you're right,' said Ken worriedly.

So did I. Desperately.

But Alucia never returned.

CHAPTER TWENTY-SEVEN

We waited impatiently in the tavern for some hours. When the landlord finally appeared, Ken summoned him over. He came quickly, probably hoping we were about to enrich him even further, an oily smile pasted on his face. 'Everything satisfactory, gentlemen?' he enquired. I don't think he called many of his customers 'gentlemen'.

'Yes, but we seem to have lost our companion,' said Ken. 'The, er, youth we were with last night. Could you find out if any of your staff saw him leave? And if so, when exactly?'

The landlord looked at me. I held my breath. I'd paid him extra money last night not to mention to Ken my arrangement with the room – and the 'boy'. I could see the wheels turning behind his eyes. He was thinking: *How am I going make more money out of this situation? Which of these two men is going to pay me the most to cooperate?*

His mental wheels were turning with painful slowness. I was going to suffocate before he made a decision. Then, finally, he said to Ken, 'I'll be happy to ask about your missing young friend. I'll do it right now.' As he left he shot a meaningful glance at me. I read it only too clearly. I was going to have to pay dearly for his continued silence. I didn't care. I started breathing again.

This sub-conversation had passed Ken by entirely; he was sunk in gloom. 'Jad, think again,' he pleaded. 'She must have given you *some* indication last night that all was not well. Search your memory. Did she say anything out of the ordinary? Did something happen that may have caused her to run away?'

Both questions were tough ones. My own mental wheels

began to turn with painful slowness. My head throbbed. *Had* anything happened to cause her disappearance? Well, she'd had sex with me. But surely I wasn't *that* bad in bed? She'd appeared to enjoy it as much as me. As for her saying something out of the ordinary, I don't think Ken would have cared to learn that his beloved had confirmed her age was three hundred years plus. Then I remembered my dream, hearing her talk to someone else in the room. Perhaps I hadn't been dreaming after all – but either way, I couldn't tell Ken about it.

However, there was *something* I could reveal that wouldn't give away my own guilty secret. 'She did get upset at one stage—'

'Because of something you said?' he asked in an accusing tone.

'No, it was nothing to do with me. It was what a soldier told us. Well, he was a deserter from Lord Camarra's army, as we're supposed to be. He'd heard we were fellow deserters and felt obliged to pass on some information to us.'

'What information?'

'He told us that Lord Camarra was still alive. He was pretty adamant about it. And Alucia took the news rather badly.'

Ken frowned. 'Just how upset was she?'

'Pretty upset. But it didn't seem to last too long; she was soon back to her normal self – unless she was putting on an act for my benefit.' Damn good act, I thought, as I replayed our love-making. 'She didn't give any indication that she was considering going off on her own because of the news about Camarra.' Which was true – unless *everything* she'd said and done after the deserter had filled us in *had* been an act. But why had she run away – fear of Camarra? That seemed unlikely, somehow.

At the end of two hours of futile waiting, Ken announced he'd had enough. 'I can't sit here twiddling my thumbs like this. I have to do something. Let's search the town for her. Perhaps she did just go for a walk, and then something happened to her. There are plenty of unpleasant people filling the town at present. By the gods, let's hope she hasn't been seized by a gang of vigilantes!'

'Let's hope not,' I agreed. It was a grim thought, but I doubted that was what had happened.

'Are you coming?'

I nodded, even though I was pretty sure it would be a waste of time.

When we returned to the tavern, hot, dusty and worn out, it was mid-afternoon; the landlord confirmed that our young friend had not turned up in our absence. We had a beer each and discussed what we should do next. Ken suggested the obvious, that we should check out the air-car. I knew we had to, but I'd been putting off the moment: if it wasn't where we'd hidden it, it would mean that Alucia really had gone. I wasn't sure I could cope with that truth yet.

We'd concealed the vehicle in the barn of an abandoned farm some five miles from the outskirts of Tarantio; the three of us had walked to the town. Ken and I decided the urgency of the situation justified hiring horses for today's journey – except no one had any available, for love nor money. We ended up buying two – from the bloody landlord of the tavern, naturally. Our genial host must have been very in with the gods . . .

I was more than half-hoping that when we reached the barn we'd find Alucia waiting for us, a big grin on her face. But the barn was deserted, and where the air-car had stood, there was nothing, just the concealing layer of old hay scattered about.

I looked at Ken, but he'd lost it. He just kept shaking his head and asking, 'Why? Why has she done this to me?'

Why has she done this to *us*? That's what I wanted to say, but I wisely kept the extent of my misery to myself.

'So what do we do now?' I asked him. 'She could be anywhere by now.'

'We'll return to the tavern and wait for her,' he said firmly. 'She'll come back. I know it. As soon as she's accomplished whatever it is she's set off to do.'

'Any idea what that might possibly be?'

He shrugged. 'Perhaps she's gone to finish the job with Lord Camarra.'

Stupidly, that hadn't occurred to me. 'But if she's gone to try and kill Camarra, why didn't she want us to help her?'

'Trying to protect us,' he suggested. 'She didn't want to endanger us in such a rash enterprise.'

'Really? That's never stopped her before. Ever since we met her, we've been endangered by her rash enterprises. And by the gods, you're the last person to complain about other people's rash enterprises. You practically invented the genre.'

Ken's eyes narrowed. 'Don't push your luck with me, Jad. You're not my favourite person these days.'

The feeling is entirely mutual, I muttered under my breath.

For two weeks we waited in that wretched tavern before we finally had to admit to each other that Alucia wasn't going to walk in the door. During those two weeks, the obnoxious landlord got even richer, and we did serious damage to our livers.

Finally, late one night, Ken said resignedly, 'She's not coming back.'

'Doesn't look like it,' I said.

'So it's back to Capelia—'

'I suppose so—'

'Shit,' muttered Ken.

I raised my mug of beer. 'I'll drink to that.'

'You have earned my gratitude, Jad,' Lord Krader growled. He didn't sound very grateful.

'Thank you, sire,' I said. We were once again in his trophy room where, so many months ago, he'd given me what I was so sure would be my death sentence: the bad news that I was to accompany Prince Ken on his mission of madness. Ken and I had arrived back at the castle three days ago, but this was the first opportunity I'd had to speak to Lord Krader alone.

'I must admit, you've surprised me,' he said. 'I feared I

would never see my son again. You two were gone so long –
much longer than we expected. But somehow you kept him
alive.'

I put on my modest face. 'I can't take the full credit for that,
sire. The Prince saved my life on more than one occasion.'

'I'm sure he did. But obviously your influence, born out of
your natural-born cowardice, acted as an anchor to my son's
normally headstrong and reckless actions.'

'Well, you *could* put it that way, sire.' Though I'd rather he
hadn't.

'But I do have a grievance with you, Jad.'

'You do?' I asked, surprised. I wondered what it could
possibly be – perhaps the fact that I had survived along with
Ken?

'My son is not the same carefree young man who left here
with you.'

'He isn't?' Was Lord Krader accusing me of switching the
original Ken with a double? Did he know about clones?

'Please don't try and tell me you are unaware of these
changes, Jad,' Lord Krader said warningly. 'The young man
who departed with you was an exuberant, cheerful fellow. The
young man you've returned with is sullen and withdrawn. He
is like a stranger to me.'

'Well, sire, we have been through a lot these past months.
We've seen some pretty terrible things and we had some *very*
close calls. There were times when we truly didn't expect to see
the dawn again.'

'That is to be expected, but he refuses to discuss these
experiences with me. Instead, he is prone to long and moody
silences. That is not like him at all. I've also noticed that you
two are no longer the best of friends, as you once were. On the
contrary, there seems to be an air of hostility between you. So
Jad, tell me exactly what happened. I want an explanation for
these changes in my son.'

'Ah, right,' I said and searched the room for inspiration. My
eyes once again settled on the head of the griffin. It seemed to
be laughing at my predicament. I turned back to Lord Krader.

On the whole, looking at the griffin was preferable. I was going to have to tell him something: time for a temporary excursion into the territory of truth, a land I rarely visited nowadays.

I took a deep breath and said, 'We met a young woman on our travels, Lord Krader. I'm afraid the Prince became quite, er, smitten with her.' Nice safe word, *smitten*.

'Smitten? What do you mean by *smitten*?' demanded Lord Krader, his eyes boring into mine. He obviously didn't think it was a safe word at all.

Damn. I glanced briefly at the griffin. It was definitely smiling at me now.

'I'm afraid, sire, that Ken . . . I mean, Prince Kender, sort of, like, fell in love with her. Badly.'

Lord Krader's face darkened. 'I trust, Jad, that you jest.'

'And break the habit of a lifetime, sire?' I said and laughed.

Lord Krader, alas, didn't. It was time I put that joke out to pasture. 'I'm afraid I speak the truth, sire. Prince Kender proposed marriage to her.'

'He *what*?' bellowed Lord Krader.

I flinched. 'He intended marrying her when we returned here, sire.'

'But he's betrothed to Princess Petal!' Still in full bellow.

'That sort of slipped his mind, sire. I did try and remind him, but, well, you know the Prince. Once he makes his mind up about something, it's hard to get him to listen to reason.'

I thought my head was going to end up next to the griffin's, but Lord Krader, after smouldering for a while, finally nodded and said, in a much quieter tone, 'I know what you mean. Who was this woman who so entranced my son?'

'Her name was Alucia. She was the daughter of a wine merchant—'

Lord Krader's face darkened with anger again. 'My son intended marrying a *commoner*?'

'Well, technically she was a commoner, sire. But there was nothing common about Alucia, believe me. She was an extraordinary person.'

Lord Krader was now regarding me shrewdly. 'Aha. Some of the pieces begin to fall into place.'

'They do?' I said in alarm. Had I, in my nervousness, let slip the less-than-minor fact that she was an Elite? I was fairly certain I hadn't.

'She was very attractive, this Alucia?'

'Yes, sire, she was.'

'So you desired her yourself,' he said with a knowing smile. 'That's the reason for the bad feeling between you and my son. Am I right?'

'Forgive me, sire, but that's not entirely correct. I *was* entranced by Alucia, but Prince Kender remained unaware of this. I never told him. I believe that his displeasure with me stems from his belief that it was something I said that lay behind her sudden disappearance.'

'She disappeared?' he asked, his face revealing a flicker of relief. 'Where? When?'

'In Tarantio. That's in the domain of—'

'I know where Tarantio is,' said Lord Krader curtly.

'Well, we were staying at a tavern there during our journey back to Capelia. On the first night, Alucia simply vanished. No one at the tavern saw her go. The Prince and I searched the town for her the following day, but we never found her. We stayed at the tavern for a further two weeks hoping she'd return, but she didn't. We have no idea what became of her.' I decided not to mention she was disguised as a youth at the time. That would only lead to more awkward questions.

'I see,' he said slowly. 'So what does my son believe you said to her that caused her to suddenly leave?'

'Uhh ... well, I told her about the Prince's arranged marriage with Princess Petal, sire. It came as a surprise to her; for some reason, the Prince had neglected to inform her of his betrothal to Princess Petal.'

'She was very angry when she learned of this?'

'She was certainly annoyed, yes, but I don't think she was angry with the Prince to the point of running off by herself.

303

She was as much in love with the Prince as he was with her.'
So much for my sojourn in the territory of truth.

'You're still young and naïve, Jad. She sounds to me like a
cheap adventuress who was after my son's title, privileges and
wealth,' said Lord Krader.

'No, she wasn't like that all,' I said, even as I remembered
that her intentions towards Ken were indeed less than
honourable. 'Anyway, her disappearance remains a mystery to
both Prince Kender and me.'

'The important thing is that she has gone, and is no longer
involved in my son's life,' he said. 'But even so, I shall bring
the date of his wedding to Princess Petal forward. The sooner
he marries her, the better.'

Uh oh, I said to myself. 'Sire, may I beg a favour?'

'Depends what it is,' he grunted. So much for being indebted
to me.

'When you inform the Prince that he'll be marrying Princess
Petal sooner than he thought, I'd appreciate it if you didn't
mention my name in connection with your decision,' I pleaded.
'He's angry enough with me as it is.'

'Hah!' he said, and his shoulders shook with amusement.
'We'll see, Jad, we'll see.'

Optimistically taking that for a 'yes', I said, 'Thank you,
sire.' Hoping that our private chat was at an end I waited
expectantly to be dismissed, but Lord Krader kept his beady
eyes boring into mine.

'Anything else you'd like to get off your chest, Jad?' he
asked in his rumble of a voice.

'About what, sire?' I said nervously.

'About your trip with my son,' he replied and gave me a
meaningful look. 'I have a strong feeling that you and the
Prince are holding back certain things. Are you?'

My armpits became soggy with sweat. On our long and
often perilous journey back to Capelia, Ken and I had
concocted a joint story of our experiences; this highly edited
version of events was what we had related to Lord Krader and
his advisors on our first day back in the castle. We described

joining up with Lord Camarra's army, the expedition to the Citadel and the devastating attack by 'Elite' secret weapons that scattered Camarra's forces. We had survived by sheer luck. There had been no mention of our adventures with Alucia, the air-car, the aliens, our journey outside of Urba in the Sprite, the attack on the aliens, the return to the Citadel and so on.

No wonder Lord Krader had sensed we were leaving something out!

Our story had concluded with the news that the remnants of both Camarra's and Megus's forces were busily fighting each other and were unlikely to pose an immediate threat to the rest of Urba, though a future threat from the victor couldn't be completely dismissed.

'I'm still waiting,' said Lord Krader.

'Just trying to remember if we left anything important out, sire,' I said. Like, among other things, the fact that Urba is actually a giant spaceship. Little details like that. 'But no, sire, we didn't.'

He gave a snort of disbelief. I waited anxiously, but then he said, 'Very well. For the time being I'll give you the benefit of the doubt. But I'll be asking my son the same question. So you've been warned—'

'Yes, sire. But there's nothing further to add.' Nothing you'd believe, I added to myself.

Again I waited to be dismissed but he still wasn't finished with me. 'Given any thought to your own future, Jad?'

I knew what he was referring to: my professional future. I was no longer his court jester; in my enforced absence I'd been supplanted by someone new, a member of a group of travelling players who'd visited the castle. Lord Krader found him very amusing and made him an offer he couldn't refuse. Ironically, it was the same group of travelling players that Ken, Alucia and I had encountered months before. I learned of my unemployment on the night of our arrival back at the castle, when Lord Krader held a feast to celebrate Ken's safe return. The new jester made an appearance during the festivities. I had to admit he was funnier than I'd ever managed to be, but I was still annoyed that I'd been replaced, even though I no longer had any real interest in being a jester. I was more annoyed that he'd inherited my old quarters. The new jester, whose stage name was Pratus, very kindly let me sleep on the floor of Harius's tiny, book-filled study – which had previously been *my* study. Marvellous. I bring the Prince back alive and find out I've lost my home in the process. I was not happy.

I would have stayed in Tiri's room, but that was another situation that had radically changed in my absence. When I'd finally succeeded in tracking Tiri down, which wasn't easy seeing that she was hiding from me, she tearfully admitted that there was a new man in her life: Radfern, the stable-master's muscle-bound, incredibly stupid son. The Curse of the Horse had blighted my life yet again. I had intended giving Tiri the diamonds I'd taken from the Citadel but, understandably, I feel, I changed my mind.

'No sire,' I told Lord Krader, 'I haven't yet given much thought to a new profession.'

'Well, don't take too long about it.'

'I won't, sire.' I assured him.

Lord Krader considered me for an uncomfortable length of time and then said, 'You've changed too, Jad.'

'I have?' I assumed he'd observed that I'd matured since he'd last seen me. Become more adult, self-assured, confident . . . more *manly*. I began to preen a little.

'Yes. The broken nose. It suits you.'

Ken and Princess Petal were married two months later. I wasn't surprised that Ken didn't ask me to be his best man; that signal honour went to his new best friend, a high-born captain in the army, a member of the Castle Guard. I did attend the wedding ceremony, though, and noted with satisfaction that Ken was the glummest-looking groom I'd ever seen.

By the time of the wedding I'd moved out of the castle. I had plenty of gold, not to mention a lot of very valuable diamonds, so I'd rented a room in one the inns in the town. Lord Krader didn't seem to mind; I suspected he was glad to see the back of me. I spent most of the time polishing up my magic act. A long-term plan was forming in the back of my mind, but it had yet to crystallise.

With Pratus's permission, I'd taken a selection of books from Harius's library. Without his permission, I'd also raided Harius's herb collection. After treating myself to a new pipe, I was once again enjoying his special herb. Life was not all bad.

It was an odd feeling, being back in Capelia. Within weeks Ken and my bizarre adventures had begun to feel increasingly like a dream. I had to keep reminding myself that it had all really happened: that we had seen for ourselves that Urba was a giant vessel speeding through a limitless void. And that the world as we'd previously perceived it was an illusion. It wasn't easy to deal with; from time to time I would make sure the door to my room was securely bolted, then take a cloth bundle from its hiding place, unwrap it and hold the Elite weapon in my hand. Whenever I did this I would think of Alucia – odd that this deadly weapon was the only solid memento I had of her. How romantic!

I wondered if Ken did the same thing with the weapon he still possessed – or had he convinced himself that everything *had* all been a dream – including Alucia?

There was one other reminder of Alucia in Capelia: the Elite Compound. I visited it occasionally, though I kept a safe distance from its walls. With the power restored, its automatic defences had been reactivated; on the day that occurred, three soldiers on guard duty next to one of the Compound walls had been instantly killed. Since then, no one had dared to approach it. Many people believed that the Compound had been reoccupied, even though there was no visible sign of any Elite.

Staring at the Compound would remind me of the Sprite ship deep below the building. Alucia had been so keen to reach it; what had changed? Had she found another Sprite and attacked the alien ship one more time? It was possible; there'd been no indication of any further incursions by the aliens. Or perhaps Alucia's original theory had been right and they'd all starved helplessly to death on their disintegrating vessel . . .

I rarely visited the castle, other than to make the occasional courtesy call on the gracious Lady Kalina. It was on one such visit, some four months after Ken and I returned, that Lady Kalina asked if I had heard the latest news. In my relative isolation, I was pretty ignorant about recent developments in the rest of Urba.

'My husband only received the news a couple of days ago,' she said. 'It was a despatch from one of his spies, about the fate of two powerful warlords who posed a threat to all of Urba—'

'Lord Camarra and Lord Megus,' I said.

She nodded.

'Prince Kender and I met both of them during our travels,' I said. 'Great pair of fellows. I trust something awful has happened to them.'

'They were about to form a truce and combine their forces. This was months ago. The two men, each accompanied by a couple of their generals, no one else, met on neutral ground. There are conflicting stories as to what actually happened during the meeting, but everyone agrees that it resulted in the death of Lord Megus and the disappearance of Lord Camarra, who's never been seen since. The rumour that subsequently spread like wildfire was that the two men were attacked by an unknown assassin . . . a woman.'

My pulse quickened. More than that: it pounded in my head like a bad hangover. For the first time in months I felt marvellous.

Lady Kalina leaned slightly forward, her expression concerned. 'Are you all right, Jad? Your face looks quite flushed.'

'I'm fine, your ladyship,' I assured her. 'More than fine.'

'The news pleases you?'

'Very much so.'

'It pleased my husband also.'

'I'm sure it did.'

'It appears that the threat of eventual invasion is over. The two armies have fragmented into small, squabbling groups.'

'That's really wonderful news,' I said, adding 'in more ways than one' to myself. I sat there thinking hard, and came to the decision that I'd known for months I would have to make: I was going to search for Alucia. And I wouldn't stop searching until I found her.

Lady Kalina coughed gently, breaking my reverie. 'Jad, are you quite sure you're all right?'

'Lady Kalina, I'm going away again,' I said slowly. 'I don't know for how long. I'll be leaving in the next few days.'

'I'm sorry to hear that, Jad, but I know you haven't been happy here since you returned. Where are you going?'

'I don't know exactly.'

'And how will you live? How will you support yourself?'

'I have some money. Spoils of war and all that. But if that runs out or I manage to get robbed, I'll work as a travelling entertainer.'

'As a jester?' she asked, doubtfully.

I laughed. 'No, your ladyship. Don't worry, my jestering days are over. I'll concentrate on being a magician from now on.'

'A wise career move,' she said dryly and smiled.

I cleared my throat and said, 'Can I ask a favour of you, your ladyship?'

'You know you can. What is it?'

'Would you mind not telling anyone else about my plans? At least not until some time after I've departed.'

'If you wish. Take care, Jad.'

'Thank you. I will, your Ladyship.'

Still flushed with excitement, I left the castle and went straight into town to buy a horse, and all the accompanying bits and pieces. This time I knew exactly what I needed.

'I want a horse that is obedient, gentle and friendly, and who positively enjoys being ridden,' I told the owner of the stable.

The man took the piece of straw he'd been chewing on out of his mouth and said, 'You talking 'bout a woman or a horse?'

'A horse,' I said impatiently.

'Don't matter, really. No such animal in either species. Take my wife, for example—'

I sighed and said, 'You missed a golden opportunity. There was an opening at the castle until recently for a new court jester.'

Two days later I left town before dawn. My horse, called, according to the comedian stable-owner, Black Lightning, was definitely not obedient, friendly or gentle, and had taken an instant dislike to me. But I was a much more experienced rider than I used to be and I was fairly certain that I'd convinced him who the boss was in our relationship.

I'd been travelling at an easy pace for a couple of hours when I heard the sound of hoof beats behind me. I looked over my shoulder, but the trail I was on was windy, and I couldn't see anyone through the trees. I began to feel alarmed. I'd chosen this particular trail because I'd been assured it was rarely used; that meant that whoever was on the horse I could hear was deliberately following me.

If Lady Kalina had broken her promise and told Lord Krader about my departure, would he send someone after me to fetch me back? But why would he care what I did? Even so, I urged Black Lightning to go faster. This time obedience came to the fore: he more than obliged, he broke into a wild gallop.

I'd been through all this before: hanging on desperately as a bloody horse went berserk beneath me. My attempts to slow the bastard down only increased his speed. All thoughts of my mystery pursuer fled as images of my violent death by horse and shattered skull filled my mind. I lost my grip on the reins and held onto the saddle instead. Then the inevitable happened. We came to another bend in the trail and parted company; the galloping horse went one way and I went in the other direction—

I landed hard on my back. Once again I was both stunned and winded. I supposed I should be grateful I hadn't landed on my nose again.

I lay there unable to move or breathe. Had I snapped my spine? Then I heard a horse approaching. It stopped by my side and a familiar voice said, 'As skilled a horseman as ever, eh, Jad?' The laugh that followed was also familiar.

Damn. It was Ken.

When I was able to breathe again, after Ken had helped me to my feet, I leaned against the side of his horse and gasped, 'What the fuck . . . are you . . . doing here?'

'I'm coming with you, Jad. My mother told me what you were up to. She was worried about you. Little did she know her words would be the catalyst for my own sudden departure from Capelia—'

My swimming head continued to swim, sickeningly. I struggled to understand what he was saying. At last a crucial phrase lodged in my consciousness. 'You're coming with me?'

'Well, of course I am.'

'But what about Princess Petal? Your *wife*?'

'An excellent reason to leave Capelia. She never stops talking, but she's got nothing to say. And when I make love to her, she lies there with her eyes shut and mutters prayers to the gods. So boring, like Capelia itself. So when I heard you were leaving, I decided I had to leave as well. I realised I would have to find Alucia—'

'Alucia?' I said, weakly. 'You want to search for Alucia?'

'You heard about Camarra and Megus?'

I nodded reluctantly.

'It *had* to be Alucia – I'm positive it was.'

'Well, you can't—' I began, but Ken interrupted again.

'It was her – and you're going to help me find her, Jad.'

'I am?'

'Well, I hope you will.' He thrust his hand out to me. 'Can we put all the bad feeling between us behind us?'

'I suppose so.' I shook his hand. My handshake was as weak as my voice.

'And forget all that Prince stuff,' he said, graciously. 'From now on, we're equals. Hell, when my father discovers what I've done, he'll probably disown me. And speaking of my father, we'd better get moving, in case he sends out a party of men to bring me back. Feel well enough to ride yet?'

I nodded, still speechless.

'Good. Let's go and catch up with your horse.' He mounted his own, reached down and helped me up behind him.

As we set off, he said over his shoulder, 'Why were you leaving Capelia?'

'Uh—' I said.

'Don't bother. I already know the answer.'

'You do?' I asked worriedly.

'Yes. You were bored, like me. Once you get the smell of adventure in your nostrils, nothing can ever be the same again.'

'Right.' Actually it was the smell of Alucia that lingered perpetually in my nostrils, but I wasn't going to tell him that. Not yet anyway. Not until we found her.